The [illegible]

Bo[illegible]wo:

A Curse of Smoke and Flame

Jennifer L Rothwell

Green Cat Books

FIRST EDITION

Published in 2021
by GREEN CAT BOOKS
19 St Christopher's Way
Pride Park
Derby
DE24 8JY

www.green-cat.shop

ISBN: 978-1-913794-70-5

Dedication

For my sisters.

You can rule the world.

CONTENTS

Author's Note

Many of the locations in this book exist. London really does have Roman ruins and an old temple. Walbrook River is real, and people really did believe that the River Fleet had magical healing powers! The London Sewers, Black Mary's well, toshers and mudlarks, and Lundonwick; they are all real in one way or another.

Similarly, there are characters in this story who really lived and whilst I have taken some creative liberties with these places and people, they are all worth learning about. William Lilly, Robert Hooke and Christopher Wren are people you can read about in any library.

Alchemus J. Fiddle would encourage you to do so, for in reading lies true magic; the magic of learning.

Prologue

London, 1651

The stars appeared like tiny eruptions in the night sky over the city. They were teasing at first; winking behind the curling smog that the great city belched out of its chimneys and smokestacks but as the night grew deeper, the stars grew more confident and they blazed bright and clear in the blue-black sky.

The astrologer leaned out of the window of his lodgings and cast his eyes towards the heavens. A cool breeze bearing the bite of the salty river ruffled his hair and beard as the astrologer's long, deep sigh joined the night air.

Beneath the window, the parchments and scrolls upon his writing desk flapped a little and he glanced down at them, at the charts and numbers and symbols they bore, and he shook his head in disbelief before looking out at the dark city.

London was a vibrant disgrace; a plague-ridden wonder of a city. Its inhabitants scurried around the overpopulated streets like the rats that ran amuck beneath.

But how he loved this city.

How he thrived upon its cadences and rhythms, the parliamentary alliances ebbing and flowing like the tides of the Thames upon its shores. He had longed to be a part of its pulse. Growing up on the farm in Leicestershire had taught him one thing; hard work and perseverance were essential to success.

'Learn your lessons, William,' his father would say to him. 'It's the best I can give you.'

Indeed, William Lilly Senior had given all he could to his son, sending him to the best grammar school he could afford, to give him the education that had been so vital to the success which William Lilly the junior now enjoyed.

Success that he now bitterly regretted.

He pulled himself back into his chamber. It was a sparse but comfortable room near the Houses of Parliament where he spent most of his days.

Had he envisaged his future on that week-long walk from his home town to London, he might have turned back.

Knowing what he knew now made him sure of it.

William Lilly slumped down onto the uncomfortable wooden chair that creaked like his bones. He fought the urge to study the charts again, but he couldn't help himself. He had to be certain.

To a layman observer, the charts would have seemed a work of witchcraft, what with their astrological symbols and their numerologies. Notes around one particular circular chart read 'Gemini' and 'fire'. At the centre of the circle read the number '1666' and it made William Lilly shiver, for he knew all too well that 666 was the number of The Beast and it made this prediction all the more frightful.

Turning to his oilskin notebook, he continued with the sketch he had been working on. It was almost abhorrent to look at and he knew that to publish it would invite scandal at best, horror at worst.

His success as an astrologer and a seer of the future meant that his works garnered an admirable audience, one that he had juggled carefully. To work with both parliamentarians and royalists was a coup but as he added the finishing touches to his drawing, he could see the future troubles he would face.

The drawing was of a raging fire with flames reaching higher than the men who tried to douse it unsuccessfully with pails of water. Above the blaze, a pair of twins fell headfirst into the inferno, clutching on to one another for dear life.

William Lilly stared with wide eyes down at his work, but he was no longer seeing the drawing. Instead, he saw what the stars had shown him; a great fire was coming. It would raze London to the ground. The fire would begin in 1666 and it would change the face of the city...of the world.

To share this prediction in black and white, with all of its meaning clear for any reader would be the end of him. A vision of his reputation in tatters passed through his mind. Once the prediction came true, as he knew it would, they would blame him and accuse him of arson. It would be the tower for him. The stars warned him.

But he had no choice. He had to publish this prediction, but he could not find the strength to write the words. Instead, he had drawn the picture, layered with meaning.

For many who saw his drawing, the twins would be a symbol of the star sign Gemini, commonly known as the astrological symbol of London. To those who knew such things, this prediction would simply mean that London would fall into flame in a great fire, and this was true; the stars spoke of such a catastrophe. But William intended another meaning to his prediction and this other meaning turned the prediction into a prophesy.

London would fall victim to a great fire, the stars said. And when that happened, it would bring forth a pair of twins not of this world but of another. The fire would be commanded by them, for they would be of fire and not of fire. And they would bring forth a flash of flame so mighty, that all the world would be left in embers and ashes.

The old astrologer's eyes regained their focus. Once again, he peered up to the stars through the murky glass of his window.

'Heaven help us,' he whispered, as he saw Gemini burning in the sky. 'They will destroy us all.'

1

Digging Deep

The boy could not tell if his eyes were open or closed. Darkness was like a living entity sprawling out around him, swallowing any kind of illumination. No breeze either, only oppressive warmth that seemed thickened somehow by the relentless stench of the murky tides beneath. He had been so surprised to learn how warm it was in UnderLondon. It continuously felt like a muggy summer's day and as the days and weeks had passed, he had lost any sense of what the seasons were doing to the world above.

'Would you like a light, laddie?'

A Scottish brogue cut through the darkness and the boy's lip twitched a little.

'I don't mind the dark, Cap'n,' he mumbled.

'Och,' said the voice.

It was a peculiar noise that sounded like irritated phlegm, yet it was a sound he had grown used to hearing. Captain Bonny Kildare had directed her mucus in his direction from the moment he'd set foot on the ship.

'You might like the dark, lad, but I cannae stand it. It invites despair and I won't have you feeling sorry for yourself again.'

There was a squeak of leather and then a flame, bright and dancing, fluttered out of nowhere. Immediately, the captain and the boy were bathed in firelight. She was dressed almost entirely in leather, from her black waders that covered her feet to her thighs to the fitted umber-coloured coat she wore. A tartan shirt was nipped into a leather lace-up corset, revealing the lean, athletic body of a woman in her forties, who had long since grown used to the life of the sewers.

'Tha's better, laddie,' Captain Kildare said softly, her ash blonde hair catching the light, so it looked like strands of gold were woven through the braids that fell out of her red bandana.

'Mudlarks'll find us now,' the boy said lazily, his eyes avoiding Captain Kildare's unwavering stare.

'We all die one day,' she shrugged a single shoulder. 'Death by mudlark isn't the worst way to go.'

She was joking, but the boy couldn't find the humour. Instead, he found only a memory of cold, dead eyes staring up at him from behind a glass cage where only moments earlier, those eyes had been begging him to save them.

'No,' he whispered. 'Not the worst way.'

Under his feet, the barge creaked in its narrow dock. Frothy brown sludge slapped against the wood and scraps of metal that made up the Skimmer.

Captain Bonny Kildare's sewer barge looked impossible, like it was a paper boat that had been folded up so many times that it couldn't possibly float any longer. But float she did.

He felt the leather clad hand of the captain wrap around his shoulders and squeeze him.

'Listen,' she said; her voice was gentle but firm. 'When I agreed to take you on board this ship, I swore I wouldn't stand for any rich boy nonsense. Now I don't claim to know what you've seen or done or been through, neither do I care, truth be told, s'long as you don't be dwelling on it. But this here looks like dwelling to me, and there's nought better for melancholy than hard work.'

He rolled his eyes and shrugged out of her hold.

'I have no magic,' he muttered through gritted teeth. 'What can you expect me to do on a magician's ship?'

Captain Kildare's conjured floating flame brightened in her anger before dimming back down to its cosy little light.

'I expect you to pull your weight, laddie,' the captain said, in a voice that could have made a dire wolf cower. 'Or I'll throw you overboard, and don't think that I won't. Ragstone and Baz have known it be done enough.'

From above them, in the darkness, a deep, laughing voice called down to them.

'She ain't a liar by no mistake. Nasty way to go, lungs full of sh-'

'Thank you, Baz,' Captain Kildare interrupted.

'I have no magic,' the boy said again, the frustration in his voice struggling to be contained.

Captain Kildare reached down into the shadow at her feet and held up a bucket.

'Och, emptying the privy spoils don't take no magic,' she smiled mischievously. 'Or is the son of Corbin Godspell too good to throw pirate turds in the boiler?'

The boy snatched hold of the bucket handle with his bare hand. They had grown callused and hard since he'd removed the gloves, the mark of a magician and a painful reminder of what he no longer was. The stink from the bucket made his stomach turn, but he didn't dare show it.

'Corbin Godspell was not my father,' he growled, squaring up to the captain and thrusting his face towards hers.

'Now there's the spark,' Captain Kildare said, eyes squinting as she looked deeply at his blue eyes.

She pulled up her leather gauntlets and turned on her heel, taking the floating flame with her.

'The ship needs fuel to depart in the morning. Get to the privy. And Linus, don't forget to use your hands. The best spoils are found when you dig deep.'

The boy waited a moment, listening to the sound of the captain's boots fading into the bowels of the Skimmer. Darkness crept in once more, filling the air with its mystery. Above him, hiding somewhere in the rigging, Baz was whistling a lively but dirty little ditty that had become very familiar to Linus in the month since he'd joined the crew of the sewer pirates.

Sighing, he made his way towards the privy, his feet knowing exactly where to step and his hands reaching for the ropes and beams to steady himself at precisely the right time. Captain Kildare may not have liked darkness but it suited Linus just fine. Darkness hid the horrors that light illuminated. Darkness hid tears.

Linus Godspell had never expected his life to have taken such a desolate turn. He had been used to wealth and riches, the best education magicians could offer and political training for his role within the Magistry, the magician's parliament.

Corbin Godspell, his father (or so he had thought) had been the Grand Vizier and ruler of the Magistry of London and all of the United Isles of Great Britain. But more than that, he'd been the Firelighter, the magician's sacred leader and protector of the Flame of Magic, the powerful source of all magic here on the First Plane.

Such grand titles; titles that Linus was supposed to inherit. His future had been mapped out for him from the moment he'd been born. No, that was a lie; from the moment he'd been taken.

The story of his birth was still a shock to him. He still couldn't quite believe that he had been born a twin to his sister Felix, a girl he had never met until the day she'd saved his life.

The same day he'd been drained of his magic.

The same day he'd pushed his father to his death from the White Tower of London.

Linus remembered her now, her hair as raven black as his own but wilder, more untamed. She had the same blue eyes above a slightly wonky nose and rather startling black spirals over her cheekbones. They were the mark of the Drow, witch elves now hunted to extinction and no doubt inherited from their mother, but there was no denying the resemblance. Felix Spark was the name she had been given after she'd been saved, only moments after their birth and the murder of their parents. Shylock Larkin, his father's man servant had secretly delivered her to safety at a commoner's orphanage and he had risked his life to protect Linus every day afterwards, until he too had been killed.

Neither Linus or Felix had ever known of one another's existence, or the tragedy that had befallen their parents.

They had been murdered by Corbin Godspell, the man Linus had called father but who had actually been his uncle; a man who was jealous of his brother and had killed him and his Drow wife simply to gain his titles...and the Sacred Flame.

Linus had been taken as an heir for the simple reason that he was a boy. Godspell had ordered Felix be killed, for he had no need for a half-breed girl. What cruel irony, then, that Linus had been terrible at magic. Felix, it seemed, had been rather powerful from the moment she'd discovered she was a magician and a Drow. It was thanks to her that his life had been saved when Godspell had tried to kill him, though as a consequence, he had been drained of what little magic he possessed.

Now Felix was the Firelighter, and he the commoner.

How fate plays its little tricks.

After everything that had happened, he was now here, a skivvy boy aboard a sewer pirate ship, scooping excrement out of the privy with his bare hands and trying not to breathe through his nose.

But he didn't hate his sister, nor did he blame her. In fact, when he thought of her, he felt a curious ache somewhere behind his ribs, but he couldn't stay at the Citadel with her after she'd saved him; not in the place he had once thought to rule. Not after Paris Lovelock told him everything. Everything and more.

From somewhere overhead, Baz's whistling reached its crescendo and he heard Ragstone raising his voice to telling him to be quiet in far less delicate language.

Linus sucked a lungful of air through his mouth and got back to work. The ship needed fuel and the privy wasn't going to empty itself.

2

Small Steps

'Eugh, I must be cursed,' Felix Spark mumbled under her breath, as she sank further down into her rather uncomfortable chair. Nobody heard her above the hum of magicians' voices that droned on about inflation rates and national spending, voices that interrupted one another, full of their own self-importance. Nobody that is, except the dire wolf.

He lifted his snout from where it was resting in between his outstretched paws on the black and white tiled floor. If it wasn't for his size (and his teeth), he'd look no different to a shaggy grey dog.

Lifting his golden eyes, he smiled ruefully at Felix.

'You wanted to come,' he said pointedly, only no words came out of his mouth.

Rather, they sprang up in Felix's mind like a thought in his unmistakable secret voice, deep and gruff.

'Stocks have plummeted, and our European exchange rate is diminishing,' shouted a voice through the din, and Felix rolled her eyes.

'Definitely cursed,' she whispered, smiling down at D.W, the name she had affectionately given the wolf who was, despite his fearsome demeanour, her closest friend.

She began to twirl a tendril of her black hair around her fingers, noticing its coarseness against her skin, and was still thankful that she no longer had to wear the gloves that were the magicians' trademark. The magic that magicians wielded was so hot that it could scald their skin yet Felix, as the new Firelighter, had no fear of the burning flame that gave her the power of magic. It lived within her, along with the furyfire that had saved her life...and her brother's.

D.W lifted his head and rested it on her knee comfortingly, knowing that the memory of the White Tower caused her pain. He could feel it inside her, like a storm cloud about to pour down.

Felix scratched at his ears and smiled gratefully at him.

'I had no idea it would be this dull,' she admitted in her mind, knowing he could hear her.

'That's politics,' D.W shrugged, flopping his pink tongue outside his mouth and leaning into her scratching fingers and wagging his tail.

The source of their boredom was a meeting of the magisterians in the Magician's Shield, a chamber at the heart of the Citadel. It was home to the Magistry, the parliament and political seat of the magicians of London. With its lofty, domed glass ceiling, polished floors and circular arrangement of seats staggered to the rafters, it resembled both a cathedral and a theatre with a platform at its centre where Felix sat, growing increasingly restless. It was here that the Magistry debated the future of the country, shouting across at one another, their voices echoing and heated as they argued over the Magistry's finances. They paid no attention to Felix and the dire wolf at all.

Felix slumped further down her seat. It was an ornately carved wooden seat, uncushioned and worn down by the backsides of all the previous Firelighters who had gone before. Her father, Everard Godspell had sat in this chair...and so had her uncle, Corbin Godspell.

His death a month earlier had left the seat empty for Felix to claim, along with all of its associated titles of Firelighter, leader of magicians and wielder of the Sacred Flame of Magic and the Right Honourable Grand Vizier, chieftain of the magicians and commoners of the United Isles of Great Britain. And to think...only a few months ago she'd been a nobody; a commoner under the care of Nanny Maude at the orphanage in the Commoner's Quarter.

Immediately, she shifted her thoughts away from Nanny Maude. The memory of her was still too gut wrenching to dwell on. Remembering the empty shells of the orphans' clothes, the only evidence of their deaths left behind after the lamia attack was seared inside her mind's eye and brought the furyfire too easily.

She'd had her vengeance.

The lamias were locked away, her uncle was dead, and the truth had been revealed to all, magician and commoner alike. The truth was vital. It meant freedom.

A shudder rippled through her body as she thought of her uncle's broken corpse, shattered like eggshells on the cobblestones beneath the White Tower. Her brother Linus had stolen her chance of killing him herself, but even so...how glad she was that Corbin Godspell was dead.

Imagining him sat in the same chair that she was in now sent a fresh wave of revulsion through her and she stood abruptly, the dire wolf's snout slipping from her knee.

The chatter in the chamber halted instantly and all eyes shifted to her.

Aubrey Dovepeace, Felix's advisor and Speaker for the Magistry tilted her frizzy red head as she regarded Felix. Eccentric as always in her purple dress and yellow velvet gloves, she waited a beat before speaking.

'Felix?' she asked gently. 'Is there something you wanted to add?'

Felix exhaled, grateful that at least Aubrey didn't insist upon calling her 'my lady' like everyone else in the Magistry did.

'Uh,' Felix began, feeling her face flush. Whenever she blushed, she could feel the fire in the spirals on her cheek burn. It was a near constant reminder of the mother she had never met and a frequent nudge towards the final words of Alchemus J. Fiddle.

'Go to the Glade,' he'd said before he died. It was his parting gift to her; an enticing hint that the home of the Drow sisterhood where her mother had come from still existed. Corbin Godspell had slaughtered the Drow after he'd murdered Felix and Linus' mother, just moments after she had given birth to them. Now the name Calantha Godspell was just another aching longing inside Felix and the tantalising suggestion that there may still be Drow surviving in the Glade was like a new gleaming pearl locked away in her mind. But she had duties here, first.

'Fiddle's memorial,' she blurted out. 'I'd like to talk about that. We haven't moved forward since our last discussion.'

The members of the Magistry began to mumble, but Aubrey held Felix's gaze.

'A solution was not forthcoming,' Aubrey said, with a frustrated arch of her eyebrow.

'Alchemus J. Fiddle was an outlaw,' said Mungo Fogwether, Minister for the London Meteorological Society.

'Here, here,' came the murmur of agreements.

'Lady Felix exonerated Alchemus J. Fiddle and his crimes against the state,' shouted a young magisterian named Zayne Amini.

'He committed no crimes,' Felix said quietly, but everyone in the chamber heard her. 'He was fraudulently condemned by Corbin Godspell, the man who murdered my parents and so many more. Anything my uncle ever said should not be taken as law. His whole reign is a blemish on the history of this country and every truth he told you is a lie.'

Felix scanned her eyes over the Magistry. They were a collection of nearly 200 members, each with a Ministry or a Guild to manage to ensure the smooth running of the country. From the Press and Public Relations Guild to the Ministry of Cuisine, there was a department to control everything.

No, not control. Not anymore.

Felix was working hard to ensure that no man or woman, magician or commoner was a victim of control. The first thing she had done as Grand Vizier was to release a public dossier named the Truth Papers, an accurate recording of the events that took place in the foggy years of Corbin Godspell's rule. Whether people believed it or not was their right. Felix was not fool enough to expect everyone on the United Isles to renounce her uncle. He had been a powerful man for a reason; his manipulation and control commanded fierce loyalty, but that loyalty was bred of fear. Felix would command no such fear.

'Alchemus J. Fiddle was my appointed Magister and that of my brother,' she continued. 'He was the trusted advisor of my mother and father and the secret ally of Shylock Larkin, my uncle's advisor and member of this Magistry. When Corbin Godspell died, I gave each and every one of you the option of resignation with full acquittal and generous retirement. You chose to stay, to advise and support me as the Grand Vizier. I believe you all want to make this country truly deserving of the greatness we claim in its name. I have forgiven all of you the mistakes of your past and I welcome the new voices of the future, which the public have selected to reinstate our lost honour. But do not think that because I am young, that I have no will.

'Alchemus J. Fiddle delivered me to you and fought for the freedom we all now enjoy but that he never saw. Whether you liked him or not, he deserves remembrance, and we will honour his memory.'

Aubrey Dovepeace regarded Felix with her unwavering eyes. Squinting only slightly, she nodded slowly before giving her attention back to the Magistry.

'A memorial then, as Lady Felix requests,' she said firmly.

Felix smiled lightly at her choice of words. She was fully aware her 'request' had sounded more like a demand, and she sat down, secretly chastised. Aubrey, no matter what anyone thought of her, was wise.

'What do you propose, Felix?' Aubrey continued.

Felix looked down at D.W, who gave her an encouraging nudge.

'Fenton House, Fiddle's home,' she said quietly.

'Alchemus left it to you and your brother,' Aubrey reminded her gently.

'I know, but I have more property than I know what to do with. I think he'd like it to be a library, for magicians and commoners alike.'

Aubrey nodded. The magisterians turned their heads back and forth between Felix and Aubrey like they were watching a tennis match.

'My lady,' a woman chirped from the higher seats of the chamber.

Felix looked to her, scanning her brain for her name. Carla Hardsmith; League of Antiquities.

'Forgive me, but Fenton House was left to both you and Lord Linus. We would need his approval before we grant your bequest,' she said.

Around her, heads nodded in agreement.

'But my brother isn't here,' Felix swallowed.

Aubrey flicked her gaze towards her again.

'Unless your brother ...forgive me...unless your brother *dies*, you have no right to overrule his right of ownership,' Carla Hardsmith explained.

Her face was pale. Felix trawled her memory of the book of faces she'd been given a few weeks ago. Hardsmith was an old member of the Magistry. Her votes had always been in favour of the antiquities she protected, not Corbin Godspell. She had three children, the eldest at Eton. Easily pledged allegiance to Felix. Her husband had been a COPP for Godspell. She was widowed.

'Thank you, Mrs Hardsmith,' Felix said, 'for your honesty. You can always speak plainly here. As Lord Linus has chosen to exile himself, does that not invoke the abdication of responsibility clause?'

A mumble of surprise stirred in the chamber and Felix jutted her chin forward a little more, catching Aubrey's small smile in her direction. They still underestimated her, it was clear, but Aubrey had been preparing her well. Felix would not be blind to her role. She didn't know much yet, but she was learning.

'No,' came a voice to Felix's left.

Ah, Maleficent Howl from the Law Lobby. Previous Godspell supporter. Accepted acquittal. Difficult.

'The law clearly states that unless a signed notice of abdication of responsibility is given, then simple absence is not enough. Unless you can get Lord Linus's signature, you'd better hope he dies.'

Felix balked a little and again started the mumbles of surprise. Anger fizzled in Felix's skin as she looked at the watery blue eyes of Maleficent Howl hidden behind square glasses. Her head bobbed a little on her long neck and she held Felix's gaze with certainty.

'Careful,' the dire wolf whispered in her head. 'She's just testing you. I can feel her curiosity.'

'Miss Howl,' Felix said as calmly as she could, in spite of the lump of dislike she held in her throat. 'I thank you for your counsel. My brother will return when he is ready, I'm sure, and I hope he comes back to us alive and well. I believe he was well educated in the ways of the Magistry, Miss Howl, and knew the members of his father's Magistry well. You were for my uncle, were you not? What stories could Linus tell me about you, I wonder?'

Felix felt the magic within her swell and glow, and she let it, knowing it would make her eyes and the spirals on her face shimmer with fire. But Maleficent Howl stared back placidly and simply bowed her head a little.

'Once again, we have reached an impasse regarding Fiddle's memorial,' Aubrey's clear voice cut through the heavy silence. She looked regretfully at Felix.

'I'm sorry, Felix,' she said. 'The law is the law.'

It was already growing dark outside when Felix left the Magician's Shield. D.W was loping at her side, his claws tapping against the tiles as he walked. The corridor was dim, lit by floating orbs of warm yellow light that drifted above their heads and it made Felix sleepy, though it wasn't all that late. Her grumbling stomach told her it was dinnertime, but she couldn't be bothered to navigate her way down to the kitchens, and there was no chance that she'd ask the staff to serve her. Tonight was an especially busy night, anyway, and she didn't want to add extra work on to the magicians and commoners who worked below the stairs.

She had still not grown used to the array of servants who worked in the Citadel. Aubrey had told her that to remove them would put them out of work and Felix didn't want that for them; but even so, as someone who had grown up making her own slop soup and using sour bread to mop up every last drop in the tin bowl, and then cleaning the plates of over twenty orphans, having people serve her a seven-course meal on silver platters each evening didn't sit well with her.

She felt defeated and the day was not yet over. Her afternoon at the Magistry had not gone well, with all three of her proposals blocked by one law or another. The Borderlock, though open for the commoners to enter the city freely, would still be manned by the Commoners Order Police Patrol, a force that could not be disbanded or even renamed to show some semblance of unity. Her suggestion of a separately governed commoner parliament was also rebuffed, once again blocking the rights that she so wanted the commoners to have. And Fiddle's memorial was once again left amongst the dismissal papers, thanks to that awful Maleficent Howl.

'It'll take time,' D.W comforted. 'You can't change the world overnight.'

'I know,' Felix sighed, scratching at his ears. 'But I don't feel like I'm much use to anyone at this point.'

'At least you got the orphanage approved.'

She smiled gladly, pleased at the reminder of her one triumph. Nanny Maude's orphanage would be reopened, with meaningful funding and an extended state-of-the-art property that the many orphans of the Commoner's Quarter would benefit from. And the schools there too were being funded again, with no restrictions on the education of the commoners. They would learn their history, unfiltered by the Magistry as her own education had been. In fact, the whole of the bill she'd put forward had been accepted. Free education, rights to health care and the introduction of a small benefit system meant that the commoners would see some changes to their poverty. She had called it Maude's Bill. Nobody apart from D.W and Nigel had recognised the meaning. Maude's husband had been called Bill.

Small steps.

"Are you ready for the state ball tonight?' D.W asked, to change the subject, glancing up at her. He heard her internal groan.

'I guess so,' Felix nodded.

'It's part of the job, you know,' D.W said, rubbing his ear against her leg.

'Yeah, I know,' she replied. 'But I'm not exactly a social butterfly, and I have to wear an awful poofy dress that Aubrey picked out from Grieves and Hawkins.'

'You, in a poofy dress?' the dire wolf grinned, supressing a chuckle.

'I know,' Felix groaned, but she struggled to hide the smile.

'Is Nigel coming to witness this?'

Felix lowered her face to hide her shy blush. Nigel had been Fiddle's apprentice, taken in after his parents had died. He and Felix had become fast friends but his loyalty and his belief in Felix had meant he had become something more. Their relationship was fledgling, but it made Felix shine.

'No. Balls aren't really his thing. But's he's taking me out tomorrow night,' she grinned.

'A date?' D.W asked in a mock gasp.

Felix nodded, biting her lip happily.

The dire wolf smiled, his tongue lolling out of his mouth.

'Where's he taking you?' he asked.

'I don't know, actually,' Felix said, a small frown creasing her brow. 'I'm meeting him at the London Library.'

'Ah,' D.W said.

He looked up at her and tilted his head. Nigel had taken over Fiddle's role as StoryKeeper of the London Library, and he'd been coming to the Citadel to join them for dinner most days, but it had not gone unnoticed by the dire wolf that Felix had been avoiding returning to library. He could sense the girl's excitement at seeing Nigel, but he felt her apprehension too.

'Fiddle would like that,' he said, pushing his head against her leg again. He saw her sad smile.

'Yeah,' she thought, but he could hear her. 'I know.'

3

The State Ball

Felix stared at herself in the mirror and took a shaking breath. The girl staring back at her barely held any resemblance to the wild-haired, jean-wearing commoner who had first stepped foot into the Magistry of London only a few months earlier. In her place was a girl with shining black hair, smoothed down into soft waves. Her eyes were bluer and sharper, enhanced by the dusting of gold Liberty Linnyshaw had brushed around her eyelids and around the thin, black spirals that twirled over her cheekbone and forehead. The dress, she had to admit, was beautiful even if it did make her feel like a meringue. It was corseted and uncomfortable with skirts that ruffled all the way down to her feet, but it shimmered with flecks of gold and the hem was orange and red; when she moved, it looked like she was trimmed with fire.

'Sorry, I'm looking for Felix,' the dire wolf said, nudging his pink nose through her dressing room door. 'Scruffy-looking thing, mad hair.'

'Shurrup,' Felix said with a laugh, carefully running her hands over her dress.

'You look great, kid,' D.W said, sitting down on his back legs and grinning toothily.

'Hmm,' Felix said, biting her lip but then she pulled up her skirts a little, revealing her scruffy trainers underneath.

D.W rolled his eyes and chuckled. 'You can take the commoner from the Quarter, but you can't take the Quarter out of the commoner,' he said, shaking his head.

'Too right,' Felix grinned.

'Knock, knock!' came a voice from behind the door.

It was pushed open slightly and Aubrey's orange frizzy hair entered before her face did.

'Oh, Felix,' she said, folding her arms and appraising her. 'You look lovely.'

'Thanks,' Felix said twiddling her fingers awkwardly.

Aubrey looked down at them. 'Gloves?' she asked

'Aww do I have to?' Felix moaned. 'I hate wearing them.'

'I know,' Aubrey nodded, opening a drawer and rooting through a pile of gloves that were still wrapped in their Grieves and Hawkins packaging. She pulled out a pair made of gold lace and buttoned at the wrists.

'These will do,' she said, helping Felix pull them on and fasten them. 'Your guests will expect you to be wearing gloves, Felix. As the Firelighter, it's important that you maintain the traditions.'

Felix sighed and rolled her eyes.

'Fine,' she said. 'What else should I expect tonight, then?'

'Lots of visiting dignitaries,' Aubrey said, straddling the stool in front of the dressing table. 'Representatives from every nation, but nothing too surprising. You met most of them at your coronation.'

'Right,' Felix nodded. She flexed her fingers in her gloves and frowned, mentally going through the names and faces she had memorised.

'There will be a few new people,' Aubrey said tentatively. 'Nobles, the families of the Magistry members, whom you've not had chance to mingle with yet. It might be a little awkward. With the commoners, I mean.'

Felix nodded and rested her hands on her hips. For the first time, a selection of commoners had been invited to the Citadel as guests. They would be mixing with the magicians as equals, and this had been the subject of controversy in the newspapers. The Monacle had said Felix was 'subversive' in their article. The Town Cryer had been less kind; they'd said she was 'plain crazy'.

'Just tell the COPPs on duty to keep the peace,' Felix said. 'And no violence or magic is to be used towards any guests – magician or commoner. I mean it.'

'Noted,' Aubrey agreed. 'Are you ready?'

'As I'll ever be, I suppose,' Felix said without enthusiasm. She looked down at the dire wolf, who was grinning up at her as though he was laughing at some small joke she wasn't in on.

'What's up with you?' she asked.

D.W shrugged and wagged his tail.

'We've got a surprise for you,' Aubrey said, standing up and going to the door. She adjusted her glasses and raised an eyebrow.

'Oh?' Felix said, feeling her neck flush.

She wasn't used to surprises. She'd had few good surprises in her life. Gifts were a rare thing growing up in the orphanage, even at Yule. Nanny Maude used to knit them hats and scarves if she had money for the wool, or else she would give them oranges and, on one particularly excellent year, a bag of cinder toffee each.

Aubrey opened the door of the dressing room. There, stood in the firelit hallway, was Nigel. He was dressed in a burgundy suit with a bow tie and new, brown leather gloves. His auburn hair was slicked to the side and his glasses gleamed. In his hands, he held a corsage of beautiful red flowers.

'Good evening, m'lady,' he said with a shy smile.

'Nigel, you look….' Felix began, smiling so widely, it made her cheeks ache.

'You too,' Nigel said, looking her up and down. 'You look…dazzling.'

Felix felt her spirals beginning to glow and she looked down to the floor, embarrassed and happy.

Aubrey and D.W glanced towards one another and smothered their smiles and giggles.

'We'll see you both down there in 5 minutes sharp, Felix,' Aubrey said, and then she and the wolf left the room, closing the door behind them.

'I thought you hated balls,' she said finally.

Nigel shrugged and stepped into the room. He cleared his throat a few times and Felix felt strangely powerful that she had this previously unknown ability to make him nervous. With fumbling fingers that made the leather of his gloves creak, Nigel opened the plastic box that held the corsage. A beautiful scent immediately filled the room. It smelled of cinnamon, smoke from the fireplace, gingerbread, brimstone and cinder toffee, all at the same time. Felix breathed it in, as Nigel slipped the corsage over her wrist and then held her hand.

'It smells beautiful,' she said, inhaling the scent again.

'I made it smell like you,' Nigel whispered, rubbing the back of his neck.

Felix looked at him and for a moment, he struggled to meet her eyes.

'Thank you,' she said, pulling him closer. She leaned up and kissed him on his cheek.

'We'd better go,' Nigel said, his lips tugging at the corners. 'Aubrey will have a fit if you're late.'

'Just one more minute,' Felix said.

Nigel turned to her and squeezed her hand. He leaned his forehead against hers.

'Thank you for being here,' Felix whispered.

'Of course,' Nigel said. 'I wouldn't leave you to face this circus alone.'

Felix grinned and breathed out a laugh.

'Ok,' she said after a few moments. She took a deep lungful of the fragranced corsage and immediately felt calmer.

'Showtime,' she said.

The Citadel was a sprawling glass and stone palace, which had long been the pride of the magicians, and Felix could understand why when she stepped foot into the ballroom. It was a large, octagonal room with a vaulted ceiling which had been painted to look like swirling galaxies and nebulas up, beyond the sky. They shimmered and moved, and the painted stars twinkled, each one sending down a beam of light so that the entire room seemed to be lit by a huge mirror ball. At opposite ends of the room, the huge fireplaces had been lit with scented wood, which provided fragrance and light and warmth.

A temporary balustrade had been erected around the rim of the room, allowing the guests to circulate around the room from a height, and which led down to a main staircase, connected to double doors which were opened by the Citadel servants whenever a guest arrived. They were opened, now, as Felix and Nigel entered, and the room fell silent as they were announced.

'Her most esteemed highness, Grand Vizier and Firelighter, Lady Felix Godspell, with Nigel True, Storykeeper of the London Library,' called out a magician, in the official midnight blue livery of the Citadel servants. Felix cringed at all the titles that came before her name, a name which still felt unfamiliar. She had been raised as a Spark, the name given to all orphans who did not know their parents. The name Godspell was one which still brought forth memories of her uncle, and yet Aubrey had said it was important that she reclaim it for her own and re-establish the honour of the Godspell family.

Felix spread a tight smile across her face, and she gripped harder on to Nigel's arm as they entered the ballroom. Guests gave a polite applause, and they began to bow or curtsy as she and Nigel passed them. Felix felt the embarrassment spreading over her; her cheeks were practically neon.

Slowly, music began playing and conversation started up again. Though Felix could feel eyes upon her and Nigel from every angle, she sighed in relief as she saw the familiar faces of her friends. Standing near the long table of hors d'oeuvres and canapes, were Aubrey and her wife Liberty and their good friend Sigbert Goodnight, chatting to an old lady dressed in a fusty, faded grey dress, embroidered with ugly pink flowers. She was ungloved and holding a little girl's bare hand, tugging her away from the dire wolf who was sat next to the table, eyeing up the mini macaroni and cheese rolls.

'Nell!' Felix said warmly, kissing the old woman on both cheeks. 'Thank you so much for coming. And you, too, Gertie.'

'Hmm,' grumbled the old woman, but the little girl named Gertie squealed in delight.

'Lady Felix!' she said. 'Ooh, you look pretty!'

'So do you,' Felix smiled. 'And don't call me 'lady'. We shared a cell together, I think that makes us good friends!'

Gertie grinned. Felix was happy to see her cheeks were fuller and pinker and that her blonde hair was clean and brushed. She looked like she was even wearing a new dress and new shoes.

'Are you enjoying school?' Felix asked. She crouched down to be eye level with Gertie, who nodded animatedly.

'Oh yes,' she gushed. 'We're learning about magic now in science and venephysics. Last week we did about gravity, too. And the school dinners are nice. I have custard every day!'

The dire wolf licked his lips as she said this.

'I like custard,' he said, and Gertie laughed, even as Old Nell pulled her away, eyeing the wolf's teeth nervously.

'Still not natural,' she said, shaking her head, and Felix couldn't help but laugh.

Old Nell and Gertie were commoners, who had once been part of a small resistance against the magicians, and they had been locked up with Felix, Liberty and Sigbert Goodnight in the Tower of London. Together they had escaped, and Old Nell and her friends had helped Felix overthrow Godspell. Nell didn't much care for magicians but was especially nervous around the dire wolf who was usually invisible to commoners' unmagical eyes. When he'd magically removed a veil from himself, making his visible to commoners, Old Nell had nearly fainted at the size of him.

'Did anyone else come?' Nigel asked, looking around.

'From the quarter?' Old Nell asked, looking him up and down and shaking her head in disgust at the colour of his suit. 'Only a handful. They're about, somewhere. Most was too scared still, what with them COPPs around.'

Nell nodded to the magicians dressed in blood red coats and top hats, who were parading around the balustrade. They had once been the security force tasked with the commoner's order and they had been violent and cruel to them. It was said that their red skin was caused by the blood of the commoners, which they used to stain their skin. Fortunately, this practise had now been banned, if it was ever true in the first place. The COPPs' skin was no longer red, though they still stuck out menacingly, like red blades slicing through the crowds. Felix looked at them and frowned. She hated the COPPs too. She patted Old Nell's hand and turned to the others.

'Sigbert, Liberty,' she said, smiling.

Liberty Linnyshaw was Aubrey's wife. Her long hair was prematurely silver, and she looked ethereal in a gown which matched the shade perfectly. Sigbert Goodnight on the other hand, once the master spy of the rebellion, looked dashing in his emerald-green velvet tuxedo with matching cape. He bowed deeply at Felix, his wide smile making his handlebar moustache tap against his cheek.

'Lady Felix,' he said, with a flourish and a wink.

'Hey Sparky,' Liberty smiled.

'This is all rather grand, isn't it?' Felix asked, looking around.

Nigel handed her a glass goblet filled with a cloudy liquid. It smelled of lemons and Felix smiled at him in thanks.

'Just for you,' he whispered in her ear, making goosebumps erupt all over her skin.

'Tell me about it,' Goodnight said. 'Last time I was in this room, I was being dragged through it by the COPPs. The night we tried to assassinate old Corbin, wasn't it, Lib?'

Liberty nodded and a little colour left her cheeks. She had not been the same since her incarceration in the Tower. Aubrey quickly changed the subject.

'There's a few people you have to meet,' she said to Felix, manoeuvring her away from the group.

Felix looked over her shoulder and gave a half wave to her friends. D.W had his paws on the table, batting a macaroni cheese roll towards his mouth. Felix giggled.

'Focus now, Felix,' Aubrey said in a whispered bark. 'This is important. Best behaviour.'

Yes ma'am,' Felix replied, smiling ruefully when Aubrey fixed her with a hard look.

She guided Felix towards a group of magicians who were clustered together drinking smoking Ashwater. Their suits were black and suspiciously dusty.

'Gentlemen,' Aubrey said, plastering a smile on her face. 'Good evening.'

The magicians turned and immediately bowed at Felix who gave a half curtsy in return.

'Your eminence,' said an older gentleman with a white moustache and white hair that framed a large bald spot on his crown.

'How do you do?' Felix asked politely.

She recognised the man from the folder Aubrey had made her study for weeks. Duncan Ellis, principal of the Ardere Academy, the university of magicians on the Second Plane.

'Well, thank you, Your Grace,' he said kindly. 'What a marvellous evening. It's a joy to be celebrating your accession.'

'Thank you,' Felix returned. 'You are very welcome, Principal Ellis. How fares the Ardere?'

'Oh it continues to educate the finest magicians, as ever, Your Grace.'

'Please, call me Felix.'

Principal Ellis smiled an avuncular smile.

'Felix,' he nodded. 'I hope the academy shall welcome you for study, soon.'

Felix looked to Aubrey in confusion, but Principal Ellis explained.

'Your name has been down for attendance at the Ardere since before your birth. Yours and your brother's. Though, of course, he may well find, ah, other education more suitable now....'

'Now that he's lost his magic, you mean?' Felix finished rather harshly.

Principal Ellis bowed his head in apology.

'I was terribly sorry to hear not only of his loss of power but also of his disappearance,' he said. 'I hope he returns to you soon, safe and well.'

Felix softened.

'Thank you, Principal Ellis,' she said graciously.

She looked at the other magicians behind Principal Ellis. Most of them lowered their heads a little fearfully, and Felix swallowed down her frustration. Her uncle had ruled with fear and she refused to do the same. She wondered how long it would be before people understood that about her. But one magician in the group was regarding her with interest. He was younger than the others, and there was something about his face that was familiar, though Felix could not recall seeing his face in Aubrey's folder before.

'Forgive me, sir,' Felix said. 'I don't believe we have met?'

The man stepped forwards and gave a short, sharp bow of his head.

'We have not,' he said in an accented voice.

'Gaspard,' Principal Ellis said with a warning tone, and Felix heard Aubrey's gasp next to her.

'Gaspard Nyxon, at your service, My Lady,' the man said, holding his arms behind his back.

'Nyxon?' Felix said in surprise. She looked to Aubrey, who was flustered and angry, her arm flapping at her sides like an indignant chicken. The effect was somewhat amusing.

'This is Professor Gaspard Nyxon, Your Grace,' Principal Ellis said, placing a hand firmly on the younger man's shoulder in an attempt to pull him away. 'He is the head of the Tempus consortium and he is also in charge of the Shadowguard, the academy's world-renowned guard, which I'm sure ...'

'Yes, I've heard of the Shadowguard, Principal Ellis,' Felix said. 'They are a force to be reckoned with. This is down to you, Professor Nyxon?'

'Yes,' Gaspard said, nodding his head once. 'I believe you know my father, My Lady? Dr Morell Nyxon.'

Felix swallowed and took a steadying breath.

'I do,' she said tightly.

Dr Nyxon had worked for her uncle. He was a famed venephysicist, studying the physics and science of magic. He had been the one to build the machine that used the Sacred Flame of Magic to try to convert commoners into magicians. Under

Godspell's command, the machine had also been used to experiment on prisoners held in the Tower of London. The machine had killed many. It had almost killed her and her brother. It was the same machine that had drained Linus of his power. After Godspell's death, Nyxon had been arrested and imprisoned. His trial was still underway, though the evidence against him was damning. He would spend the rest of his life in prison.

'I speak now in his defence,' Gaspard continued.

Immediately, Principal Ellis stepped forward to intervene, but Felix held up a hand to stop him.

'Let him talk,' she said. Inside, she could feel the swell of irritation and anger. Dr Nyxon had been ruthless. He had killed children. But he had been under the boot of Godspell, too. Felix knew that fear was a very powerful motive.

'Thank you,' Gaspard said. 'My father has committed many crimes, I know this. But I ask for mercy. Let him be returned to his home in Slovenia. Let him serve his sentence there.'

Felix sighed and looked at the polished, tiled floor beneath her. The anger was beginning to flame inside her, flickering like the hem of her dress.

'Slovenia's sentences are much more lenient, Professor Nyxon,' she said in a quiet voice. 'And many of the crimes which your father has committed have no equivalent in Slovenia. What sentence would be given in Slovenia, for the misuse of the Sacred Flame of Magic, when Slovenia does not have a law for this?'

Professor Gaspard Nyxon gritted his teeth. Felix saw his jaw tighten. She became aware of an audience watching their interaction.

'I must be fair and consistent, Gaspard,' she said more softly. 'Your father committed awful crimes for which he must be punished. You will find that imprisonment has changed since the rule of my uncle. He will have rights. Regular exercise, healthy meals, a chance at rehabilitation and you may visit him as often as you like. You have my word.'

'He was a good man,' Gaspard said in a heated whisper. 'Your uncle corrupted him.'

'I know,' Felix nodded, regretfully.

'He should be given a second chance. Please, My Lady.'

To Felix's horror, Gaspard Nyxon fell to his knees in front of her, and raised his clasped hands. Felix looked around. The faces of her guests were on her back. Whispers spread around the room like a tide. She felt Nigel and the dire wolf step towards her. Their presence provided a little comfort.

'I beg for mercy for my father,' Gaspard pleaded.

Felix's throat was dry, and her eyes flickered to Aubrey, who looked horrified. Behind her, Liberty was pale and trembling, as she recognised the son of the man who had tortured and killed so many of her friends.

Felix crouched down to the floor and kneeled in front of Gaspard, clutching his hands in her own. There was a collective gasp from the guests.

'Gaspard, she said quietly. 'We are not accountable for the actions of our family members and so I hold nothing but respect for you and what you are trying to do. You love your father, I can see that. But your father showed no mercy to the hundreds – *hundreds* – of commoners and magicians whom he killed. To let your father, is a mercy in itself. Be satisfied with that.'

Gaspard's dark eyes hardened, and he pulled his hands out of her grasp. For a moment, Felix thought he would yell at her, or even try to hit her. Instead, he stood up in one fluid movement and looked down at her, fighting a sneer.

'I thank you for your time, My Lady,' he said, though Felix heard the choke of his words.

He gave a small bow and turned on his heel, leaving the ballroom chattering and whispering behind him.

Principal Ellis reached down to Felix and helped her up, stammering his apologies but Felix shook her head, silencing him.

'He's in pain,' she said. 'He's doing what he can. We all are.'

As soon as the music began playing again, the principal made his farewells, leaving early. Aubrey apologised to Felix and took a frightened Liberty to her room to try and calm her down.

Felix managed to smile, and she mingled and made small talk. Platters of food were passed around. Drinks were poured. Music played. Felix danced with her guests.

Soon the night was over, and Felix stood by the door, shaking hands and accepting kisses on her hand as she said curtseyed and said good evening. Only when the ballroom was empty did she go to Nigel and the dire wolf. D.W was happily eating the last scraps of food from the table and Nigel was sat in a chair, unfastening his bow tie.

'What a night,' he said. 'You ok?'

'I think so,' Felix replied, resting on Nigel's knee and tipping her head onto his shoulder. She felt strangely bruised by the whole evening.

'You managed that really well,' he whispered to her.

'You think?' she asked, looking at him. 'I felt really awful. He was so sad.'

'He was angry,' D.W said, with a mouthful of custard tart. 'He had a temper to rival yours.'

'Really?' Felix asked. 'He held it together, then.'

'Hmm,' the dire wolf said, licking his chops. 'Maybe.'

'You know, you danced with every single male magician tonight,' Nigel said with a pout. 'Except me.'

'Well that won't do,' Felix grinned. She climbed off his knee and held out her hand to him.

'May I have this dance?' she asked.

'Who am I to turn you down, m'lady?' Nigel beamed.

'I'm going to puke,' the dire wolf said, rolling his eyes.

But Nigel and Felix either didn't hear him, or chose not to listen. From nowhere, music began to play.

4

The Festival of Fire

The next day was Saturday and Felix was relieved to have a day free of Magistry meetings and dress fittings and press gatherings. She was excited for her date with Nigel, and it seemed that the whole Citadel was buzzing after the State Ball. The staff were unusually cheery and there was a sense of anticipation in the air. Even the day's newspapers couldn't bring her down, with their reports about her being either 'merciless and unyielding' to 'stoic and strong'. Felix tossed them into the fire as soon as she saw them.

By early evening, she was nervous. She had never been on a real date before but more than that, she hadn't been back to the London Library since Fiddle's death. She decided to walk there to quell her nerves, and she'd been pleasantly surprised that Aubrey had agreed to let her go without any accompaniment. Even the dire wolf stayed at the Citadel, wishing her a good evening and giving her an encouraging nudge as she left.

The London Library was often overlooked by the passers-by who hurried in the orb light through chilly St James' Square. Away from the riot and fuss of the busier Trafalgar, St James' Square felt calm and forgotten, a little glen of green amidst stone houses that stretched lazily into the smoke screen sky. Squeezed into a corner, the London Library could have been sleeping for all its quiet grace, and yet Felix knew that behind its unassuming brown door and grey windows, the rooms whispered with stories; literally.

Behind those walls, huddled in front of the great fireplace in the Reading Room, she had learned that she was a magician and saw, for the first time, the Drow spirals that circled on her cheekbone and spread tendrils over her forehead.

Felix smiled at the memory and felt the tug of sadness as she pictured Fiddle sprawled, in his refined way, in his oxblood armchair sipping cinnamon tea and smiling serenely with his glistening eyes that were younger than his wrinkled face.

The library had been his home and refuge, keeping him safe throughout his fugitive years and protecting him like it was a living force. It had been her home and refuge, too, until she had been moved unceremoniously into the Citadel, the rightful seat of the Firelighter and Grand Vizier.

This was the first time she had been back since she had left it on the night her uncle had died. She had meant to come back for her belongings, but Aubrey had Thaddeus collect them for her instead. She had meant to come back to go through Fiddle's things and sort them accordingly. She had meant to come back to oversee the restocking of the History Room.

She had meant to come back. But somehow, she hadn't.

The air was colder than it had been the first time she had stood here with D.W, looking at the library from the edge of the gardens and questioning what waited for her in there. Pulling her frock coat around her tightly, she remembered the library card that had brought her here in the first place and wondered if it was still in the pocket of her jeans back at the Citadel, still stained with her brother's blood from inside the chamber.

No. Stop that.

Felix shook the images out of her head even as the warmth of the Sacred Flame shimmered inside her. Or maybe it was the furyfire. She still couldn't quite distinguish between them, and they blended together to create a fizzing sort of sensation that rippled through her when she forgot herself.

A slight movement caught her eye and she looked up sharply to see the door of the library opening slowly. Nigel leaned against the door and tilted his head.

'Are you coming in or what?' he said softly, but Felix could hear him in the silence of the square.

An easy smile spread over her face and her feet took her towards him of their own volition and led her up the steps.

'Hey,' she whispered.

'Hey,' Nigel said, giving her his lopsided smile. 'Come in.'

He took her hand and her bare fingers folded around his gloved hand. He was wearing emerald-green leather gloves today, buttery smooth and well worn. Felix knew they had been Fiddle's. He'd worn them the first time she'd met him, but she didn't say anything.

'How you feeling today?' Nigel asked, as they walked past the checkout box and into the Reading Room. It opened up in front of Felix like pages of a familiar book. Immediately, the welcoming smell of cinnamon and fire, Nigel's lemonade and the deep musk of old books enveloped her. She'd been an idiot to stay away for so long.

'Ok. Aubrey and Sigbert have a hangover,' Felix smiled, shrugging off her coat.

As always, the fire was blazing in the room, the lamps were lit and the clock was ticking, a little frantically, above the fireplace.

'Oh? Too much Ashwater?'

Nigel sat down on the Aubusson rug in front of the fire and held his hand out to her to pull her down to him. Glancing momentarily at the empty armchair, she cuddled into his chest and nodded.

'Yeah. Aubrey's been in a foul mood today as well. Keeps going on about taxes and international relations and ceremonies and all that. Not really my thing. Especially on a Saturday.'

Nigel chuckled as he began to curl a lock of her hair around his fingers.

'So make it your thing.'

'I'm trying,' Felix said. 'Yesterday I asked the Magistry about opening the Borderlock and letting the commoners into the city to live and work.'

'And?'

'We'll see. You know, when I became the Firelighter and the Grand Vizier I thought I'd have a lot more say in how things are run. Turns out it's a lot of sitting around and asking for permission to do things.'

'You know what Fiddle would say, don't you?'

Felix looked up at him and shook her head.

'He'd say 'better to ask for forgiveness than permission'.'

Felix laughed and nodded.

'Yes, he would say that.'

She stared into the fire and let herself unfurl. It was like she could breathe, finally, after holding a lungful of air for far too loon.

'I'm sorry I stayed away so long,' she said quietly. 'Now I'm here, I don't know why I did.'

'It's ok,' Nigel said, kissing the top of her head. 'I do. I'm glad you're here though. So is the library. She's been a moody old thing without you...though I don't think she's missed your outbursts.'

Felix swatted Nigel's shoulder.

'Hey, I'm getting pretty good at controlling my temper! D.W even said he can't smell the anger on me anymore.'

'Hmm and what does he say your anger smells like?' Nigel asked playfully.

'Like brimstone and ash, apparently.'

'Well to me, you smell delicious,' he said into her hair. 'Are you ready for our date?'

'Yes!' Felix said excitedly. 'Where are we going?'

'I'm taking you into the heart of the city,' Nigel grinned and stood quickly, yanking Felix up with him. 'You should see London at night. It really comes alive.'

It was something of a thorn in Felix's side that she had never had chance to fully explore the Magistry of London since she'd stepped off the locomotron from the Commoner's Quarter several months earlier. She'd been kept hidden away in the library for several weeks for her own safety, and what little she'd seen of the city had been during an illicit adventure to the Monument where her parents' ashes had been secretly placed in memorial to them by Fiddle. That excursion had led to her capture and consequent imprisonment in the Tower of London, so it was no surprise that Felix felt wary as she walked through the dimming streets with Nigel at her side. His excitement was infectious, though, and she soon stopped casting glances over her shoulders, but she spread her hand over her face for a moment to perform a glamour charm that would make her Drow spirals invisible to passers-by. They were a unique and defining trait that made her instantly recognisable, and she really didn't want any undue attention.

London was a mesmerising city. It lured her like siren's song until she was held captive by its beauty and charm. It was a city that ran on magic and steam, electricity and what seemed like sheer willpower. Orbs of light hovered above them, casting ethereal shadows through the ever-present silver mist that descended from the sky and travelled down the streets like a cautious tourist. Just like she had done when she'd first arrived, Felix could not help but look up. It amazed her that the magicians in the street, engrossed in their evening copies of The Monocle or The Daily Moon kept their noses down, never glancing upwards at the metal bridges overhead that connected the sprawling old stone buildings. Stone archways led from balconettes to wooden platforms, intersected by iron galleys that led to staircases that spiralled around tower blocks. Felix, curious as always, longed to climb them, to ascend to the rooftops of London where she could see magicians, small as ants, traversing the high walkways.

'You hardly need to walk on the ground at all,' she whispered, gazing into the smoky ceiling of the city. Nigel looked at her then followed her gaze.

'Yes, it's pretty impressive,' he nodded. 'When you can't build outwards, you have to build up. Plus, it was convenient for the skyships...before Godspell banned them of course.'

'Skyships?' Felix spluttered.

'Sure. My aunt said they were all the rage on the second plane. Your father tried to introduce them for a time, but they weren't tremendously popular. It's too built up here. But it'd be cool to see them back if you felt so inclined, Firelighter Felix.' Nigel grinned at her. Felix looked up again and shook her head in disbelief.

'How is Aunt Vessania? Set any more curtains on fire?' Felix asked.

Nigel's aunt was the only family he had left after his parents had died when he was four. He rarely talked about them. She didn't want to press him on the subject, but she lapped up any information Nigel gave about his family eagerly.

'Batty,' Nigel smiled fondly, but there was a wariness in his voice. He absently took Felix's hand and started swinging it as they walked slowly up Waterloo Place. 'I was thinking of moving her into the library actually... now that it's emptier. If you didn't mind?'

Felix saw him swallow nervously, and he flicked his eyes to her quickly to judge her reaction.

'It's your library now, Nigel,' she said softly and squeezed his hand. He squeezed it back and she felt the tension leave him. 'I'd like to meet her.'

Nigel nodded.

'You will,' he said tightly. 'Soon, I promise.'

Felix sighed, cautious of pushing him. Nigel had secrets. She only wished he'd share them with her.

Despite the library being so close to the very centre of London, it surprised Felix when they turned into Trafalgar Square only a few minutes later.

The square was impressive. It was a vast collection of grand lion statues and elaborate fountains, leading towards stone steps that arced around the old National Gallery, which stood perched on the north side. It's fluted Doric columns and white dome reminded her a little of the Citadel, and she added it to her mental to-do list to ensure that it was reopened, and the artwork returned to it from the labyrinthine hallways of the Citadel and its underground vaults. Her uncle had burned and destroyed many pieces, taking only the artwork created by noted magicians through the ages, but Larkin, rest his soul, had seen to it that at least some of the masterpieces had been secretly stashed below ground.

Thousands of people filled Trafalgar Square; magicians in their long coats and their menagerie of strange hats milled around, talking and laughing in crowds. She saw children running through the fountains, the steam floating above the water, telling her it was warm in the chilly air. They played happily, squirting each other with the water using their magic to fling droplets at one another. Stalls and market vendors paraded their wares to passers-by.

'Ashwater! Come and get your Ashwater! Special brew from the Ashfjord!'

'Cinder toffee! Sticky cinder toffee!'

'Tosher Trinkets – precious charms from Lundonwick!'

Dancers blew fire from their mouths, their bodies snaking around the flames which twirled playfully with their wielders and at the very centre of the square, a pile of logs and wood rose so high around a column that Felix didn't know how she'd missed it. But what thrilled her most, was seeing commoners mixing with the magicians. They were wary, that was obvious, and they clustered together in small groups, taking tentative sips of Ashwater and honeymead, but they stared, wide-eyed in amazement at the wonder around them.

'What is all this?' she breathed, spinning around and trying to take in a hundred different things.

Excitement hung in the air, like the musky smoke which smelled like cinnamon and spice.

'It's the Festival of Fire,' Nigel laughed. 'Surely you read about this in your daily briefings?'

'Well, yes, of course,' felix nodded. 'But I didn't realise it was such a huge thing. All I heard was that it was small parade and a fair for the kids.'

Nigel shook his head, grinning.

'It's a 6-day festival to mark the Great Spark, when magic and magicians first came into this Plane. Magicians across the country will be celebrating this day! And commoners, too, thanks to you.'

Felix looked at Nigel curiously. A memory of Fiddle's voice rang clear in her mind.

'Only the Firelighter and the Privy Council know why magicians entered into the First Plane, and why.'

Fiddle's voice was still painfully fresh. He'd said those words to her when he'd taken her to the Second Plane, the world behind worlds and the place where magicians had come from. This world, the First Plane had belonged to the commoners before magicians found their way here. For centuries, they'd lived amongst the commoners in secret until her father, Everard had made their presence known in the Great Revelation. There had been peace, for a while. Until her uncle had seized power.

But Fiddle had refused to tell her how magicians had come here. 'It's a secret,' he had said.

'The Great Spark?' she cocked her head to one side.

'It's just a myth really,' Nigel said, pulling her to the cinder toffee cart. 'They say that the first Firelighter opened the first hatch into this plane and caused a great fire in the city, bringing magic with it which then spread throughout the world!'

The first Firelighter? A great fire?

'Are you talking about the Great Fire of London? I thought that fire was started by a baker?' she asked, thinking back to the inscriptions she'd read on the Monument.

'That's what the commoners think,' Nigel winked and then he laughed. 'It's just a story, Felix. Magicians chose this day because it was already a festival for the commoners. All Hallows' Eve? Though I think it used to be called Samhain, an old fire festival. Even the commoners celebrated fire once upon a time.'

Felix nodded, but an uneasy feeling was creeping through her body, reminding her of how much she didn't know...of how much Fiddle had never told her. Hadn't her uncle said that much to her in the Tower?

'Ahh Felixia Solis...so you don't know everything'.

'It's just a bit of fun, Felix,' Nigel shrugged. 'I think every culture, creed and faith on the planet merges their holidays and festivals together. Any excuse for a party! You want some cinder toffee?'

Felix looked at his happy green eyes as he held out a brown bag of warm, sticky, amber-coloured honeycomb and smiled. He was right. It was probably nothing to worry about, but she'd ask Aubrey about it all tomorrow. Now she was the Firelighter, she had a right to know about the truth of this, surely? And she'd ask about Felixia Solis too, whatever that was. For now, though, she was with Nigel. She grinned and took a piece of cinder toffee and popped it into her mouth.

At eleven thirty, the bonfire around the column was lit to loud 'ooohs' and 'ahhh's from the gathering crowd. Nigel pulled her close and Felix snuggled into the warmth of his chest, feeling the glow of the fire searing into her secret spirals. The bonfire was built around a tall stone column with a statue of a man at the top, though the flames didn't seem to be damaging it at all.

Felix looked around at the firelit faces of the magicians around her, all peering up with gleeful eyes at the statue. There must have been hundreds of people there, circled around the bonfire and throughout the square for as far as the eye could see.

At midnight, bells began to chime.

'Wait for it,' Nigel whispered to her, and she felt his smile against her head.

The bells rang twelve times, and all was silent save for the crackle and hiss of the burning wood.

'Look!'

Felix jumped, and looked towards an excited little boy perched on top of a magician's shoulders. He was pointing his finger at the top of the bonfire. Felix looked towards it and gasped.

The stone man on top of the column was moving! No...not just moving. He was dancing! His stone legs were doing some sort of jig atop the fire!

'What?!'

Nigel's answering laugh made Felix begin to giggle, as she watched the statue dancing on top of the flames.

A mighty roar stole her attention and she turned quickly towards the noise, along with the magicians around her, and her mouth fell as she saw the giant white lion statues stretch into life, their stone jaws wide and roaring.

'I told you London really comes alive at night,' Nigel shouted over the cheers of celebration. 'Do you like it?' He gazed earnestly into Felix's eyes, searching for approval.

'Nigel...it's magic,' Felix whispered. 'All of this, being here with you, without Aubrey over my shoulder all the time, just being *me* for once...I love it. Thank you.'

Overhead, fireworks flew up into the sky and illuminated the square with dazzling colours. But Felix didn't see them, nor did she hear the explosions of noise as they burst across the sky. She saw only Nigel as she reached for his face and kissed him.

Happiness unfurled inside her and burned through her body, lighting the spirals that had been hidden by her glamour. They glowed yellow, and then a blazing orange as the heat of her joy swept through her.

'Lady Felix?' A voice interrupted their moment. 'Hey, it's Felix!'

She pulled away from Nigel instantly, her bliss turning to dread as the blur of faces began to swarm around her, bees around their queen.

'FELIX!' they cried. 'It's the Firelighter, she's here!'

'Lady Felix!'

All the attention was on her and the reappearing black spirals on her face; the dancing statue and the roaring lions were dismissed as the crowd surged its way towards Felix. Panic choked her, as she felt gloved hands reaching out in her direction. She pulled away from them only to fall back into more outstretched arms.

'Nigel!' she cried out, but she had lost him. From somewhere, she heard his voice calling her name, but it just mingled with the myriad of voices that shouted for her in the crush.

'Please!' she called. 'Please leave me alone!'

But the wave of people kept on battering towards her.

She felt it coming before she could stop it.

It was like feeling ill, feeling the wave of nausea rising up out of your stomach and pouring out of you. Only this was furyfire and it engulfed her wholly, until she was a firebird emerging from the nest of magicians surrounding her.

Their cries of fear and horror choked her more than the smoke that billowed out of her mouth and nose. Thick and fast, the lava inside her blood pounded in her heart and merged with the Sacred Flame she guarded there. It exploded within her and the power of it lifted her from the ground. Shrieking in pain, the Flame seared through her skin, every pore alight with the blue and red inferno that came from deep inside her.

She couldn't stop it. She knew she couldn't. It had to burn out the way it had done in the Tower, when she'd taken the Sacred Flame into herself. She had no choice but to let it burn her alive, knowing it would not kill her, though she wished it would. The pain was unbearable.

Screams of terror pierced through her own cries. Looking out through eyes aflame, she saw faces filled with horror as parents shielded their children from her, as magicians fled from the square and commoners cowered in fear. Below her, on the ground, she could see Nigel, the only still figure amidst the panic, looking towards her with horrified eyes. He was shouting to someone. Who?

It was Aubrey. She was running against the crowd towards her, and there was Thaddeus too. Had they been here the whole time, watching from afar?

Felix was burning from the inside out. The Sacred Flame scorched every cell and the furyfire made her heart burn, but it was the betrayal that hurt her most, the realisation that she would always be treated like this; watched over, protected and shielded, forever guided like a little girl. Never alone but constantly lonely. It was the last thing she thought before everything went black.

5

Paris

The man flicked a crumb of sour bread off the corner of the newspaper and shook his head. A lock of grubby grey-blonde hair fell into his eyes, and he brushed it back with gloved fingers, lingering over the ugly scar that fell across his wrinkled brow, remnants of the botched stitch job that Kildare had performed. He'd thought of using a glamour charm, but he'd rather taken a liking to the scar, thinking it gave him a somewhat devil-may-care aesthetic. Certainly, it helped him fit in amongst Lundonwick, what with the ne'er-do-wells and criminals who haunted the murky streets of the shantytown beneath the western reaches of the Magistry.

How are the mighty fallen.

If his father could see him like this, dirty and disfigured, lingering amongst the lowlife-infested sewer pirate town, he'd disown him. That is, if his father hadn't already been disowned by his son all those annums ago; disowned for refusing to let his son make his own decisions about his future life.

Another life. A life that had been once been his for the taking and one he'd refused for good reason.

It didn't matter now. His father was long dead. A heart attack, they'd told him. He'd believed them, of course, as would any ten-annum-old boy who was mourning the loss of his estranged father. Oh, how he'd regretted the emancipation he'd fought for and hard won, when he'd found out his father had died crying out his only son's name.

'Paris! My son, forgive me. You were right,' he'd called out. Or that's what Arthur Godspell had told him; Arthur Godspell, who had died in exactly the same way as his predecessor a few decades later. A heart attack, they'd told Arthur's son, Everard.

Lies.

At twelve-annums-old, Paris had seen the post-mortem examination report the healers had carried out on his father. He had it filed away in his memory. He'd always been rather good at remembering things; it was a skill, a talent, a magical predisposition to see things exactly as they were, or are...or...oh who knows. All he could say with any certainty was that he knew things that others didn't.

Paris Lovelock was far smarter than anybody ever gave him credit for. He was alive, wasn't he? Had he become the Firelighter, as he was meant to, as was his right... he'd have died just like the rest.

The post-mortem report had said that his father, Deacon Lovelock, tenth Firelighter, sixth of his line had traces of arsenic in his blood, which had led to his heart failure. The report was embargoed by the Privy Council, just as it was thirty-six years later when the eleventh Firelighter, Arthur Godspell had died.

And then, when his son Everard, the twelfth Firelighter was murdered and his brother Corbin took the title, the truth was covered up again. Paris had borne witness to their decision, being as he was, part of the Privy Council himself.

Let Alchemus Fiddle take the blame for the murders...and he, Paris, had voted in favour of that decision, too. Alchemus, who was reaching too high and too earnestly for equality; an equality the Privy Council did not want to grant. Alchemus, who should have known that as well as Paris did. As a peer on the council, Alchemus knew that the elders who made up the high recesses of power at the Ardere Academy were decades behind their younger, more idealist counterparts.

Alchemus always was a fool, albeit a wise one.

He'd put faith in the Spark girl and here she was, the fourteenth Firelighter, overthrower of that imbecile Corbin Godspell and heroine of the commoners. Paris was impressed by her; he couldn't deny it, though her interest in the commoners was dull. Even when he'd been Corbin Godspell's skivvy in the Department of Commoner Care, he'd found the plight of the commoners to be insignificant in the grand scheme of things. But Felix Spark, born of the commoners, made of Drow and magician, a trinity of power, was here to unite the peoples and the planes as the 'Rightful Firelighter'.

'And yet she is dressed in 'borrowed robes' as the bard would say,' Paris whispered, staring the newspapers' sketched image of Felix, glowing like a fireball at the Festival of Fire a few days earlier.

'Firelighter Felix Sparks Fear at Fire Festival' the Monocle's headline read, and Paris once again shook his head in pity.

She would die soon.

It was inevitable.

He picked up his crust of sour bread and finished eating it before folding the newspaper under his arm. It was time to go. The Skimmer would be docking in an hour, and he had secrets to share and old friends to meet.

6

Something or Nothing

She was dreaming. He could see. It hurt him to feel her anguish. He had tried hard to avoid prying into her dreams, but he was made to sense lost souls and Felix never felt more lost than in her dreams. They were vivid shards of images that cut into his own thoughts like glass. Impossible to ignore.

The dire wolf yelped at Felix's bedside, willing her to wake, trying to reach her with his voice but she was so deep inside herself, and he could not follow her. She had been asleep for days. Her eyelids fluttered constantly.

Flashes of doors. Strange, haunting music. She was pulling at a door with spirals engraved in the wood. They moved like snakes.

'Let me in!' she cried over and over, but the door wouldn't open.

Dead orphans stood behind her, stepping out of the orphanage door.

'You could have saved us, Felix,' sobbed little Raji.

Five years old. A delightful, beautiful little girl, Nanny Maude had written.

'You left us. You're a magician now. Is that why you didn't come back to save us? You don't care about us anymore.'

'No! No, I did come back! I tried!'

'You failed.'

The orphanage door slammed shut. Felix couldn't open it.

'Please someone help me!' she screamed.

'Felix I'm here!' The dire wolf shouted.

But she couldn't hear him.

'You don't know everything, then,' Godspell's voice dropped over the room like a heavy silk curtain. Shadows.

'Fiddle, please help,' she begged.

A green door now, with columns on either side. She banged on it with blistering fists.

'Felixia Solis...Felix,' Godspell purred. 'Felixia. Solis.'

'They hurt us, Felix. Why did you leave us?' Raji cried.

The orphans began to fade, their skin peeling to ash.

'Please!' Felix screamed.

The green door opened. The midst behind it was bright and warm.

'I never thought I would be naming you, little one,' Fiddle's voice spoke softly, as though from a memory. 'Wake up.'

The green door slammed closed.

Felix's eyes snapped open and before she could scream, she vomited. The dire wolf howled for help, though he had barely opened his mouth before Nigel had burst through the door. He held her hair back from her face and soothed her as she threw up beside her bed. Aubrey rushed in seconds later, relief softening her sleep-deprived face. In the hallway outside, D.W heard Liberty Linnyshaw's worried thoughts and felt the concern from Thaddeus, but it was Imelda the healer who bustled through and pushed everyone out of the way.

'Let me get to her,' she said, and shooed Nigel out of the way.

He looked on nervously whilst Imelda rubbed Felix's back and held a bowl under her mouth.

'That's right, honey, get it all out. You're home. You're safe.'

'Can't you stop it?' D.W asked, as Felix wretched again.

'Better to get it out,' Imelda answered, but as she rubbed at Felix's back, her healing presence slowed the heaves of Felix's stomach until she was bent over the side of her bed, breathing raggedly.

D.W saw her screw up her nose at the stench and he looked at Aubrey. She nodded and she motioned a scrubbing action with her hand and the mess next to the bed disappeared.

Imelda removed her gloves and placed her hands on the Felix's head and closed her eyes. D.W tried to hear what she was thinking, but healers had a command of magic that was tied with touch and not thoughts. Whatever she was doing was working though; he heard Felix's chaos begin to calm.

'You slept for two days,' he answered her passing thoughts. 'You're in the Citadel. Everything is ok.'

Felix nodded at him and smiled gratefully.

'She wants water,' he said, and heard Liberty outside in the hallway saying she'd get some.

'What...' Felix tried to speak, but her voice was a mere croak and she winced painfully.

Nigel knelt down next to her immediately. The dire wolf smiled as he heard Nigel's thoughts of concern and care for her.

'The Sacred Flame took hold of you,' Aubrey explained slowly. 'It mingled with your furyfire, just as it did in Godspell's machine but this time, it was much more powerful.'

Felix looked at Aubrey with an unspoken question in her gaze. Aubrey, expressionless as always, blinked and nodded her head.

'It will get stronger,' she said softly, answering Felix's imploring eyes.

D.W listened carefully, sensing rather than hearing the worry inside Aubrey Dovepeace, before Liberty's gambolling footsteps broke through as she burst into the chamber with a jug of water, sloshing it all over the carpet and splashing D.W's snout.

'Here,' she said breathlessly, holding out the jug, which was now half empty and dripping onto the carpet.

One by one, they began to laugh, the tension breaking as the nerves that had been on edge whilst Felix had been sleeping dissolved.

'You gave us quite a scare, Miss Felix,' Thaddeus said in his sonorous voice.

He was tall and broad, his shoulder's nearly the width of the door. The dire wolf tried not to hear Imelda's inappropriate and rude thoughts about him.

Felix smiled and leaned back against her pillows, accepting the glass of water that Liberty handed her.

'Sorry,' she said ruefully. 'I thought I had a handle on my temper these days.' She frowned for a moment, and winced as the pain of the spiral markings on her face creased.

'I don't think it was your temper, Felix,' Aubrey said quietly. 'You were threatened, and the Sacred Flame defended you. Tell us, what were you thinking when you were caught in the crowd?'

Felix thought for a moment and looked at Nigel. He was still kneeling by her side, his gloved hand clutching hers tightly. His face was pale, highlighting his freckles and the dark shadows under his eyes. She noted that he needed to sleep. They all did.

'I was thinking that I wanted to get away from them all. The crowd. I was frightened.'

Aubrey nodded.

'I think the Sacred Flame is becoming attuned to your emotions. You need to be more careful.'

'I'm sorry, Felix,' Nigel spoke for the first time. 'This would never have happened if I hadn't taken you out.'

'I have to agree,' Aubrey's voice was harsh. 'It was foolish. She's the Firelighter and the Grand Vizier. She can't be running around London without protection.'

'Aubrey,' Liberty interjected gently, resting her hand, in aquamarine gloves, on her shoulder. 'They're young. Don't you remember what it's like to be young?'

Aubrey sighed and patted Liberty's hand, taking it in her own and kissing it quickly in a rare moment of affection between the two.

'Besides,' Liberty continued. 'You were there to protect her.' She motioned to Aubrey and then to Thaddeus, who was leaning against the door frame as though he was holding it up.

Felix looked at them both, her eyes darting from them to D.W and then to Nigel who she glared at with accusing eyes.

'You had them follow us?' she demanded, struggling to hide the hurt in her voice.

The dire wolf shifted his weight from one paw to the other, reading her thoughts carefully. Nigel cast a wary glance at him.

'Well...I...yes,' he nodded. D.W felt the crushing disappointment inside Felix.

'The only sensible thing you've done,' Aubrey quipped, her lips a firm line.

Liberty gave her a dig with her elbow.

'It was to keep you safe, Felix. I didn't tell you because I didn't want you to feel like you were under supervision or something,' Nigel explained.

Felix studied him, then glanced at everyone else.

'Ok,' she whispered, but the dire wolf could feel the undercurrent of betrayal behind her words.

Silence crept into the room, and they all stood around the Firelighter with a veil of tension above them. Felix swallowed, her throat sore and dry, still, and she battled against the ugly feelings that fought inside her. It wasn't anger, though she felt irritated. It wasn't frustration, though she was certainly exasperated by the lies and secrets that she still seemed to fall victim of. It was resentment; a sickly, churning emotion that tugged inside her stomach, threatening to pull her down into darkness. Suddenly, she didn't want any of them to be there anymore.

'I'd like some rest now, please,' she said quietly, looking down at the blush pink and black spiralled baby blanket that she had only now noticed was draped over her bed.

'Have this tonic then,' Imelda thrust a canister of transparent liquid to her.

'What is it?' Felix asked, sniffing it.

'Fleetwater,' Immelda said. 'Cures pretty much anything, and it's incredibly rare so don't waste it.'

Felix looked at the unassuming liquid and swallowed it. It tasted earthy and faintly metallic, but she immediately began to feel better.

'Right, now everybody out!' Imelda said, clapping her hands together and ushering Aubrey and Liberty and Thaddeus out of the door before leaving herself.

Reluctantly, Nigel stood.

'You're sure you're alright?' he whispered to her.

Felix nodded and tried to give him a reassuring smile. He leaned down and kissed her forehead and left with the others. Only the dire wolf stayed. Felix looked down at him cautiously.

'Don't,' he said.

Felix blinked at him.

'Don't what?'

'Don't push them away.'

'I'm not.'

D.W stepped closer to the bed and stared up at her with his large golden eyes.

'They love you and you need them. You deserve them, so stop finding ways to deprive yourself of them. Stop punishing yourself.'

'Stay out of my head,' Felix said.

She wasn't threatening but the dire wolf stepped back, giving her space.

'You're lost again. I can't help it,' D.W shrugged his shackles.

Felix shook her head, and the wolf could see the slight glisten of tears in her eyes.

'Please just go,' she begged.

The dire wolf whimpered in sympathy for her pain, which he could feel as though it was his own, but he padded slowly out of the room, turning back only once.

'You belong here, Felix, no matter what you think. You always have.'

He walked away, leaving Felix in peace. When she knew that he was gone, she pulled up her baby blanket and buried her face into it.

'You're wrong,' she murmured, as she cried. 'I don't belong anywhere.'

On the third day of her recovery, she realised they were keeping the news from her. Though she was feeling stronger, Imelda insisted she remain in bed, resting and Aubrey would not disobey the orders of a healer, especially when it came to the health of the Firelighter. Rest meant a reduction in her duties. No more Magistry meetings. No more daily briefs. No more morning reports and no more newspapers. Felix figured this was because her actions at the Festival of Fire had not been reported in a flattering light. The thought made her feel cold. She wanted to be a ruler who was respected and admired, not feared. Her uncle had dominated the country with an iron fist, and he had been despised because of his rule of terror and more than anything, she wanted to avoid this at all costs. And yet here she was, locked away once again, as she had been most of her life, because of fear.

Only this time, they all feared her.

By day five, she was allowed to leave her chambers. Felix was quietly elated. She roamed the Citadel as though she had been given the gift of sight and was seeing it all for the first time. It was really quite beautiful, though honestly too large for her. Frequently, as she wandered from one oversized, over-decorated room to another, she wondered if it might be put to better use.

She was mainly left alone, and she was grateful for this. Nigel worked daily at the library and was too careful with her, when he came to visit in the evenings. He was preoccupied with moving his aunt into the rooms at the library and though Felix was curious to meet her, she felt a strange sense of unease whenever Nigel mentioned his batty aunt Vessania, and she could never quite put her finger on why. Perhaps it was the stories Nigel told about her; about how she would spend a morning talking to a lamp and then spend an afternoon completely catatonic aside from erratic bursts of laughter, but there was something about her that made Felix's scalp prickle.

The dire wolf kept his distance from Felix. Their last conversation had cut too close to the nerve for her liking, and she was irritated at his ability to read her thoughts. She practiced keeping them hidden, imagining a sort of helmet around her head, shielding her thoughts but this drained her. She was learning that much of her power came from her emotions. Fiddle had always told her this would be the case; she was after all, a Drow. In the Citadel Reading Room, she read about them in the few books she could find about their lore. Godspell had slaughtered them and had practically abolished all memory of them, burning the texts which documented their history, but a few traces remained. They were witch elves; a race of female warriors who drew their power from their feelings. It seemed they were quite feared, as the consequences of their anger resulted in chaos and destruction. Their sadness could wilt flowers and crops. Their love could calm seas and cause magic to glisten, making everything glow with a fiery warmth. There were few males and those who were born into the Drow were weak, but they were never mistreated. Rather, they were the labourers and the builders, the tradespeople and the artists. They were loved and raised to fight well using their own talents, but from what Felix could gather from her reading, the Drow were a matriarchy of strong, fierce, powerful women who were mysterious and unfathomable.

Her newly gleaned knowledge made her ache for her brother. What did he know of his heritage? Perhaps it would comfort him to know that his lack of magic was never his fault, simply his inheritance? But no, how unfair it seemed that she got the lion's share of the magic he had worked so hard for it for his whole life. Magic he had now lost completely, because of her.

The Drow were an odd lure for her. Felix felt a sad longing to know them, but it was with anguish that she thought of the spiral door in her dreams; the door to the Glade, the ancestral home of the Drow.

'Go to the Glade,' Fiddle had said.

But she was afraid to go. She was afraid of what she would find there; something or nothing. Not knowing was easier. Not knowing was safer.

The Citadel was monstrously large. By day six, Felix realised that she still had not seen half of it. Many rooms she avoided because they had been her uncle's rooms. His office had been cleared of his belongings and now sat empty, save for a large Aubusson rug on the floor. His parlour, morning room and personal dining area were locked, and the furniture covered in ghostly white sheets. A bitter taste blossomed in Felix's mouth whenever she passed them.

His bedroom was the only room that had remained untouched. She had ordered it to be left alone, thinking that perhaps Linus would want to have something of his father's. Nobody had understood this, but she knew that he would, at least. Despite everything he had done, Godspell was the only father Linus had ever known. And so, the scurry girls cleaned it dutifully but otherwise it was left alone.

Until Felix opened the door.

It was smaller than she had expected. The ceiling was low but domed, with constellations carved into the dark wood. They shimmered with a warm orange light, giving the room an unexpectedly comforting feel. At the centre of the room, under the peak of the dome the bed lay, immaculately made with expensive looking sheets in a deep shade of burgundy. A fireplace yawned emptily in front of the bed with another beautiful rug stretched just before it. The walls were lined with bookcases, and they were filled from floor to ceiling with books and scrolls and parchments. A large window to the right of the bed was draped with velvet red curtains, held back by gold rope, and cushions on the sill of the window made for a comfy reading seat. Behind the bed was a desk with a red leather inlay, neatly ordered and sparse.

Felix liked it. The room seemed to sigh as she entered it, as though it had been waiting for her to come and visit. Slowly, gently, the books began to wake up and whispered their words to her.

Stories?

It surprised her. She had expected books on politics and policies, on history, and dry, hefty tomes about finances.

But no.

Stories.

She read their spines, tracing her finger over each one tentatively and as she did, their stories flashed in her mind as she heard snippets of their words. Shakespeare's plays. Murder and betrayals, comedy and history but most of all, love...who was Shakespeare? She wanted to read him.

More stories. A great white whale, vampires and demons, 20,000 leagues under the sea. Mad scientists...well she didn't want to know much more about them. She knew what mad scientists could do. She found more modern stories. Ruby slippers and witches, an enchanted wardrobe, two boys on a raft down a river, a locked garden, a black horse running wildly.

These were the commoners' banned books. What was it Nigel had said once? Commoners wrote wonderful stories. 'That's real magic to me.'

'Yes,' Felix whispered. She felt the swell of words around her and breathed them in. She understood what Nigel meant. This room felt like the London Library; a safehold and haven, womb-like with its amber light.

So what was her uncle doing with a room like this? It betrayed everything about him.

She walked carefully to his desk, her heart thrumming in fear of being caught, though really, that was silly. The Citadel was hers now and that meant this room, too, was hers. Yet she felt like she was trespassing, that at any moment Aubrey would come bounding into the room and tell her to get out. No. Not Aubrey. Godspell. In his room, in his space, he felt close by. It was as though his ghost was sleeping in his bed.

Felix held her breath as she ran her hands across his desk. Leather, indented and rough with the echoes of correspondence written upon it.

'What was the last thing you wrote here?' she whispered.

As her words floated on the air, a shadow appeared, like it had formed from her very breath. She jumped back, alarmed, and she cried out as she saw the dim form of her uncle hunched over his desk. But he was a wisp; insubstantial and fading at the edges. Felix ran her hands through him and found herself touching nothing but air.

Fascinated, her pulse racing, she watched him. He was tired and unkempt, his oily hair falling out of place as he ran his gloved hands through it over and over again. His face was distressed. Felix crept around him and knelt down, looking up curiously at the face of the man who had tried so desperately to kill her...who had killed her parents and stolen her brother. In his room, he looked younger, and she realised then that this had been his boyhood room. She could see his name, Corbin, had been carved, with childish letters, into the leg of the desk, the flesh of the wood now dark and dirty, but still pale enough to make out clearly. Next to it, the name Everard.

She hardly dared to breathe, in case it broke the magic. She asked the question in her mind and the magic answered.

Childhood laughter. Two boys running around the bed. The dark-haired boy, the younger one threw an expensive looking ornament at the older boy, who laughed and turned it into bubbles. He ran through a door on the left. Felix hadn't noticed it. Adjoining rooms. They had adjoining rooms. But this door shimmered with magic.

The younger boy followed but halted at the shut door.

'Everard! Not fair. I can't use hatches yet. Wait for me!' He opened it and stared fearfully into the midst, then ran through shouting his brother's name.

The wisps disappeared, leaving only the faint shadow of Corbin Godspell leaning over his desk. He was no longer a child, but a weary eyed man.

Felix could not breathe. She was starting to see spots, and her body felt fizzy and unattached to her mind.

She followed her uncle's gaze. He was staring down at a fragment of paper. It was practically see-through, but upon it was a name he had written with the gold pen at the side of his left hand.

Alchemus J. Fiddle.

His handwriting was strangely childlike; not much different to the names carved into the desk.

Underneath his writing, flashes of words sprang up. Too many to focus on. They were fragments of conversations, each one containing Fiddle's name.

Felix inhaled deeply. Tracing paper. The last thing her uncle had done at his desk was to trace Fiddle's name and he had found it active. She felt queasy, remember the fear of Trace words in the quarter, of how her teacher Mr Gelding had been taken because he'd said something forbidden.

Her uncle rose suddenly, swiping his hand over the paper to erase the name. It became an innocuous piece of parchment. Picking it up, he shoved it angrily into a drawer in his desk, ran his hands through his hair once more and walked straight through Felix at his side. She clamped her eyes shut as he did but when she opened them, he was gone. The room was empty once more, but it hummed with magic; with memories.

Felix pulled out the desk chair and slumped into it, breathing hard. The spots in front of her eyes began to fade and her heart rate slowed.

She was staring at the drawer.

She watched herself open it.

She saw herself take out the Tracing paper and lay it in front of her on the desk.

She let her hand reach for the gold pen from the inkwell and she unscrewed the cap.

Her hand hovered over the paper.

Beneath her hand, though she did not move a muscle, the name began to write itself.

Immediately, flashes of words rose up from the depth of paper, masses and masses of them. Too many to read, and all tangled with the name. She caught only a few words and phrases.

'Awful...'

'Demon...'

' ...instils terror.'

'...is just as bad...'

' ...should abdicate!'

'better off without...'

'...sparks fear...'

Felix leaned back in the chair. She thought of her uncle's face. Had he felt this way? Had he felt this same sense of betrayal?

She rose suddenly, swiping her hand across the paper to erase the name. But despite the blankness of the sheet which she stowed safely back in the drawer, she could not wipe away the image of the words that people had said, the words that had been written in the newspapers, nor could she dissolve the name she had written: Felix Spark.

7

Lundonwick

Linus had sea legs. After weeks on the Skimmer, feeling the swaying dips and swells of the water beneath them, solid ground felt strangely unsteady. He was also still adjusting to the light. As soon as they'd docked in the underground city, Captain Kildare had given him an old pair of spectacles with darkened lenses. It seemed that the commoners used to wear them to block out the sun and it was funny to him that he was wearing them underground, with no natural light to speak of, just the constant glow of the fire lamps, orb light and the old electric wiring that made glass bulbs glare.

He rested his hand on an old barrel that had once been filled with ale, in an attempt to stop himself from swaying, but he knew he needn't bother. Half of the sailors in this town were swaying with liquor or poppyblood, or both. In fact, he'd look distinctly out of place if he didn't look intoxicated in some way. But that was the charm of Lundonwick. People wore their personalities proudly. They flaunted their flaws with gusto. Lundonwick was honest.

What few people in the city above realised, was that there was a whole other city below. It had become something of an obsession for Linus to trawl through the old maps of the underground subway system that had once been called the 'tube', and how they had now been joined with the sewer system to create a warren of waterways that surreptitiously snaked underneath the Magistry. At some point in the early reign of his father, the tube system had been destroyed. The tracks and platforms had been disassembled and every tube line had been flooded. But the waters had quickly subsided, as nature took over. The hidden rivers of London had joined with the new waters of the tube lines and over time, the magicians who had been driven underground had connected the waterways with the sewers.

Ah the sewers. Linus would never, ever have thought that he would find such beauty in a system made for disposing of excrement. But the Victorians had known how to build beauty into their industry. There was symmetry in their bricklaying and the pure, spherical perfection of their design meant that the sewer ships, often made of old canal barges and sometimes even the reformed train carriages, sailed through them with ease. They were also surprisingly large. In the shallows of the sewers, the crew had sometimes jumped into the mucky waters to tug the Skimmer along, and he had always been awed by the sheer scale of the tunnels. They were cavernous with delightful surprises illuminated by the dusty shards of light, cast down by the grids of the city way above. Porcelain tiles, hand-painted and weathered with artful cracks had stood the test of time and water and waste. Carvings, graffiti from the old sewer workers and the toshers, from the golden days before magic.

A feat of remarkable industry and science.

The sewers were a living history book and there was nothing more humbling that wading through the waste of the people; magic or none. The sewers were the great unifiers of the whole world. Rags or riches didn't matter. Every time a toilet was flushed, whether chipped porcelain or polished marble, it all ended up here.

It wasn't just the sewers or the old tube lines that made up UnderLondon. There were the rivers, too. The Thames, of course, but also the Fleet and Lea, Effra, Tyburn, Moselle, Rom, Brent, Muswell, Westbourne, Quaggy, Peck, Falconbrook, Neckinger...and so many, many more. Some were mere streams, others gushing tributaries that were like the veins of the city. And they were owned by the sewer pirates, by the Houdinis, by the criminals, by the mudlarks, by the abandoned, the forgotten; they were the lifeblood of UnderLondon, who called this labyrinth their home.

And now Linus was one of them.

Now he was a Sewer Pirate conscious of only an eternal night, of eerie shadows in ancient Roman ruins forgotten by those above, of the shrill quark of the ever-threatening mudlarks, of subterranean waterfalls and lakes lit by bioluminescent creatures, of fossils and bones, of entire cities built in caves and dripping caverns.

Cities like Lundonwick.

Linus ducked into the Dutch Courage tavern and pulled up a stool at a table just inside the doors. From here, he had the best view of the people passing by and he didn't want to miss his friend.

He ordered a pint of ditchmead and an Ashwater chaser from the young bar girl, and drank deeply, relieved that they soothed his swaying stomach instantly.

The tavern was one of many that made up the shantytown of Lundonwick. It wasn't a town, really, but a great city heaving with people, vomiting up markets and taverns and ramshackle houses built into the caves or above them. The city was evidence of the human instinct for survival. It didn't make any sense and yet it thrived. Like the city above, it had run out of room to grow outwards and so had grown upwards, into the ceilings of the caves, with staircases and bridges and wooden elevators. Magic was less powerful down here, though few knew why, so the magicians were less reliant upon it. That was perhaps why Linus felt so comfortable amongst them; his magical destitution was not so obvious here. Still, he slipped on gloves; coarse, patchwork leather ones Baz had loaned him, so as not to become too conspicuous.

In Lundonwick, the people, too, lacked sense. They dressed, in many ways, as one would expect pirates to dress. Hats and boots and frockcoats, with an array of artfully styled facial hair but even they broke free from the norm; the boots were waders; thigh high, made of rubber or thick leather, often with loops that reached up over their shoulders. The clothes themselves were made of oilskin, waxed leather and whale skin, and the hats ranged from wide brimmed to knitted balaclavas. And of course the gloves; always the magicians' gloves. No finery down here though; these gloves were practical and hardwearing, made for the life of a sailor.

They drank, these people, day and night. With no sun or moon to guide them, they lived in a state of eternal happy hour. The drinks were cheap and vile, and poppyblood stained the teeth and tongues black of many. The Houdinis were the only ones who lived in limbo, for they came and went between both UnderLondon and the city above. When their circuses were closed down and chased out of Piccadilly or Oxford, or Holborn or Finsbury, or any of the other circles where they established their circuses, they encamped down below and took stock of their wares, bartered for poppyblood before braving the upperlands again.

It was a dank, disgusting metropolis...and Linus loved it. His weeks of melancholy aboard the Skimmer had transformed into delight and elation and hope.

Hope. Because Paris Lovelock had confirmed it. Because Paris Lovelock had the proof. Because Paris Lovelock had promised him they could save her.

He ordered another ditchmead, and his mind wandered back to the day after his father's death, when he had been kept locked in a room in the Citadel by that Dovepeace woman, who his sister knew. Some tall man with a handlebar moustache named Goodnight had taken care of him, and Linus could not lie and say he was mistreated, but he felt like he was a prisoner in the home which had been taken from him by invaders. It didn't matter that they had saved him, and his sister, from death. or that they treated him gently and kindly. They had kept him from Felix, telling him she was in a deep sleep. Maybe she was, but how could he trust them, these revolutionaries, these rebels whom he had always been taught were the enemy?

Their mistake had been to put him in a room next to Paris Lovelock.

Paris had been captured by them a few days earlier. Linus had known nothing of this. He had been imprisoned by his father in the Tower, just as his liberators were imprisoning him now.

They were all the same.

But what his captors had not considered, was how well Linus knew the Citadel. It was his home and he had played in these rooms all his life, learning their secrets and their hidden hatches and their private tunnels. His father was a paranoid man. Each room had an escape hatch somewhere. His father had commissioned them soon after he became the Firelighter. Some were magical, others less so. Linus couldn't use magical hatches anymore; he'd soon realised that. But he could pull back the bookcase and use the door behind it that led into the adjoining room. Cliché perhaps, but then his father had never been particularly creative.

He laughed as he remembered Paris' face at seeing him appear out of a bookcase. The man had yelped before throwing his own head back and laughing loudly; a deep, sonorous laugh that came from his belly.

Linus had met Paris innumerable times and had never particularly liked him. He was not quite old but not quite young either; he hovered around middle-aged in some intangible way that gave him a mysteriously charming quality. But the charm was superficial. His smile was oily. He spoke in proofread speeches and manipulated monologues. And yet he was so familiar and comforting to Linus in that instant, that the boy had fallen to his knees and hugged him hard, weeping at the injustice and the frustration and the betrayal of it all.

They talked.

After a while, Linus forgot that Paris was a practised talker and he forgot to be wary of him. He noticed the shackles around Paris' hands and feet, bound with magic but not immune to a simple screwdriver. Linus freed him.

Paris thought he was going to die soon and so he told Linus everything. Everything and more.

It was then that Linus planned to escape. With the help of Paris, they could run away. Paris had contacts. Paris knew people. You didn't get to be Paris' age in politics without being friends with some shady types.

And so, Linus and Paris ran. He never had the chance to see his sister. He never had the chance to explain it all to her. He only hoped that soon, she would understand. Soon, she would know that he was doing this for her. For them. For everyone.

Because Felix was cursed.

Because Linus was cursed.

Because between them, they would destroy everything. The First Plane, the Second Plane...all of it. The Sacred Flame of Magic would grow out of control, fuelled by the dangerous magic that Felix already had inside her, inherited from the Drow. The Sacred Flame of Magic could not be held inside her for long. It would break free from her, burst forth and set all worlds ablaze, consuming all life, razing the city just as it had done when it was brought forth into this Plane. Only this time, it would burn the world. It was already starting. The Festival of Fire had been the beginning.

Because the Sacred Flame of Magic could only be controlled by the Firelighter.

And Felix wasn't the real Firelighter.

8

The Missing Chapter

Captain Bonny Kildare had limited patience for dry land. It was too solid and too permanent. All her life, she'd lived on the swabbed decks of ships and barges, and it was often said of her, by her crew, that she had bilge water in her veins, rather than blood. She knew it wasn't always said affectionately, but then Captain Kildare commanded only loyalty and hard work from her crew. A captain had little time for friends, and she had not commanded The Skimmer for nigh on fifteen years because of her ability to make friends. She was formidable and she had wits enough to know what was said about her under the deckhead, for she had once said similar things about the captains she'd worked under as a skivvy girl, then a bosun's mate, then a bosun, then a mate before rising further to become the quartermaster and eventually a captain of her very own vessel. She'd sailed more than just the sewers and could navigate better than anyone. Most of her crew knew only the sewers, though some, like Flint, had sailed the seas as a merchant for many years. Nobody else had ventured out of the safe maze of the sewers and the rivers and tube lines. Pinks, stunted and shy, was growing up having never seen daylight and Baz was now almost completely blind, but sight was not a requirement when you sailed through tarry days and nights that had naught to distinguish themselves from one another.

Few knew the sewers better than Bazalguette. He was a strong giant of a man, practically born in the sewers, it was said. They said he was the son of a Houdini wench (though how anyone knew this was a mystery), birthed and placed in a basket then floated on the River Effra at Vauxhall, and the sewers had taken him. Baz joked that he'd been raised by the crocodiles and mudlarks, but it was the toshers that took him in. Toshers, who worked the sewers scavenging for ancient coins, who had found Baz and said if he lived the night, they'd see it as a sign from the river gods and take him in. Baz had survived and the toshers took him, trained him. He grew strong, carving out the tunnels of the sewers, diving into the subterranean lakes for the most valuable treasures. His pitch-dark skin meant he could sink into the shadows unseen, so he had the advantage on other tribes whom he would steal trinkets and treasures from, slitting a few throats for good measure. Baz became the tosher's god and a legend in the sewers even before Godspell flooded the tube lines, before the Houdinis and miscreants of the surface poured into the underground to escape persecution. He sailed on Kildare's ship as her quartermaster, purely because he wanted to. The captain knew he had treasures and wives aplenty wherever it was that he returned to on leave. Bonny Kildare admired him, and of all her crew relied on him most.

But each of her crew were vital and she valued them. Ragstone, her bosun, was a hefty barrel of a man, pockmarked and bearded with a cigar hanging from his lip incessantly. He was a scoundrel and, if the rumours were true, a gambler of very ill and violent repute. She had seen him play enough games of Quest to know that the rumours were accurate.

And then there was Flint. Ashton Flint. Once a merchant in the Magistry's fleet, turned gentleman thief, perennial charmer and too clever for his own smug boots. Far too often he had winked in Bonny's direction. Too often he had crossed the boundaries of his role, officially the 'first mate' by his own insistence, despite no longer being on a merchant's ship, though he was a jack of all trades on the Skimmer, truth be known. Flint had been victim of the floggings of Baz many times, and the scars on his back had been tattooed to look like the branches of a tree, that grew from the base of his back up to his neck. Every new lash became a new branch and he laughed out loud each time the whip came down and the blood trickled down his back.

But he was loyal. His unexplained anger at the bureaucracy of the world above made him fierce, and his charm made it much easier to dock and trade and barter. Still...Bonny eyed him carefully, though she had to admit, he was very easy on the eyes.

Pinks was eleven years old and the only other girl on the ship. She was a mute but was small and quick, wriggling up rigging faster than any of them and bright as a button with ropes and knives. She had a deep red scar from her right ear, across her jaw and down her neck where her father had tried to kill her when she'd refused to be sold to a bawdy house a few years back. Bonny had seen it happen and saved her life. It was by far the most sentimental thing she had ever done, and she'd regretted it often afterwards when caring for the sick child. Now though...now she would throw herself into the Thames for Pinks.

She'd taken Linus on board because of Flint. It was all his fault. They'd docked in Lundonwick for supplies, and supplies only, but Flint had come back from the market with a new waistcoat and a skinny, sullen-eyed boy who looked about as useful as a dead kipper. She'd noticed his bare hands immediately and had refused. Not that she had anything against commoners; on the contrary, she pitied their lot and was hopeful that this new Firelighter, the Spark girl, would turn things around for them as she had promised to do. But Flint had insisted, explaining who Linus was and that Flint's old pal, Paris Lovelock, had paid for Linus' bed and board indefinitely with a heavy bag of tans. Bonny needed the money. The Skimmer, beauty though she was, was old and worn; hardly seaworthy, though in fairness she had never been made to sail waters. Bonny had taken Linus aboard with a sneer, and a pledge from Flint that he owed her a favour. He had a debt to Lovelock, Flint had said. If he took Linus, then that debt was paid. Bonny never questioned Flint's debts or favours. As a gentleman merchant of the Magistry, he was as twisted as they came and frankly, Bonny didn't want to tangle with the world above too much; it had disappointed her one too many times.

It was because of Linus that they were here again, in Lundonwick, only a moon and a half after they had first taken the boy aboard. It made her nervous to be away from the Skimmer, to be walking surefooted on the smooth rocks and sand and silt of the underground city but in truth, she knew it was important to be here. Besides, Linus had proven himself a hard worker, despite his lack of magic and his melancholy had been cured through graft and purpose. She rather liked him, though she would not say it and she chastised herself for her misty-eyed perspective. Captain Bonny Kildare was getting soft.

The Dutch Courage tavern was in the deep bowels of Lundonwick, about as far from water as it was possible to get. Bonny followed the winding alleyways and barrel-lined streets towards the caverns, where the pub had built itself. It was the darkest part of the city and the oldest. Limestone stalactites hung down, twinkling with the electric lights that they used down here. Bonny didn't trust electricity, preferring magic or honest fire but the city was buried so deep down in the earth, that magic was faint and the fireglow orbs she relied upon were mere glimmers, like starlight in a polluted sky.

Their laughter was the first thing she heard. Ragstone's gruff, sandstone chuckle carried through the alleyway, telling her his days of gambling had been productive and sure enough, when she saw him, he was thumbing through his Quest deck and rolling his (loaded) die in his hands, with a grin splitting his mouth where an expensive cigar rested.

They were all there, even Pinks, tucked away in the corner, sitting on a barrel with her feet barely touching the floor. There was one addition to the party; a man who could have been anywhere between fifty and seventy, was reclined gracefully (or as gracefully as he could be on a three-legged stool), sipping on a steaming glass of Ashwater. His fair hair was a tad too long and his suit, midnight blue and made to measure, was showing signs of wear that did not seem to fit with the air of superiority that he wore, as well as the gold, ruby encrusted spectoccules resting in his pocket. She could see Flint eyeing them enviously.

'Paris Lovelock, I presume,' the captain said, and all eyes turned to her immediately.

The comradely atmosphere at once halted and the crew stumbled to their feet quickly, save for the gentleman who looked up at her bemusedly.

'Cap'n,' the crew mumbled in turn, only sitting when Bonny had pulled up a stool for herself.

'At your service, Captain Kildare,' nodded Paris Lovelock, taking Bonny's hand in his own and kissing the scuffed leather of her knuckles.

Captain Kildare seethed silently and snatched her hand back, motioning to the waitress to bring her a pint of ditchmead.

She observed her crew. Their few leave days in Lundonwick had done them good. Flint was shaven and clean, with a cockeyed expression that told her he had drank well, and a new top hat which spoke of good trading, or stealing, she wasn't sure which. Pinks, thank goodness, was smiling, and the dark circles under her eyes had faded a little. She kicked her skinny legs against the barrel carelessly and it irritated Bonny, but she didn't say anything. Linus, too, seemed perkier though he was restless. No doubt he was eager to share his news.

Only Baz seemed as agitated as she felt. His pale, blind eyes flickered, and he stroked the raised skin of the artfully crafted scars on his arms. Like Bonny, he preferred to be on the Skimmer.

'To business then?' Paris said, as soon as Bonny had her drink. His command annoyed her, and she took a deep, long drink before setting it down, wiping the froth from her lips and nodding.

'Linus, if you please?' Paris motioned to the young boy politely with his hand, and he crossed his legs the way only a gentleman could.

Bonny licked her teeth and breathed hard.

'Thanks, Paris and thanks everyone for meeting me here,' Linus began.

Bonny noticed a strange light in his eyes that she had not seen previously, and she leaned in, curious.

'As you know, Felix, my sister, has become the Firelighter, and much has changed since the reign of my father. By all accounts, my sister is trying her best, and I believe she can do a lot of good. I don't know her well…' Linus hesitated and looked down at his bare hands.

'I don't know her well, but she saved my life and I want to repay the favour. Paris here has given me vital information ... information that would mean his certain death if the Privy Council found out that he'd revealed, and it is because of this information that we're here.'

At this point, Linus pulled out a yellowed and creased piece of paper. It was a mere scrap and yet Linus held it as though it was a sacred text. Looking closer, Bonny saw that it was a page torn from a book and she squinted to get a closer look. Linus laid it out on the table for everyone to see. The writing was old and ornate, difficult to decipher.

'Read it for me, will you lad?' Baz asked.

Bonny was grateful. She could read but not well.

'It's a page from a book called "The Firelighters: from 1750 to Present Day". It was published seventeen years ago and is a detailed record of all the known Firelighters up to Everard, my real father. Godspell had them all destroyed when he took power, because he believed that too much knowledge about our past was dangerous. But a man named Alchemus J. Fiddle kept a copy and hid it in the London Library. When Everard was murdered by his brother, Paris here sought it out and took this page from the book.'

'Odd thing to do,' Ragstone mumbled.

Bonny bit her lip, her curiosity burning. 'Go on,' she urged Linus.

'This is what the page says,' Linus said, and he began to read.

The Firelighter Curse

The rumoured "Curse of the Firelighters" has been subject to much conjecture from the Privy Council and interested magicians for centuries. Little proof has been offered to support the claims, though testimony has been given from excommunicated members of the council. This testimony is often discredited, due to the incapacitation of the mental state of its ex-members, who are usually extremely aged and frequently in the throes of death.

Simply put, there are those who believe that the Sacred Flame of Magic will only truly answer to a single lineage of magicians, and that any Firelighter who is not of the correct lineage, who attempts to control the Sacred Flame will be cursed to die an untimely death.

A quick perusal of the timeline of Firelighters as documented in this text will illustrate that the Firelighters of our past have indeed met with unfortunate and untimely endings.

The first known Firelighters to have been documented, the Lovelocks –

'Hold up,' Captain Kildare interrupted. 'Lovelock? You?' She looked directly at Paris who smiled insincerely and nodded his head.

'Why yes, Captain. My family were the Firelighters for over two hundred years. I, myself, was intended for the title until I refused it, as you will see if you will please keep your focus.'

Bonny clenched her fists so hard that the leather of her gloves cracked. She felt Baz's hand rest fleetingly on her thigh to calm her. Gritting her teeth, she nodded to Linus, who carried on reading.

The first known Firelighters to have been documented, the Lovelocks, have had more than their fair share of unfortunate deaths. Horatio Lovelock choked on a chicken bone, his son and heir, Sheldon, was strangled by a burglar and his son Horatio II tripped down the stairs, after meeting his mistress. Ichabod Lovelock was killed in a duel by his brother John, who then died mysteriously of an illness which saw him locked away in the Bell Tower of the Tower of London for most of his remaining annums.

It should be noted that the curse of the Firelighters does seem to be circulated by the Lovelock family. Certainly, Deacon Lovelock, the last Firelighter in the Lovelock lineage, died of natural causes aged 80 annums old. His only son, Paris, abdicated his inheritance aged 10 annums, as stated earlier in this book.

'My father did not die of natural causes," Paris interjected. 'I have seen the autopsy report and there were traces of arsenic found in his blood. The same poison was later found in his successor, Arthur Godspell, upon his death. Arthur's son, Everard, as we know, was murdered by his brother, Corbin, who has very recently been killed by his own nephew, Linus Godspell. His niece now resides upon the chair of the Firelighters, and I have no doubt that she, too, will befall an ugly death.'

'This sounds like a conspiracy theory,' Bonny mumbled.

'Yes, it does rather, doesn't it?' Paris nodded in delight. 'But I assure you madam...it is not conspiracy. I have proof.'

'What proof?' Flint asked, his eyes still lingering on the ruby spectoccules.

'All in good time, Ashton,' Paris smiled. 'Linus, if you will.'

The Curse of the Firelighters has now become the stuff of myth. So much so, that it is a mere story told by grandmothers to their grandchildren at bedtime. Most magicians hold no stead in the story, and it is fading from memory. For the purpose of whimsy, we have accrued testimony from excommunicated members of the Privy Council who corroborate the stories.

'There's a curse, alright,' said Hector Thorburn, a member of the council from 1974 to 1986. 'There's a whole subsect of council members who know about it. Four of them. The Fire Four we call them. They know all the secrets. Secrets about secrets about secrets. But it's not the curse you should be asking about. Where did magic come from, eh? That's what we should be asking. Who was the first Firelighter? How come nobody ever talks about that?'

Hector Thorburn was 97 annums old and died only two hours after this testimony was given. It can easily be dismissed as the ravings of a very old and sick man, but there are parts of his interview which echo the words of Nathaniel Gonzales, a magician who was imprisoned by the Privy Council in the early 1970's. He kept a diary before his death, which was read and copied by a maid, who later disappeared.

'The foursome met tonight, I am sure of it. It is they who will decide my fate. Perhaps the curse is not just for the Firelighters but for all magicians, for I feel the dark cloud of death resting upon me, upon us all. Their secrets will be the death of us.'

There was silence around the table as Linus stopped reading. They were each thinking of the words that they had just heard. It was Ragstone who spoke first.

'I don't understand,' he said, folding his brawny arms.

Pinks nodded her agreement. Bonny was frowning, her brain trying to fathom the meaning of what she had heard but she, too, was confused.

'The history of our origins, of the Firelighters, of magic is very blurry,' Paris nodded. 'The council want it that way and we have always kept secrets.'

"We? You mean you're on the Privy Council?' Flint asked in surprise.

Bonny detected a faint nervous twitch in his eye and she chuckled internally.

'Yes, I am...or was. I was to be the next Firelighter and I declined it. As such, I was given a place on the Privy Council. I believe very much in this curse. I believe my father and all those who came before him were victims of it, just as those who came after him have been, too.'

'So you're not trying to take the title back, then?' Bonny asked. 'You don't think that you're the true Firelighter?'

'Heavens no!' Paris exclaimed, with genuine shock on his face.

Bonny was now even more confused.

'Madam, I think you have misunderstood me. I was on the Privy Council, not because I want the wealth or the glory, although one has become accustomed to them. I did not work for Corbin Godspell because I believed in him or his cause. I believe there is a greater purpose to my life, greater even than that of being

Firelighter, which as you have learned, I did not want. I rather enjoy living and didn't want the curse to rob me of my life. No. The sole purpose of my life has been to seek truth. To seek the answers to the questions that most magicians have forgotten to ask. Think, Captain. Why is the title of this book that this chapter has come from dating Firelighters only to 1750? What is this Great Spark? This Plane which we call the First was barren of magic once; how did magic enter this world?'

'I...I don't know,' Bonny admitted.

'Because you have never been told!' Paris burst out, angry now. 'And worse, you have never been taught to ask. Our own history and heritage has been filtered and we have all been brainwashed into thinking that it doesn't matter, that we have magic and superiority. Good grief, the council simply adored the power Corbin Godspell had over us all, over the commoners. Nobody asked questions when he was in power. But knowledge is the only true power that is worth having. And I have learned a few things in my years on the council.

'The Fire Four are real. The Curse is real. And there is much, much more. I can tell you everything; where magic comes from and how it came into this Plane, this Great Spark the book speaks of.

But more than this, Captain. The reason why Linus helped me escape the Citadel? The reason why he abandoned the sister who saved his life? The reason why you're all here now at Linus' insistence? It's because I know who the first Firelighter was...who the real Firelighter is. And now, I can prove it."

.

9

The Many Faces of Vessania True

'So she's how old?' Felix asked, running her clammy hands over her hair which wasn't behaving, as usual. Not for the first time, she mentally threatened to cut it all off.

'72,' Nigel smiled, taking Felix's hands away from the ruffles on her oxblood shirt, which she was now trying to straighten. 'You'll be fine. She'll love you.'

Nigel kissed her knuckles and Felix took a deep breath.

'She might not remember you though,' Nigel continued. 'She's a little...different.'

Felix nodded her understanding and tried once again to quell her nerves.

It wasn't that she didn't want to meet Vessania True, Nigel's only living relative; it was just that she didn't really know how to act around families and Vessania was Nigel's family, even if it was only her alone.

Nigel didn't let go of her hand, though they hadn't even left the grounds of the Citadel gardens. Aubrey had insisted that, after the Festival of Fire, they use the hatchway in order to leave the grounds and Thaddeus, who was quickly becoming less of an illegal hatchmaker and more of an official one (perhaps a good job for him, Felix mused) had created a hatch in the garden which led to the London Library, where Vessania now lived.

Felix was grateful for this. It meant she could go outside and leave the rooms of the Citadel, and the way Thaddeus had winked at her when he'd told them where the hatch was, told her that he'd placed it in the gardens on purpose.

The gardens were beautiful and, of course, expansive. They were private, though really they should be opened to the public to enjoy, especially on a crisp and clear evening like this one.

'Tell me more about her,' Felix said, enjoying the cold air on her face and the darkening blue grey light of the early evening.

Nigel glanced at her briefly and shrugged, but his jaw clenched.

'She's my father's sister and she took me in after my parents died. She was always a little odd, but the loss of my father completely devastated her. She's never been the same, but I don't remember much of her from before that anyway, aside from knowing a few stories about her. She wasn't sure who I was when I went to live with her. It took her two annums to even remember my name.'

Felix squeezed his hand tenderly. Nigel was only four when his parents had passed away. He didn't talk about it, but Felix often got the sense that Nigel had been there when they'd died.

They arrived at a gardener's shed, which was painted with gloss and had a small window next to the door. This was the hatch that they were to use, but before either of them reached for the door, Nigel pulled Felix to face him.

'Look, Felix. My aunt is…' He hesitated and ran his hands over the nape of his neck. A faint flush spread over his face and Felix saw now that he was nervous, too.

'She's not really normal,' he finally said, and he shrugged apologetically.

'What do you mean?'

'She's not dangerous or anything. But she doesn't really see a lot of people and, well…you'll see, I guess. But she's all I have left of…of…'

Felix put her fingers over his mouth to quieten him.

'It's ok,' she whispered and kissed him gently where her fingers had been. 'Let's go.'

Nigel sighed shakily and nodded. He reached for the door and opened it. Inside was the darkness of the midst. Felix groaned.

'I hate hatches,' she muttered, but she stepped inside and pulled Nigel in behind her.

When she stepped out of the door on the other side, she was in a familiar room. Books lined the walls and the musky, familiar smell of heat and stories greeted her.

'The Story Room,' she smiled, as Nigel followed her out.

He shrugged his right shoulder shyly. 'Our favourite room,' he said.

The moment was pierced by a loud, operatic voice wailing somewhere in the library.

'What on earth is that?' Felix cried, slamming her hands over her ears.

'That would be Aunt Vessania,' Nigel said through gritted teeth.

'Is she ok?!' Felix made to leave the Story Room, but Nigel's nonchalance stopped her.

'She's singing,' he said, struggling to hide his amusement, but his shoulders were stiff.

Felix followed the tuneless howls which sounded, if she was honest, like a dying cat, and ended up outside the door of a small room, which Fiddle had often used as a parlour of sorts. Felix had been in it a few times, but it had been Fiddle's private living space and she had never really wanted to intrude, preferring the kitchens in the basement or the Reading Room.

'Aunt Vessania?' Nigel called out, knocking on the door three times in quick succession.

The dying cat sounds stopped instantly.

'Erik? Is that you?'

Nigel winced. Erik was his father's name.

The door burst open, and Felix beheld a tall, graceful looking lady with elegant features and strings and strings of pearls draped around her neck. Her hair was like wisps of steel neatly pinned back into a bun and her eyes, which were a strange lilac sort of colour, glowed with excitement.

'Oh...Nigel. Of course. Enter, enter, enter. Careful that the door doesn't bite you. It bit my fingers earlier!'

She held up her hand and two of her fingers had been roughly bandaged together with a dirty bit of cloth. The fingers were bent into an ugly shape.

'Oh!' Felix cried out when she saw them.

Nigel rushed forward and took his aunt's hand in concern. 'Aunty, you trapped your fingers in the door. They're broken. I can fix them.'

'Nonsense, the door bit me. With its TEETH. What sort of place have you brought me to, that the doors bite the houseguests? Honestly. It's just rude!'

Vessania flung herself down dramatically onto the chaise longue in front of a small but ornate fireplace. She was wearing a strange tunic which, upon closer inspection, turned out to be an old pair of curtains. Felix could see that the sash with tasselled ends was being used as a belt.

'It's also rude to stare,' Vessania said, her eyes hawklike and resting on Felix's face.

'Oh. I... sorry, I'm -'

'Don't care," Vessania said, shifting her head away and thrusting her jaw up petulantly.

'Aunty, now who's being rude? This is Felix.'

He had finished mending his aunt's fingers. Although he wasn't a healer, he had managed to straighten the bones so that they were no longer bent at such a hideous angle.

'Felix. Felix? Felix who? I don't know a thing about you!' She clapped her newly healed hands delightedly.

'She, uh...likes to speak in rhyme sometimes. And I have told her about you,' Nigel said, tilting his head as though he was apologising.

'I'm Felix Spark...er, Godspell,' Felix corrected herself, holding out her hand. She noticed that Vessania didn't have any gloves on.

'A Spark, eh? Orphans get that name when nobody knows where they came from.'

Felix swallowed but her mouth was very dry. She nodded.

'Yes, Ms True, that's right. I am an orphan.'

Vessania had not shaken Felix's hand, simply stared at it as though it, too, might bite her. Felix lowered her arm.

'No gloves, Erik, no gloves. A commoner, that's what she is. A commoner like Nancy.'

'It's Nigel, aunty,' Nigel said very quietly.

'Nancy?' Felix asked.

'My mother,' Nigel replied.

'Oh,' Felix breathed.

A dozen questions flooded Felix's mind, but she held her tongue. Nigel's mother had been a commoner?

'Sit, Aunty, let's have some tea. I've brought Felix here to meet you.'

'Common as muck is a commoner's luck,' Vessania chanted, allowing herself to be lowered back down to the chaise longue.

Nigel flicked a wrist and the tea set in the corner began to serve hot tea. The scent of cinnamon filled the room.

'I'm not a commoner,' Felix said, taking an armchair tentatively at the side of the chaise longue; she was realising that she needed to move slowly around this odd lady.

'I am a magician, but gloves make my hands uncomfortable.'

'Me too, me too, me too!' Vessania cried out happily. As she did, sparks flew out of her hands and landed on the rug in front of her, where they fortunately faded into ashes quickly. Felix remembered how Nigel had said she accidentally set fire to things occasionally.

Nigel gave Vessania a cup of cinnamon tea, then handed one to Felix before taking one for himself. He sat in the only other chair in the room, a hardbacked writing chair near a desk at the lace curtained window. For a few minutes, all were silent.

'Don't like her,' Vessania said suddenly.

'What's to like?' Vessania replied. But this voice was different, accented somehow.

'Have you seen those markings on her face?' Vessania asked.

'Drow witch,' the other Vessania answered.

'Drow witch is a Drow b-'

'Aunty, stop!' Nigel shouted firmly and Felix jumped, her teacup clattering against its saucer.

Slowly and very menacingly, Vessania turned her face towards her nephew. As she did, her whole appearance changed. Instead of elegant, she became fierce. Growing several inches, both in height and width, Vessania True became a bulbous-nosed, hag-haired warrior of a woman.

'Shout at me again, boy, and I'll skin you,' the new Vessania said.

Her voice, once again, was different. A strong, northern lilt made it seem somehow more threatening.

'Oh do calm down,' Vessania said to herself.

It was the accented voice again. Felix couldn't quite pinpoint the accent. Russian maybe?

Nigel set down his tea and put his head in his hands. Felix had never seen him look so tired and careworn. Is this what he had grown up with? No wonder he had taken refuge in the library with Fiddle.

'Ms True?' Felix asked; both the hag and Nigel looked to her. 'Ms Vessania True? May I speak to you please?'

Nigel's mouth dropped open.

'And why should I speak to you?' the Russian voice asked.

It seemed so out of place coming from the giant woman in front of her. It was much more refined, much more sane.

'Because it's polite, isn't it?' Felix grappled for an answer. 'It's polite to talk to your guests face to, er, face.'

Almost imperceptively, the woman on the chaise longue began to change again. She shrank down until the curtain tunic swamped her. What remained was not the hag, nor the tall, elegant opera queen, but a slim, sinewed old lady with a sharp nose and Nigel's eyes.

'Fetch me my glasses, Nigel. I want to get a better look at the girl,' the real Vessania True said, quite clearly and a little formidably.

Nigel still had his mouth open and was staring at the woman in disbelief.

'Now, Nigel. If you catch a fly, I'll send a spider in after it and we all know how much you dislike spiders.'

Nigel scrambled to his feet and to the desk where he found a delicate pair of wire rimmed spectacles. He passed them to his aunt, who put them on and squinted through them.

Vessania True stood and walked very slowly towards Felix, as though she was testing out her feet to see if they still worked. Her arms were bony with the skin hanging from the muscle after years of disuse, but she folded them as she regarded Felix.

'There, now,' Vessania said, her accent getting thicker with every word. 'I can see you.'

'Ms True,' Felix said, hoping her voice didn't betray her. 'How lovely to finally meet you.'

'Felix the Firelighter,' Vessania said. There was a slight tremulousness to her voice that revealed her age. 'What an honour.'

She spoke with a hint of sarcasm which made Felix bristle, but she swallowed it down.

'The honour is mine, Ms True,' Felix said politely.

Now she was looking Nigel's aunt, his *real* aunt, in the face, she didn't know what to do next. Vessania seemed to know this, and she smiled thinly. Her eyes glimmered with lilac light. They were such strange eyes.

'You think because I am here, that you have power,' Vessania said. 'You have power, it is true. You shine with it. Those spirals on your face shimmer with your mother's magic. But I am not here because of your power, so swallow down your arrogance, girl. I do not answer to you.'

Felix felt as though she had been slapped. Her eyes prickled with tears. What on earth had she done to this woman to invite such obvious disdain?

Suddenly, Vessania threw back her head and laughed. It was cackle in the voice of the hag faced Vessania, the kind that Felix thought that wicked witches in story books had.

'Aunty, please...' Nigel began, but stopped when Vessania turned to him.

'Wretched boy!' The northern voice screeched. 'You dare speak to me with your filthy commoner blood?'

Nigel cowered away from her, and Felix's tears turned to anger.

'You will not speak to him like that again,' she said, and her voice was low and thick with smoke.

'Careful with that temper of yours, girl. It will damn us all.' Vessania's eyes flashed as she spoke with the sane, Russian voice and Felix felt confusion wash over her.

Maybe it was the lost expression on Felix's face or the exasperated, pained sigh of Nigel behind her, but Vessania softened.

'Forgive me," she whispered. 'Both of you. It is hard to know who you are, when you have so many voices inside.'

Vessania resumed her seat on the chaise longue.

'You are a twin, are you not?' she asked Felix, who nodded cautiously.

'Perhaps then, you will understand. Erik and I were twins. Nigel has told you about his father, Erik? Yes? When he was killed, I felt his death as though it had happened to me. I have felt his loss like a splinter in my heart, all these years. Nigel has not told you how they died, his parents? Nor will I. It belongs to Nigel. I have stolen much of his youth and I will not steal his words. Or yours...I can see the words you want to say to him...to Nigel. Say them, child, whilst you can. We waste years holding back the right words and saying the wrong ones. I told Erik the wrong words. My words were hate and spite, and curses of death upon them both, him and his girl. Him and Nancy. Nancy, the commoner girl he loved, for whom he was ready to give up his whole world. And then he died. With her. And I never got to unsay those words.

'We have many faces that we wear, each of us. Madness is the inability to recognise our true selves, did you know that? You, the Firelighter, the commoner, the magician, the Drow; the light and the dark. Who are you really, my dear?

'You are a lighter of fires, girl, but you are not the Firelighter. We are never who we think we are.'

Vessania True stood, with effort, using her knuckles to push herself up. Nigel helped her and she pushed him away. She placed her bony hand upon his cheek.

'My dear, dear boy,' she said gently. 'You will not listen, as your father did not. But take heed of my words. This one is not for you. She will bring you only death.'

Vessania True removed her wire rimmed spectacles and walked to the desk. By the time she placed her spectacles upon it, she was tall, elegant and singing a haunting aria, which scratched like nails upon Felix's heart. Vessania turned and gasped dramatically, as though she hadn't known Felix and Nigel were there. Seeing Felix's face, she hurried over and took Felix's hand in her own and patted it.

'There, there my dear,' she said comfortingly. 'You oughtn't listen to the other one. As our family crest says, "True eyes speak true lies".'

'What does that mean?' Felix asked, tears winning out.

'Hmm?' Vessania asked, starting to circle around in a waltz. 'Oh, I haven't the faintest idea.'

10

The Spiral Door

The gardens were dark when they stepped out of the midst of the hatch. Neither Nigel nor Felix had spoken since they left Vessania warbling in the parlour. Felix's eyes itched with drying tears, and she felt exhausted.

Shadows of the statues and porticoes of the gardens stretched in the moonlight, and Felix could see a puff of grey mist every time she breathed. Autumn was fading into winter, and the falling frost seemed to seize her heart. She felt as hard and as cold as the stone sculptures on their pedestals that lined the path back to the Citadel.

Nigel tried to reach for her hand, and she heard his sigh as she stepped away from him, folding her hands under her arms. She knew it would hurt him, but she couldn't help it; she wanted some distance. She needed to think.

'Felix,' Nigel began, as they entered the Citadel.

She turned to him and saw his ashen face, and she knew then that it was over. It had to be. She wasn't the one for him.

'I'm tired,' she said, surprised that her voice sounded so clear and normal.

How could it be that every part of her, usually so full of fire and heat, was now so cold? She was shivering with it.

Nigel stepped towards her, but she moved away, shaking her head.

'She's crazy, Felix. She doesn't know what she's saying.'

'It doesn't matter,' Felix sighed. 'Let's just get some sleep. We'll talk tomorrow.'

Felix tried to smile reassuringly at him, but it came out as a grimace. She desperately hoped he'd refuse and just reach out for her, hold her and warm up the deep freeze that seemed to be spreading its way through her. Even the spirals on her face, which always burned mildly, were growing heavy, as though they were hardening into ice. If she cried now, her teardrops would be icicles.

But he didn't reach for her. He didn't hold her. Instead, Nigel looked at her helplessly then turned his face down at his shoes and nodded his head resignedly.

'Tomorrow, then,' he said at last, and Felix was relieved.

'Good night,' she said.

It was so formal. Had they ever spoken to one another with such stilted words before?

'Good night,' Nigel whispered, and his voice cracked.

Felix turned away and left him. She walked quickly, feeling his eyes on her back, feeling his pain. She fought the urge to run or to look back.

Felix didn't go to her chamber. Instead, she made for the drawing room. Closing the door behind her, she let the air she'd been holding in her lungs go and her knees almost buckled.

The dire wolf was curled up on the rug in front of the glowing fire, the remnants of a bowl of macaroni cheese at his side. He looked up at her as soon as she closed the door.

'What happened?' he asked, his furry face one of concern, as he stretched out his magic into her mind. She could feel him probing and she shut him out, imagining the metal helmet around her brain.

'It didn't go very well,' Felix said weakly, slumping into an oversized plush sofa and pulling a huge cushion over her and cuddling it.

D.W padded over and rested his chin on her knee, his tail drooping. He tilted his head, waiting for her to continue, but she didn't. She was staring into the fire, his lost girl, eyes red rimmed and bleak.

'You can figure it out,' he said.

He was trying to hear her thoughts, trying to see into her mind, even though he knew she hated it. But how could he comfort her if he didn't know what was wrong? How could he make it better? Her pain was as real for him, as though he had a dagger in his chest.

'Maybe,' Felix smiled sadly, reaching down to stroke his head. 'Can you do me a favour?'

'Anything,' he said, his tail wagging a fraction.

'Can you go and get Sigbert Goodnight for me?'

The dire wolf tilted his head questioningly at her, but she said no more. He tried again to hear her, but she was like a firmly locked door. A flash of irritation passed over her features and she shook her head a little, asking him to stop. D.W was confused. This girl was hardly a girl anymore. She was a steel vice of a woman and yet somewhere, still in there, was the lost and frightened girl he had found on the streets of the Magistry. She'd been happy, found and safe for a while, but now he could sense her again inside this hard shell sat in front of him. Every fibre of him felt aching; it was his purpose to find lost souls. The magic he was made of, sought out the lost as instinctively as his heart thudded in his breast

'Of course,' he said, dipping his head. He loped towards the door.

'Oh, and D.W?'

He turned to her.

'Could you, er, sleep somewhere else tonight? I just really want to be alone,' she smiled apologetically, and the dire wolf tried to hide his hurt.

'Maybe you could go to...to Nigel? I'm pretty sure he could use a friend.'

The dire wolf struggled not to yelp. Her words hurt. Not that they injured him, though he was bruised a little that she didn't want him with her, but he could feel the pain inside her voice. She was hurting badly and trying so hard not to show him. Why was she hiding from him?

'Of course,' D.W said. 'If that will help you?'

'Thank you,' Felix smiled, but it didn't reach her eyes.

The dire wolf jumped up and with his paw, he pulled down the door handle and left the drawing room, wondering what Sigbert Goodnight could do for his girl that he couldn't.

As the door closed, Felix stared into the embers of the fire. It wasn't as late as it felt, but she was so tired. Sleep was calling her name, but she wouldn't rest her eyes yet. Moving quickly so as not to drift off, she dropped to her knees in front of the fire and reached into it, picking out a lump of coal that glowed orange with dying fire. It didn't burn her hand. She was as immune to fire as a mermaid is to water.

The lump of coal was charred around the edges, leaving black marks against her skin. At its centre, fire flickered stubbornly, refusing to go out. Felix took a deep breath and let her eyes glaze over, seeing the coal, but not really, until the tiny particles of magic revealed themselves. Most magicians needed spectoccules to do this, to see the magic within things, but she was the Firelighter, despite what Vessania True said, and she held the Sacred Flame of Magic inside her; magic obeyed her. She willed the particles to move and change, forcing them to become something else. It was the way magic worked and it was all just a trick, an illusion. The lump of coal would always be coal, but for now, thanks to her, it looked like a huge, glittering ruby, still glowing with the ember's fire.

Felix held it to her chest. She felt empty. Tears were coming again and by sheer force of will, she stopped them.

A knock on the door startled her and she stood quickly, straightening her clothes.

'Come in,' she called out.

Sigbert Goodnight, dressed in a powder-blue suit, entered. He had an impressive handlebar moustache, and kind eyes which looked bewildered as he looked in at her.

'Lady Felix?' he said, stepping through the door. 'You asked to see me?'

This man had been held captive alongside her in the Tower of London, once. He'd been part of the rebellion against Godspell, with Liberty and Aubrey and Fiddle and was, despite his outlandish outfit, a rather good spy. Felix trusted him. There was nobody else she would trust more with her request.

'Goodnight, yes. Thank you for coming,' she said, beckoning him to take a seat on the sofa as she sat down. 'I need your help with something...and you must promise me it will be a secret. I need your word. Nobody must know.'

It was nearly midnight when she finally crawled into bed. She hadn't undressed; she simply wanted to close her eyes and shut out everything that had happened. Vessania, the Magistry, the Festival of Fire, Nigel...all of it.

Felix slept.

Felix dreamed.

She was in the room with the doors. The room of ways out. Once, this had been a nightmare and it still was sometimes, but tonight it was exactly where she wanted to be. It was a room that was ruled by her feelings. If she was afraid, like she had been after the festival, it was a taunting, hellish place of memories and hatches that opened up and let in ghosts of her past, and with doors that could not be unlocked.

There was the old, dirty door of the orphanage, behind which lived her memories of Nanny Maude and the orphans. But tonight, they slept, and she left them undisturbed. The green, ornate door with the columns was Fiddle's door to his home, Fenton House.

She had learned that only memories lay behind the doors; she could merely go back into her past to visit them. They gave her both comfort and pain but Fiddle's door, too, remained closed tonight.

Other doors were there; the splintered, rotting door that led to memories of Godspell. It had disappeared for a while but it was back again, thankfully quiet and inoffensive now, though it used to bang and creak, sending dust bursting out in a cloud. Another door; this one from the library, which was full of soothing voices, a rapidly ticking clock and the scent of lemonade.

New doors would appear occasionally. There was now a mahogany door, beautifully carved with a polished handle. It led to Vessania's parlour and Felix swallowed, looking away from it. Some doors hadn't been opened before, and Felix knew these were either doors from her past that she couldn't remember, or doors from her future. They didn't scare her anymore. They would open when they were ready...or when she was.

She was ready, now, for the spiral door to open.

It was a beautiful door made of white wood and was rough, like the bark of a tree. Black spirals curled across it, burned into the wood and they shifted like leaves on a breeze.

This was a hatch which led to the Glade, the ancestral home of the Drow.

'Go to the Glade,' said Fiddle's voice from behind his green door.

'I am,' whispered Felix.

Cautiously, she stepped towards the spiral door. It had opened before, just a crack, but never more than that. She had never been ready for it to open, she knew that now.

As she walked closer, the door changed. It became a mirror. Felix stopped, looking into her reflection.

The last time she had looked into this mirror, she had seen a side of herself she had not liked. Her face in the glass had been cold and hard, defiant and almost evil. Yet now, as she looked for that expression, she saw only a sad, pale child with a tangle of black curls around her, clutching a dusty rose blanket that was beautifully embroidered with the same spirals that had appeared on her face when she turned sixteen. Had that really been only a few months ago?

Felix looked at the little girl.

'You're sad,' the child spoke.

It was a statement, not a question. Felix nodded at the mirror.

'Here, take my blanket,' the little girl said. 'My family left it for me so I could find them. It always makes me feel better.' She held out her little hand which clasped the blanket firmly.

Felix almost choked on the lump in her throat. She reached out to the glass, felt her hand sink through it until she was touching the soft material.

She took a step. Then another.

The door opened, as she walked through the mirror. Gently, with a slight creak, the door closed behind her.

11

Everything, and More

Linus was not sleeping as easily as his sister. Deep underground, in the sepia light of Lundonwick, he was too excited to sleep. A sense of purpose filled him, replacing the magic that had been taken from him and it gave him a power he had not felt before. He felt determined and confident, certain that he could fulfil this task and save the fate of Felix and the Magistry...of everyone.

He rolled over in his bed, an uncomfortable, lumpy affair with no pillow and likely worth less than the tan he'd paid for it in the Dutch Courage tavern. In the beds next to him, Ragstone and Bazalguette slept easily, their occasional snores serving only as a distraction to Linus' eager brain.

Paris had proved it. Proved that there was a curse, that there was another Firelighter line, that the Great Spark was real!

'That's not proof,' Captain Kildare had scoffed, when Paris had finished telling them. Sure enough, there was nothing physical he could show them, no book or diary, no written account of everything he'd learned. But he'd sworn it was all truth. Nobody believed him. Even Linus was unsure. But then Paris convinced them.

Just downstairs, at the small table where they'd sat in the Dutch Courage tavern, drinking Ashwater and ditchmead, Paris and told them everything and had given them irrefutable evidence that what he told them was truth.

Only a few hours ago, Linus had learned everything....and more.

He hadn't thought much of it, when Paris requested a candle from the bar girl and lit it with a snap of his fingers, before he'd told his story. After all, the magic orb light was dim, and the electricity flickered this deep underground.

'There are some things you need to know first,' Paris began in a hushed voice.

Everyone had leaned in, listening carefully to each word as he spoke.

'The Privy Council is made up of thirteen magicians. We always met once a month at the Ardere Academy on the Second Plane, in a chamber that hid our faces from view. There's no rule which says we can't reveal ourselves to one another, but many members chose to keep their identities hidden. I know...I knew only a handful of the council members by face. Some I have guessed at but in truth, I wouldn't be able to point out most members even if they were sat at this very table.

'The council's role is to watch and keep ancient secrets safe. They are, I suppose, the living memory of magicians and each member has a secret to protect. No one member of the council knows every secret, so that the ancient knowledge of the magicians is never jeopardised. It's a nice theory but magicians, even those on the Privy Council, are corruptible, just like commoners.

'The secret I was given to protect was actually regarding them, the commoners. It wasn't really one secret; rather I was given access to the lost texts of their history. Forgotten and crumbling holy texts, diaries of influential and historically important people, legal documents, land deeds...any type of document you can think of, I've seen it. I can tell you where the old commoner stories of Robin Hood come from, what happens in the plays of Shakespeare's lost Second Folio...and why it was hidden. I can show you maps that lead to the Templar Treasure and the Holy Grail, piles and piles of eyewitness accounts of ghosts and mermaids and vampires.

'Well I could, before I was excommunicated.'

'They chucked you out?' Flint had asked with a wry smile.

'Yes. You see, there is only one real rule that the council have: nothing and nobody will ever endanger the secrets of the Privy Council. Each member takes an oath upon their initiation. That oath binds them to secrecy. If ever a member is captured, imprisoned or tortured, they are immediately excommunicated and unable to reveal their secret. I don't mean that they are bound by some moral and honourable ethic; oh no, I mean that they physically cannot speak, nor write, nor communicate in any way the secret which they have sworn to keep. It's rather clever magic, but not without its inefficiencies. The magic does not stop you from revealing your secret voluntarily, whilst you are in service, for example. I suppose the council once believed the word of a magician was enough to bind his honour. But as I said...magicians, like everyone, are corrupt.'

Paris had smiled mischievously and taken a sip of his drink.

Linus had not been as surprised by the story so far as the others had been. Being the son of Corbin Godspell, Firelighter and Grand Vizier, had meant he had some knowledge of the Privy Council. He knew they were a law unto themselves and did not involve themselves with the rule of the Firelighter. That was why they had never intervened when Godspell had killed his brother, or when the commoners had been subjected to such abysmal treatment. It was likely that they placed council members within the Magistry, just as Paris had been placed in charge of 'commoner care', a role he'd barely acknowledged, but Linus knew that it was merely to keep an eye on things, to document and witness rather than to involve themselves.

'I joined the Privy Council when I was but ten annums old. Within my lifetime, council members have come and gone. Some, I have known and others I haven't. Some I have respected and some I have despised. It has taken me over fifty annums, but I have learned some of the secrets that they swore they'd never tell.

'The first is that of the Great Spark. It's not the best kept secret of the Privy Council and one which you have no doubt heard of.'

'The Festival of Fire?' Captain Bonny Kildare had interrupted, and Paris had nodded and continued.

'Yes, Captain, the Festival of Fire is a holiday to celebrate the birth of magic on the First Plane. Magicians across the globe celebrate the opening of the first hatch, of the first fire, of the first Firelighter, yet it has become such a mythic idea, synonymous only with festivities and drunken bafoonery, that nobody ever thinks that it couldn't actually come from something true. Yet it does. And this secret is the first one I was able to discover, many years ago when the secret's keeper revealed it after too much drink and poppyblood.

'The Great Spark entered the first plane in 1666. On Pudding Lane, as the story goes, a baker swept out the ashes of his oven before he retired for the evening. Unbeknownst to him, the remnants of his fire contained embers which kindled the straw and wood of the thatched bakery.'

'I heard it was a maid who left a candle burning,' said Ragstone.

Paris had tried to speak but found that words could not leave his mouth. Frustrated, Paris had tried again, and it became clear that what he wanted to say was a entangled with his secret that he could not tell them. He'd banged his fist down on the table in anger before continuing, testing out each word tentatively.

'The history books state that the fire raged through London for days, destroying the city. Testament of it was recorded by the great diarists of the time, Samuel Pepys and John Evelyn.'

The words had slowly become strangled in his throat again and Linus realised that Paris had read those documents; he had seen the diaries.

'This is all common knowledge,' Linus had said. 'That is, it's all commoner knowledge. Before my father...before Godspell destroyed their history books and before you and he controlled their education, they knew all of this. But you know more, don't you? There's more to the diaries than the commoners ever knew.'

Paris had been able to do nothing. He couldn't even nod his head.

'Ok then, tell us the secret that isn't yours. You say that this Great Fire was, what, brought magic into this Plane?'

'Yes,' breathed Paris, able to talk again. 'I can confirm that the Great Fire of London was no ordinary fire. It was caused by the opening of a hatch from the Second Plane.

'We all know that the First Plane in which we sit right now, knew no magic before the hatch was opened. It is too far from the Third Plane, where magic originates to be penetrated by the particles of magic. If you know anything of venephysics, the study of magic, you'll know that magic is microscopic; tiny particles of fire that shape all things. The Second Plane, the home and birthplace of magicians is steeped in those particles. Well, when the hatch was opened, the magic burst in and took hold. It was a true baptism of fire.

'The fire razed London to the ground. A city which had taken an age to build was destroyed in a matter of days. The people of the First Plane had never seen fire like it; it could not be doused, it could not be extinguished. It raged on, surging with power, the particles of it creeping into the rivers, the smoke carrying them into the air, so that the whole of this world became scalded with magic. London, our Magistry, became the epicentre of magic on this Plane, for it is here that it originated.'

'Who opened the hatch?' Linus had asked. His voice was barely a whisper.

'The man who became known as the Firelighter. The first of them,' Paris had smiled slowly. 'You'll know him better as Thomas Farynor.'

There had been silence around the table, and Paris' smile faded.

'Thomas Farynor?' he'd said again, but the crew of the Skimmer looked at one another blankly, shrugging their shoulders.

'Goodness, you are a bunch of philistines,' Paris had huffed, folding his arms.

'He was the baker who caused the fire,' Linus had said quietly. 'Only in the commoner history books, his name is pronounced differently... Thomas Farriner.'

'He was no baker,' Paris had shaken his head. 'He was a magician from the Second Plane, sent by the Privy Council to explore an opening in the fabric of their world. It was as though a curtain was opening, a crack appearing, revealing a glimpse into an unknown world. Farynor begged to go, begged to use magic to open a doorway through to this new world. He had no idea of the devastation he would cause. He was both a destroyer and a creator.

'The hatch he created opened up on Pudding Lane, wherein he flooded the world with fire. Afterwards, when the commoners documented the fire, he...he...changed...blamed...' Paris' words had caught in his throat and his face had reddened. It seemed to cause him physical pain, until Flint had shaken his shoulder violently.

'So Thomas Farynor was the first Firelighter?' Linus had said, leaning back in his chair and knotting his hands behind his head. 'Wow.'

He'd exhaled loudly, and it seemed to him that he and the crew bore a great weight upon their shoulders. Who else, but them and only a handful of other, more prominent magicians knew this secret? What would happen to them, if the Privy Council ever found out that they knew? Which led to the question: why was Paris telling them this? Because of a conspiracy theory? What Linus really wanted to know was how to stop the curse.

'So what of the curse?' Captain Kildare had asked, echoing Linus' thoughts, as her eyes narrowed at Paris in suspicion.

'The curse exists,' Paris had insisted vehemently. He'd slammed his hand down on the table again, shaking it and causing a few droplets of wax to fall from the candle into the small metal boat which was collecting the wax beneath it. A few other customers had turned to look at him curiously, before carrying on with their drinking and debauchery.

'It exists,' Paris had repeated, more calmly. 'There is a book. I cannot tell you...it's part of my secret. A prophesy...I can't. I can't say any more. But the curse is real, and it will befall any Firelighter who claims the Sacred Flame of Magic as their own...unless they are a Farynor. Don't you see? When Thomas Farynor opened that first hatch, he gave magic a new home. Magic owes him a debt, and it will answer to only him and his bloodline. Linus, neither my family nor yours can be tracked back to the Farynor's. I've done the research. We are not and never have been the Firelighters.

'Magic is a force; it may not be sentient, but it is living, and it exists. If it has been patient thus far, it is only because it awaits its true Firelighter.

'Listen to me, all of you. This secret is one that I have worked hard to discover and one I do not tell lightly. Its secret bearer is recently dead, and though he did not give me this secret himself, I know he would want you to hear it, especially you, Linus. Especially you.

'Magic is not meant to be part of this world. It was never meant to be here. Magic lives on the Third Plane, in a nebula of fire and dust and gas. The power of that nebula descends down to the Second Plane, where it fuels life. Between the two, there is balance. When Thomas Farynor brought magic to this world, the balance was tipped.

'Imagine it like a see-saw. The nebula and the Second Plane were equally balanced; a natural eco system of magic falling in the Plane, like rainwater, before evaporating back into the nebula, the way water ascends back into clouds. But when magic was brought into the First Plane, that eco system was destroyed. Magic must now flow through the Second Plane and then into the First; the see saw is unbalanced. There is too much magic in the Planes and not enough in the Nebula, which means-'

'Which means magic is running out,' Captain Kildare had said tightly. Paris had nodded gravely.

'But nature finds a way,' he'd continued. 'And nothing is more natural than magic. The nebula is seeking out the magic from the Planes; it is moving closer. It has already started to engulf the Second Plane. Up in the Ashfjord, the colours of it shimmer like the northern lights. But the nebula is pure magic, pure fire and power. When magicians and commoners alike come into contact with pure magic...'

'They die,' Linus had breathed. He had seen it happen.

He had seen his father use a single small piece of pure magic, the Sacred Flame, on commoners and magicians and it had killed them all. All except Linus and his sister.

'My father was trying to use pure magic to turn commoners into magicians,' he'd explained.

'Your father knew what was coming,' Paris had said gently, and Linus had looked at him in disbelief.

'Your father knew that the nebula was getting closer, and he believed that magicians, being made, as we are, from magic, could survive it. By converting the commoners into magicians, albeit against their will, despite it resulting in many deaths, he really thought he was doing something good.'

'My sister. Felix, she survived the Flame. She took it into herself and she protected me. How could she have done that, if she isn't the true Firelighter?'

Linus had been conscious of nobody but Paris in that moment. Silence surrounded them as Paris looked into his eyes over the flame of the candle.

'She has Drow blood, Linus. A Drow witch uses magic differently and is made of magic in a different way to magicians. She is also a strong magician, one who can use the Flame and wield it, but it will become too strong for her to control. It's already started. You know what happened to her at the Festival of Fire.

'The Flame will no longer be patient with a caretaker. Magic awaits. It needs its true Firelighter...because only the true Firelighter can close the hatch between this world and the Second Plane and return magic to its home. Only the true Firelighter can correct the balance. We simply must find him.'

'Wait a minute,' Bonny Kildare had interrupted, breaking the trance that seemed to have fallen over the table. 'How do we know any of this is true, Lovelock? You say this is proof, but it's all just words. That's not proof!'

At this, Paris had smiled lazily and taken Flint's glass, which had been drained of Ashwater long ago. Into this glass, Paris poured the wax from the boat of the candle, which was now almost burned down.

'Because this is candoil. I trust you know what that is?'

Bonny's eyes had widened, and she'd nodded with an impressed smile.

'A truth candle,' she'd replied. 'Words spoken over its flame must be said in candor, or else...'

'Or else my tongue will be burned out of my throat when I drink its oil,' Paris had finished.

But Linus had paid no heed to this. He needed no candle to know that Paris had spoken honestly.

'Paris, how did my father know the secret of the nebula?' he'd asked desperately. 'Please don't tell me...don't say he was the secret's keeper? He can't have been on the Privy Council?'

Paris had held the glass of oily liquid to his mouth. He'd answered before drinking.

'No, he wasn't on the council, nor was he the secret's keeper. But the secret's keeper did tell him, rather foolishly, when Corbin was a young man. I think the keeper hoped it would push Corbin to be a better person; instead, it simply gave him the intent to seize power. Fiddle always did place too much trust in the wrong people.'

'Fiddle?' Linus had repeated. 'Alchemus J. Fiddle? He was the secret's keeper?'

'Yes,' Paris had replied. 'He was entrusted to guard one of the most important secrets the Privy Council has. The secret of the nebula has always fallen under his protection. He even named your sister after it.'

'Felix?'

'Yes, Linus,' Paris had said slowly. Then he'd poured the candoil into his mouth. He'd grimaced at the taste, and looked pointedly at the captain before he'd explained, clear voiced, with his tongue still intact.

'The nebula, bringer of magic and of death, is called Felixia Solis.'

Linus pushed the scratchy blanket away and sat up, the bed creaking under him. It was pointless to try and sleep. His mind was running over everything Paris had said again and again, his thoughts running away into an imaginary future, where he was the hero who had saved the world. He didn't need magic; he didn't need a title and riches and power. If he could just do this one thing, this one, huge thing...then he would have proved to himself, his sister and his dead father that he was worthy.

A faint tapping on the door interrupted his fantasy and he looked at Baz and Ragstone, but they were both sleeping soundly. The tapping came again, a little louder and Linus went to the door and opened it just a crack. Captain Bonny Kildare was stood in the hallway, fully dressed, with bright eyes despite the shadows forming under them.

'I didn't think you'd be sleeping, lad,' she said in a hushed voice. 'Walk with me.'

Linus pulled on his boots quickly and quietly, and left his crewmates snoring.

Captain Kildare led Linus out of the Dutch Courage tavern and into the deserted streets of Lundonwick. She said very little and walked very fast so Linus, who suddenly felt sleepy, struggled to keep up with her. They passed drunkards keeled over barrels, unconscious and drooling in their dreams, and waiflings curled up in corners, huddled against one another for safety or warmth, Linus was unsure which. The electric lights were still casting their yellow, flickering light and the orbs floated here and there; there was nothing at all to distinguish the night-time and yet it was as though night came with a heavy blanket that weighed down over the city, sending its inhabitants to sleep. Linus had no doubt that if he was to go back up to the surface, it would be night-time there, too. Somehow, night had found Lundonwick and infected all who lived there with sleep.

All except Linus and Captain Bonny Kildare.

When she reached the dock where the Skimmer was moored, Captain Kildare stopped and sighed, as though she could breathe more easily by the water. She sat on the uneven slats of the wooden dock, her feet dangling over the edge and hovering inches above the water beneath. Linus sat down next to her and waited for her to talk.

'I don't trust Lovelock as far as I could pitch him, but I can't deny he speaks true,' she said.

Linus smiled down at the water; Captain Kildare wasted few words and he admired her for it.

'He's not so bad,' Linus said. 'But yes, he's telling the truth.'

'Can't argue with candoil,' Captain Kildare shook her head, speaking more to herself than to Linus. 'There's much he don't know though, laddie, you have to admit.'

Linus nodded because she was right. Paris, for all his discoveries and knowledge, didn't know who the true Firelighter was or where he could be found. He'd confessed that when he'd tried to track down the descendants of Thomas Farynor, following the bloodlines of his daughters, the trail had gone cold in 1788. Paris had hinted, though he couldn't actually tell them, that there were records that indicated his only son had had a child before his wife had died, but that the records had been doctored. He couldn't tell them how he knew, his secret stopped him, but he was adamant that there was hope of a descendant. He had no idea where he may be, though.

There was also the Fire Four. Paris had absolutely no proof that they existed, just a strong conviction that he was right. Linus had no reason to doubt him. Everything Paris Lovelock had promised him had been delivered and he had been true to his word at every point.

'I do trust him,' Linus said softly. 'And I've seen what the Sacred Flame can do to people, Captain. If there's even a small chance that we can stop Felixia Solis then we have to at least try, don't you think?'

Captain Kildare looked at Linus intently. She had a habit of doing this when she was considering a person.

'Och,' she replied, and rolled her eyes. 'Why don't you just go to your sister? She's the Firelighter now, so oughn't she be able to do something about it all? By your own words, you said she was decent enough.'

Linus had thought of this and he sighed. He could go to Felix and tell her everything. He thought that she'd probably even give Paris a chance to redeem himself. He'd read of her fairness and generosity to her father's old cronies at the Magistry. But in truth, he didn't want to go to Felix. She had saved his life, and she had liberated the magicians and the commoners from the reign of Godspell, sure enough. But she had also taken his birthright. What had he now, compared to her? All he had was this. He didn't want Felix to take that from him, too.

Saying any of this to Captain Kildare felt impossible. Saying the words made him sound so petty and foolish, so he simply shrugged a shoulder. He could feel the captain's eyes boring into the side of his face and his cheeks began to redden.

'A man's worth is not measured by his ego, laddie,' she said quietly. 'It is measured by those who love him.'

'I don't have anyone left who loves me,' Linus murmured.

'That could be true,' Captain Kildare nodded, and Linus looked at her, hurt, but she flashed a rare smile at him, and Linus laughed a little.

'If you trust the damn man, I'll help you,' she said, nudging her shoulder against his. 'But I'll not risk the lives of my crew. That means your life too, lad. The Skimmer needs her skivvy boy.'

She stood up in one swift movement and Linus scrambled up next to her. He couldn't help but grin at her.

'Thanks, Cap'n,' he said, wondering if she'd punch him if he tried to hug her.

He decided that she probably would but did it anyway. Captain Kildare stiffened as Linus wrapped his arms around her awkwardly, then patted his head as though he was some sort of exotic poodle. Linus pulled away, embarrassed.

'Er, I have no idea where we should begin,' he said, clearing his throat.

'Probably at the start,' Captain Kildare smiled, straightening her hat as though she meant business. 'We're dealing in secrets and rumours, so we need someone who sells both.'

'You know someone?'

Captain Kildare shrugged knowingly.

'I know somewhere. We need to go to the Midevil Market,' she said.

'You mean medieval?'

'Och, no lad, I mean what I mean,' Captain Kildare frowned at him. 'The Midevil market is where the scum of UnderLondon lurk.'

Linus glanced at her in confusion.

'Sounds friendly. Why would we go there?'

'Because it's the best place to go for a secret or two...and it's fun.' Captain Kildare winked at Linus and jumped from the dock onto the deck of the Skimmer, pulling at the rigging knots to loosen the small, patched sails.

'Go wake the crew, laddie,' she called out to him, her eyes shining. 'Magic awaits!'

12

The Glade

The midst was black and cold, and Felix hated it. She thought for a moment of staying within it, of hiding in the darkness forever, but her fear pushed her onwards until she found the door on the other side. Groping for the door handle, she found a rough, wooden latch which she unhooked. The door opened and a slit of light cut through the dark. Felix pushed the door and stepped out into the moonlight.

She had been to the Second Plane only once before. Fiddle had taken her to show her the dense magic that occupied every leaf, every blade of grass. It had taken her a while but eventually, she saw it; each tiny, glistening particle of fire had revealed themselves to her like they were telling her their secrets. It had been one of the most beautiful things she had ever witnessed; a piece of art come to life.

Moonlight seemed only to enhance the magic. She walked out of the hatch, which looked like a makeshift door carved out of the bark of a white tree which was thick and fairly squat, with a great muddle of branches that stretched out above her head, heavy with pale red leaves. Felix had never seen a tree like it. When she looked carefully, she could see the buzzing pinpricks of magic clustered together so that it seemed like the tree was not completely solid. That was the wonder of the Second Plane; nothing was quite substantial. Everything could be anything if she willed it so.

The door she had opened closed slowly, and its hinges blended with the bark of the tree so well that she could no longer see where the hatch was. Felix swallowed nervously, committing the tree to memory so she could find her way back.

That is, if she ever went back.

She was standing in a small glen, surrounded by white trees. The grass was long and wild, reaching up past her ankles. When she moved, her long skirts rustled and made the grass sigh, sending up motes of magic that glittered like fireflies. Rays of silver crept through the branches and the leaves, coating everything in a soft gossamer veil of light.

It was beautiful and calming but it wasn't the Glade. Felix knew this. She trusted that she would feel it when she found it, that her mother's blood would sing in her veins when she found her way to the place where the Drow had come from.

Felix started to walk. She had no idea which direction she ought to go, but she felt giddy with freedom. Nobody knew she was here; she could go anywhere, do anything. Laughing at the thought, she began to run, tripping and stumbling over her skirts. She didn't care. With magic, she shore off the thick fabric of the clothes that bound her and she kicked off her buttoned shoes until she was running barefoot, dressed only in a thin, gauzy underdress, through the high grass, bubbling with happiness. On her face, the spirals glowed, sending warmth flooding through her body and it melted the ice that had taken hold of her after Vessania.

This was happiness. This was bliss. It filled her with lightness so that she felt like air, and it lifted her off her feet. She bounded in great, wide steps and each one took her several feet into the air, through the decorations of leaves above her so that she could see for miles.

Had she ever felt such joy?

Yes, you have, the little voice in her mind answered. With Nigel.

Felix crashed down, leaden again. The forgotten hurt blossomed in her chest, like wine on a spilled sheet.

Nigel, whom she had left behind.

She sank down into the grass. In shock, she looked around her as though only just realising where she was and what she had done. Spinning her head around, Felix couldn't recognise which way she had come from; the trees all looked the same and each direction looked like a tunnel of white trees filled with moonshine, fading into grey and then black and then nothing.

'I lost the hatch,' she whispered, her hand rising slowly to her mouth at her mistake. The glow left her spirals, and she clenched her fists, angry at herself. But the hatch didn't matter. Those behind it didn't matter, not anymore. She had come to find the Glade. Fiddle had told her to go there. Perhaps the Drow still lived. Perhaps they would welcome her and perhaps...perhaps she would belong there.

She climbed to her feet and walked on, trying and failing to navigate her way through the white forest. The spiral door had led her here, so the Glade must be close by, she reasoned. Unless it truly had disappeared. Unless Godspell had been right and had really slaughtered every last one of them, apart from her. Felix thought of Calantha, the mother she had never known. She thought of how she must have felt, dying on her birthing bed, watching her babies being taken from her, the last words she ever heard being ones of hate and murder. The horror of it stole the breath from Felix's lungs and she wobbled, feeling faint and tired. Nearly falling, she reached out her hand to balance herself and it found a rock; a large boulder of a rock, haphazardly placed in between the trees. Had it been there a moment ago? Felix couldn't be sure, but she was grateful for it now, as she rested her forearms against it and tried to stop the spots from swimming in front of her eyes.

It was a strange rock. It seemed more like an oversized gemstone, like a huge hunk of silver quartz. As the spots faded, she saw spirals carved into it. Tracing her bare fingers over them, they began to move, the little flecks of fire moving and merging together until they formed an archway, carved into the surface of the rock.

Felix jumped back. The rock was growing. It was pushing the trees next to it and they arched into the others around them, until all the trees surrounding her were twisting and leaning into one another. Beneath her, the ground stretched and as she looked down at the earth, she saw it moving with magic, like thousands of insects were crawling through the grass. Felix flattened herself against the gem-rock, which was now taller than she was.

Breathing hard and trembling, she saw the forest opening up into a clearing of wide-open space. The moon shone down with its full force and having no leaves to filter it, the light was almost blinding. Moonlight was brighter here and as Felix looked up at the moon, she saw how round and full and perfect it was, and how much larger it was than it ever appeared on the First Plane.

Slowly, the trees stopped moving and the ground stilled. Felix gasped as she looked out at the clearing.

'It's the Glade,' she whispered. 'It's really here.'

Felix stared at it in disbelief. She had found it; how she'd found it she had no idea but here she was, standing at the edge of wild, magical, empty beauty.

Too empty.

There were no homes or even ruins of homes. When Fiddle had first told her about the Drow, she had foolishly imagined elves in treehouses but there weren't even any of those. There was just...nothing.

Gooseflesh rippled across her skin. The gemstone rock behind her was cold and the grass between her feet was dew-kissed. Felix rubbed at her arms, feeling stupid for getting rid of her clothes. Feeling stupid for all of it. How many times would she be wrong? How many times would she have to fail before she learned that it was better to give up and stop trying? Angry and bitter tears crawled down her cheeks, but she didn't wipe them away. There was nobody here to see them.

She shivered and felt the familiar, soft weight of her baby blanket being gently draped over her shoulders. Felix pulled it around her gratefully, and then immediately jumped away from the rock and pushed the blanket away from her.

'What the-?' she cried out, flitting her eyes around to see who was there, but she couldn't see anybody.

Felix swallowed loudly, casting her eyes down to her blanket which was strewn innocently on the grass, soaking up the dew. She picked it up, inspecting it cautiously. It was definitely her blanket, the one her mother had intended for her, the one Shylock Larkin had wrapped her in when he saved her life, the one

Fiddle had left with her on the doorstep of Nanny Maude's orphanage. But Felix had left it on the First Plane. When she'd taken the blanket from her reflection in the spiral door, she'd not carried it through the midst with her...had she?

Again, she looked around the Glade.

Empty.

'Hello?' she said, annoyed at her fear-filled, hoarse voice. She called out again, louder this time.

From behind her, she heard a shuffle. Flinching, Felix turned around very slowly until she was looking back at the rock, with its curious spiral archway carved into it. It took her a moment, but then she saw the large, dark eyes and a young woman peeping out from behind the rock. Dark, thick eyebrows were arched curiously on a forehead which was marked with violet-black spirals. Felix knew they were not tattoos. She had no hair, and Felix couldn't tell if this was because she had shaven it or if she simply didn't have any.

'Hi,' Felix whispered very quietly, hardly daring to move else she scare away the girl.

The dark eyes watched her. They were so dark, Felix could not tell where the pupils were and where the irises began. Trying hard not to shake, Felix gingerly lifted her hand up to her face and pointed at her own spirals. She noticed for the first time that they were pounding, like her heart and that they were tingling.

'Drow,' she said softly, tapping her finger against her cheek. Then, she extended her hand in the direction of the girl, pointing at her and she said, again, 'Drow.'

Tentatively, making no sound, the girl stepped out from behind the rock. She was taller than Felix and slimmer too. Felix immediately thought of the word 'willowy'. She was also completely naked, but the violet-black spirals covered every inch of her skin, which was darker, too, than Felix's own.

The Drow looked at Felix, as though she was an ornament in a curiosity shop. She began to step soundlessly around her, sniffing her and very timidly touching Felix's hair. Felix let her. She could smell the scent of soil and metal and something else that she couldn't place, but it smelled...cold. Like the smell of ice or snow on the wind.

Eventually, the Drow came to face Felix again. Her eyes lingered over the spirals on her cheek and forehead and the girl reached out to touch them. As soon as her skin touched Felix's, her spirals seemed to stretch and yawn and sigh. There was no other way of describing it; Felix closed her eyes as the sensation of wholeness rinsed through her.

It was delicious.

When the girl removed her finger, Felix felt bereft and wanted to cry out at her to stop, to do it again, but she didn't. The feeling confused her. She had never felt anything like that before. It was as though she had suddenly become aware that she was missing a limb that she'd never known she'd had.

In front of her, the Drow also looked confused. Then she spoke. Felix didn't understand her. It was another language, one that used vowels and open sounds and was like a song to hear.

'I'm sorry,' Felix whispered. 'I don't understand.'

The Drow frowned, marring her beautiful face and Felix saw that her spirals moved with each expression.

She began to walk away from Felix.

'No!' Felix cried, and the Drow stopped.

She tilted her head, beckoning Felix to follow her. Felix clutched her blanket tightly and walked behind the Drow, who took long strides and stepped around the gemstone rock and disappeared behind it. Felix froze, looking behind the rock. The Drow had gone. She looked around again at the Glade and then back to the rock. Taking a deep breath, she stepped into the shadow behind the rock and she too, disappeared from view.

Behind her, the trees untwisted themselves. They drew back up, riding the tide of the earth which chased itself back towards the shrinking rock. By the time the silver light of the moon began to turn gold with sunlight, there was no sign of the Glade, of the Drow or of Felix.

13

Sense and Scents

The dire wolf jerked awake. For a moment he was disorientated, but in the thin sliver of dawn's light, he recognised the familiar surroundings and scent of the London Library. He was curled up on a scrap of rug next to Nigel's bed. The pokey room was not as cosy at Felix's chamber back at the Citadel, and his bones ached as he stretched.

What had woken him?

Nigel was a dark lump under his blanket, his shape rising and falling evenly as he breathed. In sleep, his auburn hair was a tangle of curls against his pillow and his mouth was open. When the dire wolf peered into his dreams, he saw visions of Felix.

Felix.

D.W sat on his haunches. It felt strange to be away from her. He realised now that her voice and thoughts and dreams had become so much a part of his daily noise, that he'd forgotten the sound of the others who needed him. He could feel them now that it was silent; the lost of London. It was early so it was almost calm, but the instinct to go to those he could sense was strong.

Too strong.

Since he had met Felix, the dire wolf's instincts had forced him to stay by her side. He had grown to care for her, and he chose to stay, but he had nearly always felt the pull of her. There had been times, when she was happy and settled, that he'd thought she didn't need him anymore, but the pull always came back. Felix would be lost until she truly knew who she was. D.W knew that, sometimes, knowing yourself took time and he was willing to give her that time; at some point, he would have to follow his instincts, but he would stay with Felix until that day came...and maybe even beyond that.

Dire wolf yawned, stretching his jowls. He circled the rug, which was difficult as there wasn't much room. It suddenly felt like a cage. In his dreams, Nigel was chasing Felix, begging her to stay.

Something wasn't right.

The dire wolf searched for Felix's voice. It was as familiar to him as his own thoughts, and he would recognise it anywhere. Even if she thought in images or let herself dwell on her emotions, he could sense her at any distance.

He could not sense her now.

Trying again and fighting the rising panic, which was making him pant, D.W strained to hear her through the other voices and dreams. He could hear crying and prayers and pleading voices begging for help and could see nightmares and memories and feel the uncertainty and fear and pain of London's lost, but Felix's voice was not in any of it. Nothing resembling her thoughts or dreams or even her worst nightmares were tangled in the knotted sounds he could hear.

'Nigel!' he growled, jumping up and throwing his front paws on the bed, dragging back the blanket with his teeth. 'Nigel, wake up!'

Nigel stirred and made an indistinguishable noise and a rude gesture, before pulling a pillow over his head.

Dire wolf pounced onto the bed and snarled ferociously over Nigel, baring his teeth and sharpening his ears. Turning over, Nigel started away from him.

'What the...? D.W? What are you playing at?'

Sleep fled from Nigel's eyes, replaced by fear as he clambered back against his headboard.

'It's Felix,' D.W practically shouted, ignoring Nigel's wince at the volume of his voice invading his mind. 'She's gone.'

The fright in Nigel's eyes enhanced, becoming terror, as though a deep fear had been realised. Despite the weight of D.W over him, he scrambled out of bed, dressing haphazardly.

'Gone where? What's happened?'

'I don't know,' D.W answered shaking his head. 'I can't hear her. She's just a space in the noise.'

Nigel looked frantic as he hopped, pulling on his boots. Grabbing his gloves, he ran from the room.

'Come on,' he shouted to D.W. 'We need to get to the Citadel.'

Together, they bounded up the stairs to the doors of the Story Room, which Nigel flung open. They disappeared inside the blackness in front of them and practically fell out of the door on the other side in the gardens of the Citadel.

They raced into the building. Nigel's thoughts were loud and desperate.

'No,' they cried. 'No, no no no no! Let her be here. Please, please let her be here.'

The dire wolf understood his urgency. Last night, Nigel had told D.W what had happened with his aunt Vessania and what she had said to Felix. They both knew Felix well enough, to know what sort of effect it would have on her. Despite the people who loved her deeply, despite those who admired her and valued all she had done, despite her power, Felix still saw herself in the worst light. Vessania's words would have hit their mark, planting seeds of doubt and uncertainty and both Nigel and D.W had fallen asleep with restless nerves, thinking about how they could reassure Felix and bring her back to warmth and the comfort of belonging.

'We belong together,' Nigel had said in the firelight of the Reading Room. 'I see her. Do you know what I mean? Whoever she is, whatever she is, anything she could ever do or say, I want to be her witness. I want to be there. I...I love her. If she leaves me, I don't know what I'll do.'

Now, his fears seemed to be becoming reality.

The dire wolf was much than Nigel and he bolted up the stairs, taking several at a time in large leaps, and he skidded on the polished floor. The sounds from his claws on the tiles, and the thudding of Nigel's shoes was enough to wake the Citadel's sleepers. From their chamber, Aubrey and Liberty stepped out, tying sashes around their dressing gowns. Further down, Thaddeus opened his chamber door, rubbing his sleepy eyes.

'What on earth is going on?' Aubrey shouted, but D.W paid no attention to her.

He sprinted past her, to Felix's chamber door at the end of the corridor and barged into it, using his size and weight to crash the door open off its hinges.

Smell of Felix. Brimstone and ash. Undeniable static of her magic. If he had been human, he would have had goosebumps.

The bed was slept in, that was clear. There was an indentation of her head on the silk pillow and the sheets were ruffled. Her scent was fresh and unmistakable. She had been here, and recently. Dire wolf jumped on the bed, sniffing at it. There was another smell. It was faint and not quite real; almost like the memory of a scent...but that wasn't possible. It was like the smell of morning frost.

Behind him, Nigel nearly fell as he grabbed at the doorframe. He was breathless, and D.W could hear his heart skipping in his chest.

'Felix!' he shouted. 'Is she here?'

Nigel's eyes scanned over the room. He had forgotten his glasses, so he had to squint a little but as he entered the room, D.W heard his despair. The boy walked slowly to the bed, looking down at it. Maybe if he looked hard enough, he'd see her; she'd be there.

'Felix,' he whispered.

'Will somebody tell me what on earth is going on?' Aubrey's voice boomed into the room. 'Do you know what time it is?'

Her bright red hair was in disarray, and without her glasses and the bright colours she usually wore, she looked smaller. Liberty, who was standing at her side peeked into the room and rested a hand gently on her wife's forearm.

'My love?' Liberty said softly and nodded her head towards Nigel. 'Look.'

Nigel was still staring down at the empty bed. His hand reached down to touch the silk of the pillow. Slowly, he held up a single, dark strand of Felix's hair.

The dire wolf felt the deep, slow cut of his heartbreak.

'Felix,' Nigel said again, his voice tight with hurt.

He turned to look at Aubrey and Liberty, his eyes wet and shining. It was betrayal that he felt most. Betrayal that she had left him. Again. That she had not thought they were strong enough.

D.W yelped, not just with Nigel's pain, but with his own as Nigel fell to his knees by the bed and said, with breath catching in his throat,

'She's gone.'

Cinnamon scented steam rose up from the cups in front of them. Untouched, the tea grew cold until Liberty touched each one and made them steam again.

They were in the drawing room. D.W had said it was the last place he had seen Felix and between them, he and Nigel had explained all that happened the evening before.

'Could she have gone back to the Quarter? The orphanage maybe?' Liberty asked. Her white hair was pinned back out of her face, which was lined with worry. Her eyes kept flicking up to Aubrey, who was pacing the floor in front of the unlit fire.

'No,' D.W said. 'She isn't anywhere on the First Plane. I'd hear her if she was.'

Thaddeus opened the door and all eyes turned to him. Behind him, Imelda the healer looked concerned.

'Sigbert Goodnight is nowhere to be found,' Thaddeus said. 'The night COPPs on duty outside the Citadel said they saw him leaving just before dawn.'

'They've searched the grounds too,' Imelda said, joining Liberty on the couch. 'Just in case. There's no sign of her.'

'What did she want with Goodnight?' Aubrey asked, directing her hard eyes at the dire wolf. She was fierce, but he knew that she was afraid for Felix.

'Felix didn't tell me,' he replied. 'She said she wanted to be alone. I thought she just needed a little time. She's been guarding her thoughts from me.'

Aubrey tightened her hands behind her back and her mouth was a firm line. Once again, she began to pace.

'Should we contact Old Nell in the Quarter? Rally the troops?' Imelda asked.

Aubrey nodded. 'Yes, send word to them and tell them to keep an ear to the ground. We may need the Touch Papers team to gather information, but it must be kept quiet. If the Magistry hears that the Firelighter and Grand Vizier has gone missing, there'll be hell to pay.'

Imelda nodded and scooted from the room.

'Thaddeus,' Aubrey barked. 'I'll need you to check the hatchway. I want a record of all the hatches used and by whom in the city in the last twelve hours.'

'On it,' Thaddeus said, and followed Imelda out of the drawing room.

'Why would Sigbert leave, too?' Liberty asked softly. There was confusion in her voice; she and Sigbert Goodnight had been colleagues and friends for decades.

'I don't know,' Aubrey admitted, her shoulders slumping. She sat next to Liberty and wrapped an arm around her comfortingly.

'I think we ought to assume that Sigbert has something to do with this, good or bad,' she said as gently as she could. Her wife nodded, but the hurt was evident on her face.

'What about the Second?' Nigel said.

The others turned their eyes to him. He'd been standing by the window, staring out at it for a long while, and he hadn't spoken since Felix's chamber. Now, he turned to face them. His green eyes were bloodshot and swollen.

'D.W, you said you'd be able to hear her if she were on the First Plane, but what about the Second?'

Aubrey and Liberty looked to the dire wolf hopefully, but he shook his head.

'I'd be able to feel her there,' he explained. 'It's complicated. I just can't sense her at all. It's like there's a hole in my mind where she used to be; I can't hear her anywhere, not on this Plane or on the Second. Wherever Felix has gone, she's somewhere that I can't feel her anymore.'

Nigel swallowed with difficulty and folded his arms. He turned again to the window.

'Felix,' he whispered as the rain began to pelt at the glass. 'Where are you?'

14

Lillith

Felix was somewhere dark. Dark and cold. She was shivering in her gauze underdress, and her bare feet were splashing in sludge that she couldn't see. Her arms were outstretched, scuffing against sharp, wet rocks on either side of her. She could hear trickling of water, echoes of small stones falling against the rock as she knocked against them with her hands and feet, and she could hear the echo of the Drow's footfalls ahead of her. It was the echoes that gave her the only reassurance that she wasn't alone, that she was still following the strange, tall girl from the Glade.

'Where are we?' Felix called out, knowing it was pointless, that the girl didn't understand her, but her voice was a comfort in the darkness.

It resounded, asking her question back to her. From ahead, the strange song-like language replied, sounding further away than she'd thought. Stumbling, Felix growled and snapped her fingers. As she did, an orb of light illuminated the tunnel. Immediately, she wished it hadn't.

Tiny white spiders were crawling along the wall. Felix drew her arms towards her body and gasped, a dozen imaginary itches springing up all over her body. She wasn't afraid of spiders, and these ones were as small as money spiders, but to see so many of them made her cringe. The orb light made them scurry back into little cracks and crannies of the rocks and Felix could see the Drow deeper down inside the tunnel looking back at her in bewilderment, as though confused as to why she would need a light and be so startled at seeing spiders. Even so, when she continued to walk, she did so at a slower pace so that Felix could keep up.

The tunnel was long and at times, so narrow that Felix had to stoop a little. At one point, the Drow had to bend over at a ninety-degree angle to fit through. As they walked deeper into the tunnel, Felix saw gemstones sticking out of the rock walls, glittering in the light of her magical orb. They grew larger the further they went...and so did the spiders, until eventually they were the size of her palm. Felix inspected them as best she could whilst she travelled. They were all white, the spiders, with a pinkish patch at the front which she soon realised, with some queasiness, were their eyes. But the spiders were harmless and, curiously, they were webless. She detected no wisps or sticky cobwebs anywhere; indeed, it seemed that the spiders lived in the holes and cracks of the walls, next to the gemstones.

Felix had never seen the kind of gems which grew in the tunnel. They were more than just crystals and quartz and amethysts and rubies and sapphires and emeralds, although there were plenty of these. They shimmered like rocks dipped in glue and children's glitter, like shards of glass which trapped starlight. The water which trickled over these gems seemed to collect their pigment so that even the droplets were glistening.

In time, after what felt like hours, the tunnel began to open up. The jagged ceiling changed from low hanging stalactites to sharp icicles dripping and dangling, quite perilously, overhead some fifteen or twenty feet above their heads.

Sheets of ice covered the ground, creating a more even pathway which burned Felix's bleeding feet. She was bitterly cold and had started to tremble violently, her breath pouring out in white clouds. The Drow looked at her and cocked her head to the side, before reaching out her long, slender finger and quickly tapping Felix's spirals. It was not a lingering touch like earlier, and there was none of the blissful, wholesome feeling she had instilled when she'd touched Felix last time, but slowly, a warmth began to spread through Felix's limbs, like a spring thaw, emanating from the spirals on her face. Within a few minutes, she felt quite cosy.

A little awestruck, she bowed her head awkwardly in thanks. The Drow must have understood her intent, because she too nodded and held up a hand, beckoning Felix to take a seat on a fallen stalagmite. Felix got the sense that she was telling her to wait, so she obeyed, watching anxiously when the Drow disappeared from view, into the mouth of an adjoining tunnel.

Felix took a deep, icy breath. She thought she must be in shock, for she looked around the cavern with a detached sense of curiosity. She should be feeling joy, surely, at having found a living Drow, or perhaps even fear at being in an underground cavern crawling with spiders, in some secret lair on the Second Plane. But she felt neither of those things. Instead, she felt calm, even serene. Above her, the orb of light floated as though it, too, was curious about its surroundings. Its light shone on the gemstones, causing prisms of colour to cast down over Felix. She was sat in a rainbow. Her pot of gold at the end of it, was the discovery that she was not alone; she was not the last. Carrig, her leprechaun friend on the Belfast would have been speechless, and she giggled when she imagined his expression that she had found her own Fortuna.

Sounds of movement coming from the adjoining tunnel made her tense, and she stood quickly, wary of the darkness which loomed in the entry way. The sound was not the Drow's delicate and steady footsteps, but a pounding of some kind...and voices. Sing song, soft and luring voices which Felix couldn't understand, but she recognised their expressions of interest, surprise and wariness.

The pounding, she realised, was the sound of many feet. It grew louder, and Felix shrank back down onto her makeshift seat and tried to calm her breathing. The Drow she had followed appeared first, motioning to others behind her. She was smiling and nodding at Felix in reassurance, and Felix let go of the breath she was holding but gasped again as she saw them.

Dozens of them.

Spilling out of the tunnel eagerly and filling the cavern, Felix beheld the Drow. They were tall, beautiful and hairless, each of them naked, their skin covered with spirals and swirls in varying shades of black; all of them looking at Felix as though she was mesmerising, as though she was the miracle.

The Drow clustered around her, looking up towards the floating orb light, shielding their black eyes with their arms and talking to one another in their strange language. They reached for Felix, stroking and caressing her hair in wonder, gently touching her spirals with their fingers and each time they did, Felix felt that glorious sense of oneness; of feeling whole.

Suddenly, they broke contact and fell silent. A reverent hush fell over them and the crowd which had formed around Felix parted, creating a pathway. Felix looked up and saw a woman, older than the others though still in her prime, her face creased with experience like the page of a well-read book. Her eyes were black, too, but there was a trace of blue within them, and she was the only one of them who had hair; long, silver tendrils tumbled down her back and over her shoulders and through them, her black spirals shimmered with an emerald tint.

This woman walked slowly towards Felix with sure steps, her face wearing an expression of astonishment. When she reached Felix, her gaze was deep and penetrating, and her arms lifted to Felix's face and she made to cup Felix's face tenderly, though she did not touch her. She fell to her knees in front of Felix.

'Sweet child,' the woman said, with a trembling lip.

Felix looked down in confusion at this woman but as she laid her hands on Felix's face, bliss filled her. The spirals on her face sighed as they were touched by the woman's hands, whose own spirals swirled and danced, uniting with Felix's own. Sweet pleasure flooded through Felix's body, each cell ignited with a deep sensation of wellbeing. Nothing mattered now except this feeling. She didn't have to worry, to care about anything anymore. All would be well.

'I am Lillith,' the woman said. It was a voice of comfort and care and tender, tender love and when she spoke, Felix could feel it in every part of her body.

'Welcome home.'

Felix followed Lillith in a daze. Around her, the Drow spoke in excited, hushed whispers and their talk was as soothing as a lullaby. It filled Felix's head with a gentle fog, making her eyelids heavy and her limbs leaden. She felt wonderfully calm and safe, even walking down the darkened tunnel; towards what, she didn't know, but it was fine, because she was home. Nothing could harm her here; not darkness, not white spiders and certainly not the women who circled around her like a protective shield.

The magical orb of light she had conjured was forgotten in the cavern, and Felix let the darkness embrace her. It was strangely comforting and intimate. Against her skin, she felt the Drow brushing against her and each time their dark skin touched hers, she felt tiny little purrs of pleasure and joy.

Home.

Had a word ever held such meaning and intensity for Felix as it did in that moment? All her life, from her annums in the orphanage with Nanny Maude to the time she'd spent with Fiddle in the library, she had never felt the sensation of acceptance and homecoming which she felt now. Even the memory of them, of Maude and Fiddle, did not cause her pain down here. There was no pain. No anger, no sadness, no deep fear...just love. It had swept her up and cradled her and it came from these women, from Lillith, from all of them; her sisters. She understood now why they were the Sisterhood of the Drow. She felt, with every touch, each embrace, that she knew them all. It was like they were connected, somehow.

'Our home is deep in the earth,' Lillith's voice said in the darkness. Her words were said carefully, as though she had learned the language in phrases from books.

'You've been down here for sixteen years?' Felix asked.

Her curiosity, always burning, had not diminished. She remembered from her reading that her uncle had driven the Drow to extinction from the day of her birth, when he had taken power.

'Yes,' Lillith answered. 'We have found safety in the deep earth. We are shielded from those who would harm us. I saved those whom I could, but we lost many. Come, we are nearly there.'

Felix wondered where 'there' was, but she followed silently until, once again, the tunnel opened out. Her mouth fell open as she beheld a city unlike any she had ever seen. If she had once imagined treehouses when she thought of the Drow, she must have had some kind of intuition.

She was on a ridge, looking out at what she knew was impossible and yet here it was; trees grew from the foundations of the rocks, their roots entangled with the stone. They were taller than any tree she'd seen before, creating a canopy of leaves above a trickling stream, which flowed from the strange gemstone walls and snaked down towards a city carved from rock and wood. In the vast cliff faces, caves glowed with dim, blue light, illuminating the moss-covered bridges between the walls of rock. Where branches grew out of the stone, homes had been built there, too; intricately woven leaves and branches had been bound together to create roofs, whilst balconies and wooden porches hung over the vast drop to the crags below.

Everything was growing, alive and of the earth. What resources they had, the Drow had used. Looking closer, Felix saw a water wheel further into the reaches of the stream which spread out into a small lake. At its head, a waterfall dove down even further below the city. The trees were heavy with ripe fruit and to the left Felix saw a small field of crops, tended by the only men she had seen so far.

Light shone timidly from cracks in the rocks far, far above but it was filtered by a brume, which seemed to twitch and jolt. Squinting her eyes, Felix shuddered when she realised that it was a curtain of vast cobwebs hanging between the rocks and cliffs, with spiders larger than D.W crawling along them.

'They are our white widows,' Lillith explained gently, resting her arm on Felix's for a moment. Instant tranquility spread through her like a balm. 'They will not hurt you. They protect us.'

Felix nodded, but could not resist flicking her eyes upwards warily, as Lillith led her and the other Drow down a narrow ridge path and through the wild canopy of trees.

'It's so beautiful,' Felix whispered in awe.

She giggled when she saw small Drow children peeping down from the rafters of the green ceiling, pointing down at her and waving shyly.

'It is our home,' Lillith smiled at her. 'And now it is yours, child.'

Felix fought down a lump in her throat at her words. As though sensing her emotion, the Drow women who had been following behind in a hush surged forward in concern, huddling around Felix with eyes full of worry. With each stroke of their hands on her face or her arms, Felix's feelings of sadness faded.

'They feel your pain and they feel your woe,' Lillith explained. 'The Drow can...empathise? That is the word? Yes? The Drow can empathise with each other very, very deeply.'

'Yes, Fiddle said the Drow are ruled by emotions,' Felix nodded, wiping her eyes sloppily with the back of her hand.

'Fiddle,' Lillith repeated back to her, and a slow smile spread across her mouth as though a memory had taken root in her mind and was growing. 'Alchemus James Fiddle. He is a friend to Drow and was kind to your mother, Calantha. He warned me of your father's brother.'

'You knew Fiddle? And my mother? Then you know that I'm...' Felix trailed off; she was still not quite used to claiming her titles.

'You are the daughter of Calantha, our sister, and Everard, the Firelighter who was...murdered? The Drow have no word for this, for murder. Alchemus told me of your birth and of your brother's birth, when he warned me.'

'You knew about us? Me and Linus?' Felix asked.

Shadows of hurt passed over her face at the thought that the Drow had abandoned them both. Again, the Drow pressed around her but this time, she pulled away from them seeking only an answer to her question. Lillith spoke in the strange language with soft, lilting sounds and the Drow nodded, leaving them both immediately with soft strokes of farewell to Felix.

'I thought you were both dead,' Lillith explained when they were alone, her dark eyes wide and imploring. She reached for

Felix's hands and clasped them earnestly. 'I did not know you were alive. Calantha had passed on to earth at the hands of the usurper, Corbin Godspell. My sisters and I were being hunted. Alchemus said we must hide and escape, so we did. We trust Alchemus. He is our friend. He did not tell us of you...Felix? That is your name?'

Felix raised her eyebrows in surprise and nodded.

'I can know you,' Lillith said, but she looked confused for a moment, struggling to find the words to convey what she wanted to say. 'When Drow touch, we can see one another and know one another. Do you understand?'

Felix nodded slowly. She tried to 'see' Lillith but all she could feel was the sensation of love and warmth.

'Fiddle is dead,' Felix said; the words were thick and dense in her mouth. 'I'm sorry to tell you.'

A shock of anguish clouded Lillith's face, and she closed her eyes.

'We will weep for Alchemus,' she whispered.

Felix felt the regret and grief sweeping from Lillith's hands into her own. Finally, here was someone who felt pain the way she felt pain...someone who understood.

'You are the Firelighter, now,' Lillith said, peering into Felix. 'You have been uncertain.'

Felix dropped Lillith's hands and pulled away, nodding. She folded her arms. The confusion of Vessania's words and the conflict she felt about her responsibilities lunged out from deep inside her, and she did not want Lillith to see it. She didn't want Lillith to feel her shame.

Lillith watched her carefully, with concern.

'You have known much pain, sister,' she said, with sadness ringing in her voice. 'Pain is a burden you need not share alone any longer. We will have a Drowning.'

'A Drowning?' Felix asked. 'What's that?'

Lillith smiled and her spirals shimmered with their emerald glow.

'You will see,' she answered. 'But first, you must rest. You are weary. You will stay in my home, and it shall be your home. Come now, sister Felix. There is nothing to fear anymore.'

Felix sighed, relief and exhaustion rushing through her simultaneously. She reached for Lillith's hand like a small child reaches for their mother and she let herself be led to Lillith's home.

Her home.

Felix slept dreamlessly for almost twelve hours. Waking, she stretched, feeling a lightness in her limbs and mind that she couldn't recall feeling before.

Her room was small but comfortable. It had been built into the wide branches of a white tree, which grew out of the cliff face next to a large cave which made up the rest of Lillith's home. It seemed to be the largest of the caves, higher than the others and Felix wondered if that meant that Lillith was their leader. She certainly seemed to be.

There were no windows because there was no need for them; the room was open, sheltered by leaves and woken web netting above which twinkled in the light. It was cool with a slight breeze but not cold, and the pillows and bedsheets, spun from spider silk, had kept her warm.

Felix yawned and she heard a giggle from behind her room. There were no doors, she'd noticed. Everything was sort of open and it was a little unnerving but then, the Drow were naked and seemed to know no shyness from one another. Turning, she saw the first Drow girl who had led her from the Glade to the cavern. She was peeping out from behind a branch, watching Felix curiously. The girl looked only a little older than Felix and she smiled at her, waving in embarrassment.

'Melantha,' came Lillith's voice, with a little chuckle.

She said something Felix couldn't understand and the Drow girl scurried away, giggling again.

'She is eager to know you,' Lillith said, smiling down at Felix as she entered the room. 'All your sisters are.'

Felix averted her eyes. She was acutely aware, suddenly, that Lillith was naked; all the Drow were, save for her and it made her feel all the more conspicuous, yet she knew she would never dare remove her thin underdress.

But Lillith stood in front of her proudly, waiting for Felix to feel comfortable until, after a few moments, Felix glanced up at her timidly.

Lillith, like the others, was dark. Her skin wasn't black like Thaddeus's skin, nor did it have the olive tones of Felix's own. It was almost a charcoal colour; a sort of blue-grey, the colour of summer night sky. The spirals on her skin curled around most of her body and their green tinge made them seem almost snake like. With her long silver hair, she was truly a sight to behold.

'Our spirals give us power, therefore our bodies are our power,' Lillith explained quietly. 'We do not hide our power.'

Felix smiled a little, but she thought of the furyfire she had so often quashed inside her, and of how many times she had been told to control it by Fiddle and Aubrey and Nigel. Absently, she rubbed at her own spirals on her face.

Lillith came to sit on the bed next to her. Her height made Felix feel a little cowed and she wondered how she had not noticed it earlier. In fact, she had lost most of the calm serenity she'd experienced with the Drow. Alone now, with Lillith, Felix felt the all too human shades of doubt and panic casting their shadows over her.

'Shh,' Lillith soothed, stroking Felix's hair. 'We will talk. You have questions, I sense. And if you will let me, I have queries for you, too.'

'You first,' Felix said, clearing her throat.

Lillith's proximity and nakedness so soon after waking, made her feel nervous.

'Your brother, you called him Linus. Where is he?' Lillith asked, tilting her head.

She gazed at Felix intently, barely blinking and Felix had the feeling that she was being read. It reminded her of the way the dire wolf probed her thoughts sometimes, and she felt a flare of irritation.

'I don't know,' Felix said tightly.

Lillith nodded and shifted away from Felix with a sigh. A wave of hurt drifted from her and Felix gritted her teeth, annoyed at herself for feeling so defensive to this woman who had shown her nothing but warmth and compassion.

'Sorry,' she mumbled. 'I don't know why I'm being rude.'

'You do not trust,' Lillith shrugged. 'It is ok. You will, in time. We can give you time.' She smiled kindly and Felix shuffled on the bed, swirling a lock of her hair around her fingers. She took a deep breath and explained all that had happened since her birth. When she talked of her brother, she explained his disappearance and told her how she had saved him from their uncle's cruel experiments with the Sacred Flame.

'And now it passes to you?' Lillith asked quietly. 'A heavy weight for a young woman to carry.'

Felix dipped her head and shrugged a shoulder.

'It's my responsibility,' she said.

'But you are here,' Lillith murmured, lifting Felix's chin with her finger. 'And your brother is missing. You say he had help? That he has gone away with someone? Who? A lover?'

Felix couldn't help but grin and she chuckled, lightening the atmosphere in the room.

'Not as far as I'm aware,' she replied. 'He left with a man from the Magistry, Paris Lovelock.'

Lillith's black eyes narrowed and her whole mood darkened. The emerald of her spirals surged bright and glowing.

'Paris Lovelock?' she repeated, her voice low and deep. She seemed to swell with power, and Felix swallowed audibly.

'Err...yeah. You know him?'

Lillith nodded her head once, her lips thin and set in a hard line. The anger poured out of her like heat and in her eyes, fire stirred. But no sooner had it appeared, it left, the anger dissipating and the heat absorbing back into Lillith, as she breathed out a long, deep exhalation which smelled vaguely of sulphur.

'Unfortunately, I do know him,' she said, with a smoky voice.

Felix's heart was racing. She had never witnessed furyfire in anyone else before and to see it brewing in Lillith was truly terrifying. She remembered the dire wolf cowering in front of her, the crowds of the Magistry running from her at the Festival of Fire and she understood, now, why they had been so afraid.

'Paris Lovelock is not a man to be trusted. His tongue spills lies,' Lillith continued. As though sensing Felix's anxiety, she rested her hand on her arm, easing her nerves.

'That he is with Linus, a brother of the Drow, makes me feel fear for your brother.'

'I've been trying to find him,' Felix said in anguish. 'Really. I've sent-'

'I will help you,' Lillith interrupted her, and she held up her hand to cut off Felix's words. It was a movement that was both final and intimidating. 'I will help you find brother Linus and save him from the lies of magicians.'

Felix balked. Lillith spoke as though the word 'magicians' left a foul taste in her mouth. But Felix was a magician, as well as a Drow and Lillith knew that. Felix couldn't deny that those words hurt her, just a little but then, Lillith had suffered at the hands of magicians like Corbin Godspell. Surely, she had as much right as anyone to dislike magicians. After all, hadn't Felix once felt the same way? And besides, she was offering to help find Linus.

'Thank you,' Felix breathed. 'But...I mean no offence or anything, but how? Nobody even knows you exist and you're pretty hard to miss.' She motioned to the spirals on Lillith's limbs, and the woman laughed. As she did, a white spider, a little larger than the size of a saucer crawled up and over onto her shoulder, pushing long silver strands of hair away with its legs.

Felix gasped and recoiled, her shoulders raising to her ears, and she tried to wipe the disgust off her face, especially when Lillith turned her face towards the spider and began to nuzzle it.

'I have my ways, sister Felix,' Lillith said with a smile. 'Our white widows do our bidding.'

She lifted her palm to the spider, and it crawled onto it trustingly. Lillith moved her hand slowly towards Felix who was now almost clambering out of the bed.

'Hush child,' Lillith chastised. 'Aradia will do you no harm. Take her.'

Felix fought the urge to jump up and down and brush her hands all over her body; each part of her was bristling with itches. She sucked in a breath and stretched out her hand. As soon as the spider placed one of its legs on her finger, Felix squealed but she dared not move her hand. Lillith's black gaze was upon her again, like a headmistress watching her naughtiest student.

The spider, Aradia, tentatively placed her ballet slipper feet onto Felix's skin and slowly crept into Felix's hand. She filled it easily. Her pink eyes made Felix mouth frown in revulsion but after a moment, Felix grew braver. She lifted the white widow closer to her face to inspect it. She really was quite soft and such a delicate weight in Felix's palm.

'Good,' Lillith nodded as though she had secretly triumphed. 'The white widows' venom is poisonous, but they will not bite us for to do so is to die. It is a balance, yes? The Drow do not fear nature and her creatures, Felix. We work in this special balance, like the white widows do with their venom. Our power is not like magician's power. Our type of magic comes from the earth, for we are of the earth. We are made of magic just as Aradia is, just as every creature on the Second Plane is made of magic.

'Tonight, we will have a Drowning and you will see what the Drow can do. And we will find Linus, Felix. We will bring him home.'

'Thank you,' Felix whispered, her eyes not leaving the spider on her hand.

Lillith rose to leave, and Felix panicked suddenly.

'Wait, you're going? But I have questions about the Drow. About your...our power.'

She climbed awkwardly out of bed, trying not to disturb Aradia who was inching her way up Felix's arm. It was oddly ticklish and not altogether unpleasant.

'I know, child,' Lillith said, smothering a laugh at Felix's squirming. 'The Drowning will answer them, I promise.'

'Wait. Er, take Aradia with you, will you?' the spider was now on Felix's shoulder, one leg outstretched at mischieviously tickling her face.

'I think she likes you,' Lillith laughed. 'But very well. Come Aradia.'

The white widow immediately scuttled down Felix's arm and then, suspended on a thread of web, floated down to the ground. Felix couldn't hide her horror as the spider crawled up Lillith's body and then nestled into her hair.

'Not sure I'll get used to that,' Felix rasped.

Lillith grinned. 'You will,' she said. 'I'll send some food and drink to you with Melantha. I have no doubt she will want to see you again.'

'But I don't understand the language,' Felix said.

'Do not worry,' Lillith replied as she left the room. 'The Drowning will make it all clear.'

Felix shook her head in frustration as Lillith left. She scratched her nails over her arm where Aradia had been crawling up in and shuddered again. So far, the Drow had proved to be very odd and a little unnerving, in spite of their obvious care for her. It would take a while for her to learn their ways and she so desperately wanted to learn. She doubted she would ever feel comfortable being naked and as for the spiders? Well, that was definitely not going to feel normal any time soon. A smile drifted over face when she thought of Nigel, usually so stoic, running away from the Map Room and screaming like a small child after finding a spider. He would definitely hate this place, she thought to herself, chuckling. But the memory of Nigel saddened her and the hurt which she felt and had briefly forgotten reared inside her again. She shook away the memory and swallowed, turning her attention to Melantha, who was grinning and coming towards her, holding a platter of fruits and a wooden cup filled with the clearest, most twinkling water Felix had ever seen.

Better to keep her focus on the Drow. Better to think only of her new home and the life she would create here.

As Felix drank the water, which was both sweet and crystal cold, she thought about the Drowning. *What on earth could it be?* she thought to herself, wondering what new secrets it would uncover.

15

Mudlarks and Markets

In the heart of the city of London, resting in the shadows of old St Paul's, lies the Guildhall and its accompanying art gallery. Its white stone façade, built in the gothic style of the medieval fifteenth century, had borne witness to pomp and prestige for nigh on eight hundred years. Here, laws had been written and unwritten, prominent people in power had been sentenced to death, even a queen had once stood trial for treason within its walls.

Now, it was a shell of a building, rotting into ruins since Corbin Godspell had swept the gallery clear of its fare and built the Citadel, its extravagant neighbour only minutes away.

But the Guildhall's decrepitude hid a secret.

Beneath the vaulted ceilings of the Great Hall, beneath the oval room which had once been the Chief Commoner's Parlour in the reign of Everard, beneath the stained glass of the East and West crypts, lay an ancient amphitheatre which predated even the first Firelighter.

The Roman ruins of the Guildhall bore the weight of the building and its history like Atlas holding the heavens on his back. The crumbling stone circle with tiered steps, which served as seating had once been the pulse of Roman Londinium; home to gladiator tournaments, animal fighting pits and festivals in praise of their gods. It had sunken deep beneath the earth, as time had laid its years upon it. London had grown around it and eventually above it until the amphitheatre had fallen into memory and then been forgotten completely.

Except by those in UnderLondon.

Now, the wreckage of the amphitheatre was host to new tournaments and different festivities.

Now, it had become the Midevil Market.

The Skimmer sailed along the Walbrook River and then onto the flooded route of the red central line before it emerged on the banks of Bank, the old tube stop which had once serviced the Bank of England above.

'We walk from here,' Captain Kildare shouted down to the crew, and they set about securing the rigging.

Linus took a deep breath of anticipation.

'You've been before?' he asked Ragstone, who was hauling rope over his shoulder then looping it around a windlass and turning the handle.

'Aye,' Ragstone said, managing to nod without the cigar on his lip dropping onto the deck.

'What's it like?' Linus called out, as he jumped from the starboard deck into the sludgy shallows of Bank. The water and muck came up to his chest. He caught the mooring rope which Ragstone hurled to him and began to pull on it. Slowly, the Skimmer started to drift towards him.

'Dodgy place,' Ragstone smiled, as though he couldn't be happier to be mooring in a place that had 'evil' in its name.

'Exactly how dodgy are we talking?' Linus asked, panting as the Skimmer finally hit dirt and scuffed against the ground. He secured the rope to a mooring bollard with a cleat knot and rested his hands on his hips.

'These aren't just Houdinis and gamblers, lad,' Ragstone replied, jumping onto the bank, with one hand resting on the bulkhead as he flung his legs over in one swift movement.

'We're talking good, honest evil folk. Assassins, bandits, poisoners. You want one, you can find them at the market.'

'Cap'n says it sells secrets, too,' Linus said.

Ragstone nodded grimly. 'High price to pay for secrets,' he said.

Linus looked at him questioningly, but he would say no more.

'This is disgusting,' Paris mewled, as his feet hit the silt. 'And it smells foul.'

He lifted his feet up and inspected his shoes, which had once been the shiniest of patent leather but were now dripping with effluvious slime. Behind him, Pinks was laughing her silent, breathy laugh. She kicked up some of the dirt with her rubber boots and laughed some more.

'Enough, Pinks,' Captain Kildare called down from the ship.

Pinks looked up at her then back to Paris, and promptly stuck out her tongue.

'Cap'n?' Bazalguette called down from the masthead.

He was gripping it with his thighs and leaning backwards, looking into the darkness they had come from.

'What is it, Baz?' Captain Kildare shouted up to him.

Flint emerged from below deck carrying a duffle bag on his shoulder and looked up to Baz, then into the pitch black.

A shrill 'quark' broke through the air and Baz hunkered into the rigging.

'Mudlarks!' he cried down. 'Take cover!'

Suddenly, a bird with a long, thin beak tore out of the shadows and swooped down towards the deck of the ship. Flint threw down his duffle bag and dove on top of Captain Kildare. The mudlark jabbed at the empty air where only a second earlier, the captain's head had been.

'Run!' Captain Kildare screamed at the crew on the bank. 'Follow the bank. Make for the market walls!'

Linus, Paris, Ragstone and Pinks did not hesitate. They raced along the thin strip of land between the walls of the tube line and the sewer water, splashing in the shallows. Behind them, they heard the cries of the captain and Flint, and the echoing bangs of Flint's guns. Pinks stalled, looking behind her to the ship. Paris grabbed her just as a mudlark lunged, its knife-like beak only inches away from her face.

'Run, you stupid girl!' Paris screamed at her, and he held her hand as he dragged her through the mud, but her little legs could not keep up with him. Quickly, he pulled her up to him and hoisted her over his shoulder.

'There!' Linus cried. 'The walls!'

He was looking at a vast wall that reached high above, disappearing into the pitch black of the underground shadows. Two wooden effigies of great giants stood twenty feet tall at either side of a great stone doorway, holding torches of fire and huge spears.

'Let us in!' Linus called out, waving his hands up at the walls.

Above him, he heard the screech of a mudlark and in the firelight of the torches, he saw its leathery wings spread wide, stretching wider than the wings of a harpy eagle. Another joined him and together they circled around, preparing to dive again like vultures.

Linus did not stop running, even when he saw the wooden giants turn and form an X across the doors with their spears.

'Open the doors!' he screamed out again, flinging himself in the dirt as a mudlark plummeted down towards him.

The giants stood still, their spears blocking their entry into the amphitheatre.

Ragstone, Paris and Pinks ran at the door, pushing against it breathlessly and ducking down as the mudlarks soared towards them, jabbing them with their beaks. Pinks screeched in pain as a mudlark sliced at her arm. Blood flowed out and fat, dark droplets fell to the ground where the mudlarks flicked out their long, thin tongues and licked it up. Paris pulled Pinks underneath his arm, sheltering her between his body and the wall. The mudlarks poked their beaks into Paris' back.

'Arrgh!' he cried out, but he did not move away from Pinks who clung to him, trembling.

'Please!' begged Linus, shoving his shoulder against the stone.

'Gogmagog! Cornelius!' Captain Bonny Kildare bellowed out as she ran out of the darkness towards them, holding smoking guns aimed up at the mudlarks with both hands.

Behind her, Flint limped as quickly as he could, his own arm aiming a barrel gun towards the birds.

'Guardians of London, open the brook's wall!' she cried to the giants.

She fired a gun at the mudlarks thrusting their beak at Paris' back. The gun did not shoot bullets, but an almighty burst of flame which ripped through the leathery wing of one of the mudlarks. It let out a deafening squall and, struggling, flew up, back into the air, its wing incandescent with the fire from the gun. The other took flight, hovering near the doors and looking towards its squawking accomplice.

The giants slowly pulled their spears away from the door and stood aside. As they did, the stone doors of the amphitheatre opened.

'Inside!' ordered Captain Kildare, grabbing Flint's arm and resting it over her shoulder as he hobbled.

The crew didn't need to be told twice. Scrambling in the mud, Linus and the others dashed inside, their arms over their heads as the other mudlark, angry at his partner's injury, attacked. Just in time, the giants swiped their spears together and the mudlark's headless body fell onto the mud with a squelch.

Then, the giants turned back to their positions and remained still as the stone doors closed, shutting the crew of the Skimmer safely inside the walls.

They crashed onto the ground, falling into one another, breathless.

'Pinks?' Captain Kildare called, lifting herself out from under Flint's weight. 'Pinks?!'

'It's ok, she's here,' Paris said in a strained voice.

Blood was soaking through the back of his blue suit jacket as he unpeeled the girl from him. She was whimpering and holding her arm. Bonny rushed over to her and sank to her knees, inspecting Pinks' wound.

'That'll leave a good one,' she said softly.

The captain passed her hand over Pinks' skinny arm and the bleeding stopped, but the wound was an open, nasty gash with globs of skin and salt around its edges. Linus had to look away. He was reminded instantly of a butcher He didn't care for blood.

'We need to get this cleaned up,' Captain Kildare said. 'We need a healer or some Fleetwater, if we can get some. But you'll live.' She smiled at Pinks and wiped her tear-stained face. She looked up at Paris.

'Thank you,' she said sincerely.

Paris nodded, but winced at the movement.

'I rather think I need a healer myself,' he said offhandedly, but Linus could see the tightness in his jaw. Colour was draining from his face quickly.

'Here.' Captain Kildare turned him round and, as she had done with Pinks, ran her hand over Paris' back.

The blood stopped seeping into his clothes at once.

'You have a habit of patching me up, Captain,' Paris said, gritting his teeth as Captain Kildare removed his jacket.

He had several dark slashes from his shoulder blades down to the base of his back, and the material from his blood-soaked shirt was sticking to the wounds.

'So it seems,' Captain Kildare agreed. 'These look bad. You'll have to come with me and Pinks to a healer. You too, Flint. Ragstone, I'll need your help with them.'

'Wait, what about the market?' Linus asked, trying to hide his annoyance.

It wasn't their fault at all, but he really didn't have time for delays.

'Baz will go with you,' Captain Kildare said, flashing a chastising look at Linus, which immediately cowed him.

He looked down at Baz, who was sitting on the dusty ground, his elbows resting on his knees.

Like the rest of them, he was badly shaken.

'He'll be ok,' Captain Kildare said. 'And he doesn't need eyes to be of use. That's right, isn't it, Baz?'

Baz grumbled a response and nodded.

'Fine,' Linus mumbled. 'Err...thanks. For getting them to open the doors. What are they?' He jutted his chin towards the wall, in the direction of the giants.

'Gogmagog and Cornelius? They're giants; ancient protectors of old Roman London,' the captain said. 'They answer only to their names.'

She hoisted Flint to his feet and inspected his leg, frowning.

'Get going now,' she said to Linus. 'Seek out Black Mary; she should be able to help, but she won't make it easy, just so's you know.'

Captain Kildare ducked her head under Flint's shoulder, and he leaned his weight on her. Ragstone did the same for Paris.

'Sorry, kid,' Flint shrugged at Linus as he hobbled next to the captain.

'We'll meet back here in two hours,' the captain said.

Linus nodded, but his frustration was evident. He kicked at a pebble in the dust petulantly. Paris sighed and shook his head, like he was disagreeing with himself.

'I'll go with the boy,' he said. 'I'll get to a healer later. You owe me an Ashwater first though, Linus.'

'No,' Captain Kildare said firmly. 'You need a healer now.'

'With all due respect, madam, I am not a member of your crew. I am here for Linus. I'll go with him and Bazalguette.'

Captain Kildare looked him squarely in the eyes, and Linus wasn't sure who had the greater will. The Captain looked as though she would give him a few extra injuries to go with his wounds from the mudlarks, but Paris stood equally as firm, which must have been difficult given the cuts on his back.

'Och,' Captain Kildare finally spat out. 'Fine. But on your head be it, Lovelock.'

Without wasting any further words, she marched off into the shadows of a pathway that circled inside the amphitheatre walls, Flint limping at her side. Ragstone swept up Pinks in his arms as though she weighed less than a feather. He winked at Linus before he followed the captain.

'Have fun,' he smiled, with his cigar miraculously still hanging off his lip.

Linus exhaled loudly as they disappeared from view. He nodded his thanks at Paris, who gave a stiff nod back.

'You alright, Baz?' Linus asked the blind man.

Baz was still sat in the dust.

'I could use a drink,' he muttered quietly.

He looked ashen, and Linus wondered if the stories about him being the tosher's legend of the sewers were really quite true.

'Ok, then,' Linus sighed. 'A quick drink, but then we have to find this Black Mary woman.'

He reached down and pulled Baz up by his clammy hands. With Paris leaning on their shoulders, they made their way into the shadows of the amphitheatre.

They had to walk slowly because of Paris, following the half-light of the amphitheatre round for a good while, before they got to the entrance of the Midevil Market. When they did, Linus halted and stared, in a strange mix of delight and disgust at what he saw.

The market was crammed with stalls, each with dusty rafters stretching over the wares of the sellers. Stalls were set up around a wooden platform at the centre of the amphitheatre, where it looked like an auction was taking place. Raggedly dressed children, commoners it seemed, were being paraded on the platform with shackles around their neck, which glowed with a spell of magic that bound them. Below, finely dressed magicians were bidding on them along with tall, pale men and women with red eyes and sharp teeth. The fear in the childrens' eyes was haunting, and Linus wondered if Felix knew that this was happening. Wishing he could do something to stop it and knowing that, without magic, he couldn't, he made a mental note to make sure he told his sister about the market. Maybe she would put an end to it.

Tending the stalls surrounding the auction platform, there were pock-faced magicians with sneering lips and squinting eyes, cloaked and hooded with some wearing spectoccules and shouting out prices.

'Ten vims,' one shouted at Linus as he stepped past, holding out a blood-red candle which had a black flame that smelled distinctly of burning flesh.

One of the magician's eyes was obscured by a green lens of his spectoccules. When Linus shook his head, the magician lurched back, offering the candle to thin air next to him.

Linus looked at him like he was mad.

'He's selling on the Second Plane, too,' Baz whispered in Linus' ear, as though he could see what was happening. 'The Midevil Market sells there as well as here, but secretly. It's too dangerous for them to set it up on the Second. The Ardere comes down pretty strong on them.'

'The academy?' Linus whispered back.

Baz nodded. Linus' shoulders slumped as he thought of the university on the Second Plane. He was supposed to have attended the Ardere Academy, starting only a few months earlier. His name had been down for it from birth, and he'd always anticipated his years there, hoping it would help him develop what little magic he'd been born with. But now, he would never see it. He'd never see any of the Second Plane now that he had no magic.

'It's not all that wonderful,' Paris said in consolation, but it was with a heavier weight upon him than Paris, that Linus continued his observations of the market.

It smelled foul. The stench of human sweat and flesh, and the familiar reek of excrement rose like a mist above the market. Added to the animal scent of goats and dogs and cats, and the swampy aroma of frogs, snakes and lizards, it was altogether unpleasant.

'I have a secret for you,' a wizened hag with missing teeth screeched out at Paris, grabbing his shirt collar.

She cackled noisily, as an old owl flapped its wings on a perch behind her. Her stall seemed to sell all kinds of creatures in misshapen and tiny cages; some were empty, and Linus knew they were filled with magical animals that he could no longer see without his magic. He pulled Paris away from the woman when he saw a jar of tarantulas crawling over one another.

'Er, we're ok thanks,' Linus said, shuddering.

They continued to weave down the thin, winding streets of the market until they came to an open aired tavern, where hooded magicians were drinking from steaming cups and pints of ale.

'There,' Linus said in relief.

His shoulders were aching from Paris bearing down his weight on him, and he was thirsty after their escape from the mudlarks.

Dropping Paris down on a stool, he ordered three Ashwaters and began tapping his foot impatiently.

'Where do you think this Black Mary is?'

Faces turned to them. Scars and glowing eyes and teeth that looked like fangs. Linus swallowed.

'Keep your voice down,' Paris mumbled, shifting his eyes around at their new observers.

'We're not going to get anywhere if we don't ask,' Linus hissed at Paris. 'Have you always been such a coward?'

The barkeep delivered their drinks, eyeing them carefully before leaving.

Bazalguette downed his Ashwater in one gulp, and the three sat in an awkward silence. Linus sipped his drink, the burning at the back of his throat soothing his irritation.

'I'll ask around,' Baz said, standing. The colour had returned to his cheeks. 'I know some toshers who trade here. I'll find them.'

Linus nodded, ashamed for his outburst. He watched Baz merging with the crowds, his blindness providing no hindrance to his surefooted steps.

Paris was fingering the chipped glass of his Ashwater and looking into the steam. His scarred face looked thoughtful and white with blood loss.

'It's an awful thing to be hated and thought a coward, simply because you value your own life,' he said quietly.

'I'm sorry,' Linus muttered. 'You're not a coward. You wouldn't be here if you were.'

'All my life, I've sought the truth. Perhaps I haven't cared enough for the little things. The commoners in my charge when I worked for your father, were cast by the wayside. Those children...' He looked towards the auction platform.

'I could have put an end to that. I could have guided your sister and helped her. But I placed too much value in the commoners' history and their past rather than their present horrors. I should have done more.'

'You're doing more, now,' Linus said, but he felt embarrassed.

He was taken aback by Paris' confession. He had always thought him a vapid and superficial man, concerned only with his own comfort. Linus trusted him because he'd saved him from the Citadel and had given him knowledge that could help him save his sister, but he'd always thought Paris was helping him purely to for his own glory and recognition. It had never occurred to him that he had another agenda, one that might be greater than himself.

'You know something, don't you?' Linus asked very quietly. 'Something you can't tell us. Something in the commoners' texts? Is it about the curse?'

Paris' face was pained as he looked at Linus. With great difficulty, he tried to move his head, either in a nod or a shake, Linus couldn't tell but he saw the truth in Paris' eyes.

'Thomas Farynor, The Great Spark which caused the fire of London, you and Felix. There is something which connects you all,' he whispered urgently, but his voice trailed off as the words were choked in his throat.

In anger and frustration, Paris threw his glass on the ground.

'Oi!' yelled the barkeep, but his voice was swallowed by the sudden sounds of screams.

Linus and Paris jumped up from their seats, turning to the auction platform where the screams came from. The shrill sound spread through the market, growing louder as more and more people shrieked.

They were shrieks of pain.

Then, slowly, as though it was following the screams, wisps of black smoke snaked through the maze of the market.

'Look,' Paris breathed, pointing out his gloved hand to the platform.

Upon it stood a man, draped in a brown, hooded smock. His face was covered and his hands, wrapped in black, leather gloves, were joined together as though in prayer. He looked, Linus thought, like some kind of monk; a monk with black curls of thick smoke emanating from him and his joined hands, chasing the vendors and customers of the market through the winding streets.

'What...?' Linus began, but he stopped when he saw Bazalguette running towards them, his speed separating him from the horde of marketeers who were scrambling away from the smoke.

'With me!' he cried out to Linus and Paris. 'NOW!'

For the second time, they ran.

Bazalguette was athletic and fast, and he used his strength to barge people out of the way with a force that frightened Linus. He struggled to keep up but raced after Baz, looking behind to make sure Paris was with them. From the right, a tendril of smoke touched his bare hand and Linus howled in pain. It was as though his skin had been dipped in acid. Blisters, red, raw and weeping appeared immediately. He lunged away from the smoke, looking for Paris who was struggling to run with the wounds on his back. Linus doubled back and grabbed his arm. Tugging Paris with all his might, he bolted after Bazalguette who was screaming at them to hurry.

Around them, the smoke stole away its victims. It gripped hold of them, pulling them back into the clouds of black ash and smoke as they screamed. Stumbling with Paris at his side, Linus saw the magician with the spectoccules covering one eye, falling into the scorching smoke with high-pitched squalls of pain. His skin blistered and peeled away, blackened by the smoke.

'Come on!' he cried to Paris, pulling him along again.

His thoughts drifted to Bonny and the others, and the commoner children at the auction but he blocked them out. He couldn't think of them, now. He had to keep running.

Bazalguette was leading them to the edge of the market. The shrieks were fading, either with the distance or because there was nobody left to scream. But the smoke still flooded the market, and it was curling around the streets. Everywhere he looked, Linus could see smoke. The acrid, dry smell of it, of scorched flesh filled his lungs and he began to cough.

Ahead, Baz was dashing towards a large ditch filled with glassy, black water. The smoke was starting to obscure Linus' view. Soon, the smoke would be in front of him, and he'd have no escape. He pulled Paris along harder, but the man suddenly seemed like a dead weight. Linus spun around to him and saw that he had stopped running.

'Go,' breathed Paris. He loosened Linus' hand from around his arm. 'You won't make it with me.'

Linus stopped tugging at him and looked at him with horror.

'No, get up. Get up right now!' Linus yanked at Paris' arm again, but he refused to move.

'Get out of here, boy!' Paris yelled.

Behind him, the smoke swirled at the open wounds on his back. Paris cried out in pain. The smoke wrapped around Paris like a hand, clutching him tightly.

Linus could not move. He watched, helpless and frightened. Paris fell to the ground with tears of agony rolling down his cheeks, singeing his face in the heat.

'Linus,' he begged hoarsely. 'The Ardere...'

The words caught in his throat. His flesh was blackening and charring as it burned. The smell was indescribable.

'William....Lilly's...diary.'

The words jammed in his throat but, with great effort, with pain more agonising than the blazing smoke, he forced them out.

'Linus...go!'

Paris pushed forward with one final breath of life before his body fell to the ground. Linus found himself shoved forward with a magical force that spun him around in the air. When he looked back, Paris' body was gone, consumed by the smoke which was floating menacingly towards him.

'No! NO!' he shouted into the smoke.

Linus felt strong hands looping under his arms. He screamed and cried, calling Paris' name as the smoke blocked his view. It surrounded him.

'Linus!' came Bazalguette's voice through the fog of his grief. 'The lake! Dive into the lake!'

But Linus had no command over his body. All he could see was Paris's face burning in his mind, the light leaving his eyes the way it had left Murphy and Mortimer's in his father's machine.

So much horror.

He felt himself lifted into the air. For a moment he soared, and he wondered if this was death.

Then the sharp slap of icy-cold water.

Then blackness.

16

Black Mary

Linus sank down into the freezing depths of the lake. The coldness shocked his body, so that he hardly had strength or even the instinct to attempt to swim. Above him, he heard the muffled splash of water as Baz dived in after him.

Light glimmered, a small twinkle at first, then flaring into a glowing orb as Baz projected his magic ahead of them. It shone down on a large transparent dome deep beneath them, which covered the whole of the lakebed. Linus kicked his legs out in surprise and treaded water for a moment, but he felt the current sucking him down towards the dome. Baz swam past him and mimed a swimming action with his hands and pointed down towards it.

Confused, with lungs rapidly beginning to burn, Linus let the current pull him down into the depths and he swam as quickly as he could. He could hear the blood pumping in his ears and his head was feeling dizzy and wavy. Just as he thought he would pass out, he reached the dome. His hand swiped at it as he swam and he realised it was a bubble; a giant, clear bubble deep at the bottom of a black lake.

With no time to question it, Linus swam inside. The air embraced him, and he breathed deeply and greedily, sucking oxygen into his lungs and feeling it course through his blood. A few seconds later, Baz burst through with a splatter of water. He gasped a little, but he was far more practised in swimming the waters of UnderLondon and so he recovered himself much more quickly than Linus.

'Come on, lad,' Bazalguette said, lifting Linus to his feet. 'Save your grief for Paris. Now's not the time.'

'What was that up there?' Linus sniffed. 'And where are we?'

He looked around the bubble and found it to be completely empty, save for Baz's floating orb and the silty earth of lakebed, with a hole in it at the centre of the dome. The hole was the size of a manhole, and as Linus peered down it, he shuddered, for it was narrow and dark.

'Felt like a Shadow to me,' Baz said in a low voice. 'Nasty buggers.'

Linus shivered and not just because he was wet and cold and traumatised, but because he knew what a Shadow was; he had several of them represented by cards in his Quest deck. Shadows were dark magicians who used their magic for deathly deeds. They came with many powers, and each Shadow card in his Quest deck had a different attack power. Some breathed fire, some smothered with ashes, some simply had the ability to cause invisible but very severe pain. But he had no cards like the Shadow he'd seen in the market. Linus hoped he'd never witness him, or any Shadow, ever again and he wondered why on earth the Shadow had attacked everyone. But then...Ragstone had told him the market was full of evil folk.

Had anyone survived? Had the crew? Linus felt a dark panic rising in his chest.

'Down here, Linus,' Baz said gently, as though sensing the boy's fear and anguish. 'This is Black Mary's well.'

'Black Mary? You found her?' Linus said with a flicker of hope.

Baz nodded. 'Technically, so have you. You're sort of...in her.'

'Beg your pardon?' Linus blinked.

'The lake,' Baz explained, and he motioned around. 'The lake is called Black Mary.'

Linus turned around slowly, looking first at the dome and then into the gloom of water behind it.

'I don't understand,' he said, horrified at the frustrated tears that pricked at his eyes.

He pushed the heels of his palms into his eye sockets to stop them. His father had always thought crying was weakness. 'Never let anyone see you cry, my boy,' his father had said to him once. 'Nobody cares for your tears. Especially me.'

'The captain said Black Mary was a woman,' he mumbled, once he trusted his voice.

'No,' Baz said. 'She didn't.'

Linus tried to remember exactly what Captain Kildare had said, but he couldn't. It was a sharp, tiny hurt to think that she couldn't recall her final words to him.

'You need to go down the hole,' Baz continued, edging around it.

'Hold on,' Linus said, holding up his hands. 'I'm not going down that and how exactly can you see it?' It had occurred to him that, since diving into the water, Baz had been able to find him with his eyes and had focused on what little there was to see in the giant bubble.

Baz tried not to let the grin spread too wide over his face.

'Ok, so the toshers told me the Black Mary is fed from several rivers, including the River Fleet...and as you know- '

'Fleetwater heals all ills,' Linus finished, nodding in understanding.

It was one of the first things he'd ever learned about the sewers and rivers of London. Fleetwater was expensive, though, and unless they went straight to the source of the river, which they rarely did, it was hard to get hold of.

'Wait,' Linus said. 'Do you think...?' He looked up out of the bubble and into the lake.

Baz knew what he was thinking and shook his head. 'Paris is gone, lad,' he said gently. 'There's no healing him now.'

Linus sniffed again.

'The cap'n,' he began weakly; the words caught somewhere in his throat.

'If I know Bonny Kildare, and I do, lad, she'll have gotten the others to safety. Don't fret for her or the others. You've a job to do now, boy, so best be getting on with it.'

Baz tilted his head down to the hole and Linus gulped audibly.

The hole was narrow. It looked as though it was just about wide enough for Linus' shoulders, but there was no chance that Baz would fit down it. If Linus did go down it, he'd be going alone.

'What exactly is down there?' he asked Baz.

'Toshers called it a well. Said Black Mary's well held secrets about secrets,' Baz shrugged.

'Right,' Linus nodded. 'And I get out....err, how?'

'Sure you'll figure it out,' Baz smiled and wrapped his arm around Linus' shoulders. 'Enough yabbering. Go on, off with you.'

He nudged Linus towards the well. With a clenched jaw, Linus sat on the lip of the hole and dangled his legs down into it. The air was cold and clammy, and penetrated his boots. With a deep breath, as though he was about to dive under water, Linus plunged down into Black Mary's Well.

He didn't fall far until the well curved and caught him by the seat of his trousers. Then, he slid down, unable to stop his cry of surprise. Linus looked up and saw the tiny light of the top of the hole blocked by Baz's face slipping from view and the thin, cool air took him.

Linus was dumped unceremoniously in a heap, in a large puddle of water. Scrambling to his feet, he felt around with his hands but found the space was wide and open with the damp scent of wet soil and rock.

'I made it,' Linus called out, hoping Baz could hear him. 'I'm alright!

Linus dared not spin around to search for light. He feared he would become disorientated and be unable to find the well again.

'Find your exit first,' Captain Bonny had trained him. 'Always know your escape route. Then see what tools you have. You always have something.'

He padded at his pockets. He had some soggy matches (useless), a small blade (could be handy) and a compass (pointless if he couldn't see it). He also had a flagon of water tied to his belt, a tub of pitch peat which he often used to help start the boilers on the ship, and the clothes he was wearing.

'Right then,' he said to himself.

Linus removed his coat and shirt. Both were wet, but he'd have to see what he could do. He placed his coat in the seat of the well, hoping it would be an easy marker if he had to find it again. Then, he removed his belt and looped it round his scrunched-up shirt, until it was a ball of leather and coarse linen. It was too damp but if he could just get it alight, it'd make a good torch. He smeared the pitch peat on one side of it and laid it down gently on top of his coat, careful to lay it down sticky side up. Then, taking the matches, he attempted to light each one of them but, as he knew would be the case, they were too wet to flare.

'Damnit!' he shouted, flinging down the empty box of matches. 'I wish I had a bloody light!'

Instantly, a warm light illuminated the base of the well.

Linus froze.

'Hello?' he said hoarsely.

There was no reply, so he turned very slowly.

He'd been spat out by the well into a chamber of sorts. It was larger than he'd thought, and if he stretched his arms wide and spun around, he wouldn't touch the walls. It was roughly circular, with walls polished smooth by the flow of water over them, which pooled into the puddle at his feet. Aside from the little tunnel where his coat rested, now stained with pitch peat which dripped off his shirt, there was no exit.

The light, which was soft and not too blinding, had no source. It just....was.

'Welcome, Linus, son of Everard, to my well,' came a voice.

Like the light, it seemed to come from everywhere and it spoke in hushes and crashes, like waves.

'Who said that?' Linus called out, feeling foolish.

He peered upwards but there was nothing to see. Like the bubble in the lake above, it appeared he was in a little sphere of light with nothing above but darkness.

'I am the one whom you seek, for now. You know me as Mary of the black water, but my names are many, and many are forgotten. Only I remember, for I see much.'

'You're Black Mary?'

There was a shush of acknowledgement. The sound reminded Linus of tides against the shore.

'Wait...you're the river?'

'I am all the rivers,' the voice replied. 'I am the memory of Londinium, of Lundonwick, of the Magistry and of all before.'

'Right then,' Linus replied.

He had no idea what to say. What on earth did one say to a river, and a talking river at that? Then, his manners, never far away, returned to him.

'Thanks for the light. You, er, grant wishes or something?'

'No, but you are without magic. The river is kind. The river provides.'

'My friend, Baz; he worships the river...er, you.'

'Bazalguette, son of Herbert. I saved him and delivered him to the toshers who serve me. I have returned his sight to him. I reward the faithful.'

'Right. Good. Thanks for that.'

Linus waited, his eyes rolling around the chamber, wondering vaguely if he'd gone mad.

'You seek to know,' the voice said. 'Ask and I will speak, but there is a price. I know many secrets, Linus, son of Everard. You must ask the right questions to seek what you will.'

Linus took a deep breath and ran his fingers through his hair.

'I'm seeking the one who is the Firelighter.'

'She is known to you,' the voice replied. 'She is your sister, Felix, daughter of Calantha. There is fire inside her.'

'No,' Linus shook his head. 'No, I mean the real Firelighter, the descendent of Thomas Farynor who started the Great Fire of London.'

'I remember the fire,' the voice said in an angry, crashing wave. 'It was hellfire. It did not come from this world. It came through the world of the magicians. The world you call the Second Plane. Even my waters could not douse its flame. It was a curse upon this city. A mighty curse, of smoke and flame. It burned. For many moons, the embers charred at the good earth.

'The one you call Thomas Farynor; I did not know him. His blood was not of this world. I did not flow inside it the way I flow in those born of this world, the First. But I did flow inside his children. The fire he brought from the Second Plane gave me a voice. It gave me a consciousness which remembers. My waters flow with life, with memory because of the magic fire. Before the magician, I did not seek to know the memories. Now it is all I know.'

'I'm...I'm sorry,' Linus said.

His palms were sweating, but his bare chest was cold. Anticipation was surging through him, yet he didn't want to anger the voice by demanding answers.

'It sounds very lonely,' he offered.

The river voice sighed. 'Many people talk to me,' the voice said. 'They toss me their coins and they speak of their woes and their secret thoughts. Some throw their lives into me and their memories become mine. I listen. I remember.'

'Then you must know. You must have heard of this true Firelighter. Please! It's important.'

'Be calm, Linus, son of Everard. You speak in grief for the friend you have lost at the hands of the one they call Smokesbane, but I am not commanded by man.'

At this, the puddle of water at Linus' feet began to rise, threateningly, as though filled by a high tide. It reached his waist in one swollen wave but before he could panic, the water receded back down to his feet.

'I'm sorry, I'm sorry!' Linus shouted out. 'Smokesbane. You mean the Shadow?'

'He destroys and poisons. I do not flow in him. He comes from the Second Plane, beyond this world. His smoke touched me and it hurt. He has been sent.'

'Sent? By who?'

'That is not the right question.'

'What do you mean, it's not the right question? Of course it is! Who sent the Shadow you call Smokesbane to kill Paris?'

'Nobody,' Black Mary hushed.

Linus sighed. He felt frustrated and confused. Captain Kildare had said Black Mary would have answers. But Black Mary wasn't even a real woman and now here he was, stuck down a well, talking to a river.

I've lost it, Linus thought.

As though sensing his agitation, the river soothed him with a flurry of warm water to his waist.

'So you don't know who the true Firelighter is? You don't know anything about it?' Linus asked in a quiet voice.

For a moment, the river was quiet and there was nothing but the clapping lap of the water against stone and skin.

'There is one who knows what you seek.'

'Who?'

'You ask all the wrong questions,' the river sighed.

'And what should I ask instead?'

'That I cannot say. Wisdom must be learned not given. You must give payment, Linus, son of Everard. A secret for a secret, if you wish to know who can help you seek the true Firelighter.'

'Fine,' Linus ran through his mind, trying to find a secret. 'When I was ten, I broke my father's spectoccules. I wanted to try them on, and they broke. I blamed Shylock Larkin and my father hit him. I was sorry...I am sorry. Even now. I never got to tell Larkin that it was me.'

'That is not a worthy secret,' the river said. 'I know you. I flow in you. I will choose.'

Linus huffed and shook his head. That had been one of his biggest secrets, one he'd felt guilty about since it had happened. He'd never told anyone. He wasn't even sure he had any more secrets. Apart from the really private ones...the ones that were about girls and which made him blush.

'I have selected my payment,' the river voice exclaimed.

'Oh,' Linus said. He hadn't felt anything. 'What did you, er, choose?' He hoped it wasn't anything too embarrassing.

'You regret pushing the man, Corbin Godspell, the one you called Father, to his death.'

'Wait, what? No I don't!' Linus shouted.

Beneath him, the puddle swelled.

'The river sees. The river knows. You feel regret. You miss him.'

'I don't,' Linus said firmly, shaking his head.

Again, the river sighed.

'Ok, well you've taken your payment. Tell me the name of the one who knows who the True Firelighter is.'

'She is Hestia Windwood.'

Linus mouthed the name, but it was not familiar to him. He closed his eyes and rubbed at his forehead.

'She is of the other world. The place you call the Second.'

'The Second Plane,' Linus said, defeated.

The Second Plane was lost to him. Without magic, he could never go there. The river swirled around his feet, as though comforting him.

'Many have revealed their secrets to me, and I have seen much. There is one, Robert Hooke, son of John, who surveyed all that was lost after the Great Fire which scorched the city. Like Thomas Farynor, he was of the other world, a magician. He took the Flame which you worship from Thomas Farynor and he used it for his own means. He called himself the Firelighter. When he died, Hooke passed the Flame to his friend, Christopher Wren who passed it to William Wagstaffe, who passed it to Isaac Newton, who passed it to Horatio Lovelock, who kept the Flame within his family until Paris Lovelock, son of Deacon, chose to deny it. The Sacred Flame passed to the Godspells. This is the legacy of the Sacred Flame. London was built upon it. Robert Hooke and Christopher Wren wielded this power and because of it, London was reborn. Magic destroyed London. Magic rebuilt it. If you seek their monument, you need only look around you.'

'Robert Hooke? Christopher Wren? Firelighters, both of them? I've never heard of them. And I don't seek their monument, I seek the True Firelighter! What has any of this got to do with finding Hestia Windwood?' Linus shouted in frustration.

'Robert Hooke built a back door. An entrance to the Second Plane.'

'What? What do you mean a 'back door? Why would magicians even need one, when they can access it with Spectoccules?' Linus asked.

'That is not the right question for you to know the answer.'

Linus thought for a moment. He knew that the Second Plane was available for all magicians to access if they wanted to. Even under Corbin Godspell's reign, magicians had been allowed to go there whenever they chose, though why they would bother when it was barren and empty, was beyond his understanding. The only useful thing that the Second Plane offered these days was the Ardere Academy. But nonetheless, if magicians wanted to go there, they could, provided they were powerful enough to make the step into the world, either by using Spectoccules to see it or not.

'The back door to the Second Plane wasn't made for magicians,' Linus breathed, in sudden realisation. 'It was made for commoners. But how? That's impossible, surely? The Second Plane is made of magic and can only be accessed by someone with magic inside them. Commoners have no magic inside them at all.'

He waited for the river to speak again, but instead the water at his feet rose a little. When he looked down, an old glass bottle, corked and sealed with wax, was bobbing on the water. He reached down to pick it up, but the water held it fast.

'Payment? Ok, fine, take whatever secret you want!' he said to the water.

After a moment, the bottle was freed. Linus stared down at it. The glass was dirty and thick but through it, Linus could see a small yellow scroll of parchment. Before he could open it, the river spoke again.

'This scroll is in Robert Hooke's hand. It is a secret he gave, in payment for knowledge he deemed greater than what he paid. Robert Hooke had great dreams, but he did not foresee the nightmare ahead. Darkness is coming, Linus, son of Everard. You will need to be strong. But there is also an ember in the shadows. Take this with you.'

A small typhoon of water rose up from the puddle at his feet and flowed into the flagon of water tied to his belt loop.

'Fleetwater?' Linus breathed, screwing the lid on tightly. 'Why do I need Fleetwater?'

'The path to knowledge is oft belied with pain and suffering, Linus, son of Everard.'

'Then...I thank you.'

The river sighed its acknowledgement and the water at Linus' feet began to rise slowly. He flicked his eyes down at it, curious at first and then growing more and more afraid, as the water rose higher than it had done before.

'Wait! Stop!' he called out. 'What are you doing?'

Water was around his ears and soon he was treading water, unable to feel the ground beneath him. The light faded and Linus had just enough time to suck in a large gasp of air before the water roared and surged above his head.

17

The Dire Wolf and the Catchoo, Again

The Reading Room was quiet, save for the slow, constant ticking of the clock on the mantelpiece above the fire. The flames were high and strong, but the room felt uncharacteristically cold, as though the room has soaked up the sadness and confusion of the dire wolf and Nigel, who were sat in front of the fire, watching it burn.

They had returned to the library some time ago, but neither of them had been able to rest. Plates with half-eaten meals rested on the carpet, and on the table next to the armchair which Nigel was curled up on. Every now and then, D.W would rise and circle, stretching out his invisible antenna in search of Felix's thoughts and Nigel would look at him hopefully. But the wolf's responding expression of loss would crush the hope, and both would slump down further into their melancholy.

Felix was gone, without a trace.

Thaddeus' search of the hatchway had revealed nothing; if Felix had used a hatch, then it certainly wasn't one on this Plane. In the quarter, Old Nell and the other commoners who had known Felix had searched high and low, sending out their secret reporters from their old forbidden newspaper, The Touch Papers, but all was quiet. There were no reports of Felix anywhere. When Aubrey and Nigel and Liberty had retraced Felix's footsteps at the Citadel, conjuring the wisps of memories from its rooms, they had seen that Felix had met with Sigbert, certainly, but their conversation was muffled, as though shielded somehow by magic. Whatever they had spoken of, Felix had wanted it to remain private. She had sealed the memory and made it impossible to hear or see clearly. After that, Felix had gone to bed and then...nothing. She had simply disappeared.

Aubrey and Liberty had arranged an emergency summit with the magisterians for the morning; they all had to face the hard truth that the Firelighter had gone and taken the Sacred

Flame with her. With no named Heir Apparent, the Magistry was in a situation it had not experienced in its entire known history; they were without a leader.

'She'll come back,' Aubrey had said decidedly. But it was blind hope she was clinging to, and both Nigel and the dire wolf could see that. Nobody, not even D.W, who knew Felix better than anyone, could say for sure if they really believed that she would come home.

Nigel, in his anger and out of sheer desperation had gone to his aunt Vessania, but the Russian woman with the lilac eyes and the sane reasoning did not come forth. Instead, he received only warbled rhymes or hurls of abuse from the hag, and he'd left in defeat.

They had no other options, no other ideas. They had lost her.

'What would Fiddle do?' the dire wolf asked, for maybe the twentieth time.

He had long stopped asking Nigel, who remained quiet and hard on Fiddle's armchair. Instead, he simply repeated the question time and time again to himself. He and Fiddle had not always seen eye to eye and like all humans, Fiddle had been flawed. D.W had heard some of the secrets he'd kept from Felix, secrets which the dire wolf had also kept, for Fiddle, on the assurances that it was best for her. But the man had loved Felix, fiercely and protected her like a father. And he'd had wisdom, sure enough. So what would Fiddle do?

'He'd find her,' Nigel said. 'One way or another. He found her that time she ran away to the orphanage, remember? When the lamias had attacked?'

He paused for a moment. Casting his eyes down at the worn, deep red leather of the armchair, he stroked it fondly. D.W heard his grief for Fiddle.

'She always runs away,' he whispered.

Nigel closed his eyes behind his glasses, a frown causing a crease between his brows.

'She's afraid,' the dire wolf said. 'She only runs when she's scared.'

'But why the hell would she run from me?' Nigel yelled with such anger, that D.W yelped and jumped back in surprise.

As though the anger had drained him, Nigel sank back down into the chair and deflated. D.W licked his snout and stepped forward, sitting on his haunches in front of Nigel. Tentatively, he lifted a paw and rested it on Nigel's knee.

'She's afraid of what she feels for you,' he said softly.

Nigel shook his head, staring into the flames of the fire.

'Felix doesn't feel anything for me,' he said tightly. 'If she did, she wouldn't have run.'

D.W stared hard at Nigel and tilted his head.

'You misunderstand her,' he said. 'Everyone does. She feels so deeply, don't you see? For someone who has been lied to for most of her life, Felix is actually very easily swayed. Words affect her. She doesn't understand why people would lie, why people keep secrets. In many ways, she's innocent. Felix believes what people say because she herself would not lie. If she does keep secrets, it's to protect those around her. She both trusts too easily and yet doesn't trust at all. It's hard to explain, really. She lacks the reasoning to understand and explain her emotions; she simply feels. She takes everyone at their word, so she believes what you or I tell her and what Fiddle told her, but unfortunately it also means she believes stupid things like what Vesannia said to her, or even that damn Catchoo-'

The dire wolf stopped talking. His paw slipped off Nigel's knee and he cocked his ears.

'What?' Nigel asked, sitting up quickly. 'What is it? Can you hear her?'

'No,' D.W shook his head. 'No, I have an idea.'

Nigel leaned forward and held out his hands, impatiently beckoning the dire wolf to continue.

'The Catchoo,' he said. 'When I found Felix on the streets of the Magistry, we had to go through Piccadilly Circus as we found the little fleabag in there. She gave Felix a weird sort of riddle. I thought it was a load of nonsense, but Felix took it to heart and...I hate to admit this, but what the Catchoo said sort of...came true.'

'What, like a prophesy?' Nigel asked, pulling a face as though he thought the idea was ridiculous.

'More like a prediction,' D.W answered. 'But she was right, I suppose. She knew things about Felix. Maybe...maybe we should go see her?'

'A Houdini cat? You want to go see a trickster designed to catch you out of your money for a riddle, and ask her where my girlfriend has gone?'

D.W raised an eyebrow and bared his teeth a little.

'Alright genius, do you have any better ideas?'

Nigel lifted his shoulders and gritted his teeth. He looked around the Reading Room, as though hoping it would give him some divine inspiration.

'You know Fiddle would go,' the dire wolf taunted with a sly smile.

'Fine,' Nigel sighed. 'Let's go find the damned Catchoo.'

The tents of Piccadilly Circus were flapping in the autumn breeze when Nigel and D.W approached them. Surrounded by dirty, deserted streets, the circus was something of a shame to the magicians and yet it was never shut down. The COPPs moved the circus along every now and then but it would crop up again, plying customers with fake, overpriced charms, glamours and the cloying, addictive powders of poppyblood.

Nigel had visited the circus only a few times, usually on errands for Fiddle and once only out of his own curiosity when he was twelve. He and some friends had dared one another to go in, each one running in a footstep further than the other until a magician with crazed eyes and black teeth had chased them down the streets. Now, the circus filled him only with pity for the addicts and the helpless magicians lured into it and he kept his head down, ignoring the calls of the Houdinis, magicians who had all but lost their magic to poppyblood, who lived and worked there.

D.W led them to a central tent with an array of tattered and ragged rugs on the floor. Cushions of various shapes and sizes were scattered everywhere and long, sheer panels of fabrics hung down from the rafters of the tent. On every available surface, tarnished brass plates and lamps were piled perilously so that it resembled a run-down Arabian souk. Incense clouded the tent, creating a misty fog which made D.W sneeze.

'Stop!' boomed a loud, deep voice from the mists. 'I am the daughter of Echidna-'

'Oh shut it, you mangy rat,' the dire wolf called out. 'We know you're not a stupid sphinx, so get your tail out here.'

'Sphinx?' Nigel whispered down to D.W. 'She pretends to be a sphinx? But they don't exist.'

'I know,' D.W rolled his eyes.

From the shadows, a scrawny tabby cat with a gnarled, bushy tail sauntered out before sitting in front of them and licking her paw.

'You called?' she said, flashing her green eyes at them.

'Do you remember me?' D.W growled at her.

The Catchoo rolled her head towards him and yawned in his face. The dire wolf wrinkled his nose at the fishy smell.

'Maybe I do, maybe I don't,' she said, before stretching out her front paws and scratching at a bare patch of rug.

Nigel looked at the dire wolf and folded his arms.

'Answer me, you little fleabag or I'll use your bones as toothpicks,' D.W snarled down at her menacingly.

'Doubtful, dog,' the Catchoo said, wafting her tail under the dire wolf's nose.

'I'm not a dog!'' he grunted down at her.

It would have been quite scary had he not sneezed on her tail. The Catchoo chuckled.

'Do you remember him or not?' Nigel asked the cat impatiently.

As though noticing him for the first time, the Catchoo padded slowly over to him and wound herself between his ankles.

'S'pose I do? What'll it cost you?' she purred.

Nigel tutted and reached for his coin bag. Taking a tan from it, he dropped it down by the Catchoo's feet.

'Hmmm, let me see,' the Catchoo smiled. 'Yes, I remember the mongrel and his little friend. That's really why you're here, isn't it? Firelighter Felix and her fearsome fire.'

'What do you know of Felix?' Nigel asked.

The Catchoo jumped up and curled around his shoulders. Nigel winced as her claws cut into his skin.

'I know much. I have a fortune for you.'

'What? What is it?' Nigel asked through clenched teeth.

He tried to lift the cat off his shoulders, but she clung on to him, purring loudly in his ear.

'You have lies in your eyes,' she mewed.

'No, not about me, about Felix!'

Grabbing the Catchoo by the scruff of her neck, Nigel yanked her off his shoulders, making her yowl. He held her under her forearms and her body hung down in front of him, long and skinny. The dire wolf sniggered.

'Put me down!'

The Catchoo twisted and scratched at Nigel until he dropped her. She landed delicately on her paws and then began to clean her ears. The dire wolf leaned down towards her, a growl in his throat.

'Listen, you pathetic little –'

'Oh shut your trap, dog. I'll help you,' she rolled her eyes at D.W. 'Good grief, you're more hassle than you're worth.'

She sat still for a moment, her tail flicking.

'Go on then,' D.W barked.

'Give me a minute!' the Catchoo yowled. 'It's not easy seeing into the beyond, y'know?'

The dire wolf sneered at her but sat back, waiting. Nigel crouched down next to him.

'Felix...she has had many trials and known much heartache. I warned her the fire would consume her. I was, of course right, as I usually am. Now she has gone to burn...and to drown.'

'That doesn't make any sense,' D.W said angrily.

He pointed his snout at the Catchoo, who shook her ears and shrugged her bony shoulders.

'I only see the beyond, I don't claim to know its meaning.'

'That's it? That's all you've got?'

The cat licked her nose.

'Why, you rotten little fleabag, I'll kill you!' The dire wolf barked again and began to chase the Catchoo, but she jumped up onto one of the treacherous piles of gold plates and hissed at him.

'Wait, wait!' Nigel said. 'No, it does make sense!'

D.W stopped trying to clamber up the pile of plates, giving a small 'oof' when one of them fell on his head.

'The Ardere,' Nigel continued. 'The Ardere Academy. It literally means 'to burn'.'

He looked at the dire wolf in excitement, but the wolf shook his head regretfully.

'But it's on the Second Plane. I already told you, if she was there, I'd feel her.'

'Maybe it's shielded or something?' Nigel said hopefully. 'Look, it's the best lead we've got, isn't it? And even if she isn't there, maybe someone at the academy could help us. I don't know why we didn't think of going there in the first place.'

The dire wolf listened carefully to Nigel's inner thoughts. Tangled with his longing to find Felix and his hurt at her leaving, there was also a secret excitement; he had always wanted to go to the Ardere Academy to study but had never been clever enough, or rich enough. D.W hoped that Nigel's motivations for going there weren't selfish.

'Fine, we'll go,' D.W sighed and then turned to the Catchoo. 'But if we get there and we find a dead end, I'm coming back here and I'll skin you alive, you little runt!'

'Ooh, I'm quaking,' the Catchoo replied with a smirk. 'Until next time, mongrel.'

And with that, the Catchoo turned and presented her rear end to them, her tail held high and lofty as she sauntered back into the mist.

18

The Drowning

When nightfall came, it brought starlight to the home of the Drow. Gemstones glistened in the rocks, and the fluttering webs high above in the cliffs were sparkling with evening dew. The Drow lit candles in their home but mostly they relied upon the twinkling lights of the gemstones, which they used for functional lighting, as well as décor. As Felix looked out at the valley from her bedroom, she was awestruck by its mystical beauty, but her nerves and anticipation for the Drowning could not be distracted.

She had spent the afternoon with Melantha, and between them they had formed a haphazard language using silly little mimes which made them giggle like schoolchildren together. Melantha had taught her a few words in Drow and had openly mocked Felix at her awful pronunciation. It had been good fun, and it occurred to Felix that she felt like she had not had fun, not been silly, not been a simple, happy sixteen-year-old girl in a long time. She had never even had a girl friend to talk to, or to do any of those insignificant but meaningful things that girls often did together, like shopping or swapping secrets about the people they liked.

Even in her annums at the orphanage and at the small schoolhouse she'd attended briefly, she'd never really had a close friend. Orphans tended to keep their distance, doling out insults rather than friendship as a way of defending against further hurt and heartbreak.

Oh, she knew that she had D.W and her friends at the Citadel. For a while, she'd thought she and Imelda might become good friends. But after Felix became the Firelighter, everything changed. They all looked at her differently, seeing only her power and her titles; seeing only the Flame she guarded. She felt, a little guiltily, that she was just a pawn to them, a piece to be manoeuvred into a position of power where she could protect them all. She had often felt like this with Fiddle, too and in the newfound freedom she felt with the Drow, she realised how much she hated it, how much she despised being manipulated and used.

It was just all so complicated in the Magistry; here, in the safe womb of the sisterhood, things were simple.

She had questions, of course. How exactly had Lillith known Fiddle, and had he known she was alive and that they had survived, or had he just hoped? Why exactly did Lillith not trust Paris Lovelock? Could she really find Linus? And how had the Drow remained secret for all of these years?

But she would find answers, she hoped, at the Drowning.

Felix was curious about it. She wanted to know what it was, how it would answer her questions and she wanted to know, more than anything, how the Drow made her feel so wonderful whenever they touched her. No, that was a lie. She didn't really care about understanding it; she just wanted to feel it again.

Melantha's soft voice spoke from behind her, and Felix turned. They were ready now, Melantha was trying to tell her. Her long limbs were beckoning down to the valley where the Drow were gathering. Felix smiled and nodded, bubbles of excitement in her stomach.

As Melantha linked her arm and led her down the ridge path, Felix tried to let her questions drift away. She questioned so much and never let herself just 'be'. If she was going to find peace, she would have to accept things as they were, and try and live in the serenity which the Drow seemed to take for granted. Each of them lived by their emotions. They didn't seem to think too much about the why or how, nor did they try to reason with themselves, they just felt their way through their little world and every feeling was valid; nothing was refused. Felix was beginning to understand that her emotions were just as powerful as knowledge, if not more so and right now, she felt happy. She didn't want to question it.

They were all gathered in a stone circle, which was hidden by the waterfall at the far side of the valley. Several plinths were holding up large slabs of different gemstones and somehow, the rock and stone of the walls and ceiling had been carved and polished, so that it looked like the strong arches of a temple. Together, there must have been nearly a hundred of them and though they were few, they gave the intimidating air of warrior women with their black eyes and spiralled, tall bodies with hairless heads. Felix drank them in with thirsty eyes. There were no children in this gathering and no men either. She let the questions flit through her mind before letting them go. Drow came of age at sixteen, and the men of the race had weak magic; it made sense that only the females of age were at the gathering, she supposed. But then, there were no elderly women here either. In fact, Lillith was the oldest person she'd seen since she arrived.

Being the only one covered in a dress and with a wild tangle of black hair, Felix was conspicuous. The eyes of the Drow found her easily, and they regarded her with a hushed awe that made her feel uncomfortable, but she smiled at each face that met hers and found their returning smiles a comfort. Melantha directed Felix to sit at the front of the semi-circle of sitting Drow, which had formed in front of a platform made of cut stone. Scanning her eyes around, Felix thought that it looked a little like a theatre, not that she'd ever been in one. But the Drow, sat on the floor, cross legged, staring expectantly up at the platform resembled an audience awaiting their star, and their star was Lillith.

She stepped out, now high upon her stage and looked out at the sisterhood beneath her, the blue-ringed black eyes finding Felix briefly and smiling. Lillith held out her arms and all fell silent.

Felix bit her lip. Anticipation and excitement thrummed in the air, coming from each of the women around her and it was infectious.

Lillith began to speak. Knowing she could not understand, Felix simply let the now familiar strains of Lillith's lullaby voice wash over her. She felt the Drow look towards her and knew Lillith must have been talking about her, but she didn't feel embarrassed. Rather, a coy warmth spread through her limbs, as though it was her birthday and they were singing to her in celebration.

But then the mood turned more sombre, and Felix watched the Drow lower their heads, placing their long-fingered hands over their hearts. Confused, Felix looked up at Lillith.

'We now remember the man, Alchemus James Fiddle who saved us from death and extinction,' Lillith explained to Felix. 'Our tears and our pain at his loss honour him, and we give it to the good earth. All pain is useful, Felix. Pain and sadness are not bad things for the Drow. They show us the meaning of happiness, and grief only proves love existed. We give our...energy? Yes, our energy to the earth. Our tears will water the soil. Life will be born from sorrow.'

Felix's breath caught in her throat, and she felt her eyes shining. But she did not wipe away her tears as she usually did. Instead, she let them fall, fast and freely. Laying her own hand against her heart, she let the wound of her loss open, and the deep ache which was somewhere buried in her core unfurled, rising up into her chest. She cried for Fiddle, sobs coming from so far down inside her that she felt endless. Had she cried like this for him before? She had never been allowed to. Well-meaning loved ones had tried to protect her from this pain, had kept her busy and brushed away the stray tears which had leaked from her eyes, but they had been wrong, she realised, to do that. This was catharsis; it was purifying. It was remembering him and honouring him.

So lost was she in her grief that she did not notice the Drow curling around her. They leaned forward, sheltering her, comforting her but allowing her to feel. Sometimes, Felix thought through the swell of her tears, sometimes we just need someone to be there when we cry. We just need someone to hold us.

There was no time limit. She was not hurried along or told to buck up. The Drow waited until the last tear spilled from Felix's eye, until the last sob wracked her body. When she finally looked up, her head fuzzy and aching but her heart wondrously light, she saw that many had cried with her and she felt the sisterhood, the bond. Lillith, on the platform above, nodded very gently at Felix, her own eyes dry but sad.

'You honour him,' she said softly, and Felix sighed deeply, a divine sense of feeling understood shimmering through her.

'And now,' Lillith said loudly, 'we begin.'

Again, she held out her hands and a ripple of excitement erupted through her audience. They began to hold hands and Felix felt both her arms being taken by the Drow next to her. Immediately, deep joy flooded through her, and she closed her eyes, revelling in the pleasure of it. Lillith descended from the platform and came to kneel in front of Felix. She reached out her hands slowly to Felix's face, as she had done when they'd first met.

'Open your heart to us, sister Felix,' she whispered, and then she laid her hands on Felix's cheeks.

A surging sensation claimed Felix. It caused her to arch her back and for a moment, she was unsure if it was pleasure or pain that she felt; it was sharp, gliding and consuming and in the brief few seconds before she had to close her eyes, she saw the spirals on the arms of Lillith moving, snaking and merging with her own.

Then peace.

She felt like the final piece of a puzzle, slotted into an image that had not made sense without her. She was vital. They all were. Felix felt the skin of Melantha and the Drow next to her. She felt the coarse, calloused hands of Lillith on her face. But she could feel all of the Drow and she knew their names, each one named for a flower. It was a timeless void and each of the Drow was a star within it. She could see each one of them, feel every singular girl if she chose to. Melantha; content, curious, urgently feeling the flushes of first love for a Drow boy. Shameless longing and wanting; desire. It was beautiful and natural. Amarylintha: pregnant with child, glowing and sparkling with life. Anxious for a healthy birth, and so filled with pure love that it was blinding. Iantha: young and grieving for her mother, recently dead, furious and afraid...so afraid and lonely despite her sisters' care.

Felix knew each of them. She could see them. She could feel everything they felt. Some emotions she could not name but she felt them with a burning empathy so sincere, it was like their feelings belonged to her.

Then flashes. Images, like a broken reel of film. They flowed from Lillith and Felix let them in, curious, confused, feeling a thousand different emotions at once, and unable to claim which ones belonged to her.

Grass, so green it seemed wrong. Blue sky. A thousand Drow, happy, loving, working, living. The Glade, yes, this was the Glade. There, look. See that beautiful young girl. Her black spirals covered half her body as she ran naked through the grass. Prisms of blue in the black. Calantha. *Mother. I know you*.

The image lurched. *No*! *Come back*!

Fiddle's face, younger and worried.

'Find somewhere, Lillith! You must save who you can! He won't stop!'

'Calantha? The babies?'

'She's dead – you must go!'

Cries of grief. Pain for Calantha.

The valley, now. Building ridges from rocks, helping the trees to grow. The spiders crawl out. All eyes on Lillith.

What do you feel, Lillith? Felix asked in her mind, knowing Lillith could hear her.

Pressure. Strain. Anguish. Black, dark seed of hatred. Glimpse of something ugly. A secret.

No, child.

Back to the void. A hundred tiny stars.

Felix felt a nudge inside her brain, inside her heart.

Let us see you, Felix said Lillith's voice from everywhere. *You carry the Flame. Let us share in its power. Let us ease your burden.*

Felix felt a sensation like vines creeping inside her skin, seeking. Seeking the Flame of Magic.

'No!'

Felix lurched away from Lillith's hands, and broke free from the linked arms of the Drow next to her. Immediately, the empathetic link between them broke and she felt her mind crashing back to reality.

'No...I can't,' she said, shaking her head. 'The Sacred Flame is mine to guard. I can't just share it's power like it's cinder toffee.'

Her body felt detached from her mind. When she tried to move, her actions were clumsy.

Around her, the Drow were waking from their trance. Murmurs of confusion filled the temple. Felix swallowed down a sickly feeling in her stomach. She knew each of them, now. The intimacy was too much. She felt tainted in some way, and she wished she did not know such private things about them. Had they seen her in the same way? She thought not; the Drowning had been a showcase of others, not a revelation of herself.

'Hush,' Lillith said, gripping Felix's shoulders tightly. 'Your first Drowning is strange, I know. I should have warned you. I thought you would be able to handle it. The fault is mine.'

Felix heard the disappointment in Lillith's voice, and it angered her. She felt her spirals heating.

'The Flame is mine, Lillith,' Felix said firmly. 'I cannot share it. I will not share it.'

Lillith nodded earnestly, her silver hair rippling over her shoulders.

'I understand. I sought only to help you. We are your sisters, Felix. We want to lighten your burdens.'

Felix swallowed again, looking into the doleful eyes of the Drow in front of her. Behind her, the Drow sisterhood were looking up at her with nothing but compassion. Felix softened.

'I know you do, Lillith,' Felix said softly. 'But that is one burden I must carry alone.'

'Yes, sister Felix,' Lillith replied resignedly. 'But here, you are never alone.'

Felix smiled half-heartedly. No, never alone. That was all she had ever wanted.

So why did it feel like a threat?

19

Smokesbane

He had failed miserably. The man whom they called Smokesbane, as if that pathetic epithet was his actual name, rolled the copper vims between his fingers, flipping one coin over the other with a deft movement. At his waist, the coin bag was fat and heavy; blood money. Money he was entirely undeserving of because he had failed his mission. For now, anyway. He'd have another go when he could.

Dozens had died. At the last count, it was eighty-two fatalities, with twelve more grave injuries. Not bad, but not a personal best. But all things considered - things being that he'd been in the middle of the Midevil Market of all places, and surrounded by the most wicked (and witless) the Magistry had to offer - killing eighty-two people in the space of twenty minutes wasn't bad going. Some were kids, too; those snivelling little commoner slaves. He'd done them a favour if you asked him, which nobody ever did. No-one cared about your opinion when you were a Shadow. It was like you weren't even a person; you were just the power you had, a 'gun for hire' as they would have said in the old Western stories. He'd always liked the thought of that; he wasn't a murderer or a black-moralled devil, he was a bandit, a rogue; a misunderstood straight shooter with a crack shot.

Until today.

Eighty-two. Gone. Choked. Smothered. Burned to cinder and ash.

Would have been alright if one of them was actually the one he was after. A quick job and easy money, and he'd have been back on his boat and on to the next market or town or tribe; anywhere that needed a Shadow for some shady work. Bit of torture. Straight killing. It was all the same if it paid well, and this job had definitely paid well. Whoever wanted the Godspell boy dead, really didn't like him.

Didn't matter though really, did it? The whos and the whys were just details, and the devil was in the detail. He didn't get involved, didn't ask questions. That was why he was so good at his job. If you get involved with the job, you start wondering why you're doing what it is you're doing, and let's be honest, nobody exactly dreams of being an assassin when they grow up, but we all have to work with the talents we've got and this was Smokesbane's talent; his craft, one he'd honed and perfected over twenty-four annums and two hundred and fourteen jobs. No, two hundred and fifteen. Technically. Well, it would be as soon as he killed the Godspell kid.

He wasn't stupid. He knew who Linus Godspell was, or who he was going to be before he'd killed old Corbin. He'd read those Truth Papers the new Firelighter had released. If it was the truth. Could never tell these days. Politicians were all the same. One man's truth was another man's lie, or in this case, woman's. Not that the slip of a girl who they'd put in power was a woman, not yet. He felt a bit sorry for her really. She actually seemed decent and that meant she'd obviously be taken advantage of by someone for some reason or another. Good ones always were. But the whos and the whys weren't Smokesbane's business.

Killing was his business, and he'd been told to kill Linus Godspell and any of that crew of his that got in the way. He was pretty sure he'd got one of them; the smarmy, posh one, which made Smokesbane secretly glad. He liked it when he got a posh one. But the others had gotten away, though how, he didn't bloody know. His smoke stretched for miles and could creep through windows and under doorframes like he was the Angel of Death, and he could always feel it when he took a life. It was like...Actually what was it like? The question bothered him.

Smokesbane tried to think, and he flipped the coins between his fingers again then dropped them into the coin bag. His hands twitched, hungry for something to touch, to play with, to do; to kill. He peeled himself out of the shadows of the empty market and made his way to his boat. He'd find the boy, and the crew of that sorry excuse for a barge on his own.

What was it like?

The dockyard on the far side of the market under Covent Garden was empty, save for a few abandoned ships probably belonging to them who had died. Smokesbane contemplated taking one but, weighing up the pros (being that he'd get a bigger ship for free) and the cons (being that he'd have to move all his stuff over, not that he had that much), he decided that he was better off in his little boat. Or was it a yacht? It wasn't a dinghy (he wasn't pathetic) but it wasn't a barge either, like some of the ones bobbing on the black waters. Nor was it a skiff or a scow. Yeah. Yeah, it was a yacht. He didn't need much else than what he had. It'd served him well, like his power had. Who was he, if it wasn't for his gift? Granted, the gift of death was a bit morbid, a bit macabre but it was better than being a pipescraper or some rubbish like that. He delivered people to the pearly gates of heaven, if you believed in that sort of stuff and might have been murdering scum, but he was no heathen.

What was it like when *he killed someone? What did it feel* like? The questions were burning. This is precisely why he didn't ask questions.

The heathens were the ones who set the jobs and paid the money. The ones who spoke facelessly behind walls, with spineless words or sent messages with skivvies or whatever, whoever. Them. *They* were the evil ones. Couldn't be calling Smokesbane evil, when all he did was use the talents he'd been born with. He was just the messenger. A missionary.

Everybody has to eat somehow.

You know what it was like? He had it now. It was like the essence of the lives he took became trapped in his smoke and merged with it, added to it. Thickened it. Like he was one big giant sponge soaking up the souls of the dead and raising them up in a great sacrifice of smoke. Yeah. That was what it was like. Maybe they should stop calling him Smokesbane. Maybe they should call him... the Angel of Death.

Now that had a nice ring to it.

20

The Message in the Bottle

Linus wretched up the water from his stomach as soon as he reached the surface. It poured out of his mouth and then out of his nose, as he coughed and gagged on the acrid taste of the brackish water.

'He's over here, Cap'n!'

The gruff voice of Ragstone broke through the thick, clogged feeling in his ears and as he turned in the water, using his arms to steer himself, he saw the Skimmer in all her ugly, sludge-soaked glory floating slowly towards him, and she had never looked so beautiful. He heard other voices and a flurry of boots on deck before Ragstone threw him a rope and a lifebuoy.

Disorientated and lacking strength, Linus struggled to swim towards it but finally he grasped it and felt himself being pulled towards the ship. Through bleary, sore eyes, he took in his surroundings. He was in a river, that much was clear to him and there was no sign of Black Mary or the Midevil Market. From the depths of it and the taste of the water, it was a hidden river, long forgotten under the Magistry. At least it wasn't a sewer. He felt like he'd been under the water for a very long time, swooshed and sloshed around in nothing but wet, heavy blackness which he thought he'd die in, but he hovered on the edge of unconsciousness for a while before the current thrust him upwards, delivering him to sweet, precious, dank UnderLondon air.

'I've got you, lad,' Ragstone croaked, as he hauled Linus onto the deck.

For a moment, Linus just lay there, bare chested, soaked to the bone, half drowned but still, marvellously and miraculously alive.

But what's more, so were the crew.

'You're here,' he managed to say, before coughing up another quart of grey water.

'Let me at him,' Captain Bonny Kildare's angry voice growled, and as she pushed Ragstone aside, she leaned over Linus and inspected him.

'Och, you stupid, good for nothing little – do you know we thought were dead? Who goes down a bloody hole in the middle of a lake without breathing equipment or magic at the very least?'

'How did you –'

'Bazalguette, the moron, told us everything when you didn't come back up,' Captain Kildare said, glaring up at Baz, who was rubbing the back of his neck sheepishly.

He shrugged a shoulder and winced immediately; a tell-tale sign of the lashings he'd probably received as punishment.

'Glad you're alright, lad,' he mumbled. 'Knew you would be.'

Captain Kildare flashed him a look, so deadly that even Baz with his blind eyes could sense the daggers and he removed himself from deck.

'What were you thinking? Seriously, Linus?' Captain Kildare asked, her face crumpled in both concern and confusion.

She crouched down next to him and chucked over a coarse blanket that Flint had just brought up from below deck.

Linus shrugged.

'I wasn't, really. After Paris- wait, do you know that Paris –'

'He's dead, yeah,' Flint interrupted. 'Baz told us. Sounds like he was very brave...in the end. We'll raise a glass for him later.'

'Right. Yeah,' Linus' voice cracked. 'Well, after Paris died, Baz chucked me in the lake and, well, truth be told if he hadn't have done that, I definitely would be dead, so really Baz saved my life, Cap'n.'

Captain Kildare frowned and folded her arms, but she nodded her head once.

'Baz'd found out that Black Mary was a lake, you see.'

'He's told us all this, lad,' Ragstone said gently. 'What happened after you went down the well?'

'Erm' Linus said, sitting up and taking the hot mug of cinnamon tea from Pinks, who smiled at him shyly as she held out the mug with a well bandaged arm.

'Well it's a bit weird, really and I know how it's going to sound but...I spoke with the river.'

Flint smirked and raised an eyebrow.

'You spoke to the river?' he asked. 'Tell me, kid. Did the river talk back?'

Both he and Pinks broke into laughter and Linus, feeling hurt, dipped his head down into the cup and breathed in the warm.

'I'm going to bed,' he muttered, and he struggled to stand. Ragstone helped him up.

'Hold up, laddie,' Captain Kildare said softly, looping her arm around his waist.

Together, they helped Linus down the ladder to his sleeping quarter below deck, but not before Captain Kildare glared at Flint and Pinks.

'Privy needs emptying, Flint. And Pinks? You're off grogg rations tonight. I don't tolerate rudeness on my ship, d'you understand?'

Ragstone lay Linus down in his hammock before taking his leave. Linus saw him circling his finger next to his head at Captain Kildare as he left and Linus slumped down, pulling the blanket around him. He felt uncomfortable and shuffling, he remembered the flagon of Fleetwater tied to his trousers and the corked bottle he'd shoved inside his waistband. He pulled both of them out.

'I've got proof, Cap'n,' he said, holding up the glass bottle.

Captain Kildare pulled up a three-legged stool and sat astride it next to Linus' hammock.

'What've you got there, boy?' she asked.

'The river gave it to me,' he said quietly. 'I know it sounds nuts, Cap'n but once I got down there, the well I mean, there was this voice and it said she was Black Mary but that she had other names too. She knew lots of things and secrets, just like you said she would, and she took secrets from me too; really private stuff.

Stuff I didn't even really know myself until she said it. And she gave me information. Said I had to find some woman called Hestia Windwood on the Second Plane. But she knew I couldn't go there, see, and she started going on about some guy called Hooke and how he'd made a secret hatch I could use, a back door she called it and then she gave me this.'

He held up the bottle limply, suddenly exhausted from telling his story. Captain Kildare took the bottle from him and peered through it, tipping it upside down.

'A message in a bottle,' she said, simply. 'Have you read it?'

Linus shook his head.

'We should open it then, don't you think?'

'Wait,' Linus said, resting his hand on her gloved wrist before she started to pull out the cork. 'You believe me then?'

Captain Kildare tilted her head and licked her lips before speaking.

'Linus, you are a member of my crew. You are my responsibility and this mission you find yourself on has pulled me and the others into it, too. I told you I would help you and I'm a woman of my word, make no mistake about that. If you say you spoke to the river, then as a trusted and valued member of my crew, I will take you at your word.'

Linus gave her a crooked smile of thanks.

'But so help me, Linus. If you pull a stunt like that again and risk your life for the sake of some stupid secret, you will find yourself without a crew and a home, do you understand?'

'Yes, Cap'n,' Linus said, trying to keep a straight face, and failing.

His grin won Captain Kildare over and she smiled back at him fondly.

'I'm glad you're ok, laddie,' she said.

'You too, Cap'n,' Linus said seriously. 'I thought Smokesbane had gotten you all, and after I saw what it did to Paris, I thought...'

'Smokesbane?' Captain Kildare frowned.

'Yeah, the Shadow at the market. The river said that was his name. You know him?'

'No,' Captain Kildare shook her head. 'But I know the name. He's a paid assassin; he kills for money, not sport.'

'Yeah, the river said he was 'sent'.'

'By who?'

'She...it didn't know.'

Captain Kildare looked thoughtful for a moment.

'I don't much believe in coincidences,' she said quietly, leaning in. 'And it's too much of a coincidence that a Shadow turns up and sets his power loose at the Midevil Market on the same day you, the missing brother of the Firelighter turns up there sniffing around asking secrets about the 'true Firelighter'.'

'What are you saying?' Linus asked, puzzled.

'I'm saying...how much do you trust your sister?'

'What? You think Felix sent him? To kill Paris?'

'Paris, maybe, sure,' Captain Kildare nodded, hooking her gloved finger under her chin in thought. 'But have you thought that maybe he was after you?'

'Me?' Linus flinched. 'No...no, Cap'n. I'm sorry, I don't mean to be rude or anything but...Felix saved my life in the Tower. She protected me and risked her life to save mine. She wouldn't try and kill me now.'

Surely she wouldn't? The thought echoed in his mind.

Captain Kildare held her hands up to back off.

'I'm sure you know your sister better than I do, Linus,' she said genuinely. 'But I heard a few things at the market about her, rumours about her locking herself away in the Citadel, refusing to come out, abandoning her duties, even the commoners she always claimed to love. Public opinion is that the power has gone to her head. They say...'

'What? What do they say?'

'They say she's just like Corbin, underneath it all.'

Linus swallowed at the mention of his father. He pulled himself up in his hammock awkwardly.

'She's not,' he said, his voice hard. 'And she wouldn't do this. There were commoner children at that market. She wouldn't risk their lives, even if she was capable plotting my death or whatever it is you think.'

Captain Kildare nodded, but Linus could tell she remained unconvinced.

'If Smokesbane attacks again, laddie,' she said, 'you need to ask yourself if you know your sister as well as you think. Maybe she knows who you're searching for and is trying to put an end to it. Secrets breed, Linus. Always remember that. Truth will out.'

Linus lowered his eyes, refusing to argue any further about the topic. Felix was his twin, and they may have been torn apart for most of their lives, but he would not betray her now, not when she had saved his life. He owed her this.

'I'm sorry about Paris,' Captain Kildare said, breaking the silence. 'He was a good man.'

Linus nodded, his throat thick.

'He said,' Linus's voice cracked and he cleared his throat.

Captain Kildare gave him a moment. 'He said something, as he was dying. I think it was to do with his secret. He could barely say the words.'

'What were they?'

'He said 'William Lilly's diaries'.'

Captain Kildare took a deep breath, thinking about the words before shaking her head.

'And then he said 'the Ardere'.'

'Ok. So, if I'm getting this right, we've now two reasons to go to the Second Plane; the first is to find this Hestia Windwood the river told you about and the second is to go to the Ardere Academy to find the diaries of this Lilly fellow.'

Linus nodded, grateful that she had listened and heard him and, more importantly, had believed him. He sipped at his lukewarm cinnamon tea because his eyes were watering, and it was probably to do with all the water he'd absorbed from nearly drowning but even so, he didn't want the captain to see.

'Problem is,' Captain Kildare said, leaning back on the stool and knotting her hands behind her head. It made her hat slip forward a little over her brow. 'Problem is that you can't get to the Second Plane.'

'Actually,' Linus said. 'Black Mary did say something about that.'

Captain Kildare tilted her head and waited, folding her arms.

'It sounds crazy –'

'Most of this sounds crazy, Linus,' Captain Kildare smirked.

Linus winced. 'I know it does, ok, but she said that Robert Hooke- well she said that he built a secret hatch, a back door to the Second Plane. She said it was for commoners.'

'But that's impossible,' Captain Kildare said, shaking her head so that her red braids jiggled on her shoulder.

'I know, trust me I know. But if she's right then it means I can get to the Second Plane and we can get to the Ardere, get William Lilly's diaries and then find Hestia Windwood.'

Captain Kildare rubbed her chin with her gloved fingers and squinted her eyes. Linus could see that she was struggling to stretch her usually logical and practical brain to believe what he was saying.

'We had better open the bottle,' she said finally.

Linus pressed his lips together and nodded. He reached for the bottle that the captain had placed on top of his blanket and uncorked it. It opened with a small pop. He tipped it upside down and then pushed his finger in like a fishing hook and pulled out the rolled parchment.

It was very brittle, and the inside of the bottle had a sour smell of old wine but, despite being under water for centuries, the paper was bone dry.

Very gently, Linus flattened the paper. It was quite yellow and the ink upon it had faded a little, but he could just about read it, despite the ornate script and the outdated spelling.

'Beneathe a Monumental view of London
Lays a hatch in dark abandonne
Counte ye the footesteppes in to fyre
And burn upon a funeral pyre.'

Linus read it three times over before passing it to Captain Kildare. She struggled over it for a moment before Linus spoke the words aloud, their rhyme and rhythm helping him memorise them.

'Beneath a monumental view of London? So it's somewhere high?' Captain Kildare pondered. 'Maybe the old Clock Tower?'

'I don't think so. Big Ben was built after the Great Fire of London. The river said that Hooke was a Firelighter, one of the first after Thomas Farynor, so it'd be a very old building. Something built after the Great Fire in 1666. The river said he and his friend, Christopher Wren rebuilt most of London. He was a Firelighter too, apparently.'

'Wren? A Firelighter? Well, I never.'

'You know of Christopher Wren?'

'Certainly. You know, I feel bad for your generation. Corbin Godspell really did a number on your history education. You don't know the history of your own city.'

She shook her head pityingly before continuing.

'He was the first person to suggest a sewerage system in London but didn't get the funding for it. But he also designed the Monument, amongst other things. It was built in memorial of the Great Fire of London. It says so on its base.

'Think about it. If the first ever hatch, opened by the first Firelighter, Thomas Farynor on Pudding Lane, caused the Great Fire of London and brought the spark of magic into the First Plane, then it makes sense that Hooke chose it as his hidden hatch. Especially if what Black Mary says is true about he and Christopher Wren being Firelighters after Farynor. It's quite clever actually, the Monument. A hidden hatch, a commemoration to the commoners' history as well as being a secret homage to the origins of magic on the First Plane – all designed by two of the first Firelighters, forgotten by history. Fascinating, isn't it?'

Linus nodded, but he was no longer really listening.

When he had first escaped from the Citadel with Paris and ran away from his sister, he'd tried to keep abreast of news of her. Running away seemed so callous and cold; so ungrateful. It was a sort of penance to learn what he could about Felix and her reign, a way of checking up on her to make sure she was ok. So of course, he had read the Truth Papers. She'd released them soon after she'd taken power. In fact, it was one of the first things she'd insisted upon. Through Paris, Linus had managed to get his hands on a copy and he'd read, with a curious sort of detachment, as though he was simply reading a newspaper article, that his parents, Calantha and Everard, who had been so brutally murdered on the day he was born, had a secret grave. This grave, a memorial to them containing only their ashes, was the Monument. Alchemus James Fiddle had arranged for the remains of Linus and Felix's parents to be cremated and then placed inside the gold, flaming urn atop the Monument to the Great Fire of London.

Linus had not been to it. He'd not wanted to. His parents, whose names were just meaningless configurations of letters on paper, were phantoms to him; unknown entities that held no more meaning for him, than characters in a story. He understood the significance of it all, now. The murdered Firelighter, guardian of the Sacred Flame interred with his wife inside a monument to a Great Fire...a great fire which brought magic into the world. He had not known Alchemus J. Fiddle, but Linus appreciated his sense of poetry.

'I suppose then,' he said, with a weariness which came from something heavier and more exhausting than nearly drowning. 'We should go to the Monument.'

Captain Kildare nodded and she looked down at Linus. For a moment, she forgot herself and leaned her hand down to smooth away a lock of his black hair from his eyes.

'We will,' she smiled down at him affectionately. 'But first, rest.'

Linus closed his eyes. Only when his breathing had slowed to a calm, steady pace did Captain Bonny Kildare leave his side.

21

Bridges to Burn

Nigel and DW were sat inside a little café just off Glasshouse Street in Soho, a few minutes away from Piccadilly Circus. It was a ramshackle affair, with a layer of grease coating the windows, which was smeared with condensation. Through the grubby glass, magicians scurried past, jogging through puddles with newspapers held above their heads as they dashed from hatch to hatch. There was a chill in the air and Nigel rubbed at his arms with his hands, inwardly cursing himself for not bringing his long coat. The thin scrap of material that made up his favourite t shirt may have been stylish, but it certainly wasn't warm, and even with the candles scattered around the café weeping wax onto the scrubbed tables, Nigel was cold. It was a cold that had arrived when Felix had left. He felt the absence of her strongly as he stared out into the grey streets of London and, unbidden though not unwelcome, the memory of her dancing in his arms after the State Ball sprang into his mind, bringing with it a fresh wave of anger and hurt.

D.W sat opposite Nigel patiently, perched precariously on a wooden chair which wobbled on uneven legs every few seconds whenever he leaned down to slurp down the stew or soup or whatever it was that the owner of the establishment had slopped into a bowl for him. It was rather good, even if he wasn't entirely sure what he was eating.

The café was empty, save for an old woman who was feeding crumbs of cake to something inside her handbag, which was making unnerving belching sounds which made the waiter, a spotty teenage boy, shuffle uncomfortably whenever he delivered another slice of cake and cinnamon tea to the lady.

'I still don't think we should tell Aubrey about what the Catchoo said,' Nigel said, his eyes not leaving the window, even as he shook his head.

A frown line was forming between his brows, obscured slightly by the rim of his glasses. D.W rolled his eyes and licked his chops.

'She's worried too, you know? They all are. Besides,' the dire wolf said, 'If you really think we should go to the Ardere, Aubrey will know someone. The principal from the State Ball?'

'Principal Ellis? She probably does,' Nigel agreed. 'But if Felix has gone to the Ardere, it's to get away and escape her life here. If I tell Aubrey where we plan to go, she'll want to come and then Liberty will come as well, and then before you know it there's a whole troop marching on the Ardere and Felix will just feel attacked. I think it should just be me and you. Between us, we can talk some sense into her.'

The dire wolf snorted, and the chair shook beneath him until he balanced himself.

'When does Felix ever listen to us?'

Nigel smiled and chuckled.

'She listened to Fiddle, even when he was wrong.'

There was a faint rumble of anger behind his words and D.W could hear the bitterness in Nigel's mind. He tilted his head questioningly.

'You're angry at Fiddle,' he said.

It was a statement and not a question, but Nigel looked at the dire wolf and nodded slowly, as though admitting a shameful secret.

'It wasn't just Felix he kept secrets from,' Nigel mumbled, brushing a curl of his red hair out of his face.

D.W listened hard but rather than hearing, he saw instead slivers of memories in Nigel's mind. An argument about Felix aboard the Belfast. Slammed doors.

'She doesn't need to know!'

'Yes, Alchemus. She does.'

'What...what was he talking about?' D.W asked, as the memory went dim.

Nigel pursed his lips and folded his arms. Again, he stared out of the window.

'Fiddle was on the Privy Council,' he said. 'At the Ardere. He had a secret that was his to protect, until he was excommunicated when he went into hiding after Corbin Godspell took power.'

'What was the secret?' D.W asked, leaning in with his front legs perilously as his wobbly chair trembled beneath him.

Nigel flashed his green eyes at the wolf, and they seemed cautious. D.W tried to listen to Nigel's thoughts, but they were scrambled, like an old radio with voices being drowned out by static.

A loud belch from the handbag behind them made them both jump and the dire wolf slipped from his chair and landed with a thud on the cold, stone tiles. When he jumped back up again, Nigel's face was passive but closed; a vice that would not open up again.

'We need to go to the Ardere,' he said firmly and then he pulled out a few vims, dropped them on the table and walked out into the pouring rain, before the dire wolf had even jumped down from his chair.

They arrived at the London Library through a hatch that opened up near the wooden check out box. Steam rose from them both as the warmth of the Library welcomed them home, but the piercing warble of Vessania broke through the evening silence and it seemed that even the library winced. Nigel rubbed at his temples with his thumb and forefinger and sighed, heading towards the parlour with D.W on his heels.

'Aunty?' Nigel said, as he knocked on the parlour door.

He didn't wait for an answer and opened the door a crack and peeped inside.

Vessania the opera singer was stood upon her chaise longue with a closed umbrella in her hand, conducting an invisible orchestra in front of her. On the desk, a Victrola was playing a mournful aria and she was singing, unsuccessfully, along to it.

'Come in, come in, come iiiiiiiin!' she sang, before leaping from the chaise longue and twirling into a pas de bourree more gracefully than one would expect from an elderly lady.

'Oh you've brought a visitor! It's a little doggy! Hello doggy!' Vessania squealed, lowering the volume of the music by swiping at the air in the direction of the Victrola.

She bent over the dire wolf and smushed her face into his, seemingly oblivious to his surprised and somewhat moody growl.

'Dire wolf,' D.W murmured, but Vessania was already pirouetting away, humming tunelessly.

'Aunty, I have to go away for a little while,' Nigel said, taking a seat next to Vessania and grasping her hand. 'You'll be ok for a couple of days, won't you? I can arrange for someone to come and stay with you if you like?'

'Darling, I'll be fine!' Vessania smiled moonily. 'You take a little trip. How jolly!'

The dire wolf rested on his hind legs and pricked his ears up. Then, his bushy eyebrows fell over his eyes in a snarl, and he began to growl as the woman in front of him grew, stretching the seams of the elegant purple dress Vessania was wearing. Now, a wizened old witch was sat next to Nigel, with one eye white and rolling and the other one fixed pointedly at the dire wolf.

'Come to listen, have you?' the woman sneered at him. 'Come to hear the voices?'

'Oh do stop, Vessania. Leave the little doggy alone.'

'Ain't no doggy, you daft bat, this here's a dire wolf. They can hear your thoughts, can dire wolves. Tell me...can you hear mine?'

D.W pulled his lips back over his teeth, and leaned low over his front legs, growling menacingly. He nodded slowly, never removing his fierce eyes from hers. Nigel was watching the exchange in both shock and wonder, and the dire wolf could hear the question in his mind, loud and clear.

'What's it like? Please...what's it like in a Spinner's mind?' Nigel asked, dread lacing every word.

The dire wolf listened to Vessania. Each voice - and there were several, some who almost never came through – was distinct, and each voice told its own version of the truth. The hag in front of him spoke with rotten words intended to hurt. They were twisted and decayed until only a fraction of truth remained. The opera singer was innocent and oblivious; for her the truth was a game; something to tell when it suited her but mainly, it was as interchangeable as a child's fantasy game. Others were there; some were confused and conflicted, unable to recognise what was true and what wasn't, looking out through the hag's one beady eye and questioning the reality in front of them. Every now and then, a beacon of sanity shone through the chaos and a Russian-voiced woman broke through, her words angry and frustrated before she was pushed down again into the depths.

It was madness and insanity; the complete inability to recognise the truth of oneself or the surrounding reality. And it was cruel; each facet of Vessania True was spinning, like a roulette table, desperate to speak out, to confirm just for a moment that she existed, that she was not a frayed collection of fractioned personalities lacking a whole form.

'Yes,' the hag grinned at the dire wolf with toothless gums. 'You see. He'll see too, in time.' She motioned to Nigel next to her, and then she tugged roughly at his arm so that he called out in pain.

D.W barked ferociously at her, and the hag laughed, throwing back her head in a throaty chuckle which quickly morphed into a bell-like giggle. The opera singer had returned.

'Oh, don't mind her,' she flopped her hand down at D.W. 'Oh, darling, look! Your arm is all bruised!'

Vessania stroked at Nigel's arm tenderly and slowly, the bruising faded.

'There now,' she smiled warmly. 'Perfect again.' Then she leaned forward and kissed Nigel, her long arms wrapping around his neck and gripping him in a lover's embrace.

Nigel scrambled away, pushing her with a force of magic that left her doubled over and giggling like a schoolgirl.

'Such a prude!' she said, through peals of laughter and then she was up, twirling, motioning to the Victrola which started playing its song again.

'Enjoy your trip, darling! I'll miss you.'

Nigel and D.W lurched towards the door, and Nigel closed it just as Vessania blew them a kiss.

They stood outside the parlour door, listening to the strains of music and the squeals of singing which sounded like a bag of rats being drowned. Occasionally, another voice would speak, and the sounds of conversations sputtered through the door.

'What's wrong with her?' D.W asked, one ear flicked towards the parlour. 'She had so many different thoughts, but they all sounded different, and they were all talking at the same time. It was chaos.'

Nigel swallowed, and they started walking towards the Reading Room.

'She's a Spinner,' he said gruffly. 'She has a condition which means she lies, and she can't tell the difference between what is the truth and what isn't.'

He opened up the Reading Room doors and slumped down onto the sofa, sending a jet of fire into the fireplace. Flames rose up swiftly and heat spread through the room. At the same time, the candles lit themselves and a few floating orbs filled with soft blue light started floating around lazily.

'Over time, the lies become a net that she's stuck inside, and she can't get out of it; a spider caught in her own web. Her...personalities... are all the different sides of her, all the different lies she's told about who she is, or maybe they're who she thinks she is...I don't know. I could never really figure out how it works.'

'And she raised you? Your aunt? After your parents...?'

Nigel swallowed and nodded.

'My father was Vessania's twin. After he married my mother, a commoner, his whole family disowned him. Everyone apart from Vessania. She didn't understand why my father would choose a commoner over his family, but she couldn't give up on her brother. They fought a lot and eventually, Vessania said he had to choose between my mother or her. My father chose my mother and it drove Vessania mad. She'd always been...different. Touched, my father said, by lies. I think only he had really understood her and even after they fell out, he made sure she was cared for after my grandparents passed away. But they never spoke again.'

He conjured up a large glass of cloudy lemonade and immediately the room smelled of sweet lemons. The dire wolf jumped up on the sofa next to him and cocked his head, and Nigel poured a little lemonade onto the sofa, but before it hit the fabric, a shiny tin bowl appeared. They both took a long, deep drink.

'When my parents...when they died, Vessania was my only living relative. She wasn't in a fit state to look after me really, but she did anyway. She really did her best, but she was batty,' Nigel smiled fondly.

'It was funny at first. She'd forget things and we'd laugh, and she'd tell stories and become the characters. She'd tell me she was a famous opera singer and a ballerina, and we'd spend the day singing and dancing. Another day she was a wicked witch, and I was her captive. But as I grew up, I stopped pretending and she didn't. It stopped being funny. And soon, she started to believe she really was that wicked old witch and she'd...she'd hurt me. There were moments of clarity, though. Moments when my real Aunt Vessania would break through. It was her who reached out to Alchemus and made him honour my father's wishes that I become his apprentice.'

Nigel drank some of his lemonade and winced at its sharpness. For a long time, he was silent.

'It's genetic,' he said eventually. 'The condition runs in my father's family. There's a chance I could inherit it.'

'You're afraid,' D.W said, understanding now.

Nigel nodded and pulled his glasses off, pinching the bridge of his nose again.

'Felix doesn't know any of this, does she?' D.W asked, and Nigel's silence confirmed that he was right.

'You ought to tell her,' he said gently.

Nigel flared. 'Why? So she can get rid of me now before I become a burden to her? Before I lie to her like everyone else has? I won't lie to her.'

He tossed his glasses down onto the sofa beside him and ran his gloved hands through his hair.

'It doesn't matter anyway,' he mumbled gloomily. 'She's gone. I didn't even have chance to tell her, and I suppose now I know that she wouldn't have stuck around.'

'On the contrary,' said D.W quietly, resting his paw on Nigel's hand. 'I think if she knew how much you needed her – and I mean her, the love and friendship she can give, not her power, then she would stay with you, always. She loves you. Surely you can see that?'

But Nigel's answering gaze was one of disbelief and confusion. His mind was a cacophony of thoughts, each one contradicting the other, but they were all undeniably and distinctly Nigel. There were no lies in his thoughts or in his feelings for Felix.

'Let's find our girl,' the dire wolf said, nuzzling his head against Nigel's arm.

The boy looked over his slumped shoulder at the wolf and smiled lopsidedly, scratching him behind his ears.

'No Aubrey?' Nigel asked.

D.W shook his head.

'No, I think you're right. We do this alone.'

'Ok,' Nigel swallowed.

In his mind, D.W could hear anxiety and concern that Aubrey would soon find that they, too, had gone, but Nigel's mind was made up.

He walked over towards the black iron staircase that led up to the galley walkway along the upper shelves. Behind the staircase, Nigel reached to the very top shelf of a bookcase that was hidden in shadow and obscured by the stairs. He pulled down a copy of an old, slightly mildewed book called 'Traditional Garden Gnomes'.

'Fiddle's?' D.W grinned, and Nigel smiled in response.

Inside the book, the pages were hollowed out and held a pair of spectoccules. They were ornate and wire rimmed with an array of multi-coloured lenses that folded down over each other.

Nigel placed them on the bridge of his nose. They were heavy and cumbersome but were a necessity for him to see and access the Second Plane.

'You ok to get there?' Nigel asked the dire wolf.

'Sure,' D.W said, his tongue hanging out of his mouth and his tail wagging.

Ever since Felix and the Magistry had lifted the ban on magical creatures entering the Second Plane, he'd returned to his home several times. Nowhere was as good for a long run as the wild meadows of the Second Plane, where he could jump up and snap his jaws at firepixies and flutterbies.

The dire wolf watched as Nigel picked up his normal glasses and slipped them into the pocket of his jeans, before adjusting the coloured lenses of the spectoccules. He did this with the practised air of someone who knew exactly what configuration worked for him, and after only a few seconds, Nigel's body began to fade, particle by particle, molecule by molecule until he had completely disappeared.

D.W sniffed the air, flicked at ear towards the neighbouring parlour where Vessania was still singing and then, satisfied that all was well, he closed his eyes and disappeared, silently and swiftly leaving the Reading Room still and filled with the firecracker scent of magic.

22

The Archimedes Bohr Appreciation Society

Slingsby Buzzard, fourth annum student of the Ardere Academy, was cramming. In one hand he held a gold fountain pen over a sheaf of parchment smudged with blotches of ink which resembled a Rorschach test. In the other hand, he lazily rolled a tumbler of Ashwater so that the steaming, golden liquid teetered close to edge of the glass, but each time it seemed that he was about to spill it, he'd adeptly tip his hand a little and save it.

The barkeep watched him with irritation, knowing full well that interfering with Slingsby Buzzard would result in a wasted quarter of an hour listening to him wittering on about the 'calamitous ineptitude' of his professors at the academy, and how it was 'super inconvenient' to be given a test on a Friday morning when 'simply everybody' knew that Thirsty Thursday was a 'real event' for the students, and that Highcliff-on-Sea was 'practically overrun' with scholars and academics with their pasty, candle wax skin and their squinting, shadow rimmed eyes. And so, the barkeep kept his teeth on edge and his mouth shut, as he watched the crystal tumbler sliding across the crushed velvet glove of Slingsby Buzzard's hand.

It was true that The Scholar's Rest tavern was the hive of Highcliff-On-Sea on Thursday evenings, possibly because it was the only tavern in the only town within a twenty-mile radius of the Ardere Academy, but mainly because it offered the scholars studying there a discounted rate on Ashwater, Ditchmead and that sickly Honeygin that the girls and the hippies from Caelum consortium liked to drink. It was also true that the barkeep watered down these drinks more and more as each hour passed on a Thursday evening, so that the discounted rates didn't affect his profits, but this was a secret he didn't tell too many people about. A drunken scholar could hardly tell the difference between his elbow and his ear after a few tans had been spent; except for Slingsby Buzzard that is. He had what he said were 'refined tastebuds', practised in the detection of what he called 'balance' in his drinks, and after a particularly nasty argument in which the barkeep had lost a whole pyre to Slingsby causing him to be down on his profits, he'd learned to serve the trumped-up git the good stuff, even at a discounted rate.

Annoyingly, Slingsby Buzzard, for all his irritating emphasis on his over-dramatic exclamations (an Americanism he had never quite lost, despite his years spent travelling the world, on both the First and the Second) and his florid hand gestures which had resulted in many a broken glass, he was ineffably likeable. He tipped well and had a sort of familiar charm which meant that after one shared drink (for he was generous and frequently bought two drinks, one for himself and the other for whomsoever he might stumble upon at a table) one would feel like they had known him all their life and that he was, unexpectedly and delightedly, their new best friend. It was because of this affectionate warmth, this familial friendship and the small hope that his presence would invite that of other, more gullible drinkers, that the barkeep (grudgingly) allowed Slingsby to study there.

Slingsby Buzzard was not a natural academic. On the contrary, he was and always had been a man of action and had refused, rebuffed and renounced the world of academia altogether when his father, a self-made Texan-born magician, had insisted that he attend a university, either on the First or the Second, it didn't matter. Instead, Slingsby had travelled, taking that much coveted and most sacred of experiences: the gap year. Only it had turned into five years and within that time, Slingsby had found his joy, his passion; his 'flair', as the professors at the academy called the predispositions of talents that the students carried with them, along with their nerves and their red, embossed trunks on the first day of the semester.

Some had their affinity with fire and flame; their pyrotechnics came to them as naturally as breathing, more so than other magicians, who all (let's be honest) had a 'thing' for fire. These scholars studied in the Ignis consortium, and it was well known to everyone (except maybe to the Ignis scholars) that it was the easiest consortium, the one which let in the magicians who didn't quite have what it took to get into the others; others like the Vene consortium. Home of the venephysicists, who studied the particles of magic, it was generally accepted that they were the most arrogant of the consortiums. They weren't quite as intelligent as the Tressis consortium, but they were studying the Third Plane, so obviously they were going to be absolute geniuses (and well they knew it) but the Vene scholars really thought they owned the place, especially (or probably) because the Ardere Academy's motto was 'magia corre nelle loro vene' which meant 'magic flows within their veins'.

The other consortiums had a particular contempt for the Vene scholars but none more so than the Tempus lot, who thought that their flair of time and history was more meaningful that staring out of spectoccules or glaring into a microscope all day. 'History predicts the future' was their common phrase, and although the other consortiums frequently took their side in debates when they went up against the Vene scholars, mostly people just rolled their eyes at their incessant mooning over the past.

All the consortiums thought they individually were the best; perhaps that was what instilled such kinship and camaraderie within its scholars, and why each consortium held strong the ancient and much lauded tradition of secrecy; each one of them acted as though they were keeping grave and dark secrets that might endanger the worlds, should they ever be released to outsiders. The Poculum consortium brewed their tonics and potions and cures, the Caelum kept their noses pointed up at the skies and the clouds, and the Tellus pointed them down at the earth and the dirt, and all of them protected their findings like a mother bear protects her cubs.

But it was none of these consortiums that Slingsby Buzzard found himself inducted into four annums ago; it was his beloved Ostium, the consortium of routes and paths and doors, and the only place which would envelop a cartographer in its open arms like it was welcoming a prodigal son home.

Slingsby's flair was maps. When laid out in front of him, curling at the edges like a coy lover, they would reveal their secrets wordlessly, and they were projected in Slingsby's mind like a three-dimensional world which he could drop himself into at any point. How many spans of space and time would it take to navigate between islands and inlets on a map? Slingsby could glimpse at it and tell you. What scale would a cartographer need to use in order to correctly judge the distance between one town and the next? Slingsby could visualise it in an instant.

His particular flair meant that each place Slingsby visited, each country, land and city he navigated, was stored and filed away in his brain. Once he'd swam in the ocean, he knew the bathymetry in order to determine the bottom topography – simply put - he knew how deep the water was and how to map out the surface of the seabed. He could design a cadastral map for every farming town he'd seen, tell you exactly where laylines were and, thanks to an (extremely rarely granted) elective in geomorphology in the Tellus consortium, he'd been able to actually study the valleys at the Ashfjord up in the most northern reaches of the Second, and had become the first person to map out the mountains and lakes there (and was also how he knew when the Ashwater had been diluted by the barkeep).

But for all his flair, Slingsby didn't perform very well under pressure, and Professor Risewell had made it unquestionably clear that if Slingsby underperformed on one more test, then he'd be out of the consortium, flair or none. And so he found himself cramming from a textbook called Ptolemy's Toolbox: Mastering Maps In Minutes, whilst nursing a now cold glass of shimmering Ashwater on Thirsty Thursday before his chums arrived.

It was perhaps because of this, that Singsby failed to notice the arrival of a tall, scrawny-looking young man with a shock of outgrown auburn hair and a rather large, shaggy grey dog. Slingsby heard the jingle of the bell as the bar door opened, and 'tutted' loudly to himself when the accompanying flash of cold autumn air flipped at Ptolemy's pages, but he didn't look up. In fact, he didn't raise his eyes until he heard the loud 'heehaww' laugh of his friend Heckton Piebald. He was a large, squat teenage boy, brilliant in his flair of Plane mapping but often lacking in social graces. His laughter came now from squeezing his round middle between a chair and a table and knocking over the drinks of some disgruntled patrons.

'Awfully sorry, haaaw,' he honked. 'Didn't see you there! Bit of a squeeze, haaaw!'

Slingsby smiled an affectionate smile and only then noticed the boy and the dog sat at the bar. The lad was not dressed in the attire of the Ardere nor wearing the tie colours or tiepin of a consortium, so Slingsby looked away, forsaking him to the snobbish assumption that he was a townie.

'Heck, ol' buddy, you're late!' Slingsby drawled, leaning back in his chair and pulling over a brown leather wingback for his friend with a flick of his hand.

'Yes,' Heck bustled. 'Rallying the troops. Got distracted by supper. They're on their way – Sonja too!'

'Oh, terrific!' Slingsby said in earnest and lifted his hand to his mouth and breathed hard, testing his breath. 'You ready for Risewell's test?'

He held up his book as though it was the heaviest thing he had ever lifted.

'So, so,' Heck tilted his head. 'Perhaps Sonja could tutor you.'

Heck winked and Slingsby threw the textbook at him half-heartedly and the two laughed.

The barkeep was just delivering a round of drinks when the bell jangled once more and a group of a half dozen or so magicians traipsed in, rosy-cheeked and grinning. The barkeep tried to squash down his greedy smile.

Slingsby and Heck stood and stretched out their arms in welcome to the newly arrived students, each of them wearing long navy frock coats over their respective trousers or skirts and each with an academy tie and tiepin. Each consortium had different colours to demarcate their students and the tiepins were golden sigils adopted by their consortium.

Seemingly of its own volition, the table at which Slingsby and Heck were sat at stretched itself to accommodate its guests and chairs popped up behind perching bottoms.

'Brisk out!' said a young man with black hair growing white in an attractive way at his sideburns.

'Still warm for this side of Yuletide though,' returned another gentleman, older and more weathered around the eyes.

'Oh don't talk of Yuletide yet!' called out a pretty girl with long, curling hair the colour of polished brass. 'It's only just been the Festival of Fire!'

'And a good one at that, Sonja!' Slingsby winked at her and raised his fresh glass of Ashwater. Sonja smiled back shyly.

'Well then, chaps,' said Heck, standing clumsily and shaking the table with his rotund middle, 'I call to order the third meeting of the much acclaimed, the much envied and the very much ignored...Archimedes Bohr Appreciation Society! Huzzah!'

The students all cheered and raised their glasses, clinking them one at a time. Slingsby noticed that the tall boy and his dog had turned to face the group, a look of curiosity on both their faces. (Could a dog have an expression?)

'What's on the agenda tonight?' a small, feline-looking girl asked, with the sticky glisten from her honeygin still on her lip.

'Bohr's inspirations,' Heck belched.

'Thought we did that last time?' the older, weatherworn gentleman asked.

'No that was his influences.'

'Isn't that the same thing?

'Probably,' Heck shrugged, and necked the rest of his Ashwater and summoned another.

'Jolly good then,' Slingsby grinned, liking the sound of the phrase on his lips. 'Bohr's training in healing was likely a HUGE inspiration in his discovery of the pyron particle. I mean, he basically said in Science and Sorcery that once he'd been able to identify the particle inside the cells of his patients, he was able to then find it in everything else.'

'True, but in Venephysics: A Very Vague Guide, he explained that the pyron particle was more to do with his obsession with fire than anything to do with medicine,' said the feline girl.

'Trust an Ignis scholar to bring it back to fire,' Slingsby rolled his eyes, but winked to show his humour.

'Regardless, his identification of the pyron particle meant great things for venephysics, science and magic,' Sonja interjected.

'Certainly,' Slingsby nodded. 'Without his work, we wouldn't have been able to study the source of magic. His extraction technique was arguably the best -'

'Don't be daft, Slingsby, his extraction method is poppycock,' interrupted a dark-eyed Asian magician, wearing the purple colours of the Vene consortium. 'It was a means to an end. Extracting the pyron particle from each atom to analyse pure magic is all well and good, but it hardly allowed him or us to see the true power of it. If we had access to the Flamma Di Magica then –'

'The Sacred Flame? Are you nuts? You'd jeopardise the source of all magic!'

The Vene scholar sneered.

'You Poculum lot don't have the faintest clue about real magic, do you?'

'Thrain...that's enough. A pyre in the pot,' Heck said, folding his arms and his voice surprisingly firm.

The Vene scholar gritted his teeth and ran his butter-soft brown gloves over his forehead, pushing away a curl of oiled dark blonde hair. He rooted in his pockets and counted some change.

'I have eight tans. I'll have to owe you,' he said with a clenched jaw, tossing the coins in a tarnished tankard with a label on it, which read 'It costs nothing to be nice but costs a lot to be a rot.'

'Thrain Maxwell caught short, eh? Haaw,' Heck chortled.

Slingsby chuckled along with his friend, but his attention had now been fully diverted to the auburn-haired, bespectacled boy and his dog. Only upon closer inspection, it wasn't actually a dog, it was a dire wolf. In itself, that wasn't unusual, though they were sadly a rarity to see in the wild these days, especially on the Second, what with most of them choosing to stay on the First, even with the Magical Creature Charter being overturned by Lady Felix, but seeing a dire wolf inside a pub accompanying a boy as though he was a chum was quite unusual.

What's more, they were both listening intently to the conversation that the Appreciation Society were having. The boy, especially, looked rather ravenous for the information they were discussing and Slingsby sensed in him a thirst for more than just that of the Ashwater in his glass.

'But what you fail to see is that the Sacred Flame is just a small part of the source of all magic. It comes from the Third Plane, which is practically made of magic; that's why it's so dangerous.'

'But that's also precisely why we have no way of understanding the Third Plane, Thrain,' said Sonja, who was clearly frustrated. 'In the Caelum constortium, we're trained to look up into the sky, and beyond it, and question what is out there and what we see. You may be trained to look at the pyron particles inside everything, but I'm trained to look at the shapes the particles make when they're all together...and I'm telling you, the Third Plane is something altogether different; natural of course, but different. And what's more, at Caelum, our findings have revealed that it's getting closer –'

'Sonja, shh!' a freckled boy poked her in the ribs. 'You want to give away all our secrets?'

'Oh tosh,' Sonja waved her hand at him. 'Archimedes Bohr didn't concern himself with keeping secrets about his findings and neither should we.'

'That's not necessarily true.'

The chatter amongst the group halted and they all turned to face the thin, tall boy whose green eyes were shining with interest behind his spectacles. At his side, a dire wolf sat, his tongue flopping out of his mouth curiously.

'And you are?' Thrain raised an eyebrow and rested his polished shoe on his knee.

'Nigel,' the boy replied, nodding in greeting. 'Nigel True. This is D.W.' He motioned down to the dire wolf, who dipped his head.

The group regarded them silently, and an awkward frisson surrounded the table as their eyes flitted from Nigel to D.W's jaws.

'Forgive me,' Nigel said lowering his eyes and rubbing the back of his neck, 'I'm a fan of Archimedes Bohr, you see. I couldn't help but overhear your conversation. It was rude of me. My apologies.'

Nigel began to back away and in the pit of his stomach, he felt a deep pull, despite the flush of embarrassment that spread over his cheeks. From behind him, the American boy's voice stopped him.

'Wait, Nigel,' he called and when Nigel turned, he was standing. 'You're very welcome to join us, right folks?'

Slingsby looked around at the table and in spite of some expressions of surprise and faint terror at the wolf's teeth, they were mildly curious.

'Any fan of Archimedes Bohr is a friend of mine,' Sonja smiled kindly. 'You were saying? That Archimedes Bohr kept secrets?'

Nigel panned his eyes around the group and swallowed before pulling up a stool and crouching down on it. D.W shuffled up next to him and tried his best not to look too toothy.

'Well, yes,' Nigel nodded. 'His friend and rival, Dante Leadbeater wrote in his text *In Plane Sight* that Bohr had actually made several notable discoveries about the pyron particle and its origins on the Third Plane but had chosen not to disclose them. Or rather had been ordered not to.'

'Ooh, you mean by the Privy Council perhaps?' the freckle-faced boy asked.

'How fabulous. I do love a conspiracy theory!' Heck said, clapping his hands together greedily.

'Interesting,' Slingsby said, stroking his lower lip. 'I'd never considered Leadbeater as a notable contemporary of Bohr. I found his works to be quite parochial. I shall have to read his text again.'

Nigel nodded enthusiastically.

'You should. It goes into far more detail about the theory of the Third Plane than other books on the subject.'

'You're a Vene scholar then?' Thrain asked, a threatened pinch to his eyes.

'Oh...err no,' Nigel tried to keep the disappointment out of his voice. The dire wolf looked up at him. 'I don't actually attend the Ardere.'

'You'd do well here, I think,' Slingsby said kindly, and Nigel flushed at the compliment.

'Actually, I'm hoping to see the principal at the academy.'

'Principal Ellis? He rarely grants audiences with applicants directly...' Slingsby began but stopped when Nigel shook his head.

'No, it's not about me. It's urgent business.'

'What sort of urgent business?' Heck asked, leaning forward.

His bulk meant that others around him had to lean forward too.

'I can't really say,' Nigel faltered, looking towards D.W who gave him a nudge of encouragement. 'It's sort of an issue of national security.'

'Golly,' Slingsby said, leaning back and resting his head in his knitted hands.

He doubted that this boy, this townie and his wolf could really have such an important issue to convey to the principal, but then, people had always underestimated Slingsby and he would be damned if he underestimated anybody else. Nigel seemed a nice enough fella, though his wolf was a bit shifty, but then who was Slingsby to judge on the choice of one's companions? He looked around fondly at his motley crew of pals, all joined by their shared love for a theologian and scientist who had lived over a hundred years ago. Besides, (and this was really the deciding factor for Slingsby) if this really was an issue of national security and this boy really was someone important, well then; wouldn't that take precedent over a test on Ptolomy?

'Well stick with me, Nigel,' Slingsby grinned and wrapped his arm around Nigel's shoulder. 'I'll get you to the principal. Tonight.'

23

Hooke's Monument

Smokesbane pulled his smock around him and breathed hot air into his hands. His breath was a thin wisp of mist and it dissipated into the crisp, dark London night. Rubbing his hands together, he felt the prickle of smoke and flame within his skin waiting to be commanded but he held it back, let the smoke curl under his fingernails and then reached into his pockets for his gloves and slid his long ashen fingers back into the leather.

It was rare that he ventured to the First Plane. His back door dealings and shadowy deeds required the more claustrophobic setting of UnderLondon, but he had received his instructions. They had been less than artfully delivered. Smokesbane was not afraid of pain, nor was he afraid of death, being that he was the one that delivered it so frequently, but even so, the sharp sting of the wound at his eye made him wince each time he blinked.

'A message,' he'd been told, as the skin under his eye was torn open slowly at the command of his faceless commander's magic. 'Do not fail again.'

Above, the night sky was clear and cloudless, but the moon was a waning sickle in the sky. All was quiet. All was dark. Perfect for a murder.

No. He would not fail this time.

In the shadows of the Monument, Smokesbane waited.

The Romans of ancient Londinium may have been all but forgotten by the magicians and commoners who walked along the cobbled streets of the city, but the ghosts of their once proud and powerful architecture held strong underneath the footfalls of the city dwellers. London, old and shaped by time, hid cities beneath cities.

Linus had once been dismissive of history. Like many magicians, he had simply thought that the past was done and nothing could change it. What could you learn from those who had gone before, when they had been primitive? The Romans had been without magic; commoners. There was little to learn from them. But now, with naked, powerless palms, Linus was beginning to see that history was a sort of powerful magic, too. It paved the way for the future and those who lived in the past could teach you from beyond the grave, for their lessons always had space within the present. What a wonder it is to learn something today that was learned thousands of years ago. True knowledge, Linus realised, was found in humility; in looking at the past, the present and the future as equal sources. He understood now that time travel was possible, only not in the way he had imagined when he was a small boy. No mechanical machines could carry you back into another time. No spell could spirit you back to the past. Time travel was found in learning history, in walking the paths trodden by those who had gone before.

This lesson had never been more valuable to Linus than now, walking along the underground Roman road next to the London wall, a defence built by the Romans thousands of years ago. It led south of the amphitheatre under the Guildhall all the way to the Mithraeum, a ruin of the Roman's temple to Mithras, the god of mysteries.

The Walbrook River flowed alongside the foundations of the London wall, but Linus and Captain Kildare had disembarked from the Skimmer, parted ways with the crew who would meet them on the Second Plane and now they walked the small stone path to the temple. From there, they would emerge into the open air of the Magistry and make the short walk to the Monument, to try and decipher the rest of Hooke's message.

'What do you think it means?' Linus asked, gazing down at the parchment from the bottle. ''Counte ye the footsteppes in to fyre'?'

Captain Kildare shrugged.

'I'm more concerned with the 'funeral pyre' bit,' she mumbled.

Linus smiled and looked back at the parchment. At his side, the little flagon of Fleetwater glugged as a reminder of its presence.

'The Fleetwater has something to do with that, I think,' he said.

Captain Kildare turned and looked at him, then down at the little bottle.

'Has a commoner...a mortal ever tried to access the Second?' she asked.

Linus thought for a moment, scanning his memories of the texts and tomes he had read in his schooling at the Citadel.

'Not that I recall. It's impossible. Commoners have no magic inside them, so they are unable to access another world that is made entirely of magic. The source of magic is basically fire, you know that, right?'

"Of course," the captain nodded.

All magicians were taught this basic introduction to venephysics. You didn't need to be a Vene scholar to know that everything had a particle of fire inside it that only magicians could see and command.

'Well, if you get a lot of that fire together in one place, it can burn.'

'That's why we wear gloves, laddie,' Captain nodded.

'Yes, but have you ever wondered what would happen if you gathered together millions of particles of magic? What it could do if targeted at a person?' Linus mumbled the question.

Captain Kildare paused for a moment and ran her bottom teeth over her top lip.

'You're talking about your father's machine,' she said finally.

'Using magic that powerful was enough to kill magicians. I saw it happen. I have no doubt it killed commoners just as, if not more, easily.'

'Corbin Godspell was using the Sacred Flame though, Linus,' Captain Kildare said gently. 'I read the Truth Papers.'

'Yes, he was. But the Flame of Magic comes from the Third Plane, where power filters down to the Second Plane beneath it and then into the First. If magic can kill commoners here, on the First, where the power is at its weakest, imagine what it could do on the Second when it's closer to its origin. I don't understand why Robert Hooke would have wanted to build a back door to the Second Plane – a hatch leading to a world that would kill them.'

Captain Kildare nodded in understanding and looked at Linus in concern.

'Then...if it's impossible for a commoner to access the Second and it'd kill them even if they did, how are you going to do it?'

Linus stroked the Fleetwater.

'I think that's why Black Mary gave me this. Fleetwater cures all.'

Captain Kildare stopped her long strides and rested a hand on Linus' shoulder.

'Linus...' she began, and tried to stop the pity from invading her eyes.

She knew Linus could not bear to see it. Sure enough, he looked away angrily.

'Linus, Fleetwater heals wounds and stops pain. I don't think it can restore magic to those who have been robbed of it.'

'Then why would the river give it to me?' Linus snapped, pulling his shoulder out of Captain Kildare's grip.

'You told me that Black Mary said she was brought to life by magic, yes? Then, if the rivers of London are filled with magic, by drinking water from the Fleet, a river historically known for its healing, then surely that will put magic inside you, for a time too. So if a commoner drank water from the river, technically, they too would have magic, albeit temporarily.'

'Yes, that makes sense,' Linus nodded. 'But if that's true, any old riverwater would do. Black Mary specifically gave me Fleetwater and she said that the path would be full of pain and suffering.'

'You think she meant that literally?' Captain Kildare asked, glancing at him.

Linus shrugged the question away.

'This can't be for naught,' he said thickly. 'The curse, Paris' death...There must be some greater reason for it all.'

'I wouldn't have taken you for a fatalist, lad,' Captain Kildare smiled.

Linus chuckled despite himself.

'I'm not. But I have to believe that I'm doing the right thing.'

'Everyone does, laddie,' Captain Kildare said softly. 'Even the most evil amongst us can justify their actions when they use faith as an excuse.'

'Do you think I'm doing the right thing?' Linus asked, with a nervous glance towards Kildare.

'I guess we'll find out,' she shrugged. 'Now stop your dwelling. We're here.'

They had reached a small, curved entrance in the wall. It was so small and slight that Linus would have missed it and mistaken it for a crumbling crack had the captain not pointed it out. He peered in warily, but the gloom denied him. Behind, the captain conjured an orb of pale blue light and briskly pulled Linus aside. Crouching down and pressing herself against the wall sideways, she crept in through the entrance and Linus followed. Inside was a very narrow pathway with a low, uneven ceiling. Linus' thighs began to burn as he squatted down and shuffled along beside the captain and just as his legs began to shake, they stepped out into a long, shadowed chamber that stank of stale air and damp musk. Lifting up the orb light, Captain Kildare looked over her shoulder and grinned.

The Mithraeum was a ruin, but it held a majestic mystery, even now, thousands of years since its use as a temple.

The crumbled foundations of a wall stretched down through the inside of the chamber, with another, shallower line of stones paving the inner walls of the temple.

'Woah,' Linus said, spinning around to take in the height of the ceiling and the length of the temple.

'I know,' the captain nodded. 'It was a museum for a while.' She nodded towards a promenade that had been built around the edges of the temple.

They had entered through what seemed to be a hidden door in the northwest corner of the temple. Now that they'd stepped out of it, it looked no larger than a drain.

'An escape tunnel,' Captain Kildare explained. 'I think. I guess whatever they were doing down here wasn't popular! Come on, we're nearly at street level.'

Linus nodded and took one last look around. Excitement was bubbling in his belly. He hadn't been streetside in months and he was strangely nervous to see it again, especially this part of London which had been his home.

He climbed up the old museum steps, sticky with dust and arrived in a grey tiled foyer which glowed silver in the shafts of moonlight that shone down from the night sky.

They had timed it right; it was just shy of three in the morning and the streets would be almost deserted, although London was London and there were always some stragglers around, staggering from one bawdy house to another, drenched in Ashwater and mead. But if they were careful, they'd remain inconspicuous.

Linus was sure that her sister had people out looking for him. His disappearance had been widely reported in the newspapers which he'd managed to fish out of the sewer sludge.

The Daily Moon had branded him "Lost Linus". The Monocle had announced that "Felix Godspell Orders Search Committee To Find Lost Brother". Linus had balked at seeing her name like that. He'd wondered if she'd claimed the name Godspell now or if she still saw herself as a Spark. It was unfair of him to hope that she did; Spark was the name given to children who didn't have a family name of their own. When she'd discovered who she really was, it was her right to claim the name Godspell. But secretly, Linus hoped that she wouldn't. He wanted just one thing to cling to that was his and his alone.

'Come on lad,' Captain Kildare hissed at him.

She was near the bound double doors of the entrance. They'd been sealed to the museum long ago. It was doubtful that anybody had ever set foot through the museum doors in sixteen years, when Corbin Godspell had ordered the closure of all commoner museums and galleries. The buildings were left to moulder and rot, and the doors turned into hatches to transport magicians from one location to another in a snap. Outside, on the street, a magician would just have to open one of the double doors and they'd enter the hatchway and come out somewhere different.

'I can't use the hatches, Captain,' Linus shrugged.

'No, I need you to open the door,' she replied.

'What?'

Captain Kildare rubbed her temples with her fingers and then grabbed the handles of the double doors and pushed them open. Inside was the pitch-black nothingness of the midst between hatches.

"If I open it, it's a hatch, but if you open it...'

'It's just a door!' Linus finished understanding.

Maybe being a commoner could have its uses after all.

'Exactly," Captain Kildare nodded as though he'd stated something very obvious.

She pointed sharply at a door, her expression telling him very clearly to get on with it.

Linus stepped forwards and swallowed. The nerves in his stomach were fluttering in his chest now. He pushed at the door, gently at first but then harder once he realised it was sticky with age.

With a creak, the doors opened heavily into the moonlit streets of London.

A gush of icy winter air billowed into their faces and for a moment they shrank back. Even in the night, with a shining sliver of waning moon, the light was brighter than any Linus had seen in a long time. The streets were illuminated by the glow of blue orbs that hovered ten feet off the ground. Glowing bulbs flickered over the bridges connecting buildings high above and there was a gentle crackle and shush of firelight from inside the orbs and bulbs. Overhead, there was the occasional caw-caw of ravens, circling over the streets away from their Tower of London nests in search of a tasty night-time morsel, and there was the gentle sigh of the Thames nearby, lapping against the oozy mud of the shoreline.

The sound of London.

Linus closed his eyes and breathed. The air was thin and cold, making him cough for a moment. It smelled clean, crisp with a hint of saltiness from the river and there was the familiar cinnamon sweetness from the countless teashops that stained the air after their day's trade.

Home.

'Linus,' Captain Kildare nudged him gently. 'We shouldn't linger.'

He opened his eyes and blinked quickly to clear the blurriness, and he wiped the back of his wrist against them.

'Yep,' he said hoarsely.

He looked back and forth along the street. They were just around the corner from Canon Street. If they followed it to Pudding Lane, it'd take them straight to the Monument. Linus sniffed and began walking, no longer needing the captain to lead the way. He knew these streets well. His childhood had been spent with nannies and governesses and tutors walking him up and down the streets of London, taking him in and out of hatches as they went to tailor's shops or tea rooms or occasionally, if he was lucky, to a toffee shop for a sneaky bag of cinder toffee before supper! He'd paraded these streets with his father and Shylock Larkin, to bestow favours on business owners, to celebrate festivals and holidays and occasionally, the mourn a public loss; a well-known celebrity or a member of the Magistry perhaps.

He knew that the further you went down Canon Street on to Eastcheap, the more run down and decrepit the buildings became, how snotlings had taken up residence in the old churches and office blocks. Few magicians lived near the Tower of London. Who would want to?

Linus paced quickly and comfortably, his feet remembering the cobbled roads well. Had his sister walked these streets? Had she paraded them the way he once had? Out in the cold

November air, he couldn't seem to stop thinking of her. It seemed like every breath he took brought her closer to him. His twin. The sister he never knew. He tried to reach out to her then, to grope for an invisible rope that might tether them, but he felt nothing. He trusted her, yes but perhaps that was foolish. She'd saved his life but then, she hadn't known that using furyfire magic could shield him from the Sacred Flame's destruction. Maybe she'd just got lucky.

Captain Kildare's questions burned holes in his trust. How well did he really know his sister? Could she be looking for him, not to bring him back but to kill him? What if Smokesbane really had been sent by her?

He shook his head. There was no way of knowing. Linus tried to push his sister out of his thoughts because, frankly, he had more important things to think about.

Their main priority was finding William Lilly's diary at the Ardere. He owed it to Paris to find it, so that his secret would not die with him. There was something in that diary that Paris had wanted Linus to know – something he'd died trying to reveal. And then, there was finding Hestia Windwood, whoever she was, to see if she knew anything about the true Firelighter.

It was like a wild goose chase, flitting around from one location to another, finding clues, revealing secrets. When he had a chance to really think about it all, it all seemed so improbable, yet here he was.

The Monument was close now, hidden by the buildings behind Pudding Lane. Just a few more steps and they'd be there, at the resting place of his parents.

With leaden legs, Linus marched onwards into a secluded square, feeling Captain Kildare's presence behind him like a balm.

The Monument rose like a sword into the dark sky in front of him, impossibly tall and bulkier than he'd remembered. The towering column stood on a stone plinth, cuboid in shape with carved reliefs and words engraved into every side. Linus stopped and looked up, his head tilting back dizzyingly.

There it was; the golden urn, wreathed in delicate copper flames, a symbol for the commoners of the Great Fire Of London of 1666 which razed London to the ground. But for Linus and his sister, the urn held a greater meaning.

'It smells like magic here,' Captain Kildare mused, as she wandered around the plinth. She leaned in closer, to one of the panels where there was a curious sculpture of a girl, fallen upon the ground whilst an aged man and a woman helped her to rise. Captain Kildare sniffed it.

'Powerful magic,' she continued.

Linus couldn't smell it, but he knew that magic had a memory. He wondered if the captain could scent her sister's presence. It had been here where she had been captured by the COPPs Mortimer and Murphy; the same COPPs whose murders he had witnessed only days later. He wondered where they had been buried.

'Linus,' Captain Kildare said sharply. 'Look.' She had moved round to the north panel and was pointing at an inscription.

'Read it, lad,' she ordered eagerly.

Linus squinted at the old text. It was written with different spelling and hardly any punctuation, but he translated it as best he could.

'Ok it says: "In the year 1666, at a distance eastward from this place of 202 feet, which is the height of this...column" I think it says, "a fire broke out in the dead of night which, the wind blowing devoured even distant buildings and rushed devastating through every quarter with astonishing swiftness and noise". Then it goes on to list how many buildings it destroyed.' He paused for a moment and shook his head gently. 'Paris was right. This was no ordinary fire. It was the Great Spark – the fire which brought magic into the First Plane. The legends and stories are true, and the proof has been here all along, hidden in plain view.'

'That's often the best place to hide, lad. There's this bit too,' Captain Kildare pointed to a smaller, more modern white stone plaque, beneath the engraved panels on the plinth.

Linus ran his eyes over it quickly. 'It's strange. Neither of the inscriptions mention Hooke at all. Just Wren. I guess that means he was the Firelighter, like Black Mary said. In the past, Firelighters have been secretive and private, hidden away from the commoners until Everard – my real father – revealed magicians to the world in the Revelation. I think it's all true, Captain, everything Black Mary said.'

Captain Kildare nodded briefly, her expression carefully blank.

She waited until Linus was ready to continue, which he did with a shaky sigh.

'This one says: "This Monument designed by Sir Christopher Wren was built to commemorate the Great Fire of London 1666 ...The Monument is 202 feet in height, being equal to the distance Westward from the Bakehouse on Pudding Lane where the fire broke out-"'

'That's it!' the captain cried out, clicking the gloved fingers. 'That's what the clue means!'

Linus looked at her, confused and reached into his pocket for the parchment which had been rolled inside the bottle and read it again.

"Beneathe a Monumental view of London
Lays a hatch in dark abandonne
Counte ye the footsteps in to fyre
And burn upon a funeral pyre."

'I don't understand,' he frowned.

'Thomas Farynor opened the hatch that started the fire on Pudding Lane, 202 feet away,' Captain Kildare's eyes shone excitedly.

'Count the footsteps in to fire...' Linus said quietly, the solution dawning on him. '202 feet is the footsteps we have to count to get to the hatch!'

The captain nodded in agreement.

'Find the door!' Linus ordered her. 'There'll be a door somewhere that Corbin sealed up. The parchment says we have to go 'beneathe' the Monument, so we have to get inside and go down, somehow.'

The pair began to clamber around the stone plinth, their hands groping against the stone. As they did, the man in the shadows grinned slowly. They were exactly where he wanted them. Out in the open. No easy escape. Distracted.

He would not fail this time.

Taking his time, as though the lifting of his fingers would create a commotion of noise, Smokesbane let the toxic, black smoke curl out of his hands. It unfurled around him, blending with the darkness of the shadows and soon it began to rise, billowing around him and, like a timid animal growing more daring, began to stretch outwards into the square.

'Gently,' he commanded the smoke and it slowed, thinned out so that it was a mere sooty mist shadowing the light of the moon.

The boy and the pirate had not noticed yet. They were occupied; too busy looking for something to worry about the tendrils of smoke that spiralled towards them like snakes along the ground. It was getting close now. Any moment, the smoke would stroke them, and they would know. He would taste their pain. Their screams would merge with the raven-black thickness of the smoke he conjured.

Just a few... more...inches....

He felt the dagger pierce his chest before he saw it. Smokesbane staggered back against the black wall and lifted his hand to the hilt of the blade lodged in his heart. He raised his eyebrows in surprise. Looking up, he saw the man who had delivered his death stepping silently towards him. Tall. Thin. A rakish man, in a cloak the hue of nightshade now standing only inches away, the smoke circling around him as though he were immune to it.

'Sigbert Goodnight,' the man said.

He had a grey handlebar moustache which twitched as he talked. 'At your service.' He bowed his head, reached for the dagger and pulled it out of Smokesbane's heart swiftly.

The Shadow fell to his knees.

So this is what it felt like.

A slow ebb. A chill infecting every limb.

Peaceful.

Painful.

Blood bubbled at his lips as he began to laugh.

Sigbert Goodnight stepped away from him, his face unsure.

Smokesbane felt the life leave him but he would not die yet, not until he had done his job. With a final surge, he pushed his power out of him, from his hands, his mouth and from the gouge in his heart. Soot and ash poured out of him, thickening the smoke, giving it haste and he died laughing.

Sigbert Goodnight watched the smoke quicken as it slithered towards the boy and the captain.

'Linus!' he called out, scrambling towards them.

His vision was obscured by the smoke. Though it didn't seem to be harming him, it blocked his eyes and throat and he coughed, struggling to shout. Tripping, he clambered along the ground, reaching for the velvet pouch tied to his belt.

Linus turned and jumped back, crying out to Captain Kildare. A thick fog of smoke was inching closer to them and in the midst of it was a thin man clumsily crawling through it, yet the poison smoke had no effect on him. Linus narrowed his eyes, saw the waxed handlebar moustache that was joltingly familiar.

'You,' Linus breathed, in shock.

Sigbert Goodnight. One of his sister's men. He'd delivered food to Linus when he was recovering from the machine, before Linus had run away.

'You did this?' His voice was barely audible, and he was frozen on the spot, muddling his way through his thoughts.

Goodnight was the Shadow?

'Linus, here!' called the captain, reaching for the boy's hand and wrenching him away from the tendrils of smoke that threatened him. 'The door!'

She blasted the faint outlines of a sealed door with a shot of fire from her hands and the slabs of stone blew apart. Inside there was an old ticket office, which led to a spiralling staircase that climbed up to the top balcony. The captain ignored the dusty cobwebs hanging down and began stamping her foot on the ground to find a trapdoor.

'So help me….boy, if you don't start doing something I'll kill you myself!' she screamed at Linus, causing him to flinch.

The smoke was circling around the Monument now and the wet, crackling wheeze of Sigbert Goodnight was getting closer. Linus hurried, stamping down his boots trying to find a part of the floor that was weak or hollow.

'Here, Captain!' he said, when his foot hit a thin part of wood.

Crouching down, he ran his fingers along the cracks of the floorboard and saw small metal hinges near the edge of the wall. They were obscured by the plasterwork and sticky with dust. Captain Kildare shoved Linus out of the way and blasted a force of power at the wood, splintering it into hundreds of sharp shards. Flicking her wrist, she conjured a small ball of light and held it down.

There was another staircase inside, spiralling downwards into nothing but blackness.

'Woah,' Linus whispered, but there was no time for awe or wonderment; Sigbert Goodnight was at the door, struggling to pull himself up.

'Wait!' he cried out hoarsely, reaching for them.

Smoke clouded around him, entering the door but it did not burn or blister his skin the way it had done to Paris.

'Down, now!' said the captain, starting to descend the staircase. 'Count the steps. 202 remember?'

Linus didn't need telling twice. The spluttering man was reaching for Linus desperately, the noxious fog beginning to fill up the chamber. He slipped down through the trap door hole just as a curl of smoke reached out to stroke him.

He'd counted only three steps when he felt a leather clad hand grab his. Sigbert Goodnight was weak now and fading fast, but he held firm to the boy.

'Get off me!' Linus spat. 'You murderer! You traitor!'

For a moment, Goodnight looked confused but then he coughed, red-flecked phlegm bubbling out of his mouth.

'Your sister....sent...me,' he managed to croak out.

Linus face fell, his mouth dropping open.

His sister had sent this man. This man, this Shadow...then it was just as the captain had warned him.

Felix wanted him dead.

'Take...this,' Sigbert Goodnight choked. He was holding out a velvet pouch. 'Please...'

Above the man's head, the smoke was circling, beginning to spiral down through the trap door.

Linus grabbed at the velvet bag, feeling the captain tugging him down urgently just as Sigbert Goodnight let go of his wrist.

The instant he did, Goodnight howled in pain as the smoke burned his skin, ripped at his flesh and stripped it from his bones. In an instant, he was dead, his head and arms hanging down into the trap door.

'Move!' the captain shouted, and Linus' legs began moving, racing down the steps, his mind counting the numbers even though he couldn't shake the image of Goodnight's dying eyes out of his mind.

The smoke was chasing them, moving faster in the confined spiralling staircase. When Linus looked up behind him, he could see straight through the centre of the staircase, all the way to the top of the Monument. There was a pinprick of moonlight shining through.

'It's a telescope,' he murmured, but either Captain Kildare didn't hear him, or she didn't care.

'200, 201, 202. Here. Linus it's here!' she said, turning to him.

Linus was only a step behind her, and he almost stumbled straight into her back.

On the wall, next to the 202nd step there was a door. It was small, ancient and thin with rot, but sure enough, it was a door.

'...a door in dark abandonne..' Linus recited.

'It's time, lad. We have to go through it now.'

The captain looked up through the gap in the middle of the staircase. The smoke was getting closer. Linus reached down for the bottle of Fleetwater, hindered by the velvet bag in his hand.

Curious but impatient, he opened it and looked inside.

'It's just a lump of coal,' he said in surprise. He looked at Captain Kildare.

'I don't care if it's the bloody giant pearl of Persia. DRINK THE FLEETWATER!'

Shoving the pouch in his pocket, Linus unstoppered the bottle of Fleetwater. Without a chance to think, he downed it in one gulp.

The smoke was behind them now and it was descending down the centre of the staircase, dripping lower like black paint. There was no way forward or backwards.

Captain Kildare took a deep breath and grabbed Linus' hand.

'Here goes nothing.'

She opened the hatch and they stepped into the midst.

24

Pieces into Place

Only a few minutes away, inside the Citadel and completely unaware of the commotion taking place at the Monument, Aubrey Dovepeace was pacing inside the parlour. She rarely slept, though she tried for Liberty's sake. Her wife worried constantly; for her, for Felix, for Linus, for Sigbert and now for Nigel. After her imprisonment in the tower, after she and Sigbert had attacked Godspell all those months ago, Liberty had never been the same. She was nervous and jumpy, and Aubrey tried not to burden her any further. But Aubrey, too, was worried and her concerns spoke to her more loudly in the dark silence of the night.

During the day, Aubrey was busy. She had meetings with the Magistry, press conferences, consultations with the security services who were out looking for Felix and Linus, and now Nigel who had inexplicably disappeared. Vessania had been useless, simply repeating in that awful piercing voice that Nigel had gone on a 'little holiday'. That the dire wolf had gone with him, was a little comfort to her; D.W, at least, was faithful and loyal and would not let harm come to Nigel. Besides, he was a grown man, now. If he wanted to leave, then so be it. If he had gone to find Felix by himself, then she could not command him to stay. Aubrey knew that she had little power to command anyone, no matter how intimidating she appeared to be. At the press conferences, she had told them that Lady Felix was ill after the excitement of the Festival of Fire but soon, the Monocle had printed an article that questioned this and then soon, they were all in on it. The Daily Moon, a rag really, had printed that Felix was missing or that she had run away, renouncing her titles and leaving the Magistry without a leader. Aubrey had snorted in ridicule during the press conference. When Tabitha Bloyd from the Town Cryer had asked her who was really in charge, now, Aubrey had replied, again, with emphasis, that Lady Felix was still their Firelighter and their Grand

Vizier and was, in fact, weak and feverish but making a slow recovery. She would make a statement soon.

Lies. All lies. Aubrey Dovepeace, who had always prided herself on absolute honesty was lying to the people of the country, of the world – all of whom had their eyes fixed on the Citadel.

'Goddamn you, Alchemus,' Aubrey breathed out, pinching the bridge of her nose with scarlet leather fingers. 'Godamn you for dying and leaving me here to handle this.'

She slumped down onto the sofa and cupped her face. How many times had she sat in this room, trying to put herself in Felix's shoes, trying to think about where she would go, what she would do? But she was very, very different to Felix – it was why they worked so well together. Felix led with her heart and her passion and the fire that would make her – *was* making her - a great Firelighter. Aubrey was, however, logical and practical and she could not understand why Felix would have run away from her friends and the people who loved her deeply, rather than talking to them. Felix had been making a difference. It was slow and frustrating but change often is when it is changing for the better. Change for worse always happens swiftly because it occurs without consultation, without diplomacy and democracy. Change for good means winning people over gently, with action rather than words, guiding them but also, respecting their right to disagree. Felix wanted too much so quickly, and she was also very young and had already faced so much.

'What would you do, Alchemus?' she asked aloud.

She expected no response but still, it was a ritual she performed most evenings. Alchemus J. Fiddle had been a flawed and secretive man, but he had still managed to deliver Felix to her rightful place as Firelighter. He had still helped to overthrow a dictator. Somehow, a lying librarian, and a fugitive at that, had made everything right. But now it was all wrong again and Aubrey was the one left to fix everything. But she couldn't. Aubrey was not a tearful person. Her initial response to stress was always to find a solution and to work hard until one manifested itself. But lately, Aubrey felt the unfamiliar tightening of her throat and the sting of salt behind her spectacles. She was about to succumb to tears when an eager knocking at the door made her flinch.

'Yes?'

Aubrey stood quickly when Thaddeus burst through the door with a look of excitement on his face.

'What is it? Have you found her?'

Thaddeus shook her head.

'No. But we have something.'

Aubrey swallowed down her disappointment but encouraged Thaddeus to continue. He was tired and careworn, with sprigs of grey in his black hair that had not been there months before.

'As you know, we've been monitoring the hatchway for any unusual activity. Well something came up. A hatch was opened at the Mithraeum only a few hours ago.'

Thaddeus pulled out a folded piece of parchment from his inner coat pocket then shrugged off the leather coat, chucking it over an armchair. He unfolded it and spread it over the low table in front of the sofa. Aubrey peered down at it. It was a map, similar to the ones Thaddeus had shown her before, but it was unusual. Instead of showing buildings and roads, this one showed routes in all different colours that zigzagged and crossed over and spiralled. It looked like an old London Underground map but with far more colours and lines.

Thaddeus pointed down to a magenta-coloured dot. When he touched it, the route immediately lit up like it was highlighted in three-dimensional colour.

'This is the Mithraeum hatch.'

Aubrey looked down and traced her finger along the magenta route.

'It leads to Kensington?'

'Yes,' Thaddeus nodded. 'It does, but it's a busy hatch. That's not what was flagged up.'

'What then?'

'The hatch was opened from inside the Mithraeum, not outside on the street like it usually is.'

'Inside?' Aubrey thought for a moment. 'But the Mithraeum is one of the old museums. The door is still sealed – we haven't opened the museums in that part of the city yet. How can someone be inside?'

Thaddeus sat down on the sofa and Aubrey joined him.

'That was exactly what I thought. So I did some digging. The Mithraeum is an old Roman ruin of a temple, so I went through the old documents Godspell kept locked away in the basements and found the plan for the museum. There's a tunnel – an old escape tunnel – that leads to the sewers.'

'The sewers?'

'Yes.'

'So you think someone from Underlondon has come up and opened the hatch from inside the museum? Have you sent people to Kensington to scout around? Do you think it could be Felix, or Linus?'

'Wait, Aubrey, wait,' Thaddeus held up his hands. 'The hatch was opened but it wasn't used.'

'What?'

'Someone opened the hatch inside the Mithraeum Museum, but they didn't use it. Nobody came out of the adjoining hatch – and nobody is lost in the midst; I sent someone to check.'

Aubrey looked confused and thought through what Thaddeus was saying.

'So...what's going on then? Do you think someone is inside the museum?'

Thaddeus smiled.

'I thought that too. I went and checked myself. Took a team of hatchers and thought we'd have to unseal the door, and do you know what I found when I got there?'

'What?'

'The door was already unsealed.'

'How can that be? Are you sure it was definitely sealed?'

'Yes. The hatch was successfully used 378 times yesterday. If it had been unsealed, the door would simply just open to the museum entrance.'

'Who could have unsealed it then? I'm under the impression that only trained hatchers can unseal a hatch?'

'Yep. Magicians can't unseal hatches – unless they're specialist Ostium scholars like myself, with a licensed permission, they can fire magic at it all they want and they still won't unseal it. It was all designed by old Corbin himself, but there was one thing he overlooked...same way he always did.'

Aubrey understood now and she nodded.

'The commoners.'

'Spot on. To a commoner, a hatch is just a door and sealing a door to magicians doesn't seal a door for commoners. They have more simple methods for sealing doors – keys and locks and as you can probably predict, Godspell didn't bother locking doors with primitive things like keys.'

'So what you're saying is that somehow, a commoner has come up from the sewers of Underlondon?'

'Yes boss. But I have a theory. This commoner has come up with a magician who has tried to open the door inside the museum and found that it's a hatch – which the commoner can't use. So the commoner has simply opened the door to streetside, thus unsealing the hatch accidentally. Now who do we know that is a commoner, travelling with a magician?'

'You're thinking Linus and Paris?'

'I tell you, you're reading my mind,' Thaddeus grinned.

'Excellent work, Thad! This is wonderful! We need to send out a team of COPPs to the area and look for them.'

'I already have, Aubrey.'

'Well done. Well done!' Aubrey grabbed Thaddeus' hands in hers and squeezed them, but Thaddeus' face was not as joyful as her own.

'This is where I have some bad news,' he said, clearing his throat.

Aubrey's grip on his hands loosened.

'Go on. Just say it straight.'

'My team found two bodies at the Monument. No – it's not Linus, or Paris for that matter. The first body was a Shadow – he'd been stabbed through the heart. The second body we have been unable to identify because...well. The Shadow's smoke has done its work.'

Aubrey swallowed and nodded, trying not to imagine it.

'Aubrey...the blade that killed the Shadow was Sigbert Goodnight's. We think the body we can't identify is...well we think it might be Sigbert.'

'No,' breathed Aubrey and she clamped her hands over her mouth.

Her first thought was for her wife. Liberty and Sigbert had been colleagues and friends and they had shared horrors together in the Tower of London. This would destroy what was left of Liberty.

'There's more,' Thaddeus said softly, with an apology in his eyes. 'Sigbert's body was found inside the Monument, halfway down a hidden staircase underneath it. The stairs are hundreds of years old, it seems, but I have people working on dating them right now. There's a laboratory at the bottom of the basement which hasn't been disturbed for centuries, too. The whole Monument appears to be a telescope of some sort. If you stand at the bottom, you can peer upwards and there are contraptions that allow you to see, sort of, into the sky and beyond it. And there's a hatch, but it's a hatch I've never seen before. Definitely illegal and hasn't been used for a very long time, but one that has been made with very powerful magic.'

'Where does it lead?' Aubrey asked.

'I haven't tested it – it's too dangerous. But when I touched the brick, I saw the route. It's blurry and a hardly a safe path, though impressive really when you think about it because I don't know of anyone who has actually done it before and –'

'Thaddeus. Where does the secret hatch lead?'

'To the Second Plane.'

'But that's impossible. Hatches can't lead between planes.'

'I mean, technically it's not impossible, though as I say, I've never known anyone to do it, but that's not to say that it can't actually be done, if you had a good enough understanding of venephysics and routing, and the guts to even dare to do it. You'd be mixing densities of magic, which is dangerous stuff, because obviously the magic is denser on the Second than here. But also, why would you even need a hatch to the Second when we have spectoccules?'

'No, I don't mean that. Listen, if we think that Linus is the commoner who unsealed the door at the Mithraeum, and it was definitely Sigbert Goodnight's body then there is a rather obvious series of events here. Sigbert Goodnight was sent by Felix to find Linus...and he did, and he died protecting him from the Shadow. Which means that Linus must have gone through the hatch.'

'Ah. Yes. I see now. Impossible. Linus doesn't have any magic. How could he have used a hatch in the first place, let alone use it to get to the Second Plane?'

Aubrey inhaled deeply, her teeth busying her bottom lip.

'Exactly. We must find out. Thaddeus, we have to go through that hatch, no matter how dangerous it is.'

Thaddeus blinked the reservation from his eyes and nodded.

'I'll get it ready.'

'Good.' Aubrey stood up. She felt smaller, crushed under a heavy weight. 'But first, I must tell my wife that she has lost another friend tonight.'

Above the fireplace, the clock struck five a.m.

25

Trust

Felix no longer dreamed. Or if she did, she didn't remember them when she woke up. For someone who had been plagued with dreams of locked doors, and the secrets and monsters they hid behind them, this was something of a relief. Her sleep was now peaceful; a deep, empty sea of peace that left her rested and alert when she opened her eyes.

The only problem was actually falling asleep. Whenever Felix lay down her head, her mind would zip around, firing questions at her as though they had been gagged all day, and only in the quiet of the night could they surge into her brain.

She had taken sleeping draughts carefully prepared by Melantha, and Lillith had given her crystals that glowed with captured moonlight which were supposed to lure you into slumber, but Felix remained immune, her burning curiosity, which had always led her into trouble, blazing the moment the lights were dimmed.

How had they survived for so long without discovery?

How was Lillith trying to find her brother?

What had she meant when she said Paris Lovelock was a liar? Felix had no trust of the man either, but Lillith had spoken with such hatred, the rage pulsing from her like heat. Why was that? Had something happened between them?

Why had Lillith pushed Felix out of her mind at the Drowning?

Where were all the men?

These questions, and what felt like hundreds more performed their nightly dance for Felix, until she passed out from sheer frustrated exhaustion.

One morning, she woke to find Aradia's soft, feathery feet tickling at her nose. Felix shifted, startled for a moment, before yawning and holding out her hand for Aradia to scamper onto her palm. She was a gentle weight.

'Hey,' Felix nodded to the spider.

Aradia twitched her head a little and lifted up her two front legs, as though waving. Felix smiled.

'She wants me, huh?" Felix asked blearily, rubbing her eyes with her free hand.

Aradia blinked her little pink eyes and Felix sighed.

'Lead the way.'

She placed Aradia down on the floor and watched the spider begin to scuttle out of the chamber.

'Who'd have thought I'd be talking to a spider?' she said to herself, as she pulled her nightdress over her head and tried to tame her mass of dark hair. Defeated, she twisted it up into a bun and tucked it into itself. She had gotten used to not having a mirror, but she was annoyed at the lack of brushes and hair ties in this place. The Drow, with their bald heads, didn't need either of them of course.

Felix followed Aradia to Lillith's quarters. She had a colossal cavern all to herself, carved into the rock and elevated above all the other caves, and just above the white willow tree house that had become Felix's room. Sometimes, when she couldn't sleep, Felix wondered if her sleeplessness was because she was in such close proximity to Lillith; close enough that the woman would just have to lean over her balcony and look down through the pale leaves of the tree to see into Felix's bed.

Aradia scuffled through the carved archway that led into Lillith's chamber. The Drow, it seemed, had no use for doors. Their openness and intimacy with one another meant that there were no secrets. It was both touching and annoying to Felix, who valued her privacy far more than she had ever realised.

'Come, sister Felix,' Lillith's melodious voice called from inside.

Felix swallowed, and tried to ignore the strange iciness that spread over her fingers and toes whenever she was near Lillith.

Letting go of the breath she was holding, Felix walked inside and smiled warmly.

Her smile froze when she saw Lillith reclining in her bed, stroking the bald head of a sleeping man.

'Err…' Felix began, averting her gaze and looking anywhere but at the bed, horrified that she should walk in on what was clearly an intimate moment. 'I'll come back.'

'Nonsense!' Lillith laughed as Felix spun around, clumsily knocking over a bowl of water. Felix halted and turned around slowly, like a toy ballerina that needed winding up.

'You're obviously, err, busy,' Felix muttered, with a flush spreading over her cheeks.

Lillith looked down at the sleeping male next to her. He was covered by the blanket, as was Lillith but Felix was still uncomfortable. Yet beneath her discomfort, she was curious to see a male Drow. His face and shoulders and bald scalp were the only things visible to her and she could see that he lacked the spiral markings that the females shared.

Lillith saw her looking and she followed her gaze, running a long, delicate finger over the curve of the man's head.

'Our men do not share our special power,' she explained, emitting pity in waves. 'As with the white widows, the males of the species are weaker. Much like your brother, Linus, no?'

Felix's mouth was filling with water, and she swallowed noisily and nodded.

'Have you found him yet?' she whispered.

'Alas, sister,' Lillith answered, her voice sounding like she was inches away from tears. 'Not yet. But we are close.'

'How? How are you close?' Felix asked, braver now.

Her eyes puckered and she felt her spirals heating beneath her skin. The burst of life and energy alarmed her, and she cleared her throat. Lillith observed her blankly.

'You still do not trust," she said, disappointed.

'I do!' Felix replied, stepping forward but stopping as she saw the man in the bed shifting in his sleep.

Abashed, she stepped back, looking down at her cold fingers.

She felt rather than saw Lillith's smile.

'Does this embarrass you, sister?' Lillith asked, making a gesture to the bed and the sleeping man.

Felix grimaced and flicked her eyes up towards the bed.

'No,' she mumbled unconvincingly.

'It is a natural thing; natural as anything. A way of showing love.'

'Yes,' Felix managed.

For some reason, what she was seeing was not love. She had known love; this felt like dominion.

'You must overcome your shame, I think,' Lillith continued. 'The Drow do not have a word for this, for shame. It is a magician word, a mortal word. There is no place for it here. Take a lover; we have many fine men. Choose one that you like.'

Felix glared at Lillith aghast.

'That hardly sounds like love,' she said slowly.

Lillith tipped her head at Felix and regarded her more carefully.

'You have known love, yes?'

Felix nodded. 'I have.'

'Nigel.'

His name on Lillith's lips made Felix's heart skip inside her chest. Her skin prickled with ice, but heat burned underneath it.

'Yes.' The words were scarcely audible.

Lillith nodded slowly and a careful smile stretched across her dark face.

'It is hard. I feel your pain. It is inside your words, your skin...your eyes. You must let Nigel go.'

'I can't,' Felix choked.

Tears threatened but she forced them down, knowing that her resolve was stronger than her sadness. *I won't...* came the voice in her mind, strong and sure.

Anger poured out of Lillith like a transparent, icy mist. Felix lifted her head and looked her squarely in the face. Felix felt her spirals shimmering; she let them.

Lillith's gaze was hard and dark, and cast a shadow over the room that woke up the sleeping man. He looked towards the two women and shuffled down into the blankets, voiceless and afraid. Lillith paid no heed to him. Her attention was entirely on Felix as she rolled her eyes over Felix's nightgown, at the tangle of black curls messily twisted back. She stepped out of the bed with clenched fists and moved towards Felix with an elegance that belied her rage.

Bracing herself, Felix stood her ground. She had always been a rebel. Her nose had found trouble from the moment she was born, and she'd fallen foul of many punches in her lifetime. Nanny Maude had given her a fair few slaps for insolence, and her crooked nose was thanks to her brother smashing it when she was nine annums old, in an orphanage line up. Rather than making her angry, these memories warmed her, and she thanked them voicelessly, for preparing her for the violence of this world.

But no slap or punch came. Instead, Lillith wrapped her arms around the girl and stroked her hair.

'Shhh, sister,' she soothed. 'You have spirit. Of course you do; you are your mother's daughter. But we must master our anger.'

Lillith's hands were now woven into the matted bun on Felix's head. She gripped it hard.

'Cut it loose from yourself, Felix,' she whispered into Felix's ear.

Her skin prickled with goosebumps. This close, she smelled of damp, cloying earth.

Felix pulled away and struggled to keep her face blank and impassive, despite the pain in her scalp as Lillith clung harder to her hair.

'We will shave you tomorrow,' Lillith said, glancing over the inky tendrils of hair falling down into Felix's face.

She could not hide her horror as Lillith spoke.

'But –'

'And we will burn this.' Lillith tugged at the thin scrap of nightgown that was the only modesty Felix had.

Felix began shaking her head, but Lillith loosened her grip and cupped her face gently with her hands. Her rage was gone, replaced by a desperation, a yearning sort of feeling that thickened Felix's throat and made her feel queasy.

'You are one of us, Felix,' Lillith breathed pleadingly. 'You must stop hiding from your true nature.'

She stroked Felix's face lovingly, the way a mother strokes her child's and then she stopped and pulled away. For a moment, she seemed to shrink, losing the power and the shadow she had cast only seconds earlier. Glancing at the trembling man in her bed and the frightened girl in front of her, Lillith sighed.

'Go on,' Lillith said softly, her eyes full of apology, 'off you go.'

She tilted her head towards the archway and Felix stepped back nervously, nearly tripping over her feet. But then she turned, and she walked quickly out of the chamber, her footsteps echoing in the stone hallway as she began to run.

Lillith looked down at Aradia and shrugged her lean shoulders slightly.

'Follow her,' she said to the spider, in her voice of songs.

Lillith climbed back into her bed, patting the man gently on his head as Aradia scampered secretly after Felix.

Felix had not failed to notice that the men and boys whom she'd spotted when she first came into the valley were strangely absent from the day-to-day procedures of the Drow. They didn't join the women during the Drowning, nor did they eat with them. They had their own lodgings away from the women, closer to the fields. They kept themselves to themselves but still Felix had wondered why. Now she knew.

The man in Lillith's bed had been afraid. That much had been clear. Who was she kidding, even she had been afraid of Lillith. Felix could not forget the menace in her eyes, and her scalp was still twinging where Lillith's thin fingers had clutched at her hair...hair that was to be shorn from her head tomorrow.

Dashing away the tears with her hand, Felix marched down the zig zagging staircase hewn into the rock face and descended down to the green grassed floor of the valley. She was ashamed of her vanity. Many times she had threatened to hack off her own hair when it got too wild and bushy to tame but she never had. As silly as it sounded, her hair belonged to Nanny Maude. She had never been a particularly gentle woman but on chop days, she had been so careful with Felix's hair, brushing it tenderly until it shone like silk and snipping only a few inches from the ends. Her coarse hands, no stranger to mean jabs and rough slaps, stroked her hair almost lovingly until she softly whispered, 'there now. What a beauty you are an' no mistake'.

It was only when she'd left the orphanage when she'd turned 16, that Felix had learned how Nanny Maude had loved her, how Felix had reminded her of her own daughter, Lily; dead and gone now...just like Maude. They had died at the hands of magicians. Maude, Bill, their two little children; a whole family wiped out. And the orphans Nanny Maude had cared for, too – their fledgling lives savagely ended by lamias sent to destroy them, by her uncle.

Felix jogged towards the cornfield, past the tree canopy, past the waterfall with the waterwheel that helped power the millstone, that pounded the wheatsheaves and helped make their food, beyond the wheatfields. Her chest began to burn a little and sweat glistened on her top lip, but she kept moving, spurred on by the ugly feeling growing inside her.

She had fought so hard to overthrow her uncle. People had died to help her. Her own brother had lost what little power he had been born with, because of her.

And they trusted her.

They had given her everything – the Citadel, the titles, the land, the wealth. They had listened to her, tried to help her. Why had she not seen that before? Why had she been so focused on the things she could not achieve? She had acted like a little girl, defeated by something on her first attempt. That's not who she was; it was not the girl Nanny Maude had raised in that orphanage and it was not the woman Fiddle had wanted her to be.

And now she had left them. She had run away, abandoning them.

What am I doing here?

Felix stopped jogging but marched on, ignoring the curious waves of inquiry coming to her from the Drow she passed. She was nearly at the end of the cornfield now and the light was dimmer. There was no crystalline glow of gemstones to glaze everything with silver. Overhead, the crack between the rockfaces narrowed and only a thin slice of light trickled down to the valley floor. It occurred to her that she didn't know if it was sunlight or moonlight. She didn't know what day it was. She slept when the Drow slept, believing and trusting that it was night-time but in truth, she could not have guessed how long she had been here. It could have been days, or it could have been weeks.

Taking a deep breath, Felix walked onwards, stepping into the grey shadows beyond the cornfields. The air here was clammy and sickly, but each inhalation seemed to bring truth and clarity to her foggy mind.

In a place filled with sisters, with others who looked like her and who loved her unquestioningly, the last thing Felix had expected to feel was loneliness. Her sister Drow were with her constantly, even when she was alone in her chamber. The Drowning had left its mark; she felt her sisters inside her and near her even when they were physically absent from her side.

In the night, she would sit, knees clutched to her chest, listening to the heartbeat of the valley that was now supposed to be her home. The waterfall's ever-present gushing was like an overbearing mother's hush. The silence of the deep caverns burned too loudly but up in the rafters of the valley, the tuneless whistling of the wind through the crannies dulled everything, even the strange voiceless emotions of her sisters that lingered inside her.

With the Drow, in this new home, she felt calmer than she had ever felt in her life. From the frustrated yearning of Nanny Maude's orphanage to the confused anger of the London Library, Felix had always felt *more*. All her feelings had been coloured with anger so that she saw the world through a tinge of smouldering embers, of grey smoke. But here, her anger was extinguished. The furyfire that had once saved her life and her brother's, had left her. In its wake, was an emptiness so deep that Felix wondered if she was still whole. She didn't know how that could be, when a piece of her identity had slotted into place during the Drowning. She belonged here with the Drow, she knew that. She had sought it, secretly but fervently. It was why Fiddle had told her to come here, lying on his deathbed.

And yet...

Felix had been glad that her anger had abated, here. She had always seen it as a flaw. It was a burden she had to overcome and squash down. Furyfire may have saved her life in the glass chamber of her uncle's machine, but it had frightened her followers at the Festival of Fire, and they had seen her then for what she was a monster.

Except that she wasn't. She understood that now. Her anger was a part of her, it shaped her. She would not be the Firelighter without that anger.

Felix began to see. Her anger was a weapon, one to hone and wield, and use for good. It was a product of injustice, of hatred aimed towards her and those unable to defend themselves; therefore her anger was the fire that would burn down the world that had been built on prejudice and injustice. She had to use it, not bury it. Lillith had been depriving her of the one weapon that she had to really change things.

The valley was chillingly cold beyond the cornfields, and the jagged gash of path disappeared into deep blue nothing. As her eyes adjusted to the darkness, she saw that there were small wooden huts clustered together with meagre pinpricks of light glowing inside.

'Oh,' Felix stopped abruptly, startled.

She looked down at her hand and curled her fingers. Immediately, a flame flickered to life above her palm. It sputtered and hissed for a moment and then went out and Felix rubbed her palms together, blowing hot hair into them. She tried again and a brighter, hotter flame sprang up, illuminating the damp walls of the rock faces and the rotting wood of the dingy huts.

It was the first magic she had done since she'd arrived.

How could I forget about magic?

Shivering slightly, but not from the cold, Felix stepped forward gingerly towards one of the huts.

She was silently horrified that her brain had pushed aside her ability to do magic; it had not occurred to her until now that it was something she could do, that it was a power she had at her command. Furyfire was a Drow trait, she knew that; Fiddle had told her. But to invoke fire was a magician's gift, such was their affinity with the Sacred Flame. Felix frowned, confused. She was half Drow and half magician. Had Lillith really been trying to suppress her magic all along, trying to convince her to become Drow through and through?

Surely not.

The valley was eerily quiet. There was no sound, apart from the 'guh guh' of the flame in her hand. It was scalding her skin a little, more so than it had done before, but she put that down to being out of practice. When she'd first learned magic with Fiddle, she'd worn gloves.

'Hello?' Felix called out timidly.

There was a small flurry of noise; a waft of air that made a shredded piece of netting hung up as a makeshift curtain in the doorway of a hut begin to flutter.

Felix lifted it a little with her free hand, held the flame up and peered inside.

Children.

They sat clustered together, ragged and dirty. Their eyes were large, in faces too hollow.

'It's ok,' Felix breathed, hardly daring to move in case she scared them.

She held out a hand to placate them but still they shifted back away from her, scrambling together as their frightened eyes scanned over her spirals.

Felix backed away to show them she meant no harm, but her eyes were locked firmly upon their faces...their pale, gaunt spiral-free faces.

Boys, all.

'You shouldn't be here!'

Felix felt her elbow tugged fiercely out of the hut. Scrambling backwards, she turned to see a man who couldn't have seen more than twenty annums glaring at her in panicked anger.

'Who....' Felix began, but the man shook his head and interrupted her.

'I'm nobody. We're all nobody. You need to leave!'

Felix pulled her arm free and looked around. In the flamelight, she saw them. Some were mere boys; some were older, like the man in front of her. But none were much older than him. They were dressed protectively, to keep the chill away, in scraps of netting and woven reeds and leaves.

'What's going on here?' Felix whispered, hardly daring to ask.

The man narrowed his eyes at her. They were dark and savage, reminding her of Linus' eyes instantly.

'You are not wanted here,' the man spat. 'Now go.'

'But I can help!' Felix cried, and motioned her arm to the children in the hut behind her. 'Please! What is this? Please tell me what they're doing to you.'

The man stepped towards her, unfathomable cruelty in his eyes.

'This is where they leave us to die,' he growled. 'Us men who will not do their bidding, the boy children who are unwanted.'

'Why are you unwanted?' Felix asked, her voice shaking.

The man was so close now she had to lean back, her shoulder pressing against the children's hut.

'We are of no use to her...to them. To you, Drow witch.'

Felix swallowed.

'I'm not one of them,' she said.

The words spilled out of her mouth too easily. Too truthfully.

The man in front of her did not look convinced. He reached a finger up to her face and held it a centimetre above her face; he traced his finger over the pattern of her spirals.

'Are you sure?' he snarled.

Felix tried to control her heartbeat and the surge of anger racing through her. Anger, whilst useful, would not convince these men that she was no threat to them.

'Cadmus, stop.' From behind the bulk of the first man stepped a second, leaner and younger. 'Look at her. She isn't one of them.'

The man named Cadmus trailed his eyes over Felix and she felt it like ants on her skin.

'Yet,' he said, and it sounded like a threat.

But he backed up, allowing the second man to wrench him away.

'Whoever you are,' Cadmus continued, 'you need to leave us. You put us in danger.'

'How? Why? I don't understand."

'The spiders,' the second man said. 'The white widows. They sense you and know your scent. She'll have sent them to follow you.'

'And by 'she', you mean...'

'Lillith," Cadmus finished.

'But the white widows are harmless. They're friends to the Drow. And you are Drow, aren't you?'

Cadmus spat on the ground where Felix was stood.

'Cilix, get rid of her now," he said, his voice barely more than a whisper.

The second man, Cilix stepped around Cadmus and beckoned to Felix to follow him. Stepping around Cadmus, Felix went after him.

'We are Drow, yes,' Cilix whispered. 'But we have no power at all. They keep only the men with some power or perhaps beauty. They send the rest of us here. And the old. They send the old ones here too. This is where the white widows feast.'

Felix looked at Cilix, staggered and he nodded, confirming her horror.

'We've built some defences, burrowed deeper into the rocks. She knows we're here. Lillith. She toys with us.'

'The others,' Felix began, swallowing down sickness. 'The other Drow, in the valley. Do they know?'

'The sisterhood? They don't ask. They are trained not to ask,' Cilix said, shaking his head.

'I don't get it,' Felix said, shaking her head. 'They wouldn't allow this. If they knew, they'd help, they'd –'

'No,' Cilix interrupted. 'She is like a spider, and they are all flies caught in her web. She poisons them all with illusions of truth, but she is a liar. You must not trust her.'

Cilix stopped.

'I dare not go further. Follow the path and leave this place. Leave the valley.'

'But I can't just abandon you...those children. I can help!'

Cilix shook his head.

'We are trapped. But you don't have to be. Go. Run away from here.'

Cilix turned and sprinted soundlessly back into the shadows.

For a moment, Felix was disorientated. She felt drunk, as though she'd had too much Ashwater.

Startlingly, absurdly, the first thing that came to her mind was –

"Nigel," she breathed. Nobody except the wind heard her. 'Nigel, I wish you were here.'

But he wasn't here, and there was no dire wolf to listen to the deep echo of longing inside her, to witness and sooth her mounting fear. His insightful nudges into her mind and heart, once a growing annoyance, now seemed painfully absent. Why was it that she did not mind his knowing her, but the thought of the sister Drow peering inside the chasm of her soul had made her stomach lurch sickeningly? Had she known all along, in some deep subconscious part of her, that at its core, this place was rotten?

"What would you say right now, D.W?" Felix asked out loud.

The voice that answered was her own and she frowned, missing the gruff, deep sound of his words so intensely that she felt an ache inside her caused by no physical wound.

"Trust your instincts," she whispered to herself and she nodded, her dark hair falling into her face. Taking a moment to stroke it gently, she thought hard.

And what did her instincts tell her?

That she was a Drow. Their power felt as much a part of her as her own skin. She knew, without having to test them that her sisters would save her life, because she would do the same for them, for they were a part of her blood and she a part of theirs. It was self-preservation to protect them. She felt a deep understanding that they were innocent; they didn't know what horrors Lillith was inflicting here. She had brainwashed them and since the Drowning, she was one with them now, slowly losing the parts of herself that Lillith did not like and could not use. Felix knew that was why it was called a Drowning. She was being pulled down to the ebb and flow of their emotions, the tides of their feelings so that could no longer identify herself and she, too, was now part of the current.

Part of the web.

And yet...

The absence of those she loved, burned within her. Fear at what she'd seen in that wooden hut ignited her nerves, so that even her skin hurt. She noticed that the flame in her hand was dying, leaving scorched and tender skin. She let the fire die.

'Fiddle told me to come here,' Felix swallowed, bunching up her fists, straining to fight through the fear. 'It was his parting gift. He knew I had a piece of me missing. Why would he send me here if it was dangerous?'

'Learn to let go,' replied the voice of her reason.

It was her own voice, but they were Fiddle's words spoken with dying breaths. Had he known she would need to see this? Had he understood that she would never be whole unless she knew the complete and ugly truth? Had he known the truth about Lillith?

She had no way of knowing.

Fiddle was not infallible. He'd made mistakes; too many to count. He was not the hero from storybooks, or the father figure she had dreamed of in the dingy patch of orphanage that had been hers. He was just a man and he messed up sometimes; walked the wrong path. Didn't we all?

She had come here because he had told her to.

'You need to trust your guides,' said a voice inside her head but it was not her own, it was D.W's. It was exactly what he would say if he were here. *'Trust your instincts'*.

Felix had to trust Fiddle. She had to have faith in him. She had to believe that he had sent her here for some reason, that she could not yet see. She looked for him now, in her mind's eye.

'You have trusted me this far, Felix,' he had once said to her. *'Please trust me now'*.

And she realised then that despite his mistakes and despite his secrets, despite the pain and anger and the grief she felt towards him, she completely, absolutely and instinctively did.

'Ok,' she said to no one. 'It's time to leave.'

She began to walk back towards the valley, planning her escape as she went.

Behind her, creeping out of the shadows, a white spider reached out her legs as though waving. Then she scuttled after Felix, following and watching with her eight pink eyes.

26

To Burn, to Drown.

Principal Duncan Ellis was an old man. He wore his age well; from his twinkling green eyes to his white tufts of hair which rested over the tops of his ears. He was bald at the crown but made up for his lack of hair with a robust moustache which joined with his sideburns. His short, rotund stature, often draped in plum-coloured robes made him a less than intimidating spectacle, but this was perhaps why he had been the principal of the Ardere Academy for over thirty-five years. Instead of fear, he garnered admiration, respect and love from his faculty and the alumni of the university.

His rooms were in the third highest tower. The highest tower was given to the Caelum consortium, to examine the fluctuations in weather and the second highest to the Tressis consortium, who looked to the sky and beyond it, examining the Third Plane with their telescopes and occulums. Professor Ellis kept his rooms sparse and modest. Whilst some of the other, younger professors made their chambers homely and inviting, the principal preferred humble surroundings as they reminded him of where he had come from.

One would assume that the principal of a globally renowned academy of magic had lived a life of privilege and wealth, but this was far from true. Born on the Second Plane, he had been. The son of a travelling gypsy and his plain-looking wife, who had ridden in their caravan from town to town providing their little puppet shows and circus tricks. They had never any money to travel to the First Plane like the wealthier magicians and so they had remained on the Second, growing hungrier as their journeys between settlements stretched from days to weeks with little food. The towns were smaller. The paying customers fewer. There were times it seemed that they survived by sheer willpower alone.

His ma' had died first – the black fever. No amount of Fleetwater from the First Plane's magical healing river would have saved her. A few months after, his father had gone too – an infection in his leg caused by a small scratch from a rusted nail. Had Duncan been learned in the art of healing, he would have been able to save his da'. But Duncan had only the instinct for magic, no training, no learning and so his father had died sweating and trembling, clutching at his son's hand until he went cold and stiff. Duncan didn't know how old he had been, so he could not accurately attest to his age even now, but he imagined he was something like six annums when his da' went. But even at that tender age, Duncan knew that he wouldn't survive for long on his own. He didn't have the money to pay for a license for the First Plane, and he had no other living relatives. Finding work in the towns was folly when they were all upping and leaving for the First, so he did what he thought was sensible and walked to Highcliff-On-Sea to the university. This was logical. It was the oldest institution in these parts of the Second, and his ma' and da' always pulled in more coin after a show there. It took him the best part of eight days and nights walking to get there, on near enough no food and little water. He practically fainted on Hestia when she opened the door.

'Poor lamb,' she'd said.

She was naught but the cook's maid at the time herself, and a pretty thing she'd been at eleven or twelve, and it was because of her that Duncan survived. He was given a job as a sweep at first, because he was small and slight and because the cook thought the job would kill him, which would rid her of the burden of him. But in a place of flairs and talents, Duncan's was survival and the job gave him taut muscles and a determined jaw. After nine annums, nobody knew the turrets and spires and chimneys and alleys and bridges the way that Duncan knew them. Hestia was the cook then, and she was a shining beauty. If she knew Duncan's feelings for her, she never let on.

It was no surprise, really, when Principal Bertrand Windwood took a fancy to Hestia. She was young and beautiful and spirited, and Bertrand Windwood was older, a widower and lonely. She always said he was kind enough to her, and that it was the best someone like she could hope for. But a life as a professor's wife meant she would remain at the Ardere, not as an employee and not, as she had always dreamed, as a student. So, her meagre savings for the academy fees were gifted to Duncan.

Principal Ellis looked up at the portrait of Hestia. It was the only decoration he had on his walls, aside from his framed certificate of graduation from the Ardere itself. A Pocculum scholar – poisons and potions, of course but also cures and tonics and medicines. Even now, an old man with aches of own, he hoped his da' would be proud. But it was to Hestia he owed the change in his stars, and to Hestia to whom he raised his nightly glass of Ashwater. He was about to sip the golden liquid when he heard a loud banging at his door. Glancing at the clock on his mantelpiece above the small fire, Principal Ellis frowned a little and pushed himself out of his armchair with some difficulty.

The banging came again, louder this time.

'Principal Ellis, sir?'

Duncan groaned at the voice, a voice he recognised far too well. Slingsby Buzzard. The boy was incorrigible – always asking questions and making dramatic excuses for not turning in his assignments. For a moment, he almost didn't open the door, but the experience of his years made him too good of a principal to do that. Instead, he took a deep breath to brace himself and pulled open his heavy chamber door.

'Mr. Buzzard,' he said with a kind smile. 'How unexpectedly delightful to see you at eleven-thirty in the evening.'

His words may have been lightly laced with sarcasm, but it fell away the moment he saw Slingsby's face, and the young man standing behind him who was peering in with undisguised curiosity and badly hidden excitement. Glancing down, Duncan raised his eyebrows at the sight of a dire wolf.

'Well, well, well,' he said. 'Wonders never cease. I haven't laid eyes on a dire wolf in quite a few years and from the looks on your faces, you have something rather important going on. Please do come in.'

'I'm so sorry to interrupt you, Principal Ellis,' Slingsby gushed, 'what with it being so late and especially with it being Thirsty Thursday and all, but I had to bring these guys to see you because, if you can believe it, they have a matter of what they say is 'national security', and I don't believe I'd be doing my duty as an alumnus of this great institution if I didn't take that seriously, now would I?'

'Thank you, Slingsby. Kindly take a seat. Quietly, if you will. We don't want to wake the whole tower, do we? Now, I don't believe you are a student here, but you are familiar. Have we met?'

Duncan held out his gloved hand to the unfamiliar young man with auburn hair and smudged glasses.

'Nigel. Nigel True. This is D.W. We met very briefly at the State Ball.'

'Ah, yes,' Principal Ellis nodded.

He shook Nigel's hand and waved them through to his sitting room, and with a quick motion from his hand, the decanter of Ashwater transformed into a pot of steaming cinnamon tea and the chipped crystal glasses turned into pretty porcelain teacups.

'Please be seated. True, you say? Alchemus' apprentice?'

'How did you'

'Oh Alchemus and I go way back – or rather we did. I was sorry to hear about his death, though I am glad that his name was cleared.'

'Then...you must know why I'm here, surely?'

Duncan looked at Nigel and then at Slingsby, who was watching their exchange excitedly.

'Perhaps, though I rather think we ought to talk privately about *that*.'

'So she's here then?'

Principal Ellis frowned.

'I'm sorry?'

'Felix. She's here?'

Duncan leaned back in his armchair and crossed his leg over his knee, which was somewhat difficult with his aching bones.

'I'm afraid I don't understand at all,' he confessed. 'If you're referring to Lady Felix, I was under the impression that she had taken ill after the Festival of Fire and was recovering at the Citadel. At least, that is what the newspapers from the First say. But from your line of questioning and your somewhat disheartened expression, I'm assuming that this is not the case?'

Nigel rested his forehead in his hands and much to Slingsby's simultaneous horror and joy, began to swear in frustration. The dire wolf whimpered and rested his snout on Nigel's knee.

'I see,' Duncan nodded. 'I'm terribly sorry, but Lady Felix has never set foot inside the Ardere, though I much hoped that she would, I must admit. I feel she would make a fine Ignis scholar. Tell me, young man. What is going on?'

Duncan felt the dire wolf probing his thoughts and allowed him.

'Please do satisfy yourself that I can be trusted if you must,' he said to D.W, who scowled only a little before nodding at Nigel.

'She's gone missing,' Nigel said from behind his fingers, which still covered his face miserably. 'She's just gone. Nobody knows where.'

'Absconded!' Slingsby gasped.

'Oh do be quiet, Slingsby,' Duncan snapped. 'She is hardly a criminal, she is your Firelighter so do give her the respect she deserves.' Slingsby flushed and looked down at his twiddling gloved fingers.

'She may as well be a criminal,' Nigel said dully. 'She's taken the Sacred Flame with her.'

There was another dramatic gasp from Slingsby, silenced by a hard look from the principal.

'I see,' said Duncan, with a darkening understanding settling over his face. 'And so we are rudderless in rough seas. Tell me, why did you think she may be here?'

Nigel looked at D.W who seemed to blush, though it is in fact impossible for dire wolves to blush.

'We were given a prophecy of sorts,' D.W admitted.

'A prophesy, you say?' Duncan said warily. 'Go on.'

'It was from a Catchoo. A Houdini.'

'Hmm,' Duncan frowned. 'Rarely any merit in Houdini nonsense, and surely you know better than to trust a Catchoo?'

'We had few options,' Nigel said tightly.

'What was the prophesy?' Slingsby asked, earning another hard look from the principal.

'She said that Felix has 'gone to burn and to drown,'' D.W answered.

'I see. So you assumed 'to burn' meant the Ardere?'

Nigel nodded glumly.

'And the 'to drown' part? What did you make of that?'

Nigel and D.W looked at one another.

'Well, to be honest, we didn't really pay much attention to that bit,' D.W replied sheepishly. 'Nigel thought...we thought that this was the most logical place she could have come.'

'Hardly,' Duncan snorted.

'Excuse me?' Nigel squinted in annoyance.

'I said 'hardly' my boy. This is hardly the place that Lady Felix would come if she was in distress. She has never been before and from what I can gather, her commoner upbringing would suggest she is more inclined towards commoner education than that of magicians. I read that she rebuilt a commoner orphanage and school? Perhaps you could try there?'

'We already did,' D.W growled. 'We know her better than anyone. Don't you think we tried every single place that ever meant something to her? Besides – she isn't on the First Plane. I'd hear her if she was. I can hear her anywhere.'

'And you can hear her here, can you?'

It was a reasonable question, delivered entirely without malice but even so the dire wolf's shackles rose in defiance. He looked at the little old man with the shining white hair and green eyes and saw why he was the principal. He suffered no fools.

'Don't underestimate this one,' he said, only to Nigel.

'I won't,' came Nigel's returning thought and when D.W probed, he heard the mistrust of this man amongst the confusion and hurt and yes, the longing to be a student here.

'No,' the dire wolf answered, finally. 'No I can't hear her here either. The magic is too dense.'

The principal nodded slowly and uncrossed his legs. He reached down to the table and picked up a teacup and saucer and drank half the cup of cinnamon tea, his eyes on a portrait of a pretty lady on the wall. When D.W tried to hear Principal Ellis' thoughts, he heard only a fuzzy white noise, the same he heard in Nigel's in the café in soho.

Finally, Duncan placed his teacup down on his saucer and spoke.

'I should think that this is a rather simple riddle to solve. I would have thought Alchemus would have taught you better than this, Nigel. I know how he enjoyed his little riddles and clues. But I can see that you are emotionally involved, and perhaps that is why you can't see it.'

'See what? Please, sir if you know something, please tell us.'

'You were told that she has gone to burn and to drown. Now if you trust in this prophesy then perhaps you ought to take it literally as well as figuratively.'

'You can't be saying she has burned and drowned?' Slingsby asked, leaning forward.

Duncan shook his head. 'No, not quite. Look, I read the reports of what happened at the Festival of Fire and I also read the Truth Papers. It seems that Lady Felix is prone to fire – she has a flair for it, as we would say here. It is why I think she would make a remarkable Ignis scholar. But from what I hear about our young leader, she is also ashamed of her talents and her propensity for destruction – because yes, fire destroys. She fails to see that fire can also be a cleansing, that beneath scorched soil is new life. I sense that she has run away because she fears the destruction her power brings.'

Nigel and D.W exchanged glances and then nodded in agreement with the principal.

'However, Lady Felix is more than just a magician, she is a Drow. If she finds nothing but fear within the fire of her magic, then it would make sense that she would seek comfort in the other half of her. Perhaps she is not purely destruction, perhaps there is something more to her. Do you see?'

'So you're saying you think Felix has gone to learn about the Drow?' Nigel asked.

Duncan nodded.

'The prophesy also develops new meaning if you learn what a 'Drowning' is. It is, in fact, an initiation into the Drow sisterhood.'

'But they're extinct. Godspell eradicated them,' Nigel said, his brow creased.

Duncan rubbed his forefinger against his chin and thought for a moment. His eyes passed to the portrait and back several times. The dire wolf began to grow more and more curious about the woman in the painting. Who was she?

'I see that there are many things that Alchemus has not shared with you.'

Nigel swallowed. D.W could see the lump of his voicebox moving up and down in his throat.

'What do you mean?' Nigel asked thickly.

Duncan took deep inhalation and looked at each one of them. His eyes were calculating his options. D.W noticed a faint twitch at the edge of his moustache.

'What I am about to disclose is a matter of complete and utter secrecy.'

'More secrets. Damn you all to hell,' Nigel whispered, closing his eyes.

'You'll understand why this is a secret, my boy,' the principal said softly. 'The Drow survive.'

'What? No. They were slaughtered. Godspell killed them all.'

'Most of them, yes. But some were able to escape with the help of your master – Alchemus J. Fiddle.'

Nigel was shaking his head so rapidly, D.W worried he would give himself whiplash.

'I know this will be a surprise. Frankly I commend Alchemus for his commitment to their safety, but if he kept this a secret, it was not through mistrust of you but for their safekeeping.'

'Did you know this?' Nigel fired the question at D.W.

'No,' he barked in reply. 'No, I swear I didn't. I never heard it in his thoughts.'

'No,' Duncan said. 'Alchemus was adept at guarding his mind from prying eyes...or ears.' He smiled kindly at the dire wolf.

'Where are they?' Nigel asked urgently. 'Tell me now, please. If she's gone there, I have to go and find her.'

'Ah, that I don't know, I'm afraid.'

'Then what use are you?'

'Nigel–' D.W began, but Nigel cut him off.

'No! No. You can't tell us something like that and not know more. How can you not know more?'

'Young man, I sincerely apologise but Alchemus never told me where the Drow hid themselves. If you wish to find them, you will have a hard job on your hands, for the Drow are powerful in their own right. Once hidden, they will not be found unless they want to be. But I suggest you start with their ancestral home, the Glade.'

'The Glade is lost,' the dire wolf said. 'The few maps that existed were destroyed with the Drow. It is said only a Drow can find it anyway.'

'Untrue,' Duncan said, shaking his finger. 'The Glade is a place like all others. It can be found if one knows the route.'

'But that's the problem isn't it, old man,' the dire wolf snarled. 'We don't know the route.'

'Then I offer you one who does,' Duncan smiled serenely. 'I believe you are acquainted with one of our finest Ostium scholars, Slingsby Buzzard?'

'Say what?' Slingsby exclaimed.

He had been quiet throughout the conversation, which had somehow miraculously ignored him, and he felt like he had been spying on a glorious senate meeting or something. They wouldn't believe this back in Texas.

'Mr. Buzzard? You are an Ostium scholar, are you not? Routes and maps, paths and doors?' the principal asked with amused eyes.

'Well, yeah sure,' Slingsby spluttered. 'But that doesn't mean I know the way to some hidden home of the Drow, now does it, sir?'

'Come now, Slingsby,' Principal Ellis tutted. 'A true Ostium specialist can navigate his way anywhere.'

'Well how about I just navigate my way up to my room then, huh sir? I have a test in the morning that I really need to cram for.'

'I will speak to Professor Risewell on your behalf, Slingsby.'

'Right. Great. Wow.'

Slingsby rubbed at the back of his neck and smiled awkwardly at Nigel.

'I guess I'll go pack my stuff then, huh?'

'An exceedingly good idea. Please do take D.W with you, whilst I have a chat with Nigel here.'

The dire wolf lowered his head and looked menacingly at the old man.

'I don't think so,' he growled at him.

'My dear dire wolf. I am a very old man. If I meant any danger to Nigel, I'm fairly sure he could use magic far faster than I can, and I am certain he could outrun me. You have probed my thoughts and I welcome you to do so again. I mean you, nor Nigel any harm.'

'It's ok, D.W,' Nigel said, resting his hand on the back of the wolf's head. 'Go with Slingsby.'

Principal Ellis waved his hand at the door and it opened with a creak. Slingsby and the dire wolf looked at it and walked over, both hoping they would be called back by some dazzling change of mind.

'I guess I'll err, see you in a few hours,' Slingsby said.

'I suggest you leave just before dawn, so as not to raise questions,' the principal said.

Slingsby nodded, and he and D.W walked out of the room into the darkened corridor beyond it. The wolf looked back only once to see Duncan and Nigel staring hard at one another before the door slammed shut.

'More tea?' Duncan asked Nigel. He shook his head, but Duncan poured a cup for him anyway. 'You may need it. We have a lot to discuss.'

Nigel nodded sullenly.

Duncan pushed himself up from his armchair with his knuckles and huffed at the activity. He made his way into a small adjoining room which housed only a small single bed. Nigel heard some shuffling and the sounds of things being moved around before Duncan came back into the room holding a metal box that looked familiar to Nigel. It was the size of a tea tray and was dented and scratched but nonetheless, Nigel knew immediately what it was.

'That's Alchemus' check out box.'

'Yes,' Duncan said, puffing as he lowered himself back down into his armchair. He passed the box over to Nigel.

'Yours now, I believe? Alchemus named you his replacement, didn't he? Actually, this is what I thought you were here for; I thought Alchemus had told you to come to me.'

Nigel flicked his eyes up at Duncan and widened them in disbelief.

'Yes, I know. I am somewhat disappointing.'

'You're–'

'Yes. A fellow secret keeper. Welcome to the Privy Council, Nigel.'

They talked until they had exhausted the contents of the check out box, until throats were hoarse and until the relentless cinnamon tea no longer warmed the chill, which filled Nigel more and more. Then, it was time to leave.

Outside, the Ardere clocktower struck 5 a.m.

27

Skimming the Second

They tumbled out of a half-rotted wooden door and landed in a heap on the sandy floor. Captain Bonny Kildare kicked the door shut to the midst behind them, which had remnants of the Shadow's smoke curling through it.

'Linus?'

She lifted her legs off the back of the boy who was face down in the sawdust and straw of the floor.

'Hmph!' came the muffled reply and the captain nodded.

'You're alive then,' she said and climbed to her feet, taking in their surroundings.

The secret hatch beneath the Monument had opened up into a small wooden hut. It was ancient and crumbling with dark wooden beams hanging down into the circular, stone room revealing slices of inky blue sky beyond it, with stars twinkling like fireflies in tar. A great stone hearth remained intact but much of the walls had collapsed, replaced by tall grass, branches, bushes and brambles. The door from which they had tumbled was attached to a small section of wall, held on with one powdery orange hinge which held on the hatch precariously.

Captain Kildare took a deep lungful of air and closed her eyes. The air was thick. It almost shimmered with magic.

'We're on the Second, lad,' she sighed. 'And you survived it.'

Linus sat in the dust, his elbows resting on his knees. His dark eyes were wide, and sawdust and sand sullied his usually pitch-black hair.

'You alright?' the captain asked.

Linus nodded.

'Fine, yeah,' he replied. 'Great in fact. I feel...brilliant!'

He stood in one fluid movement and circled the room, flexing his fingers and shoulders, bouncing a little on the balls of his booted feet.

'I feel invincible!'

'Hmm,' the captain squinted her eyes and removed her bandana, wiping her brow. 'That'll be the Fleetwater then. We'll need to get you some more.'

Linus looked at her, confused.

'It will wear off soon. You have maybe a day or so I'd say. Sorry to say it, lad, but you're a mortal now, and I don't fancy seeing what happens to you on the Second without the protection of Fleetwater in your veins, so it's best that we get you some more, just in case.'

But Linus was distracted. His eyes were flitting all around the room, touching the walls and the beams, sniffing the old ashes in the fire.

'It's like I can see everything in precise detail! I can smell everything! You stink of sewers, Captain, if you don't mind me saying. Ha! So do I, though. These walls are ancient. Feel how smooth they are! Age has polished them. Reckon this was Hooke's house? Reckon I can do magic again?!'

'Woah, laddie,' Captain Kildare began, but Linus was already trying to conjure a fire in the hearth.

He pushed his hands towards it, flicked his wrists, rubbed his palms together, blew into them, pushed them towards the hearth again.

'Linus,' Captain Kildare said softly. 'I told you. I don't think any amount of Fleetwater can fix what happened to you.'

The boy's head slumped and when the captain rested her gloved hand on his shoulder, he shrugged away.

'I'm alright,' he said tightly, but Captain Kildare could see his bunched fists.

His hands were almost blackened with dirt, and rough, now, with callouses from life on a sewer ship, but there were patches of pale pink skin which made him seem entirely childlike and vulnerable. Captain Kildare ran her teeth over her bottom lip, fighting the urge to comfort him. He was a crewmember, not her child and he had taken enough liberties as it was.

'Right then,' she said brusquely. 'I'll call for the Skimmer. Get a handle on that moping, lad, if you want to stay a part of its crew.'

She turned on her heel and ducked through the beams and out of the hut.

Captain Kildare had not sailed the Second in a very long time, but she knew it well. It had seared itself into her skin and, in the dark depths of the sewers, when it made no difference if your eyes were open or closed, she had imagined she was just sleeping, sailing through the calm of the Second, the Skimmer smooth and graceful as she cut through the blue. Now, she gazed around the hut, hoping for some familiarity. There were great hulking silhouettes of mountains in the distance and there were the night calls of sea birds to the east. A faint tang of salt on the air, perhaps. And the grass was dry here, too. She knelt down and removed her glove to feel it. Although the current climate was mild, verging on chilly, this place had known warm, arid days recently. The south then. Near to the coast. The geography of the Second was similar to that of the First but there were few differences, but without knowing where the hatch had delivered them, it was harder to discern an exact location. Usually, magicians simply stepped into the Second plane, whether by using spectoccules to see it or not, and they arrived at the exact same parallel location, as though simple taking a step up into a world overlapping another. But it was a tricky business. Magic was far denser here, making it easier to see, yes, but also making this world heavier, somehow. The Second felt larger. Time, though the same here as on the First, was relative, too. Distance seemed greater; hours felt longer.

But there was no need for hatches to the Second. They were unnecessary. Captain Kildare had always used Spectoccules to step into the Second. They were attached to her belt, alongside her cutlass and pistols and she felt disorientated to have arrived here without them. She looked back at the hut, which was half obscured by the yellowed grass and thorns and shrubbery around it, like the earth was trying to reclaim it. But it had been cultivated that way. She was no Tellus scholar with a green thumb – had never cared to be. Learning hadn't ever been easy for her, but even the captain could see that the greenery had been planted there. Snaking Ivy, woodcrawl, flowering hollyoak and stinging swellweed. Defensive plants, designed to overgrow the hut. If this was Robert Hooke's home, and there seemed to be every indication that it was, then he had intended for it to be hidden from view.

'Why would Hooke want to bring commoners here?' Captain Kildare mused. 'Why would he keep it a secret?'

'Where exactly is here?' Linus asked, appearing from the midst of some stinging swellweed and wincing at the small blisters that formed on his hand.

Captain Kildare watched in surprise as the Fleetwater in his veins took effect and healed them immediately.

'The south I think,' she said, turning around and looking up towards the sun.

'The south is pretty big,' Linus said. 'Anything more specific?'

The captain looked at him with hard eyes.

'Watch your tone,' she hissed. 'Don't be getting all big for your britches just because you feel indestructible. I doubt Fleetwater would save you from a cutlass slitting you from tummy to throat and no mistake.'

'Yes, Cap'n,' Linus grinned.

'The southwest, I'm guessing. There are seabirds over yonder.' She pointed to the horizon where large blue birds flickered, hardly visible against the night sky, but their shrill hawkish cries were loud.

'Southwest? Near the Ardere Academy?' Linus asked.

Captain Kildare nodded. 'That's my reckoning.'

'That's perfect,' Linus said, starting to march off into the grass, which reached his waist.

With each step he took, flutters of seeds and magic rose up around him. The captain wondered if he could see them.

'Hold up, laddie,' she called out to him. 'The Skimmer will be here shortly.'

Linus looked around.

'Er, Cap'n, there's no water around here.'

Captain Bonny Kildare smiled broadly. Linus raised an eyebrow. He had never seen her look as joyful as she did right now.

'I know, lad,' she said with a wink.

Captain Kildare rooted inside her leather waistcoat for a moment and then pulled out a thin silver whistle. It was tarnished with age and Linus had never seen it before, let alone heard the captain blow it. In the dark, quiet of the sewers, silence was the preferred state. Mudlarks were an everyday threat and whenever they sailed too close to the Mire on the outskirts of the Magistry, you never knew what might hear you and come snaking down after you. Flint and Ragstone had told Linus horror stories about other sewer ships which had ventured out too far. Only wreckage and bones had ever been found.

'Hello, old friend,' Captain Kildare mumbled fondly to the whistle and Linus raised his eyebrow.

'Er–' he began, but the captain immediately silenced him by blowing loud and heartily into the whistle.

Linus covered his ears at the shrill sound which shook his brain. It was a long call, raising and lowering in pitch for a few seconds until Captain Kildare stopped and turned to him, smiling broadly.

'What the -?' Linus asked, but stopped when he heard a faint whistle calling back in return.

'Brace yourself, lad,' the captain said, with a grin that spread to her eyes, crinkling them at the sides.

Linus had never seen her looked so happy.

'There she blows!'

Linus looked up to the sky, where Captain Kildare was stretching out her hand. Cutting through the dark blue sky, a skyship burst forward. It looked like a jagged crack had been opened in the sky, opening wide enough and for long enough to let a skyship lit with glowing orbs and lanterns through. A gigantic, oblong balloon covered the length of the keel below it, attached with ropes and the old, patched sails which looped over the nose of the balloon. Rarely had Linus seen the full stretch of the sails – the sewers had little airflow and not enough height to fully erect them but even so, he had known the sails had a greater capacity than they had use for, but he had not expected them to be so large. Masts stretched high reaching into the balloon and then out of it at the top, surging into the sky above, the flag of the Skimmer fluttering wildly. Wings stretched out from the sides of the hull, and they looked like an accordion with oilskin stretched over long ribs of bone that moved independently, pulled with ropes and wires connected to the large wheel at the stern. As the ship descended, Linus stared, mouth open, as he made out the tall, graceful form of Flint steering the ship, his teal and gold waistcoat catching the moonlight.

'Come about!' Captain Kildare shouted up to Flint, making Linus jump.

He had heard the captain yell, sure, but had never heard the full range of her voice. Linus watched as Flint masterfully tilted the ship, the wings at the side folding whilst great hisses of air chugged from the balloon. The ship gracefully turned and settled to a hover just above them.

'Ahoy!' Flint shouted down.

'Ahoy!' Captain Kildare returned the call. 'Toss us the ladder, you plumped up dandy! I want to see my girl in all her glory!'

'Aye aye, Cap'n,' Flint grinned down, and a rope ladder unfurled towards them, stopping just a foot or so above the ground.

'Up we go, lad. Hand over fist,' the captain said, motioning for Linus to begin climbing up the rope.

He started his ascent, the rope swaying precariously. But he had no fear. The Fleetwater in his body made him feel strong. Even the cracking callouses on his hands did not slow him. He reached the gunwhale of the hull and Flint pulled him over, so that he was stood on the deck of the Skimmer once again. Ragstone, Bazalgeutte and Pinks were there, too, smiling at him, though Pinks looked nervous and unsure, having never before stepped foot outside of the sewers, let alone been to the Second on an airship.

'You alright there, boy?' Flint asked him, gripping his fist tightly and slapping him on the back.

'Yeah,' Linus said hoarsely, his eyes panning over the ship.

It was the Skimmer, sure enough, but it was like she had been unfolded and stretched out.

'Woah,' he breathed, spinning slowly as Captain Kildare jumped over onto the deck with a hand from Flint.

'Cap'n,' Flint nodded, and the crew bowed their heads and tipped imaginary hats.

'All set?'

'Yes, Cap'n. We had some issues with the airbrake but Ragstone got it going again, and Pinks patched the balloon.'

'Cloudmast sturdy? After it got blown off in the last battle it's always been wobbly.'

'Secured, Cap'n. That was definitely one of my best shots, if I do say so myself,' Flint grinned.

'Hmph,' Captain Kildare snorted. 'I let you make the shot. Lulled you and your captain into a false sense of security so I could get aboard your ship and loot it.'

'And all you got was me,' Flint laughed. 'And you're my captain now.'

'And never a finer one!' Ragstone growled happily.

'Here, here!' the crew agreed.

Pinks smiled and clapped her nimble hands.

'Where to, Cap'n?' Flint asked.

Captain Kildare looked at Linus and nodded slightly.

'The Ardere Academy. We're not far, I think.'

'Right you are,' Flint said unquestioningly. 'Ok you bunch of sewer rats! Set sail! Bazalguette, hoist the ladder and tend the airbrake! Pinks, to the cloudmast and loosen the sail. Ragstone, batten the hatches and monitor the airflow!'

'Aye, sir!' the crew responded to their first mate and hurried to their duties.

Soon, the ship was turning and they were catapulting south through the dark.

Captain Kildare breathed deeply and walked to the bow of the ship. She balanced her hipbones on the gunwale and leaned over.

'Hey!' Linus cried out and ran after her, but the captain leaned up again, grinning widely.

'Take a look, lad.' Captain Kildare leaned over again, and Linus joined her.

Stretching out her arm to the wood of the bow, Linus saw muck and dirt flake magically away from the wood. The name of the Skimmer had always been legible, it's faded golden letters engraved deep into the ashwood of the ship though faded and dirty, visible only when they made port in the candlelight of Lundonwick. Now, Linus saw it restored to its shining glory but more than that, he saw other letters forming as though they were being pulled out of the wood where they had been hidden.

An ornate, swirling letter S.

A 'k' with its kicking leg looping underneath the name to underline it.

A gentle, slanting 'y' hanging down and vining around the word.

'Hello, my beauty,' Captain Kildare said softly, and she stroked the wood. 'Welcome lad,' she said with glassy eyes, 'to the Skyskimmer.'

Although Linus had visited the Second Plane once or twice, he had never spent a significant amount of time there. His father had been a hard taskmaster, making Linus practice his magic constantly, though his grasp of it had always been weak. Most magicians learned magic by learning how to enter the Second Plane, where magic was at its most visible. It gave magicians the ability to recognise magic on the First, where it was fainter and better hidden within the fabric of things. But Godspell had made

Linus practice by getting him to try and step into the far more mysterious Third Plane. Not only was this forbidden by magical law that nobody, not even the Firelighter could break, but it was also incredibly dangerous. But Linus had never questioned his father. He'd tried and tried to enter and gotten close once, before Shylock had interrupted him.

I wish I could ask my father why he wanted me to go to the Third Plane, and why he never let me come here, Linus thought. He was standing at the hull of the Skyskimmer, looking at the Second Plane passing underneath them. It was still dark, and the weather was chilly but even from the clouds, Linus could see how beautiful and untouched the Second was. But he was unnerved by the thought. He had no care for Godspell. He wouldn't wish to *ever* see him again. Even as he frowned and clung to this, Black Mary's voice seemed to sing inside his veins: *"You regret pushing the man, Corbin Godspell, the one you called Father, to his death."*

'I don't,' Linus mumbled to himself.

And yet he could not shake the melancholy thoughts from his mind. Perhaps the Fleetwater was slowly wearing off or maybe it was the recent betrayal of Felix, whom he had trusted and defended...had she really sent Sigbert Goodnight, of all people, to kill him? And could he really believe that Goodnight had been a Shadow? It all seemed so far-fetched now that he thought about it, but he'd seen it all with his own eyes. The deadly smoke had not touched Goodnight. It had flowed around him on its way to Linus and the captain. Goodnight *had* to be the Shadow...but then how had the smoke killed him, in the end? And what was the lump of coal he'd so desperately wanted Linus to have?

He reached down to the small weight of the coal in his pocket and tapped it, making sure it was still there.

'It doesn't make any sense,' he said to himself, and shook his head.

'Land 'hoy!' shouted Ragstone, interrupting Linus' thoughts.

The boy looked up at the cloudmast where Pinks was pointing and grinning, and then turned to follow her gaze.

'The Ardere,' Linus said with a quiet gasp. 'Woah.'

Carved into the white stone cliffs, jutting out over the roaring waves of the sea was the Ardere Academy. Its steeples and turrets, bridges and domes sparkled in the moonlight. Every single bit of it was carved from the cliff face, and Linus couldn't help but wonder how long it had taken to build. This was to be the university where he studied. He was supposed to start studying there next year and his name had been down for enrolment since he was a baby. His father had been a student here, in the Vene consortium. His real father, Everard, had gone there too, as a Tempus scholar. Linus felt the churning of longing in his gut. If things had been different, what would his flair have been?

'Prepare for docking!' Captain Kildare bellowed out to the crew. 'Linus! Stop lollygagging and help Baz with the airbrake! Pinks, hoist the sail! Flint, get your arse over here and help me with this!'

There was a chorus of 'Aye, Cap'n' and then a flurry of movement as ropes were pulled, wheels were turned, sails were gathered. The ship began to tilt, her wings outstretched as she began to skim clouds, descending and turning. Linus watched the captain as she steered the Skyskimmer, as she read the dials, flipped the switches to release the air pressure and pulled the levers to balance the ship. She was like a composer and the Skyskimmer was her melody. Flint was there next to her helping but she didn't need it; she was fluid and confident, commanding her ship as though it was an extension of herself. Linus couldn't help but admire her.

The ship gracefully looped around the Ardere so that it was now coming up behind her, over the sea. Linus peered out from behind the airbrake and saw that there was a long, sharp shard of stone protruding out over the sea. There were large cleats affixed to the rock as well as piles of rope, thicker than Ragstone's thighs, curled around large fishing baskets.

'It's an air dock!'

'Never mind that, boy! Keep pulling that airbrake!' Baz shouted, pulling at a lever with all his might, as sweat dripped down his brow. 'You should never approach a dock faster than you're willing to hit it!'

Linus quickly gripped the lever and pulled down, feeling the weight of the ship begin to slow.

'Anchors away!' the captain shouted.

Ragstone, who was commanding the windlass, saluted and lowered the anchor slowly. Linus was pouring with sweat, at the effort of applying the airbrake but beneath the ship, down on the dock, he saw the small figures of guards rushing out towards the skimmer and reaching for the anchor and pushing it over the side into the sea.

'Pinks, send down the lines!' Flint called out.

Pinks ran around the ship, unravelling thin wire ropes and throwing them over the sides. Below, the guards caught them and pulled them. Linus could just about hear them shouting 'heave!'.

Slowly but surely, the Skyskimmer descended until it came to a complete halt only a few metres above the dock. The guards tied off the lines to the cleats and secured the ship.

'Ok, crew,' Captain Kildare said, as she peered over the side. 'We're here for William Lilly's diaries, remember. And we need to find out who this Hestia Windwood is...but we don't know how welcome our questions will be, so let me and Linus do the asking.'

'But, Cap'n, I'm an alumnus. I can help,' Flint said.

'Only if we need it, Flint. Until we get our grounding here, I don't want to reveal our play. I've never trusted these namby pamby scholars...no offence, Flint. Baz, lower the ladder.'

Bazalguette tossed the rope ladder over the gunwale and Captain Kildare slung her leg over, but paused as she saw a beefy, squat man with grey hair pulled into a ponytail marching along to dock towards them. He looked angry and his hands, gloved in green leather, were clenched into fists.

'Oh, hold up. Looks like we've got trouble already,' Captain Kildare said, rolling her eyes.

'That's Gaspard Nyxon. He's a professor here. Head of one of the consortiums, I think.'

'Friend or foe?'

'Not sure, but he doesn't exactly look like a welcome wagon, does he?'

'You there!' the man shouted, in a voice that was gruffer than expected. 'Come down immediately!'

'Pinks,' Captain Kildare said to the girl. 'Stay aboard and keep hidden. I don't like the look of this one.'

Pinks nodded and her smile was one of relief. She scurried below deck to the cabin.

'I say! Come down this instant! You are in direct violation of the air safety code number 678 and -'

'Alright alright! Keep yer' wig on! We're coming!' Captain Kildare shouted, and she climbed down the rope followed by Flint, Ragstone and Bazalguette. Linus brought up the rear.

'This is an outrage!' Professor Nyxon was shouting as the captain jumped from the last rung onto the dock. 'This dock is a historic monument! It hasn't been docked by an airship in over thirty years!'

He was spitting with rage as he gesticulated around him.

'What in fire's name are you doing here? Answer me!'

'We're here to see Principal Ellis,' Flint said. 'If he's still here?'

Professor Gaspard Nyxon sneered and folded his arms.

'It pains me to say he is,' he said, with knotted black eyebrows. 'But the principal is in a very important meeting right now.'

'Well, this is more important,' said Captain Kildare, stepping in front of Flint and resting her hands on her hips. 'We'll be seeing him now, unless you fancy having your gizzards pulled out of your nose?'

'Your threats won't scare me, pirate scum!' Professor Nyxon snarled, but then suddenly he froze as he saw Linus jump from the ladder rope onto the dock.

'Linus Godspell?' he whispered.

His dark eyes glittered wildly as he stared at the boy.

'Uh,' replied Linus.

Captain Kildare shot him a threatening look and shook her head almost imperceptibly.

'Save it. We've met many times before,' Professor Nyxon said to Captain Kildare. 'Linus knew my father, isn't that right?'

Linus swallowed.

'I wouldn't say I knew him. I witnessed his...work.'

'Well,' Professor Nyxon said with a sneer, stepping closer to Linus. 'How pleased she will be that I have you.'

'She?' Linus spat out. 'You mean my sister, don't you?' But then he felt himself shoved to the ground, his arms twisted painfully up his back.

'What the..?!' An invisible hand clamped tightly over his mouth, muffling his words and sealing his lips.

Around him, he heard the 'oofs' of the crew as they too were pushed down onto their stomachs. Linus twisted his neck to see what was happening. Professor Nyxon was waving his hands and binding them all magically, menace woven into his face.

'Guards!' he shouted, his voice as grating as a knife against brick. 'Take these scum to the sea cave dungeon and seal the doors. The tide rises in a couple of hours. They'll be drowned before sunup.'

Linus wriggled in protest, trying to cry out behind the tight, invisible hand.

'As for this one,' Professor Nyxon growled, lowering his pockmarked face down to Linus. 'I'll handle him. Cut the ship loose!'

Two guards ran to the ship and cut the lines and anchor with magically conjured swords, that disappeared as soon as they'd disconnected the ship. The Skyskimmer began to float away from the dock. From behind her invisible gag, Captain Kildare screamed, her eyes wide with panic as she flailed against the guard who was holding her.

Linus began to kick at the guard holding him, throwing his head back in an attempt to headbutt him. For a moment, he broke loose but Professor Nyxon smiled as he made a snapping motion with his hands and Linus felt his leg break in two. He screamed in pain but the Fleetwater in his blood immediately started to heal him. He felt the pain recede and the bone reconnect, though he made no show of this to Professor Nyxon. Linus looked to the crew, who were being dragged towards a staircase at the base of the dock by the guards. His eyes were wide, trying to convey to them that he would get to them, he would save them. Then, they were gone.

A single guard remained. His face was obscured by a cloak, a uniform which looked familiar. He was like a monk, Linus thought. *I've seen that uniform before.* It was the final thing that crossed his mind before Professor Nyxon punched him.

All went black.

On the third floor, in a large south-facing bedroom, Slingsby Buzzard and a large shaggy grey dog which looked like a dire wolf were leaning out of the open window, looking down at the dock, their faces lined with horror at what they had witnessed. They saw the great shadow of an airship floating away, out to sea. They saw its crew captured and hauled down to the sea caves. The dire wolf heard the professor call the tall, thin boy 'Linus Godspell' and then hit him. With a growl, D.W lurched to the door and bounded down the staircase. Slingsby Buzzard hesitated for a moment, wishing that all he had to worry about today was a test of Ptolemy, but then he abandoned his half-packed suitcase on his bed and followed D.W to the principal's office.

On the deck of the Skyskimmer, a little girl named Pinks peered through a porthole as she saw her crewmates and her captain pulled away by the guards. She felt the tilt of the ship as it began to keel, and she raced to the wheel and pushed at it with all of her might in the opposite direction. The ship began to right itself. Then she scuttled up the cloudmast, as quiet as a tiny mouse, and lowered the mainsail, securing it with nimble fingers. A gust of wind caught the ship and blew it back towards the dock. She leaned out over the gunwale, her face resolute. Pinks was only eleven years old. She was mute, but she was a crewmember of the Skyskimmer and she served Captain Bonny Kildare. People often underestimated her, but Pinks knew what she was capable of. Her captain had taught her well. Sometimes, the quietest of people can fight the fiercest.

Above them all, in the stone bell tower of the ancient Ardere Academy, quite oblivious to the action happening beneath, the bell tolled five times.

28

Lost and Found

Felix was rushing. The sun would rise soon, and although its light barely filtered down through the crevices of the mountain and its silver canopy of webs, it would still bring about the waking of the Drow and with them, the white widows and Felix was now fearful of both. She had dared not venture back to her room. It was too close to Lillith, who might sense her emotions even in her dreams and Felix knew that what she was feeling was treacherous. She tried to calm herself, breathing deeply and pushing her fear and her anger down, quelling them with the hope that she would soon see Nigel and the dire wolf again.

With each stumbling step away from Lillith, her mind became clearer, her vision sharper as though she had been stood in mist for weeks and had not even known it. But rushing was making her clumsy. Twice she had tripped, and she had cut her knee badly. The blood was dripping down her bare legs and onto the ground. *Could a spider smell blood?* she wondered, looking over her shoulder constantly, half expecting Lillith to be chasing after her astride a white widow. Nonsense, surely, for Lillith would not bring any harm to her. Anger, yes and perhaps a sense of betrayal but Lillith was no threat to Felix. Not Lillith, the one who had taken her in with open arms, welcoming her, teaching her and accepting her. But even so, Felix couldn't stand the thought of Lillith tempting her to stay. She could bear to hear Lillith's justification for the way those men and those children were being treated.

She stopped for a moment; the breath sucked out of her stomach at the thought of the little boy who looked at her as though she was something terrifying. At the Festival of Fire, too, people had cowered. The way the commoners had screamed in fear at the spectacle she had made of herself, the way the magicians had sneered at her in disgust and now the little boy who had pulled away in terror – these memories seared into her brain and burned there like brands.

'I won't ever be what they think I am,' she whispered to herself, her hands clutching onto her thighs as she bent over, trying to pull the air back into her lungs.

She looked up. Ahead of her was the cavern, through which she had followed her sister Drow. To pass through it now would lead back to the tunnel that would open out into the Glade.

She began to run. Her knee was smarting, and her feet were cut to ribbons from the rocks and crystals jutting out from the ground. The cavern was dark, and she conjured an orb of light, revelling in the feel of magic in her hands again, each step warming her and thawing the ice. Gemstones glittered in the rocks as she passed and she could hear the familiar scuttling of spiders on the rockface, but these things didn't stop her. Her thin scrap of nightdress grew damp from the water dripping down from the cracks, and her hair was caught on protruding stones but still she ran. With each minute that passed, she felt like she was waking up. Her head ached. It was the same ache she had on her sixteenth birthday, when the Drow markings had first appeared for she had come of age. So much had happened since then. A different life. A different person.

Keep going.

Lillith had tried to get her to forget it all. Forget Nigel, forget D.W. Forget Fiddle. They had remembered him together at the Drowning and they had honoured his memory, but that was it – she'd been told to cast him aside in her memories, to let him go. But Felix understood now. Her thoughts were clear, her inner voice something she could now recognise. How long had the voice in her head sounded like Lillith?

If you honour something for one day, it gives you an excuse to forget it the rest of the time. The best way to forget something is to remember it, Felix thought, her mind strong and clear. Something Fiddle would say. She smiled and closed her eyes, letting the grief for him flow through her. *Not all grief is bad. Grief is just a reminder of love.*

Felix laughed aloud as she cried, celebrating all the confusing, joyful, ugly, mournful contradictory chaos that were her beautiful feelings. *Her* feelings and hers alone. No longer was she being pulled down by the tangle of her sister Drow. She loved them. Yes, she loved them. She wouldn't lose them again, but she was two things at once, a Drow and a magician. She would straddle both sides of her identity proudly, the way her parents would have wanted her to, the way Fiddle had encouraged her to. Felix realised now that she didn't have to choose a side of herself, and that Lillith was wrong to try and make her stamp out her magic.

It came as a surprise when she burst out of the dim cavern and into the watery morning light of the Glade. Felix almost fell to the ground again, but she caught herself and she put her hands on her hips, gulping down oxygen and willing the stitch in her side to abate.

It was frosty and the grass was tipped with glitter. Her bare feet were instantly cold and Felix began to shiver, her heavy breath forming misty clouds in front of her face. Looking above her, she saw the growing light of the winter sunrise; a watercolour sky. Birds chirped and sang, and Felix grinned, tipping her head back and feeling her hair brushing against her back. Nanny Maude had loved her hair, brushed it so softly.

"Y'know, you and my Lily was nearly the same age? If she'd have lived, I reckon she would have turned out a bit like you.'

Maude's voice reached out of her memory and Felix smiled through the sob. It had been right there in front of her, the whole time. Her whole life spent longing for home. For family. Now all she had to do was step down into the First Plane and go...where? The orphanage? The library? The Citadel? It didn't matter. All of them were home because in each of those places she had been loved; by Maude, who loved her like a daughter, by Fiddle, who had given up his freedom for her and by her friends: the dire wolf, Aubrey, Liberty, Sigbert, Thaddeus...and Nigel. And she loved them all, too. How could she have possibly felt so lost when she had found what she had been searching for?

'Sometimes, when we feel lost it is because we have yet to find true selves,' a voice cut through the calm like a knife, and Felix spun round to face the cavern, her heart catapulting into her mouth.

'Lillith,' she said, immediately feeling the chill penetrating deeper into her bones. 'How did you know I was...'

'Leaving?' Lillith finished for her.

She stepped out of the cavern, and her face was hard and unreadable. For the first time, she was wearing clothes; a silver blue dress woven from spider silk. With her dark spirals vining around her neck and face and wrists, she was an intimidating sight to behold. It made her seem more real somehow, more human and less otherworldly. It was as though being naked had been her mask, marking her as vulnerable and harmless and now clothes revealed her to be a threatening weapon.

'Or should I say escaping?' Lillith said again.

Felix swallowed and lowered her head.

'Fortunately, I have some who are loyal,' Lillith continued, tilting her head to reveal Aradia creeping over her shoulder, her two front legs stretched out to Felix in silent entreaty. Felix nodded resignedly and looked directly at Lillith, a knot of fear burrowing in the pit of her belly.

'Lillith, I am grateful for everything you've done for me, but it's time for me to go home.'

'Home?' Lillith said, but her voice was hard, and it made Felix jump. Lillith stepped closer to Felix and began to circle around her like a vulture. 'This is your home!'

Felix swallowed. Power radiated from Lillith, and Felix knew that all she had to do was touch her and she'd be lost again, pulled down into the tides.

'This is one home, Lillith,' Felix said gently. 'But I am not just a Drow. I am a magician, too and I have people I love waiting for me and I've left them for far too long.'

Lillith scoffed and a fleck of spittle landed on Felix's cheek. Instantly, anger flared through her spirals, but she tried not to let it show.

'They don't love you,' Lillith spat. 'How could they? They don't even know you. *I* know you. Your sisters and I...we truly love you. We have seen your *soul*.'

'I know,' Felix nodded, slowly stepping away from Lillith, who saw the movement and sneered.

'Would they love the secrets you keep, I wonder?' Lillith smiled, her eyes narrowing.

Felix tried to slow her breathing. Inside her head, alarm bells were ringing. She knew she was in danger.

'Would they love you if they saw your dreams the way I do?' Lillith whispered. 'The way you wish there was a way of going back, of giving it all up? Would they love you if they saw how weak you truly are? You thirst for truth, and yet you can't even be honest with yourself! You don't want to be the Firelighter. You never did. People have *died* for you, to put you where you are now, and you don't even want it. An ungrateful, spineless coward. That's what you are. Would they love you if they knew?'

'You're right, Lillith,' Felix nodded.

She felt it was important to keep agreeing with Lillith, to keep her calm. Besides, Lillith *was* right.

'I didn't ask for any of this. I never wanted to be the Firelighter. But we all keep secrets, Lillith,' Felix sighed. 'Even you.'

'You know NOTHING of secrets!' Lillith roared and Felix jumped back, her skin prickling with adrenalin.

'I know that they are a noose around your own neck,' Felix said, trying to get Lillith to meet her eye. 'Why don't you share your burden, sister Lillith?' Felix reached out to her slowly, but Lillith's shoulders began to shake.

At first, Felix thought she might be crying but then she realised she was laughing, deep and hearty, phlegm rattling in her throat. Felix drew her hand back.

'You think you can beat me at my own game?' Lillith finally said in a hoarse voice.

'No,' Felix shook her head. 'I'm not playing any game. I just want to help. Clearly something is weighing on you. Whatever it is...please. Let me help.'

For a moment, Lillith's face grew lax. Her mouth opened and closed noiselessly, and her shoulders slumped.

'It is... so... heavy,' she whispered.

Felix stepped towards her and reached for her hand. Lillith's skin was cold and unpleasant to touch.

'Tell me,' Felix implored. 'We can fix it together. We can stop hiding down here and be free again, be rid of the white widows, stop sending the men and boys to them. The Drow can come back from this, Lillith. I can help.'

Lillith looked at Felix and snatched her hand away, her eyes hardening once more.

'There is only one thing you can do to help me,' she sneered.

'What is it?' Felix asked.

'Give me the Sacred Flame.'

Felix felt the blood drain from her face.

'What?'

'Give it to me,' Lillith spat, stepping towards Felix with burning eyes.

'Lillith – I –why? Why do you need it?' Her mouth was dry.

Lillith looked up at the sky and screamed, her fists clenched so hard that when she opened her palms, Felix could see the blood in the crescent shaped cuts from her nails.

'Do you ever stop asking questions?' she breathed, her words spraying spit into the air.

Felix let the anger surge up and out, letting her spirals glow.

'Back off, Lillith,' Felix growled at her. 'Let me go and I won't hurt you.'

Again, Lillith laughed. Felix swallowed, fear squashing down her power a little. It was maniacal laughter, the laughter of one who has lost all reasoning.

'You're mad,' Felix whispered.

'Ahh, sister Felix. You're not going anywhere,' Lillith said, her smile stretching thinly over her teeth, before she swung her arm around and hit Felix's head hard with a shard of quartz.

Blood spurted from the wound as Felix crumpled to the ground, her body still and silent as the morning sun crept higher into the sky.

29

Rescue!

The last of the bell's tolls had sounded, and Nigel was locking Fiddle's check out box when he and Principal Ellis heard the scratching of the dire wolf's claws against the doors.

'Right on time,' Principal Ellis said. 'Though I'm afraid he'll scratch the varnish off my door, and it is a rather old door.'

Nigel smiled, but it faded as the dire wolf's whining became a bark.

'Something's wrong,' he said, pushing past Principal Ellis and opening the door.

The wolf bounded into the room, jumping from the sofa to the armchair, his words pouring out in a confused flurry, obscured by barks and whines and whimpers.

'Here…took him…crew!'

'D.W, calm down, I can't hear what you're saying,' Nigel said, holding his gloved hands out to calm him, though he felt foolish doing so when the wolf was foaming at his teeth and panting desperately. Nigel wondered if dire wolves could catch rabies, but he stopped the thought instantly when D.W growled at him ferociously.

'He's HERE!' D.W cried out loudly, a mix of gruff voice and high-pitched whine.

Nigel winced at the sound.

'Who is? Where's Slingsby?'

'Yes, where is the rascal?' Principal Ellis asked, peering out of the doors into the dark corridors. 'Ah here he comes, late as usual.'

Slingsby Buzzard jumped the final four steps of the staircase and slid past the office, catching himself on the door frame.

'Come quickly!' he cried out, trying to catch his breath somewhat dramatically.

'What on earth is going on here?' Principal Ellis said, looking between D.W and Slingsby as though their behaviour was distasteful.

The dire wolf jumped up at Nigel, his paws pushing at him aggressively.

'Nigel, listen,' he said, his golden eyes wide. 'Linus is here. He's here, Nigel!'

'Linus? Linus Godspell? Felix's brother?' Nigel asked.

'HOW MANY OTHER LINUS' DO YOU KNOW, YOU IDIOT!' the dire wolf growled.

'Yep. Him and an airship crew, complete with airship and all,' Slingsby nodded, his hands clutching at his lower back as he bent over like he'd just run a marathon.

'Where?! Did you know about this, Principal Ellis?' Nigel said, moving quickly and grabbing Fiddle's checkout box by the handle and carrying it like a small suitcase.

D.W looked at it curiously.

'Don't look at me, boy, I had no idea he was here!' the principal said indignantly. 'Where are they all, Slingsby? Come on now, spit it out!'

'Professor Nyxon and the Shadowguard took them, sir,' Slingsby said, his face crumpled as though this was horrible news, but his eyes were glittering gleefully.

'Took them? What do you mean took them?' Nigel asked, looking now to D.W.

'I don't know, but I don't think it was to a hotel,' D.W snarled.

'The crew were taken down to the sea caves by the Shadowguard,' Slingsby said excitedly. 'Sir, the dire wolf is right in what he says. Professor Nyxon wasn't exactly friendly with them. He cut the ship loose and knocked the boy out himself. Always said Professor Nyxon was a bast-'

'Alright, Slingsby,' the principal held his hand up to stop him, and then looked at the clock on his mantelpiece. It was only a little after five in the morning.

'The tide will be in very soon,' he said. 'Slingsby, get down to the sea caves now and set them loose, then bring the crew back here. They might not deserve the sea caves, but I still want to find out exactly why they're here.'

He removed a metal ring that held a single key from his belt and tossed it to Slingsby, who caught it and struggled to hide the smile on his face.

'Gee, sir. The key to the school?'

'It will open any door, window or cage,' Principal Ellis nodded, with a look of regret on his face as though he would rather give the key to anyone in the world other than Slingsby Buzzard.

'Er, sir, not to present a problem rather than a solution or anything, what with me being a solution orientated person, as well you know–'

'Spit it out, Slingsby,' Principal Ellis interrupted.

'What about the Shadowguard?'

'D.W will go with you. His howl can kill lamias, so it can definitely knock out a few guards. Plus, look at his teeth!' Nigel said, looking down at the wolf. 'You go save the crew, and me and Principal Ellis will go and get Linus.'

D.W tilted his head a little at Nigel, regarding him suspiciously but if he had any cause for concern, he put it to one side and leapt out of the door.

'Come ON, Slingsby,' he barked.

'Golly....how...*exciting*!' Slingsby said, scrunching his shoulders up to his ears before turning on his heel and running after D.W.

'Professor Nyxon,' Nigel said, turning directly to the principal. 'Why would he want Linus?'

'Honestly...I'm not sure,' Professor Ellis said, with a shrug of his old shoulders.

'Is he on the Privy Council?'

'Well if he was, I couldn't tell you,' the principal frowned. 'But why do you ask?'

Nigel shrugged.

'Seems like everyone is,' he said sullenly.

'Everyone may have secrets, Nigel, but not all secrets need protecting.'

'What would he have against Linus?' Nigel asked, shaking his head. 'Have they met before?'

'I think so. Gaspard's father, as you know, worked for Corbin Godspell. I imagine their paths have crossed,' Principal Ellis replied, rubbing his gloved finger under his chin. 'Linus was due to start studying here next year before he...well, before he lost his magic, but he'd never visited the school. His father was always particularly strict about Linus, I believe. And Professor Nyxon is the head of the Tempus consortium, the commandant of the Shadowguard and a well-established member of my staff. He's not exactly popular and we don't particularly see eye to eye, but he's hardly a villain. He has lived and taught at the Ardere for many years.'

'Well, after he threw himself at Felix's mercy at the State Ball, perhaps he's seeking revenge on her by targeting her brother?' Nigel suggested, trying to piece everything together.

'Maybe,' considered Principal Ellis. 'But Gaspard Nyxon has never shown any indication that he meant any harm to anybody. Honestly, this could all just be a misunderstanding.'

'A misunderstanding?' Nigel repeated. 'You call drowning innocent people a misunderstanding? Why would he do that, if he's not got some crazy plan of vengeance?'

'We'd better go and ask him,' Principal Ellis said, jutting his chin out.

'No offence, but if Professor Nyxon has the Shadowguard at his command, we might need a little more help,' Nigel said tentatively.

'Young man,' Principal Ellis said angrily. 'I am the principal of the Ardere Academy and a member of the Privy Council. I have more tricks up my sleeve than you could ever dream of!'

'Then by all means,' Nigel said, pushing his glasses up his nose. 'Lead the way.'

Pinks looped the lines around the cleats as quickly as she could. She didn't have time to secure all of them and the Skyskimmer was veering ominously to the right in the early morning breeze, but it would have to do.

Steady girl, Pinks thought, stroking the ashwood of the ship with her leather-clad hands.

It was still dark, and Pinks sent a silent prayer of thanks to the Flame. Darkness was familiar. She knew it well. Crouching down, she scanned the dock, but it was empty. No guards had come running when she'd docked the Skyskimmer again. She peered up at the carved cliff face of the Ardere Academy. Some people said it was beautiful but to Pinks, who preferred the shift and swell of water and wood, the stone was too solid, too still. Thankfully she would not need to enter it, for she'd seen the guards pull the crew down the staircase made of rock underneath the dock. The angry man had taken Linus, but he'd carried him inside. Pinks would need the crew, Captain Kildare especially, if she was going to get Linus back, for Linus was part of the Skyskimmer too, to be sure.

Staying low and keeping in the shadow of the Skyskimmer, Pinks dashed along the dock, hardly disturbing a single pebble as she moved, for Pinks was as soundless as her tongue. She reached the staircase and peered down the steps. They were steep and narrow, curving round underneath the jutting dock. Lower still was the black water of the sea, glimmers of white foam catching in the sliver of light from the moon and stars. But Pinks didn't fear the water, nor did she fear the height. Like a spider, she crawled down the stairs. Her thin ankles and tiny feet were the perfect fit for the shallow steps. Only once did she misstep, but she righted herself quickly and quietly.

The stairs did not reach the water or the thin strip of beach that remained under the dock, as the tide slowly inched its way higher and closer to the cliff walls. Instead, the stairs led into a hole in the rock face, more than big enough for a little girl to slip through. She waited at the apex of the hole and listened. Pinks had grown up in darkness. Her vision, though piercing in dimness, was poor in light. She had not spoken a word for as long as she could remember. Robbed of these two faculties, her remaining senses had overcompensated. Her ears listened to the rushing of water inside the hole. The sound told her the depth, the width and the danger all of which were great, but Pinks was no coward. She took a deep breath and did not think again before pushing herself into the hole.

She landed exactly when she thought she would, in water that covered her boots but did not quite come up to her knees. Pinks was mute but she was not dumb. She understood water. She could swim before she could walk. The tide may not yet be in, but it was seeping in through the sand and through the rocks and crevices beneath it. Judging by the depth, she had little over an hour to find the crew.

Feeling with her boots, Pinks identified a part of the ground that was smoother than the rest – a path, well worn by boots of guards. Reaching out with her hands and feeling for the height and width of the ceiling and walls, she stepped slowly but surely along, bending only a little through tunnels. When the darkness became too thick, she conjured a small orb of light and listened again.

Cries to the east. The crew? But no, the crew would not scream. Listening harder, she realised that the cries were just the calls of nesting seabirds. But their cries were shrill and loud. Why, when they were in the dark, alone and undisturbed? Unless they were not alone at all.

Pinks smiled and followed the sounds, leaving barely a whisper of ripples behind her.

Linus groaned. His head was heavy, resting against a cold, damp wall and his nose and right eye were throbbing. His face felt wet and sticky but when he tried to lift his hands, he found them restrained behind his back, his shoulders burning in dull pain as he tried to pull his hands free.

He stopped moving and tried to keep calm. He reached back into his memory, to the classes Shylock Larkin had given him in the event of capture. As son to the Firelighter and heir apparent, it was a sensible precaution, especially considering how many times the rebellion had tried to capture or assassinate his father.

Stay quiet and still. Don't give anything away. Take stock of your surroundings. Listen for sounds or identify smells that may help you guess a location. Most importantly, do not panic.

Linus opened his eyes a crack, though his right eye wouldn't open at all because it was swollen shut. The Fleetwater in his veins was wearing low and its healing power was slowing down. He tried not to think about what could happen when the Fleetwater ran out. With his remaining eye, Linus could make out blurred outlines – a wooden chair, things hanging down from a ceiling that he couldn't see. Dim light – only a few candles. Scent of rot and cold, dank sea air. Seaweed, fish...was that the metal tang of blood? The floor beneath him was stone, but it was rough with sand and it was damp, too. The chill pervaded his bones. He was near the sea, certainly and underneath the Ardere would be his best guess. But this wasn't a sea cave; it was a chamber of some sort. Linus shuffled quietly and slowly, blinking his good eye to try and get a better view. The room began to take shape. It was most definitely a dungeon of some type. The things hanging from the ceiling were hooks and cages, and the smell of seawater came from a black hole at the centre of the chamber. An oubliette.

Swallowing as silently as he could, Linus' body beginning to tremble. What little Fleetwater that was left in his blood minimised the pain in his face, but it could not take away the fear or the cold.

There was a faint muffling sound coming from somewhere in the shadows of the room. A low voice. Linus strained to listen. Yes, definitely a voice. He shifted again, edging around the circular wall, his eye darting around, trying to pierce the blackness.

'I can't keep him here for too long,' the voice said in a hurried whisper.

It was Gaspard Nyxon's voice, and Linus was confused at his tone. For some reason, Professor Nyxon was in a panic.

'Don't you understand? Someone will find out I have him. I could lose my job, my reputation. I've already done enough of her dirty work, and I've lost enough already.'

Linus leaned around and he saw the thin, reedy silhouette of Professor Nyxon. He was holding something in his hand and talking to it. What was it? Whatever it was appeared to be communicating with him soundlessly in some way.

'How can she have changed her mind?' Professor Nyxon hissed into his hand. 'She's wanted him for weeks! Smokesbane died for this – the best Shadow I ever trained – and now I have him and she doesn't even want him? What could possibly be better than Linus Godspell?'

There was silence and then a gasp from Professor Nyxon.

'Then, once she's got it...she can free my father? She promised me she would!'

Linus' pulse was beating so loudly in his ears, he was struggling to hear. He had met Gaspard Nyxon's father in his laboratory only once. Dr Nyxon's cold, appraising glare still gave him nightmares, along with the memory of Murphy and Mortimer's dead eyes in the machine Dr Nyxon had been building. Linus moved closer, again.

'Fine...' Professor Nyxon sighed. 'What do I do with the boy then?'

Whatever the answer was, clearly Professor Nyxon found it was distasteful. He grimaced but nodded. Linus arched his neck and saw him bend down and place whatever was in his hand on a stone step that had a crumbling hole at its base. He watched as a white spider, almost as large as Gaspard Nyxon's gloved hand, crept from his palm and onto the step.

'Aradia,' Professor Nyxon said, and the spider stopped and turned, its front legs twitching. 'She made me a promise. Please don't let her forget it. I...I just want my father back. I made a bargain and I'll keep my word. Tell her I expect her to keep hers.'

The spider dipped its body in a small nod and then scuttled into the hole. Linus was still shaking, but it was horror and anger that filled him now and he struggled to keep his cool. When

Professor Nyxon stepped out of the shadows, his face haunted and grey, he found Linus glaring up at him with one piercing blue eye, hatred etched into the lines of his face.

'Awake, I see,' Professor Nyxon said with resignation, his shoulders slumping.

'I'm assuming she told you to kill me,' Linus spat.

'Yes,' Professor Nyxon nodded. 'Not quite the outcome I had in mind, I must admit but one I am equipped for, as you can see.'

He motioned around the room at the instruments of torture.

'As head of the Tempus consortium, I have an affinity for all things past and present and future. Time, you could say. Magicians spend far too much energy on the 'new' when in fact, often our best inventions can be found in history.'

He stepped over to an empty cage hanging down from the ceiling. He touched it and instantly the iron bars began to glow red with fire.

'My father spent so long working on that crazy machine – I trust you know the one? You have direct experience of it, yes?'

Linus sucked air in through his teeth. Fear and rage churned inside him.

'Yes,' Professor Nyxon nodded. 'It was too complicated, really. But then, he is a venephysicist and wouldn't be told. You know how the Vene scholars are.'

Professor Nyxon chuckled and walked to the wooden chair. Linus saw now that there were leather straps to hold the sitter in place. With a single swipe of his finger, hundreds of spikes coated in coagulated blood shot out of the wood before vanishing back into the seat.

'No, I find the older methods work the best,' Professor Nyxon continued, and circled back to stand in front of Linus.

'Why does she want me dead?' Linus asked.

His voice was choked. He thought he might be sick.

'You're of no use to her anymore,' Professor Nyxon shrugged. 'I don't claim to understand her. She simply promised me that if I sent my best Shadowguard out to kill you, she would ensure that my father was set free. Smokesbane, as a real Shadow, was the obvious choice though even he was not infallible, it seems.'

'When did he join you? Sigbert Goodnight? When did he become a Shadow?' Linus asked.

In the back of his mind, Shylock Larkin's advice resounded: *keep them talking. Always keep them talking.*

'Sigbert Goodnight?' Professor Nyxon replied. He arched an eyebrow. 'The spy?'

'Yes. He was Smokesbane.'

Professor Nyxon laughed.

'You're mistaken there, Linus,' he said shaking his head. 'Smokesbane was a hired assassin who sought refuge in the Shadowguard. I promised him sanctuary if he performed the last task of murdering you. Sigbert Goodnight is a member of your sister's Magistry, if I'm not mistaken, and one who voted in favour of my father's imprisonment.'

Professor Nyxon spat on the ground and ran his fingers over his dark hair.

'I don't understand,' Linus said. 'My sister contacted you and promised you she'd free Dr Nyxon if you cooperated, but you didn't send Goodnight?'

'Your sister?' Professor Nyxon exclaimed. 'Boy, what are you talking about? Felix has nothing to do with this.'

Linus' eyes widened and he felt a deep sense of relief flood though him.

'She ...she didn't...doesn't want me dead?'

Professor Nyxon looked at Linus and panned his eyes over him.

'Linus, I don't much like your sister. She has condemned my father to a lifetime of imprisonment when he was manipulated and threatened, and frankly brainwashed by Godspell, but whatever ideas you had about her being your enemy are all wrong. The last I heard she has been searching for you pretty desperately – even tried to find you herself, it seems.'

'What do you mean she tried to find me?'

'Well, that's just it. She's been doing everything she can to find you – she even went to the woman who hired me.'

'Who, Professor Nyxon? If you're going to kill me, you at least owe me an explanation! Who wants me dead and why?'

Professor Nyxon held his hands up in submission.

'Lillith,' he said. 'The leader of the Drow.'

'What?' Linus said, shaking his head and pulling a face. 'But the Drow are extinct. My father...Corbin Godspell...he wiped them out.'

'Not quite,' Professor Nyxon said, shrugging his narrow shoulders.

'But why would Felix go to her, to Lillith, if Lillith wanted me dead? And why did she want me dead anyway? None of this makes any sense!'

Linus was shouting now, his voice echoing from the walls. It was true, none of it did make any sense but that wasn't why he was shouting.

Make noise as soon as it is safe to do so. Shout, if you can, came Shylock Larkin's voice from his memory.

He didn't know why Lillith would want him dead but right now, that didn't matter. Better to live in ignorance than die in knowledge.

'Keep your voice down,' Professor Nyxon snapped, and he tightened the invisible restraints around Linus' wrists and back.

Linus cried out as the burning seared through his back and dislocated his right shoulder. Professor Nyxon made a beckoning motion with his finger and Linus was dragged along the stone floor, his cheek landing against the rough stone with a loud whack. He felt himself lifted onto the wooden chair. His wrists were freed, but he screamed at the pain as his arms were pulled down to the arm rests. The straps began to fasten themselves tightly around his wrists, his neck, his middle and his ankles. He could barely move and each time he tried to wriggle, the straps tightened.

'I'm truly sorry to have to do this, Linus,' Professor Nyxon said. 'But I really don't have a choice.'

He reached his hand out to swipe a finger against the wood to release the spikes.

'Wait!' cried out Linus. 'Wait, wait, wait, please, just tell me this!!'

Professor Nyxon held his hand mid-air.

'Yes?'

'My sister. Where is she now? Is she alive?'

'For now,' Professor Nyxon said. 'Lillith will take the Flame of Magic from her and then kill her. Then Lillith will free my father...but only if I do her bidding. She promised me!'

'So Lillith wants to be the Firelighter?' Linus asked.

He was sweating profusely. His skin was beginning to burn like he had a fever.

'I assume so,' Professor Nyxon nodded impatiently. 'I don't care as long as I get my father back. Don't you understand that, Linus? My father did awful things, things I can never forgive him for, but he's still my father. I know you understand me. I can see it in your eyes. Your father, too, was a monster, but that didn't stop you from loving him, did it?'

Linus eyes widened. Denial rose up to his lips, but he couldn't lie. He knew, then, what payment Black Mary had taken. A secret so deep, he hadn't even realised it was true. He had loved his father. Even now, knowing the horror of a man that he was, Linus still loved him and missed him.

Professor Nyxon didn't wait for a reply. He swiped his finger and Linus closed his eye and screamed.

The scream continued, even after Linus closed his mouth. It was a shriek of pain and it didn't belong to him, it belonged to Gaspard Nyxon. Linus opened his eye and saw that the spikes that should have burst out of the chair into his flesh, were instead pointed directly at Professor Nyxon, the tips of each rusted spike slowly grinding into his flesh, a millimetre at a time. Linus tried to move but the straps tightened again, beginning to choke him.

'Nigel, unstrap him, quickly,' said an old voice.

Linus saw a familiar looking boy with auburn hair and glasses step over to him hurriedly. The straps were unfastened with a simple click of his fingers. Linus sucked air into his lungs and slumped forwards, into Nigel's arms.

'Woah, there,' Nigel said. 'I've got you.'

'The crew…' Linus croaked.

'Safe,' Nigel said.

Linus looked into the green eyes behind the glasses. He trusted him instantly and nodded.

'Gaspard Nyxon,' the old voice said. 'As principal of the Ardere Academy I have the authority to place you under academic arrest.'

Linus lifted his head over Nigel's shoulder and saw an old man, Principal Ellis, holding out his hands towards Professor Nyxon. He was the one holding the spikes at their slow, torturous pace.

'Until you are transferred to the COPPs and the care of the Magistry, you are henceforth stripped of your privileges and your faculties.'

'Duncan, please -' Professor Nyxon cried out but with a wave of his hands, Principal Ellis took Professor Nyxon's voice, his sight and his hearing.

He also removed the spikes, leaving a hundred red pinpricks of blood all over Professor Nyxon's body. Gaspard Nyxon slumped to the floor, his mouth opening and closing wordlessly, his hands groping at his eyes, his ears and then the floor and walls around him.

Principal Ellis took three tired strides towards him and helped him up, looping Professor Nyxon's arm around his neck. Then he reached to a deep plum-coloured pocket with his spare hand and pulled out three vials of liquid. He checked the labels, replaced two and then unstoppered the cork from the third bottle with his teeth. He poured the clear liquid into Professor Nyxon's mouth. The wounds on Professor Nyxon's flesh began to heal instantly.

'Er, Principal Ellis?" Nigel said. 'I think we need some of that Fleetwater over here.'

Linus was shuddering in Nigel's arms. His skin was red and beginning to blister.

'He's burning up!' Nigel said anxiously. 'Is this Professor Nyxon's magic?'

Principal Ellis shook his head and hobbled over to the chair, with Professor Nyxon dragging his feet across the stone floor.

'This is what happens when mortals come to the Second Plane,' he explained. 'Commoners are not meant to be here. The magic burns them.'

"And burn upon a funeral pyre..." Linus said, through shuddering breaths.

'Precisely,' Principal Ellis nodded.

He helped put the remaining Fleetwater to Linus' mouth. As soon as he swallowed, the blisters sealed themselves and Linus stopped shaking. His shoulder mended and he was able to lean back from Nigel and sit unsupported.

'Thank you,' he said gratefully. 'The crew. You said they were safe? And Felix, she's–'

But before he could finish his sentence, a great big, shaggy grey wolf launched himself from the stone staircase into the room.

'I felt her!' he cried out in a loud bark. 'Felix! She's here! I know where she is!'

Nigel let go of Linus and crouched down in front of the dire wolf.

'Is she ok? Is she hurt?'

D.W nodded.

'She feels pain,' he said with a whine. 'But she is alive.'

'Where's Slingsby? We have to go, now!'

'He's seeing to the crew. We put them in your office, Principal Ellis,' D.W said.

'My, my, it is a busy day,' Principal Ellis said, giving a short, sharp slap to the blind and deaf Professor Nyxon, who was trying to edge away from him.

'She's in danger,' Linus said.

Everyone turned to look at him.

'How do you know?' Nigel stepped towards him threateningly.

'Professor Nyxon said so. He's working for someone named Lillith. He said she's a Drow and that she has Felix.'

'Lillith?' Principal Ellis asked. His face paled. 'You're sure he said Lillith?'

'Yes,' Linus nodded.

'Then we were right,' Principal Ellis said, turning to Nigel and the dire wolf. 'She went to the Glade. We need Slingsby to navigate.'

'She's far,' D.W interrupted. 'When I felt her, she was miles and miles away. We won't be able to get to her quickly.'

'Can you feel her now?' Nigel asked, his eyes wide with concern.

The dire wolf concentrated for a moment, his head tilting and his golden eyes squinting.

'No, I can't,' he said finally. 'She's gone back to wherever she was before.'

'Or she's dead,' Nigel whispered.

D.W growled at him savagely.

'She isn't dead,' he said through bared teeth.

'Whatever the case,' Principal Ellis said, trying to calm them. 'We must move quickly. Everyone up to my office. I'll make Professor Nyxon comfortable in a more reasonable cell than this. Great Flames, I had no idea he had set this chamber up.'

He shook his head in anger at himself and began to move towards the staircase, pulling Professor Nyxon along with him, who was mouthing soundlessly at him.

'Principal Ellis,' Linus called out, quickly standing up from the chair with a wobble. 'I have to talk to you.'

'Yes, yes, boy, later,' the principal said, as he hauled Professor Nyxon up the stairs.

Nigel and D.W rushed to help him.

'It's important!' Linus cried.

'Linus Godspell,' Principal Ellis said. 'It's only 7 a.m. and I have already had quite a day! I have matters far more urgent that require my–'

'I need to see William Lilly's diaries,' Linus interrupted. 'And I need to find Hestia Windwood.'

Principal Ellis stopped abruptly.

Passing Professor Nyxon to Nigel, he turned back and stepped back down into the dungeon.

'What did you say?' he asked, with eyes full of incredulity.

'William Lilly's diaries. I know you have them here. And you must tell me where I can find Hestia Windwood.'

Principal Ellis leaned against the wood of the chair, as though he little energy to keep him upright.

'Come to my office, boy. We must all talk.'

'I don't have time to talk!' Linus cried, banging his fist against the chair.

'Linus,' Principal Ellis said with a wince. 'You are welcome to look at Lilly's diaries, and I am willing to give you a great deal of information, to all of you. But...Hestia Windwood...' Principal Ellis broke off.

It seemed liked his words were stuck in his throat. He took a haggard breath. When he spoke, it was with deep sadness, as though the words would suffocate him with tears.

'Linus, Hestia Windwood is dead.'

30

William Lilly's Diaries

'You must all listen very carefully, for I am going to tell you a story,' Principal Ellis said.

He was sat at the head of a scrubbed table, which he had stretched to be big enough for them to all fit around it: Nigel, the dire wolf, Slingsby and Linus and the whole crew of the Skimmer.

Their reunion, only an hour or so before, had been sweet but swift. The crew were unharmed and all in awe, it seemed, of Pinks who had almost single-handedly freed them. Slingsby and the dire wolf had arrived in time to help them escape the rising tide, but in truth it had been Pinks who had done all of the hard work. She was sitting now next to Captain Kildare, who made no secret of holding the little girl's hand protectively, as though she would never again let her go. Slingsby had helped them navigate a quicker, undiscovered way through the caves, as was his flair, and he hadn't let anyone forget it, either. But Nigel was impatient and anxious to leave. He had stayed only at the insistence of Principal Ellis, and the dire wolf had been angry, suspicious of the hold that the old man seemed to have over Nigel, and of the fuzzy white noise he heard whenever he tried to probe Nigel's thoughts.

A floating teapot drifted around, pouring out steaming cups of cinnamon tea. Captain Kildare poured a cup for Pinks and pushed it to her, smiling when the fiery liquid brought the colour back to the girl's cheeks.

'It is a story I have not told before and I ask only that you reserve your judgement,' Principal Ellis said, joining his gloved fingers together in front of him. 'Age delivers the luxury of hindsight, and there are many things I would change if I had the chance to make certain choices again.

'As a young boy, I was very poor. I was, as you might say on the First, a Houdini; not so very gifted with magic and not educated either. When my parents died, I came to the Ardere and was granted sanctuary and work, and it was here that I grew up. I believed myself lucky. A life in the kitchens, or on the grounds of the Ardere would have been a proud vocation for a gypsy boy like me. But when I was around fifteen annums, I came into some money. Not much, but enough to afford me two annums of prep study at the Ardere, from which I could then matriculate early for further study by scholarship. I worked hard, finding my flair in the Pocculum consortium and becoming indispensable to the Academy healers. Once I graduated, I became a professor and then the principal and as my Tempus scholars would say, the rest is history.

'Yet this is merely the surface story; the respectable life of Principal Duncan Ellis, that shall be recorded in the Tempus texts. But as with all stories, there is more than meets the eye.

'You see, the money left to me was from a young lady named Hestia Windwood. There she is, in that painting. She was a beauty and I loved her. By the Sacred Flame, I loved her, but she was married to Principal Windwood. He was an old man, as I am now. Youth does not understand its fickle ways. Youth betrays us all. In my youth I saw Principal Windwood as a threat, as the obstacle to my happiness and the cage which trapped the love of my life. I see now, through aged eyes, he was only a lonely man who sought a companion.'

Principal Ellis shook his head in pity.

'Hestia and I were young and naïve. Her marriage to Principal Windwood had been beneficial for both of us. She had been able to leave me money to become a scholar, and she was a lady of society. She had been born with little magic and without schooling, she had never developed the little power she had. To be held so highly in regard by the academics of the Ardere, was something she had never expected. And yet neither of us saw the gifts we had been so graciously given. We saw only the things we did not have; we did not have one another. We began our affair in secret, but soon we grew tired of deceptions and furtive embraces in hidden chambers. Principal Windwood was growing old. We believed that his death would grant us the freedom we so wanted, to be together.

'I am, as I have said, a Pocculum scholar. My flair is knowing what compounds will cure and kill. What balance of chemicals will bring relief or torture. With Principal Windwood laying sick in his bed, I was sent to bring him relief. I told myself that what I was doing was a kindness. Better he die, better to be at peace than in his agony.

'When I poured the poison into his lips, he drank it willingly, in trust. I shall never forget his eyes as he looked at me, the life eking away from him. He pulled me to him, and he breathed his last words into my ear. Better they had been a curse than what he told me, for his dying words changed everything for me and Hestia.

'The aftermath of Principal Windwood's death brought darkness into our bed. Though free to marry me, Hestia was wary and unsure, hesitant to marry a man who could murder so easily. And I was haunted by Windwood's final words to me. Hestia and I were tainted; where once there had been love, was now suspicion and fear.

'We came to blows one winter evening. She had just told me she was with child. I was horrified. I knew the exact tonic that could rid us of the burden of a child, but Hestia wanted the babe. I was, at this time, the head of the Pocculum constortium. Principal Windwood's demise had not been unexpected, and nobody looked for a cause other than death by natural causes. Nobody saw any suspicion in me, and I was being groomed to take over as principal within the next decade, when Windwood's successor retired. I was ambitious and stupid.

'I told Hestia she could go, but I was concerned that once she was free of the Ardere and free of me, she would confess our sin…my sin, and I would be hunted and imprisoned. So I trapped her in an oath of secrecy. I made her swear that she would never tell a single living soul what I had done. If she could do that, then I would let her and the babe in her womb go.

'She agreed, binding herself to the secret and she left me, taking my unborn child with her.

Thus was born the first secret of thirteen. Thirteen secrets of the Privy Council.'

Principal Ellis paused and looked up, seeking Nigel's eyes before he continued.

'The words Principal Windwood whispered in your ear...' Nigel began. 'They form a secret the Privy Council guards?'

Principal Ellis nodded and continued.

'The Privy Council, as has become commonly known, is a council which protects the magician's greatest secrets. These secrets have been kept for the safety and protection of all...'

Principal Ellis shook his head once more.

'No,' he said. 'That is a lie. These secrets are for the safety and protection of those who seek power.

'After the Great Revelation, when your father, Linus, your real father, Everard Godspell revealed the truth of magicians to the commoners, there was a rush of discoveries. It was a revolution of knowledge, of commoner history merging with the histories of magicians. Certain things came to light; the origins of magic on the First Plane, the history of the Firelighters...more and more knowledge was accumulated, but this knowledge could bring about huge change and there had already been enough of that. The truce between magician and commoner was shaky and after a history of death amongst the Firelighters, magicians and commoners were at last united under the reign of Everard Godspell. Again, I thought that peace was better than the pain of truth. I formed a council and just as I had bound Hestia to secrecy, so too did I bind the council members.

'Each one would know only one secret. Nobody would know everything, for the one who had all the knowledge would have all the power, and power could be corrupted.'

'But don't you know all the secrets?' Linus interrupted. 'If you assigned them, surely you know them.'

'I do,' Principal Ellis nodded.

'Then tell us!' Linus said, looking around the table for support.

'I can't,' Principal Ellis said. 'I excommunicated myself.'

'What?' Captain Kildare leaned forward. 'So you are the head of the Privy Council, you know every single secret and yet you can't reveal a single one of them?'

'Not quite, madam,' Principal Ellis said, holding up a finger. 'I *was* the head of the Privy Council. Technically, I am no longer even a member, seeing as I excommunicated myself.'

'Why does that matter?' D.W asked. 'I don't understand why excommunication means he can't tell the secrets.'

'When you're excommunicated, you are bound by the oath of secrecy. The secret cannot be spoken or written willingly, nor can it be taken from you by force,' Linus explained.

'You know rather a lot about this, Linus,' Principal Ellis said in surprise. 'How?'

'Paris Lovelock died trying to tell me his secret,' Linus said, with eyes of stone.

'He was helping me.'

'Helping you with what?' Nigel asked. 'Is he why you ran away? Which was a rotten thing to do, by the way. Felix was worried sick about you.'

'Paris Lovelock,' Principal Ellis said, raising his eyebrows. 'Wonders never cease.'

'Yes,' Linus said. 'He was a good person.'

'Perhaps,' Principal Ellis nodded. 'But even your worst enemy may seem like a good person to the people who they fight for. Goodness is subjective.'

'I thought you were a good man,' Flint said with narrow eyes. 'And yet you're a murderer.'

'And you are a traitor to the Merchants' Guild, and a pirate,' Principal Ellis replied. 'Yet here we both are.'

'This isn't getting us anywhere,' Nigel shouted. 'Felix is in danger. All this talking is getting us nowhere, and I've had enough of secrets to last me a lifetime. I understand why she left. When people keep this amount of secrets from you, I don't blame her.'

'Here, here,' said D.W with a growl.

'It seems to me,' Slingsby broke through, 'it seems to me like all your paths are scrambled.'

'What do you mean, Slingsby?' Principal Ellis asked in exasperation.

'Well, you're all trying to seek something, right? You're all out on your own little quests but it hasn't occurred to any of you to ask one another for directions.'

'Slingsby, we really don't have time for your Ostium metaphors,' Principal Ellis said, rubbing at his temples with his thumb and forefinger.

'Just talk to one another!' Slingsby shouted. 'You British keep everything all bottled up all the damn time. Seriously, just tell each other the truth of things and help one another out.

Nigel, dire wolf, you guys want to get to Felix and save her from a Drow who isn't even supposed to exist, but Professor Nyxon certainly seems to know her, and he's sat in a cell with his lips sealed. Linus, you want to read some diary that the principal has and find this broad Hestia Windwood whom you, Principal Ellis, sir, knocked up and then exiled. Now if she's dead, I'd be asking the question, what is it you wanted her for anyway, Linus? What did she know?'

Linus looked at Slingsby and then at Captain Kildare. She shrugged a shoulder at him.

'He's got a point, laddie,' she said. 'S'up to you though.'

'Right,' Linus nodded. 'Ok. If honesty is what is going to save us here, then I'll go first. Paris Lovelock told us about a curse on the Firelighters. No, don't laugh. Think about it. Every Firelighter in our recorded history has died in suspicious circumstances, and Paris reckoned it was because of a curse. He'd done his own digging and had found out that this curse existed because...well, they're not the true Firelighters.'

'Nonsense,' Nigel laughed. 'You're saying Felix isn't the real Firelighter? Come on, Linus, you saw her take the Sacred Flame inside her – it saved your life! Could she do that if she wasn't the real Firelighter?'

'I'm not saying she isn't powerful,' Linus said. 'I know she is. But Paris swore over candoil that this was true, and I believe him. We all did.' Linus motioned to the crew and they each nodded.

'It's true, lad,' Captain Kildare said to Nigel.

'So who exactly is the 'true Firelighter' then?' he asked.

'We don't know,' Linus admitted. 'That's why we were trying to find Hestia Windwood. I was told she might know.'

'Do you know?' Nigel asked Principal Ellis.

'I don't know where the true Firelighter is,' he said, shaping his words carefully in case the bonds of his excommunication took hold. 'I have never known.'

Linus slumped.

'Then it's a dead end,' he mumbled.

'Why do you need to see Lilly's diaries?' Slingsby asked.

'They were part of Paris' secret,' Linus explained. 'They contain information, I think. Something to do with the curse.'

'I have them,' Principal Ellis said.

All eyes turned to him. He flicked his wrist and a small, oilskin bound book appeared in his hand. Linus stared at it, as though he was starving and it was a loaf of bread.

'I cannot tell you Paris' secret,' Principal Ellis said softly. 'But I can give you the text that contains it. I have done wrong in my life. I am old, now, and weary of the burdens of secrets.'

He looked to Nigel and he spoke slowly, with weight to his words.

'You are all young. Secrets have no place in the world you are trying to build. The secrets of the Privy Council members can be told freely, in trust. This is the one clause of the oath a council member takes; secrets breed secrets, but truth breeds trust. Do with these secrets what you will. It is you who shape the future of magicians and commoners, not I. Perhaps it is time to bring light to the dark.'

He passed the ancient text to Linus who clasped it in his hands, stroking the old oilskin. When Linus opened it, the spine crackled with age. The writing was small and written in ink, which had faded almost entirely in some places. It was filled with diagrams and charts, illustrations and notes that made little sense. As Linus flicked carefully through the pages, the book fell open at pages which had clearly been examined several times. The spine was split at this section and the page was dog-eared.

'Here,' Linus said so quietly, the others strained to hear him. 'Paris' initials. This is it. This is the secret.'

'Read it out, lad,' Captain Kildare said.

Linus nodded and began to read.

London 1651

I have seen many things in the stars and in the sky. I am in an agony of conflict. The stars have told me of a Great Fire that will raze the city of London and all its citizens therein, in the year of the beast 1666. Oh woe to know such a fate, to see such death and calamity that shall befall God's earth which He hath made, yet which shall be burned in hellfire. I have published this prophesy in hieroglyphs and horoscopes in my pamphlet yet know the wrath of the Commons Committee shall stem its circulation. Oh, I am timorous of the committee! I fear I shall be upbraided, scorned and derided, yet I must speak this truth to save us all.

All authors agree that Gemini, a pair of twins, is the symbol of the City of London, indeed much of England. I have made this known in Christian astrology, but people do not see, or perhaps they have no eyes with which to see the truth of what the stars speak of these twins.

London will fall victim to a Great Fire, the stars say. And when that happens, it will bring forth a pair of twins not of this world but of another. The Fire will be commanded by them for they will be of fire and not of fire. And they will bring forth a flash of flame so mighty, that all the world will be left in embers and ashes, for the Fire they wield will not belong to them, but to another. All who claim this Flame for their own will be cursed and in turn, they will bring a curse of smoke and flame to the world, for they will bring down a great maelstrom of hellfire that will devour us like a demon, and life shall be no more.

Linus stopped reading.

'There's a drawing here,' he said. 'Two twins falling head-first into flames.'

'I don't understand it,' Bazalguette said.

Pinks nodded her head in agreement.

'It means that the curse isn't just on the Firelighters,' Linus breathed. 'It means that if the Sacred Flame of Magic doesn't return to the one, true Firelighter, then the world will burn again, just as it did in the Great Fire. 'A curse of smoke and flame' he writes.'

Principal Ellis closed his eyes and sighed.

'You knew this?' Nigel breathed.

'I knew, yes. I protected the secret. We cannot know if Lilly was right! It could just be conjecture!'

'And you thought you would risk the fate of magicians and commoners alike on the off-chance that Lilly was wrong? Who gave you that power?' Linus asked, pushing up from the table and shouting at the principal, who merely winced.

'I told you, power corrupts. You have the secret, now. It is up to you what you do with it.'

'We have to get to Felix. She needs to know about this,' Nigel said.

'Agreed,' Linus nodded. 'I was trying to protect her, Nigel. I thought she would fall victim of the curse if she stayed the Firelighter.'

'Yeah, I get it,' Nigel nodded.

There was a sudden rapping at the door, which made Pinks jump.

'Ellis, you old trout, let me in!'

'That's Aubrey!' D.W barked, jumping over the table to the door and pawing at the handle to open it.

Aubrey and Thaddeus pushed through, an agitated young student behind them.

'I'm so sorry, Principal Ellis!' the student said. 'They just barged past me!'

'It's ok, Celine, I'll handle it.'

The table of guests stirred as they watched the woman with wild, frizzy red hair, help herself to a pot of lukewarm cinnamon tea.

'Nigel?' she said, after she had downed half the cup. 'D.W? What in flames are you two doing here? Do you have any idea how worried we've been? After everything that's going on already, we find you here and – oh sweet fire in the sky, is that Linus Godspell?'

Aubrey practically crawled across the table and grabbed Linus' cheeks in both her hands and kissed his face, pushing her lilac framed glasses skew-whiff on her nose.

'I am SO happy to see you! By sky, we're saved, Thaddeus!'

Thaddeus was stood by the door, picking suckers from his arm from swellweed, which had caused his arm to double up in size.

'You have to come back with us, you know?' Aubrey was saying to Linus.

She hadn't let go of his face yet and his mouth was all puckered up by the force of her hands.

'You're the heir apparent, did you know? Felix named you herself. All Firelighters name an heir, as well you know. And now she's missing, we're without a Firelighter and a Grand Vizier! But now we have you till we find Felix, fire protect her.'

'Aubrey wait...hold up,' Nigel said. 'There's a lot of ground to cover here. We know where Felix is.'

'You do?' Aubrey let go of Linus's face and looked around the room, seeing everyone for the first time.

'What exactly is going on here?'

'There's no time to explain, Aubrey. Right now, we have to save Felix. She's in a lot of danger and we're a long way away from her,' D.W said.

'What do you mean she's in danger?'

'She's with the Drow. With someone called Lillith.'

'Lillith?'

'Yep.'

'The Drow?'

'Yep.'

'But...'

'Yeah we thought they were extinct too but - '

'We don't have time for this!' exploded Nigel. 'Somebody explain it all to her but right now, Slingsby you need to navigate a way to the Drow.'

'Right, err. Yes,' Slingsby nodded, rubbing at his throat nervously. 'So, I'll, err, need some kind of information? Some idea of where to start?'

'She's further north, I think,' D.W said. 'Near the mountains. I felt her there.'

'Ok,' Slingsby thought, scanning his mind for everything he knew about the mountain passes. 'There are no encampments there. It's uninhabitable.'

'Well, that's where she was.'

'You could start where the Glade used to be? Before they went extinct? Or not as the case may be,' Linus said.

'It was in the forests at the foot of the mountains,' Principal Ellis said softly. 'It's abandoned now.'

'As if we're going to trust anything you say,' Linus spat at him.

'D.W, can you picture exactly where you felt Felix's presence?' Thaddeus asked, clutching his chin in thought.

'Yes, sort of. I can't see the location or anything, but I can place her in relation to where we are now, if that makes sense?'

'Right,' Thaddeus nodded.

He rooted in his pocket and pulled out a small stub of chalk.

'A chalkey?' Slingsby asked in delight. 'Splendid!'

'What's a chalkey?' Ragstone whispered to Bazalguette, who just shrugged.

'It can open a hatch anywhere you draw one,' Linus explained, remembering his own chalkey which had remained unused, along with his entire menagerie of belongings.

'Describe exactly where she is – co-ordinates will be helpful.'

The dire wolf and Thaddeus continued to talk, much to Slingsby's dismay.

'I suppose I'm not much use now,' he said, hanging his head.

'On the contrary, Principal Ellis said, kindly. 'Nigel, Linus, I have three final pieces of information that may help.'

Linus looked at Principal Ellis as though he was an insect.

'Why do you want to help us in any way, after everything you've done to keep these secrets in the first place?' he asked.

'I told you,' the old man said. 'Age changes you. It grants you new perspectives. It teaches you that life, when lived well, is precious. A life filled with sin and lies and secrets, is no life at all.'

'What information do you want to share?' Nigel asked him gently, conscious that Ellis was an old man.

'Lillith was a member of the Privy Council. She bears a secret, but she is excommunicated so cannot reveal it,' Principal Ellis said. 'Be wary of her. She was a dangerous woman, even before Corbin Godspell tried to eradicate her kind. She...wants Felix...' Principal Ellis' words became tight and muddled.

He opened his mouth, but nothing but guttural choking noises came out.

'He can't say,' Linus said to Nigel, 'it's too close to his secret.'

Principal Ellis nodded but he tried again anyway.

'Something...only....Felix has,' he pushed the words out his mouth.

'The Sacred Flame,' Linus said. 'That's what she wants. Professor Nyxon said the same thing to me before.'

'I wish I could tell you more,' Principal Ellis said, shaking his head sadly. 'But I can tell you this. Hestia was living in the Northlands, near the Ashfjord, when she died.'

'I've been there!' Slingsby smiled. 'Beautiful place!'

'I know you have, Slingsby,' Professor Ellis smiled. 'That is why you are still useful. And Linus, you will find nothing but pain on the Second Plane. Those with no magic will burn in pain here. You'll need Fleetwater, and lots of it.'

The principal reached into his plum-coloured robes and pulled out all the vials of liquid. He pushed four of them to Linus.

'There are more in my personal stores,' he said. 'Slingsby has the key.'

Linus nodded and mumbled his thanks, before looking to Nigel.

'I *have* to find Felix, Linus,' Nigel said.

'I understand,' Linus nodded. 'But I have to go to the Ashfjord. If Hestia knew who the true Firelighter is, then maybe she left some kind of clue there.'

'Then you'll go with Slingsby,' Nigel said.

'Nobody is going anywhere!' Aubrey screeched in panic. 'Will somebody please tell me, in Fire's name, what is going on here?!'

'Nigel, the hatch is ready,' Thaddeus said, ignoring Aubrey completely. 'It's not going to be perfect, but it's the best I can do. I've put you as close to her last known location as I can.'

Nigel looked down at the rectangle drawn in white chalk on the stone floor. It looked entirely innocuous.

'I'm coming with you,' D.W barked, but Thaddeus shook his head. 'I'm sorry D.W, but there's only enough chalk here for one journey.'

Nigel looked down at him.

'It's ok,' he said, stroking the wolf's fur. D.W whined and flattened his ears. 'I'll bring our girl back.'

Nigel went to the table and picked up the small metal suitcase Principal Ellis had given to him earlier. He handed it to the dire wolf, who clasped it in his jaws.

'Make sure Felix gets this if I don't make it back,' he said.

D.W's eyes challenged him, but he gave a quick nod by dipping his head.

'You'd better make it back,' he said, using his secret voice so that only Nigel heard him.

Nigel smiled and took a step towards the chalk square. He looked back at Linus, who nodded sternly at him.

'Nigel! Wait!' Aubrey shouted, but Nigel had already stepped into the chalk square and disappeared down the hatch.

In all the commotion, nobody noticed the old, frail principal slipping out of the office. He walked with slow, heavy steps towards the dock at the back of the Ardere Academy, where the Skyskimmer bobbed against her restraints.

It was a clear, crisp morning. Principal Ellis could see his breath on the air. The sea was foaming beneath him as he walked to the end of the dock and looked out to the horizon. It was a beautiful world; one he had thought he had the power to shape. He looked down at his gloves and removed them, dropping them into the sea far below him, where the waves swallowed them up. He stared at his hands. They were still calloused and rough from his manual work as a child, but they were thin and stringy with age.

The only way we can shape the future is to leave something behind better than ourselves, he thought to himself. For a moment, the old man wept; wept for his child whom he had never known, wept for the sins of his life.

Then he wiped away his tears, revelling in the way the liquid felt against his bare hands.

'Hestia,' he whispered into the breeze. 'My love. I'm coming.'

Principal Duncan Ellis stepped off the dock and plunged to his death.

31

True Lies

Nigel tumbled out of the wide trunk of a tree head-first and immediately vomited. His head was swirling from the haphazard journey through the midst, and he couldn't seem to make his eyes focus on anything. For a moment, he bent over and rested his hands on his knees and kept his eyes clamped tightly shut, trying to fight another wave of nausea.

'Come on, True,' he muttered to himself. 'Get a grip.'

He stumbled forwards, looking around the white limbs and trunks of trees around him. It was a dense forest, with pale barked trees stretching high into the morning sky, their bare branches looking stilted and naked against the blue. After a few steps, Nigel looked back, unsure which tree he had stepped out of, unsure, even, of which direction he had come from. The forest was like a labyrinth. He had taken only a few steps and already he felt lost.

And yet Felix had been here, close by, only a few hours ago. The dire wolf had felt her, had heard her cries of pain. If he spent his entire life looking, Nigel would find her.

To mark his way, he broke off a branch from a tree with low hanging branches and he charred the end so that he could mark each tree he passed with ashes. But soon he found his way back to trees he had marked, and he realised he was walking in circles.

He decided to climb a tree to try and find the direction of the mountains. If Ellis said that the Glade had been at the foot of them, then he would aim for them. But it seemed that the more Nigel climbed, the higher the tree grew.

He climbed down and jumped back to the grass angrily. A snapping branch made him halt. Nigel looked around, his senses heightened, and his hands braced to fend off an enemy with magic. But the sound did not come again.

Continuing to meander through the trees, Nigel kept his eyes on the ground and on the tree bark where he continued to leave marks. He did not look up into the branches, and so he did not see the white widow spider creeping down above him. Her legs were long and thick, white like the branches of the trees. Each leg was the size of a tree branch. Her body was round and bulbous, but well hidden by the thick trunks of the trees.

She descended lower, until she was above Nigel's head. Her great shadow blocked out the sunlight and Nigel looked up too late, for she had already spun her web around his feet and pulled him up, weaving her silk around him as he screamed.

Felix opened her eyes to darkness and the sound of shuffling. Her arms were stretched out above her head and her wrists were bound by something tight but soft. She was dangling, her feet hanging freely beneath her. Her head was splitting in pain, and she knew without feeling that there was a deep gash at the side of her head. She could feel the congealed blood that was sticky in her hair.

For a moment she listened. Aside from the sound of her own breathing, the only sound was a strange skittering noise that she could not identify. Though her wrists were bound, her fingers were free. She gripped the restraints and found them to be slightly slimy, as though they were covered in mucus. Felix took a deep lungful of air and rubbed her fingers together quickly, bringing to life a small flame inside an orb that floated down beside her. Looking up, Felix was prepared for what she would see but still, she recoiled in horror. White widows, the size of fully grown men were crawling along the ceiling from which she was hanging. They were metres away from her, but one single outstretched leg could have brushed against her hair. There must have been more than fifty of them.

As the light hovered around her, she saw that she was in a deep crevice of rock. It was unfamiliar to her, and she knew she had never been to this part of the cavern before. Beneath her was pitch black and she sent the orblight down beneath her, illuminating the ground below. It was a steep drop, one that would break a few bones at the very least, if she were to loosen her restraints. There was something else there, too. A large white sac of spider web was on the ground, laying prone in the dirt. Felix thought of how spiders usually captured their prey; how they would wrap them up in their web, after paralysing them with their stingers before then drinking the blood of their victims, whilst they still lived.

Felix glared down at the sac, wondering who could be inside it, her mind flipping through Cillix and the other men, to Melantha and even to Lillith herself.

Lillith was nowhere to be seen. Her absence was the scariest part of this whole situation. Felix felt sick at the thought that Lillith had just left her here to be eaten alive by spiders.

No chance, Felix thought. She looked down again at the drop. Better a death by falling, than being dinner for a bunch of overgrown tarantulas.

She looked up at the restraints and pulled apart the particles of magic, loosening the threads of the web one by one, until her wrists slipped through and she fell to the ground.

Telling herself not to scream out in pain, Felix hit the ground with her feet and crouched down, so the shock of impact would travel quickly and equally through her body. Immediately, she felt her left foot and ankle shatter and her right shin bone splinter. She bit down on her lip so fiercely that she drew blood, but she didn't scream.

Above her, the white widows hissed as their prey tried to escape, and they scuttled down the the walls and hung down from the ceiling on threads of sticky web. Felix rolled onto her back and sent a force of flames at them. One of the spiders caught fire and gave an almighty shriek as it fell from the wall onto its back with a loud thud, its legs curling into its body as it burned. The other white widows pulled back, some drawing into crevices in the rock, but they did not leave entirely. It gave Felix enough time to drag herself over to the white sac. It was still warm and oozy with mucus. Whoever was inside it was still alive, then. Felix tried to rip open to the web, but it was too sticky. Her nails couldn't tear it open.

'Oh, you've found your surprise!'

Felix flinched and turned quickly, wincing as the pain of her broken bones seared up her body. She leaned back against the body in the sac.

'Lillith,' she said.

Felix called on her anger to flood through her spirals and it obeyed. The power was there, waiting to be used.

'Oh but, sister, you mustn't be angry at me,' Lillith said, entering into the orblight.

She was still wearing her dress, but she was sat astride a white widow like she was riding a horse.

'Sweet fire,' Felix gasped.

'I told you the white widows do my bidding,' Lillith said, stroking the fuzzy hair on the spider's back.

Great pincers opened and shut at its mouth, and Felix's heart jumped into her throat.

'Now, I know I was a little unreasonable earlier,' Lillith said, climbing off the back of the spider. 'I was just angry. We Drow do seem to have a penchant for anger, don't we?' She let out a girlish giggle and Felix stared at her aghast.

'I thought we could strike a bargain,' Lillith continued, clasping her hands in front of her.

'A bargain,' Felix repeated.

'Yes. Tit for tat. Is that the phrase?'

'You want the Sacred Flame of Magic,' Felix said.

Lillith nodded delightedly.

'Why?'

'Hmmm I'm so sorry, sister Felix but I can't say.'

'Yeah, right. No bargain then.'

'Oh but I mean it. I genuinely can't say. My lips are sealed by oath. I couldn't utter the words even if my life depended on them. And besides, you don't know the terms of the bargain.'

Lillith stepped forward, her bare feet poking out of her silver dress like claws. Felix pulled herself away using her hands, but Lillith instead walked to the white sac. She pulled out a small blade from her belt and smiled widely at Felix, before slicing the sac in half.

Felix peered inside, hardly sure she wanted to see the unfortunate victim inside.

'Nigel,' she breathed, when she saw his face. 'Nigel!'

'Surpriiise!' Lillith said in a musical voice, holding out her arms as though she'd just performed a magic trick.

Felix lurched towards Nigel's body, her broken bones complaining, but she didn't care. She scooped him up, resting his head on her thighs, stroking his hair away. He wasn't moving.

'He can't be dead,' Felix screamed.

Tears came thick and fast, dripping down her face onto Nigel.

'Oh, don't be so dramatic,' Lillith said, rolling her eyes. 'Of course he isn't dead. But he will be, if you don't give me what I need.'

Felix looked up, shaking her head. She wiped her face sloppily with the back of her hand.

'You give me the Sacred Flame of Magic and I'll let Nigel live,' Lillith said, as though it was a reasonable bargain.

Felix glared at Lillith, barely seeing anything through the blur of tears.

'Wake him up,' she demanded.

'Hmm?' Lillith uttered.

'Prove he's not dead. Wake him up so I know you're upholding your end of the bargain.'

'Oh fine,' Lillith said, rolling her eyes again.

She leaned over Nigel and pulled a small tub out of her skirt pocket. Felix grabbed her wrist, when Lillith moved the tub to Nigel's face.

'It's anti-venom, sister Felix,' Lillith said. 'Be calm.'

Lillith twisted the lid of the tub, revealing small holes. A noxious odour rose from the tub, that reminded Felix of vomit and Mount Mudslop in the Commoner's Quarter. She forced herself not to gag.

Nigel, on the other hand, sat bolt upright at the scent, gagging and retching emptily. Felix held him, amazed that he was there, sitting in front of her, full of life and honest, three-dimensional realness.

'You're here,' she said through sobs.

Nigel held himself up with his arms and turned his head to her.

'Felix?' he said, reaching out a hand to touch her, as though she was the cause for amazement.

When his hand landed on her's, he jumped forward, lifting her up into his arms. Felix moaned in pain but held him back, crying and hiccupping and laughing all at the same time.

'How sweet,' Lillith said with a thin smile. 'Sister Felix, I can feel your joy. It pours out of you in waves. How pleased I am to reunite you.'

Felix pulled away from Nigel, her hands holding his tightly. The leather of his gloves was soft and familiar, like his hands underneath them.

'Tell me why you want the Flame of Magic, Lillith,' Felix said. 'You've held up your end of the bargain. But you must tell me why you want it, if I'm going to give it to you.'

'Felix!' Nigel said in surprise, tugging at her hand. 'No. You don't understand.'

'Hush, Nigel,' she said. 'Go on, Lillith. Speak.'

Lillith ran her teeth over her bottom lip.

'How many times....I CAN'T TELL YOU,' Lillith shrieked.

The spiders above scuttled further into their holes, causing Nigel to look up. He gasped and Felix felt him begin to tremble.

'She really can't tell you,' Nigel whispered to Felix, his eyes never leaving the ceiling. 'She was on the Privy Council, Felix. This is her secret, one she cannot reveal after excommunication.'

'Excommunication?' Felix asked.

'Yes,' Nigel nodded, swallowing audibly as the spiders began to crawl out of the holes. 'She was declared officially dead when Godspell killed all the Drow, or so it was thought. She couldn't tell you her secret even if she wanted to.'

Lillith crouched down to the balls of her feet and stared at Nigel. She pulled his chin towards her, forcing him to look her in the eyes.

'And what do you know of the Privy Council, child?' Lillith asked.

'A little,' Nigel said, pulling his chin out of her hands in disgust.

Lillith's lips spread in a wide, sinister smile.

'You have lies in your eyes, boy,' she said, and she began to cackle, clapping her hands together.

'Nigel...what does she mean?' Felix asked.

Nigel looked at her in apology.

'There's a lot to explain,' he said to her. 'Trust me. Please.'

'Oh but she shouldn't trust you, should she?' Lillith said, recollecting her composure. 'Nobody should trust a Spinner.'

'A Spinner?' Felix looked from Nigel to Lillith. 'What's a Spinner?'

Lillith gasped dramatically.

'And you haven't even told her! Oh my, my, my.'

'Told me what? Nigel? What's she talking about?'

'He's a liar, sister Felix,' Lillith sang, in her sing song voice.

'Shut up!' Nigel roared at her. 'I'm not, Felix. I swear to you, I'm not. My Aunt Vessania, she's a Spinner. She lies. She doesn't know who she really is, doesn't know what truth is. It's a condition, Felix. It's hereditary. But I've never lied to you, Felix. I promise!'

Felix swallowed, shaking her head in confusion.

'That's a lie,' Lillith said. 'You're lying to her right now. Tell her about the Privy Council, Nigel.'

'You know I can't do that!' Nigel burst out. 'That's not fair!'

'What, Nigel?' Felix begged. 'What about the Privy Council? I don't understand.'

'Felix...I...I can't.' Nigel shook his head.

Behind his glasses, his eyes were wet.

'He's on the Privy Council now, I'd wager,' Lillith said, with a shake of her head. 'One of them. Just like Fiddle. He lied to you too, didn't he, Felix? He didn't tell you about Felixia Solis, did he? But he told Corbin Godspell. I don't lie to you. I tell you the truth.'

Felix held up her hands and closed her eyes. It felt like that was the only way to see clearly.

'You're on the Privy Council?' she asked, opening her eyes and staring deeply at Nigel.

'I...yes,' he nodded.

'Do you know what Felixia Solis is?'

Nigel didn't answer. He stared at Felix, his eyes begging her to trust him. Felix bit her lip, the familiar feelings of betrayal rushing through her.

'Ok, then,' she said. 'Lillith, you have a bargain.'

'Felix, no! You can't!'

'Shut up, Nigel. Let me deal with this,' Felix hissed.

'Oh, sweet child,' Lillith said in mock concern, stroking Felix's hair.

Felix cringed whilst Lillith touched her. From behind Lillith's hair, Aradia peeped out, stretching out her legs.

Felix reached for her and Aradia climbed onto her hand. Her little weight was so soft, nothing in comparison to the great white widows above them.

'I thought you were my friend,' Felix whispered, as Aradia lifted her little leg out to Felix's face. 'But you betrayed me too, didn't you?'

Aradia shuffled her two front legs against each other. It was impossible to know what a spider was feeling, but Felix thought that for a moment, she felt the shame and sorrow of the little spider as it scurried back up Lillith's arm and into her hair.

'I have one condition,' Felix said to Lillith, her voice stern.

'What?' Lillith asked, narrowing her eyes.

'I want to know you, Lillith,' Felix said. 'The way you know me. Like a sister.'

Felix reached her hand out to Lillith's spirals. At first, Lillith pulled away.

'What are you doing?' she asked warily.

'Drowning,' Felix replied.

Her hand connected with Lillith's skin. There came the deep jolt of feeling, like she had dived head-first into Lillith's skin. Lillith resisted, barriers and walls stopped Felix from probing her way through.

It's ok, sister, Felix reassured her in her mind.

Hatred. Yes, so much hatred. Hatred for the magicians who had killed her people. Hatred for men who seemed weak to her. But hatred was fuelled by love. Oh, such deep love. Love for the Drow, for her sisters. And the weight of it all on her shoulders. Felix could barely breathe at such a weight.

Oh, Lillith.

There was pain buried deep. Memories that burned through her skull, wrought with terror and horror. Her sisters slaughtered in front of her. Their culture, their sacred texts, their forest and the good earth that they loved – all burned and destroyed. *When you don't have a history, do you even exist anymore?*

I'm here, sister Lillith.

Godspell, too. Godspell hurting her. Godspell's crushing weight on top of her.

'This is the payment I'm due, Lillith,' he said. 'The payment for keeping your sisters safe.'

Felix shuddered. She could feel Lillith's fear, Lillith's pain, Lillith's anger. And here was a secret; a knotted black web at the centre of her.

'No, you can't!' said Lillith, but Felix didn't stop.

She untangled the web, pulling strands and threads apart.

'You can't get to the secret with magic!' Lillith shouted.

'I'm not using magic, sister,' Felix said.

Lillith flung Felix away from her and the connection was lost. Felix groaned in pain as her shattered bones moved in her skin. Her face was wet with blood and sweat and tears.

'Give me the Flame!' Lillith screamed through her own tears.

She dashed them away with her hand, her spirals lit with green fire inside her skin.

Felix shook her head.

'We made a bargain!' she cried, reaching for her blade and holding it aloft.

'I lied,' Felix said. 'I don't have the Flame to give to you, sister Lillith.'

'What?' Lillith screeched.

Even Nigel looked confused.

'Felix?' he asked.

'I've not had the Flame of Magic for a long time,' Felix said quietly.

'But then...who does?' Nigel asked.

Felix paused, biting her lip.

'You...you lost it?' Lillith said in a low voice. 'You stupid, foolish child! But you've seen it now, haven't you? The secret? Do you understand now? Do you see what danger you've placed us all in?'

'Lillith – I...'

Felix stopped, for Lillith was surging forwards, the blade in her hands ready to drive deep into Felix's throat. Nigel scrambled over bleeding knees to Felix, throwing himself over her in protection but Lillith stumbled suddenly, a gasp of shock and pain escaping her lips. Then she froze, her eyes widening in horror as she slowly sank to the floor, her body twitching, her mouth foaming, until she lay still on the ground.

'Lillith?' Felix whispered.

She pushed Nigel's hands away gently and pulled herself over to Lillith's prone body. She lifted away the long strands of silver hair. There, at her neck, Aradia was crouched, her pincers wedged deep into Lillith's neck. Like Lillith, Aradia wasn't moving.

'She's dead,' Felix whispered. 'Lillith is dead.'

'But...how?' Nigel asked.

'Aradia's venom is lethal,' Felix said. 'But white widows need the venom in their bloodstream to keep them alive. Aradia killed Lillith, knowing it would end her own life.'

'I'm...I'm sorry, Felix,' Nigel said gently. 'I'm sorry for all this.'

Felix nodded.

'I know,' she said. 'I believe you.'

Nigel shuffled over to her and reached for her hand. She let him take it and squeezed his in return.

'It's alright, Nigel,' she said to him, stroking the skin of his wrists, where she could feel his pulse thumping.

She lifted his wrist to her lips and kissed his pulse. Then she turned to face him and looked into his green eyes.

'Let's go home,' she said.

32

Trust and Love

But it took a long while to get home. Felix's broken bones meant Nigel had to carry Felix, and they were lost somewhere underneath the mountains, with white widows crawling above them. When they finally broke through into the Drow caverns, Nigel was ready to drop in a faint and Felix was burning a fever. The underground caverns of the Drow were protected and bound, so that Nigel and Felix couldn't step back to the First Plane there, and they realised that D.W couldn't sense or hear them there either. Because of this, Felix asked Nigel to take her to Melantha and though he was wary to begin with, his exhaustion and concern for Felix's grey pallor was enough to convince him.

Nigel slept for a full day and a night. Melantha tended to Felix's wounds as best she could, but the Drow were not magicians; their healing was in herbs. Felix conveyed what she could of what had happened with Lillith in the broken language she had still not mastered. For as long as she lived, Felix would not forget the wails that rose up from her sisters. Their grief was shattering, and Felix felt it with them and wept for them, for their pain; they were innocent in ways Felix couldn't explain to Nigel. Nigel, who could not meet their eyes, who was shy around their nakedness, who was curious of their bald heads and spiralled skin and melodious tongue.

Before they left, Felix held Melantha's hand and showed her gratitude and love, but she also showed her the hope she held; hope that Melantha would bring the Drow into the light once more, all of them; including the men and children hidden in the mountains. When their connection broke, Melantha was pale underneath her spirals but she nodded, her jaw set tightly in firm resolve.

Felix's pain was numbed and her bones had been set, but she could not walk. In a show of solidarity, Cillix was the first to step out of the hidden mountain cracks and venture back into the

Drow caverns. Cadmus was still wary, but Felix felt Melantha's attraction to him, instantly. There were small smiles, shy glances. For the first time, Felix felt wise. Where hate brings poison, love brings the cure.

With Cillix's help, Nigel carried Felix through the tunnels and into the Glade once more. Felix left the Drow, knowing she would miss her sisters; knowing she would feel the ache of their absence for her whole life. But she knew they were safe, now. She knew where they were. Yet she also knew she would never see them again. Family, she had realised, are not always bound to you by blood. Sometimes, they are the people who see into your soul, not because they are entitled to, not because they can, but because *you* choose to let them. Felix loved her sister Drow, but her family was Nigel, the dire wolf, Aubrey and Liberty and Thaddeus, Sigbert and Fiddle, for family remains even after they have passed on.

As soon as they were above ground, they heard a howl. Crashing through the trees, the dire wolf came leaping towards them, his tail wagging speedily, his tongue hanging out of his jaws. He knocked Nigel and Cillix down as he jumped up with his front paws, licking Felix all over her face, nuzzling her with his pink nose, barking and yapping and talking to her all at once until she laughed, throwing her arms around him, breathing in his scent.

'You found me,' she whispered to him, knowing he would hear her.

'I will *always* find you,' he said back, with his secret voice.

Nigel had explained a little of what Felix had missed whilst she had been with the Drow, but it was still a surprise to see a real airship looming over the trees. She stared open-mouthed at it as its shadow passed over them, a rope ladder swinging perilously below it, as if they expected her to climb up something so flimsy, which she wasn't sure she would do even if she had working legs. With magical aid, Felix was hoisted onto the ship; she liked the weightless feeling of floating so high even less than the idea of climbing up the rope ladder.

Once aboard the ship, she was strapped to a stretcher by a gruff, bearded man with hulking muscles called Ragstone, who talked without ever moving a smouldering cigar from his lip. A tall, brusque woman with red hair and piercing eyes introduced herself as Captain Bonny Kildare. As Felix understood it, this was the woman who had taken her brother in. Weak and drowsy, Felix made a mental note to speak to this formidable woman as soon as she was able. But for now, her head ached, her bones throbbed, and sleep was a welcome absolution.

Felix slept.

She had expected to waken in the London Library or in her chamber in the Citadel but instead, Felix woke in an unfamiliar wooden bed, with four mouldering posts and dusty red curtains hanging above in a canopy. The vaulted ceiling was made of grey stone, and a small chapel window let in only a glimmer of light. The room was, save for a rug on the paved floor and an empty wooden desk.

Felix lifted herself up in her bed, relieved to find her legs and head had been healed, though her bones felt jelly-like inside her skin. She was reassured to find D.W curled up at the bottom of her bed, his paws stretched out next to her as though he had fallen asleep protecting her. She smiled and reached out to stroke his ears. The dire wolf woke with a start and yawned, his tongue unfurling out of his mouth as he stretched out his long front legs.

'You're awake,' he said, with a lolling grin.

'How long was I asleep?' Felix said, with an answering nod.

'Three days. Imelda gave you Fleetwater. Said you'd heal faster if you slept.'

'Imelda's here?'

'Everyone is here,' D.W said, as though he was slightly exasperated with this idea.

'Where exactly is here?' Felix asked, pulling the comforter up around her, for the room was chilly.

'The Ardere Academy,' D.W replied.

'We're still on the Second?' Felix asked in surprise.

D.W nodded.

'Aubrey wanted us to all go back to the Citadel, but Linus dug his heels in.' The dire wolf rolled his eyes and jumped down off the bed. 'I'll go get him.'

'No wait,' Felix said, in a voice that made D.W turn around quickly.

'What is it, Felix?'

He ignored the urge to reach into her mind to listen, thinking that perhaps she had had enough of feeling invaded during her time with the Drow.

'I...err...'

'You're nervous?' D.W finished for her.

He knew her well enough to understand her. He didn't need to listen to her thoughts.

Felix nodded.

'What do I say to him?'

'Oh, trust me, he'll have enough to say for the both of you,' D.W said, shaking his head.

'You don't like him,' Felix realised, with a small frown that caused a little line between her brows.

'I wouldn't put it like that,' he said. 'But it's close enough. Come on, I'll help you to the kitchens. Aubrey will want to see you. And Nigel, of course.'

There were several things that Felix learned, as they descended through the stone castle of the Ardere Academy. The first was that it was nearly Yule; only two days away, D.W said. The academy was wreathed in holly and ivy, and mighty evergreen trees grew out of the stone at every corner, dressed in orbs of fire and glittering frost so that they twinkled like sunlight on a lake. The second was that the academy was practically empty; students had gone home for the holidays, D.W explained, sent home a few days early after recent events. Felix looked at the wolf curiously as he'd spoken, sensing that there was more to the story, and as she limped along clutching at his fur, she fought a wave of tiredness, not because she was sleepy but because she knew that there was far more to come.

The kitchens were a riot of noise and smells. Food was cooking in several of the ranges and bacon was frying in a skillet on top of a hob. A great fireplace, large enough to fit ten fully grown men was lit, the mantle blackened with years of smoke and ash.

Felix stood at the door and peeped around, not quite ready for the barrage. There was Aubrey, bossy as always, her hair getting frizzier and frizzier as she barked at Thaddeus, who was stood next to a burned loaf of bread, arms folded and failing at hiding a smile as Imelda pulled faces behind Aubrey's back. Liberty was sat at the table, her face hollow and looking more frail than Felix had ever seen her, even more so than when they had first met in the Tower of London. Next to her was a little girl she remembered as a crewmember of the Skyskimmer, scrawny, with a face smudged with dirt. Liberty was braiding her short mop of hair whilst the little girl ate rashers of crispy bacon with her fingers. Felix smiled, liking her immediately.

There were others she recognised from the ship; the forbidding captain sat astride a wooden chair like a cowgirl, wildly gesticulating to a handsome man in a vibrant waistcoat, his charming half-smile revealing his admiration for the woman, though it seemed she couldn't see it herself. The man with the cigar, Ragstone, was eating something from a bowl, hunched over it like someone might take it from him and, low and behold, his cigar was still resting on his lip even as he leaned over to say something to a man with black skin, white eyes and a wide smile who chortled loudly, sipping from a pint glass even at this early hour of the morning.

The room was full, and yet Felix felt the absence of Nigel and Linus.

'Where are they?' she said to D.W privately, in her mind.

'The office,' he said back to her, just as secretly.

'Take me? I'm not quite ready for everyone yet.'

The dire wolf led Felix up the staircases, to an office that read 'Principal Duncan Ellis' on a gold plaque.

'Is he in there too?' Felix asked. 'The principal?'

'He's gone,' D.W replied, looking up at Felix sadly. 'His body washed up on the beach two days ago.'

'Oh,' Felix said in surprise. 'What happened?'

'He jumped from the dock,' D.W said shaking his head, a tremor of anger in his voice.

'But...why?' Felix asked, confusion marring her face.

'You'll find out,' D.W said, nudging her to the office door. 'It's open.'

Felix wasn't sure if she ought to knock. She felt like a stranger suddenly, unsure of the etiquette. She was painfully aware that Nigel now knew her own brother better than she did.

Not wanting to seem intrusive, Felix wrapped her knuckles on the ancient door. Her fingers were cold, and she wished she was wearing gloves.

The door was opened by a boy, with hair the same shade as hers. It fell over blue eyes, which looked at her warily.

'Hello, Linus,' Felix said, her voice trembling.

'Felix,' Linus nodded, opening the door wider to let her in.

Felix swallowed as she entered the office, D.W at her side. Linus was much changed. His face was older, stamped with a frown that seemed permanently etched into his forehead. Dark stubble grew over his jaw and chin and his hands, bare without gloves, were tough and hard, dirt caked beneath the nails. He was broader, too, filling his worn clothes more than he had done when he left. Had it only been a few months ago? It seemed the world had changed insurmountably since then.

Felix was thankful for the small fire in the grate and as she looked towards it, she saw Nigel sat in the armchair, his fingers steepled beneath his lips as he stared into the flames. When he turned, he smiled warmly at Felix, breaking his concentration. Felix was alarmed by how weary he looked.

'You ok?' she asked him, reaching her hand out to his.

Nigel took it and kissed her knuckles affectionately. 'Sit,' he said, nodding to the empty chair next to him. 'We've got a lot to discuss.'

Felix sat in an armchair, which felt as though it would collapse at any moment. Linus perched himself on the edge of a battered sofa and folded his arms. His eyes were narrowed as he regarded his sister, and Felix squirmed.

'I'm glad you're safe,' she said quietly. 'I was worried.'

'It's not your job to worry about me,' Linus said back, in a voice that felt heavy, like bricks.

Felix swallowed nervously. It seemed fitting to be in the principal's office; she felt like she was being scolded, though she didn't know why. She looked down at the dire wolf, comforted by the way he rolled his eyes out of Linus' view.

'Linus,' Nigel said. 'You promised.'

Linus held his hands up and slumped down into the sofa, throwing his legs over the arm with the movements of someone who was used to getting his own way.

'I don't know why you're so angry with me,' Felix said, swallowing her nerves. '*You're* the one who ran away.'

'What's that old saying?' Linus said, looking from her to Nigel. 'Pot, kettle, black?'

Felix scowled.

'He's got a point, Felix,' Nigel said. 'You *did* run away, too. Again.'

'I had my reasons,' Felix said, looking down at her hands.

'Well, so did I,' Linus retaliated.

They were silent. Each of them stared into the fire.

'I'm sorry,' Felix said finally. 'To you both. Truly. I did run away – from my responsibilities, from my friends, from it all. I was...overwhelmed. I thought that I wasn't cut out to be Firelighter. I still don't, truth be told. I never asked for any of this. But I learned a lot about myself whilst I was with Lillith and the Drow.

'There I was, surrounded by my sisters, feeling everything they felt, understanding them and knowing that they, in turn, understood me, felt everything inside me, too. And guess what? I'd never felt so isolated, so utterly alone. I felt like a voice in a crowd, losing myself.

'But I realised that I know who I am. I know that I'm this lost, frightened, angry and confused girl...woman ....but it's ok, because I'm not alone; I have you. All of you. My family. And I trust you; I have to trust you. I choose to, despite all the secrets and betrayals and lies, on both sides. Because that's what family does. Family forgives each other, and trusts each other, and relies on each other.'

'Pretty words, Felix,' Linus said. 'But trust is earned.'

'Then I'll earn your trust, one day,' Felix nodded. 'All I ever wanted, growing up in Maude's orphanage, was a family. You're my brother, Linus. I'm not going to lose you now that I've found you. If you think there is anything I wouldn't do for you, then you're mistaken.'

'You might regret saying that,' D.W whispered to Felix, gritting his teeth.

'If that's true, then you need to let me leave,' Linus said.

'I wasn't aware you couldn't,' Felix replied.

'Well can you tell that bloody Aubrey woman, please?' he spat, sitting up now and leaning his elbows on his knees.

Nigel winced.

'What's Aubrey done?' Felix asked, looking between the two boys.

'Aubrey has said that Linus and the crew of the Skyskimmer are detained for the time being,' Nigel explained.

'Detained?' Linus laughed. 'She's *arrested* us!'

'Arrested you?' Felix exclaimed, eyes wide. 'What on earth for?'

'Oh let's see, shall we?' Linus said, starting to count off the charges on his fingers. 'Piracy, illegal flight, illegal docking of an airship, destruction of public property, skipping bail, smuggling fugitives, oh and treachery to the Magistry.'

'Ah,' Felix said. 'You've been busy, I see.'

'It's not funny, Felix! I have to leave!' Linus shouted.

'I'll talk to Aubrey,' Felix said, appeasing him. 'But why do you need to leave so urgently? Don't you want to come back to the Citadel and–'

'I have to find the true Firelighter,' Linus interrupted her.

Felix stopped speaking, her mouth open. Nigel rubbed his forehead with his gloved hands.

'You...what?' Felix asked incredulously.

'Felix, you need to listen,' Nigel said. 'I tried to explain some things to do you, but this story is complicated.'

'That's putting it lightly,' D.W muttered.

'Start at the beginning, then,' Felix said, shuffling up in her chair.

'The beginning,' Linus nodded. 'Right. Well, the beginning starts right after you saved my life, Felix, and then locked me in a room in the Citadel next to Paris Lovelock.'

Felix squirmed uncomfortably.

'You weren't a prisoner, you know? It was to keep you safe.'

'That's entirely debatable,' Linus replied, and Felix heard the grumpy snarl of D.W next to her.

She motioned for Linus to continue.

'Paris Lovelock, he was one of my father's...one of Corbin's Magistry members and head of the Guild for Commoner Care, but he was so much more than that. Before the Godspells were Firelighters, beginning with our Grandfather, Arthur, the Lovelocks were the Firelighters.'

'Yes, I knew that,' Felix nodded.

'You did?' Now it was Linus' turn to be surprised. 'How?'

'I read about it in a book from the Genealogy Room in the London Library months ago,' Felix explained. 'It said that a ten-annum-old Paris abdicated the role after the death of his father and the Flame passed to the Godspell clan. It was in that book that I learned that Corbin was my uncle, but the rest was torn out. That's why I secured Paris at the Citadel. I wanted to question him about it all.'

'Paris tore those pages out?' Nigel said, looking at Linus, who nodded in return.

'They're why I went with him,' he said. 'The pages spoke of a curse upon the Firelighters. It recorded the sordid history of Firelighters from 1750 onwards. Every Firelighter died in mysterious or suspicious circumstances, and Paris believed this was because of a curse that befell any Firelighter who claimed the title and the Flame. It was why he abdicated; he didn't want to be a victim of the curse.'

'But if there is a curse, why does it exist?' Felix asked.

'A good question, and one that leads deeper into this tale,' Linus said, edging closer to her on his seat. 'Paris was also a member of the Privy Council, a group of 13 magicians each guarding a secret. The Privy Council itself isn't exactly a secret, but the information it guards is protected well. A member can be excommunicated if they're captured or questioned against their will and once excommunicated from the council, it becomes impossible to reveal their secret.'

Felix looked to Nigel, who looked down at the fire, his eyes filled with weariness. Linus continued.

'Paris had been excommunicated the moment he was held prisoner by you, so he couldn't reveal to me why the curse existed. But he had spent his life learning several of the 13 secrets of the Privy Council and he told us, me and the crew, those he had discovered, and before he died, he gave me the means to uncover his secret about the curse.

'Paris' role in the Privy Council was linked to his membership in the Magistry. He guarded secrets of the commoner's history that had been influenced by magicians. As such, we learned about the first secret: the secret of the Great Spark.'

'The Great Spark,' Felix repeated. 'You mean how magic came to the First Plane?'

Linus nodded.

'The Festival of Fire is the only thing that remains of this knowledge now, the history reduced to a mere myth. But there is truth in it, in the Great Fire of London in 1666. This Great Fire brought magic to the First Plane. Which leads us to the second and third secrets of the Privy Council. The fire started because a man named Thomas Farynor opened the first hatch from the Second Plane into the First. The opening of this hatch spread fire and magic through the First Plane, burning the city to the ground. Thomas Farynor was the first Firelighter.

'But the fire had been predicted. A commoner named William Lilly had foreseen it all in 1651, and he wrote it all down in his diary. But he also foresaw us, Felix. Twins, bringing a curse of smoke and flame to the earth. That was Paris' secret! We will somehow bring about the destruction of the First Plane.'

'But...I don't understand. Why?'

'Because neither of us are the true Firelighter, Felix. The Flame just doesn't belong to us.'

'Who does it belong to, then?' Felix asked, shaking her head.

'I don't know,' Linus admitted with a sigh. 'I was told someone named Hestia Windwood might know, but she's dead. Principal Ellis was her lover, and the founder of the Privy Council. He had some pretty shameful secrets, to be honest. That's why he helped us. He was ashamed of what he had done. I think that's why he wanted to die; to find peace and punishment. He didn't know for sure where Hestia had gone, but said she'd been up near the Ashfjord so that's where I'm headed. I have to find out what she knew.'

'So your plan is to go to the Northern Realms of the Second Plane, hunt around for some clues that might have been left by a dead woman, and then hand the Sacred Flame of Magic over to some stranger, in the hope that you stop the end of the world?'

Linus blinked.

'That about sums it up, yeah,' he shrugged.

'It will also stop the curse from befalling you, too, like it has done every other Firelighter in history,' Nigel said softly.

'But I don't have the Flame anymore, so technically I'm not the Firelighter, am I?'

'You really don't have it?' Nigel asked. 'I thought you just said that to Lillith to throw her off.'

'What's she on about?' Linus asked. 'What do you mean you don't have the Flame? Who does?'

'Well, I gave it to Sigbert Goodnight before I left,' Felix said.

'Sigbert Goodnight?' Linus asked. 'But he's dead, Felix.'

'I know,' Felix nodded. 'Nigel told me. But I trusted him, and he gave me his word that he would do as I asked.'

'What did you ask him, Felix?' D.W asked, sitting on his hind legs.

'I told him to get the Flame to Linus,' Felix said.

'To me?' Linus breathed.

Felix nodded.

'But that would make me...'

'The Firelighter,' Felix said simply.

'But I'm a...I'm a commoner. I can't be the Firelighter.'

'Do you think I care that you don't have any magic, Linus?' Felix asked. 'You're my brother. The Flame should never have come to me or you alone. We should guard it together. The magicians and the commoners should have leaders that represent them both equally.'

'You know...I thought you had sent him to kill me,' Linus said thickly.

Felix shook her head sadly.

'I saved your life, Linus. Why would I then try and take it?'

'I'm sorry,' Linus said. 'I thought...'

'It doesn't matter now,' Felix said, reaching over and touching his hand.

They both looked down at their bare fingers pressed against one another. Smiling sheepishly, they squeezed one another's hands.

'Sorry to interrupt a tender moment,' D.W coughed with a growl. 'But we still haven't established where the Sacred Flame of Magic actually is.'

Well,' said Felix shrugged, leaning back into her chair. 'I trust that Sigbert fulfilled his task.'

'He didn't give me the Flame, Felix,' Linus said apologetically. 'All he gave me was this old lump of coal.'

Linus reached into his pocket and pulled out the lump of rock Goodnight had begged him to take before he died. Immediately, Felix started to laugh.

'Linus, pass it here.'

He gave Felix the coal.

'You can't see the magic, Linus,' Felix explained. 'To you, it's just a piece of coal because that's what it was when I pulled it out of the fire. But with magic, I transformed it.'

She threw the coal into the fire where it was immediately consumed by a bright flame. A blinding light filled the room, sending heat searing through the office. Linus and Nigel covered their faces and D.W leapt behind the sofa, but Felix stared into the fire and held her hand over it. Slowly, shyly, the fire floated upwards.

'Guys,' Felix whispered. 'Look.'

Linus and Nigel peeped up, and the dire wolf peered over the patchwork cushions.

'Woah,' Linus breathed.

The fire was hovering over Felix's hand. It was so bright the fire seemed white, then blue, then red again.

'This is the Sacred Flame,' Felix said gently.

'That was inside that lump of coal?' Linus asked, and Felix nodded with a small smile.

'Woah,' he said again. 'How can I see it if it's pure magic?'

'Even the commoners saw the fire that raged through London in the Great Fire, didn't they?' Felix asked. 'And that was magic.'

Linus nodded.

'I guess,' he whispered.

'Hi,' Felix whispered softly to the Flame, as though she were meeting it for the first time.

Then she moved the Flame slowly, as though she might scare it, towards her heart. The Flame slowly sank into her, out of sight.

'There now,' she said, as though speaking to a child. 'You're safe again.'

The room was quiet, reflective.

'Linus?' Felix asked.

Her brother started, as though he had been deep in thought.

'Hmm?'

'Would you mind terribly if I had a moment with Nigel?'

'Oh!' Linus said, flushing. 'Yeah. Sure. D.W told me how it was with you two. Course. Sure. I'll be, err going?'

Linus stepped backwards, awkwardly scrambling for the door handle. He gave a small salute to Felix and Nigel, and looked at D.W expectantly.

'Come on then,' he said to the wolf. 'Unless you really want to watch them snogging.'

The dire wolf shuddered and pounced out the room. With a wink, Linus shut the office door.

Finally, Felix and Nigel were alone.

33

A Flame in the Night

'You seem tired,' Felix said, looking at Nigel.

'It's been a long few days,' he said, looking her straight in the eyes.

Felix nodded. She moved to him, kneeling on the ground between his legs, and looked up at him. Tentatively, she reached for his hand. He let her hold it for a moment and then he sniffed and pulled it away, his face a careful blank.

'I have something for you,' he said.

He reached down to the side of his armchair and pulled up a small metal box.

'What is it?' Felix asked, looking at the old, scuffed metal.

'Fiddle's check out box,' Nigel said, opening the latches. 'It's like a safety deposit box, I suppose. All the Privy Council members have one. It's mine now.'

Nigel looked at the box with unconcealed animosity.

'So he was on the Privy Council, then?'

Nigel lifted his gaze to Felix and nodded warily.

'You don't exactly sound surprised,' he said. 'Did you know?'

'He said something to me once,' Felix explained. 'The first time he took me to the Second Plane. He said there was a secret he couldn't tell me. He mentioned the Privy Council then.'

'He told me he was an excommunicated member a few weeks before he died, when we were on the Belfast,' Nigel said. 'I told him he had to tell you and give you his secret somehow. We fought about it. He never listened to me.'

Nigel looked into the fire. His jaw was set and angry, shadowed with the beginnings of a beard from where he had not shaved. Felix reached up to touch his face. It felt rough, like sandpaper.

'He left you this,' Nigel said, pulling his face away, his eyes pained, like he regretted it.

He pulled out an envelope. It was crisp and fresh, and Felix could tell it had not been sealed too long ago. Her name was written on one side in Fiddle's familiar sepia swirls. She took it from Nigel and leaned back on her heels. Moving closer to the light of the fire, she opened the letter and read it with trembling hands.

My darling girl,

There are many things I regret in my life, and I must die carrying the weight of them to my grave. But if I can be redeemed for any of my mistakes, I greet death cheerfully, knowing that in saving you, I have saved myself.

When your parents chose me as your Magister, I swore an oath to protect you, always. If I have lied to you and kept things from you, it is because I believed a lie that kept you safe was better than a truth which placed you at risk.

But I have done you wrong in this. Secrets and the lies they breed are a burden that will drive the humanity from all of us, commoner or magician.

As 1 of the 13 members of the Privy Council, I was given a secret to guard. When I became a fugitive, the night of your birth, I was immediately excommunicated from the council. I could not tell my secret in any capacity. It was locked within me, a plague rotting away at me, much like the cancer which claimed my life.

But the council has its loopholes. A member of the council, if not excommunicated, can choose to willingly reveal their secret to someone they trust. The council, though flawed, believe in the good of humanity, that a burden can be halved if it is shared.

Trust is made of many things, my dear; truth, honour but most importantly it is made of love. I named Nigel as the designee of my secret, because I saw in him the first two of these qualities. When he met you, I watched the third grow.

Tell him how you feel, Felix. Life is too short for secrets. Love and trust. These things will save us all.

Alchemus. J. Fiddle

Felix took a shaking breath and stared at the words until they became blurry. She wiped away her tears with the back of her hand. She held out the letter to Nigel, but he shook his head.

'I don't want to read it,' he said, shaking his head.

Felix tried to catch his gaze, but he avoided her. She frowned.

'Does anyone else know? About you being on the Privy Council?' she asked.

Nigel shook his head.

'D.W has guessed, I think. But he's been gracious enough not to ask me outright. I'm not sure I'd tell the truth if he did.'

'You would,' Felix said firmly. 'I know you would.'

Nigel leaned forward and removed his glasses, crushing his hands into his eyes.

'I hate him for it,' he confessed. 'Alchemus, I mean. He knew I was afraid of ending up like my Aunt Vessania. Truth has always mattered to me and he gave me this secret to keep, this lie to tell.'

'But that's why he gave you the secret, I think,' Felix said, resting her hand on Nigel's shoulder and squeezing it. 'Because you strive for honesty always. Who better to trust with a secret, than someone who would never betray him?'

He shook his head and Felix saw the fire reflecting in his eyes.

'I'm not sure what this means...for us,' Nigel said, wiping the fleshy part of his thumb under his eye.

Felix shrugged a shoulder and looked at him. His green eyes were wet, and he seemed different, vulnerable without his glasses. She sighed and reached out to him, resting her hands against his cheeks and then pressing her forehead against his.

'You have your secrets to keep, Nigel,' she said softly. 'I understand that. A secret is not a deception, but it carries its own darkness with it, its own cold night. But there is a magic that can bring light and warmth, even into the ugliest of secrets. Love. Love burns through every darkness. I love you, Nigel. And I will be here, whenever you need a flame in the night.'

Nigel raised his eyes to Felix's.

'Felix...' he began, but the words were choked in his throat.

He swallowed noisily, fresh tears dripping down his cheeks.

'I love you too,' he said hoarsely. 'That's the truth. My truth.'

'Well then,' Felix said, tracing kisses along the damp tracks of his tears. 'That will be enough.'

'No,' Nigel whispered. 'Secrets can drive us mad, Felix. We keep them locked away inside us, building little cages around them, but we trap only ourselves. I don't ever want to hide any part of myself from you. I don't...I won't become like my Aunt Vessania, spinning lies, weaving secrets until even she doesn't know what is truth anymore.'

'You could never be like your aunt, Nigel,' Felix said softly, her hand cupping his cheek.

'I'm going to tell you the secret,' he said, his eyes flicking up to hers. 'I choose to tell you...because I love you and I trust you, and it's what will keep us going.'

'That's what Fiddle said in his letter,' Felix said. 'He gave you his secret because he believed in you, Nigel.'

Nigel nodded, reflecting her smile back at her. He took a deep breath and closed his eyes, and then he began to talk.

'Fiddle chose your name. He held you in his arms when you were hours old and named you Felix. A boy's name, yes, to keep you safe but more than that. Oh, so much more than that.'

'Felixia Solis,' Felix said, not really wanting to interrupt him.

'How did you know?' Nigel asked, surprised.

'Something my uncle said to me once. But go on. I didn't mean to stop you. Who is Felixia Solis?'

'It's not a who, it's a what.'

'Sorry?'

'Felixia Solis is a nebula – a cloud of mist and gas burning above us, beyond the sky and into the stars. You already know it but by another name.'

'I do?'

'Yeah,' Nigel nodded. 'Felixia Solis is the Third Plane.'

'Then...Felixia Solis, the nebula...that's the source of the Sacred Flame?'

'Yes.'

'Wow,' Felix said. 'But why is that a secret?'

'That's not the secret part, Felix,' Nigel said, his expression growing nervous.

'Then what is?'

'Felixia Solis is getting closer.'

'Closer?'

Nigel nodded again.

'Wait. Let me get this clear. The Sacred Flame is the fire that the Firelighters wield, and it is the source of all magic on this earth, right? So if a tiny little flame like that can envelop the First Plane in magic during the Great Fire of London and, if used the way my uncle used it, it can literally incinerate people, yes?'

'Right on both counts,' Nigel agreed.

'So if the Sacred Flame is a part of the Third Plane...part of the nebula, we must assume that the nebula itself is a thousand times more powerful.'

'More like a billion, actually.'

'And it's getting closer...to us? To our Earth? Both Planes?'

'Yes, Felix. That's the secret. The Third Plane will completely destroy everything. Just like William Lilly prophesied.'

'Then they're all connected, the secrets.'

'I think so,' Nigel said, his voice cracking a little.

'Hey,' Felix said, tilting his face up. 'Thank you for telling me. You don't have to bear it alone like he did.'

'I don't know how he stayed sane all these years, knowing that the world will end, knowing there is nothing that can be done about it.'

'That's not strictly true,' Felix said slowly.

'What do you mean?'

'Ok. Listen. Fiddle sent me to the Glade. He sent me to Lillith, knowing full well that he was putting me in danger and for a while, I didn't understand why he would do that but now I do. He knew I'd find answers there.'

'What do you mean?'

'I have a secret, too,' Felix said with a wry smile. 'Lillith's secret.'

'But...' Nigel looked flummoxed. 'How? She was excommunicated! She wouldn't have been able to tell you, and there's no way you'd have been able to force it from her magically.'

Felix shook her head.

'I didn't. The Drow are a sisterhood, Nigel. Once connected, we feel everything the others feel, we learn everything about them, their thoughts, their dreams. Everything.'

'You can read their minds?'

'No, it's not as straightforward as that,' Felix said. 'It's like...it's like their experience is my experience. Like their memories are mine. It's a collective. It's called Drowning.'

'To burn and to *drown*....' Nigel mumbled.

Felix looked confused, but he motioned for her to continue.

'When I touched Lillith, it was like diving into her. It's a bit disconcerting. You sort of feel like you lose yourself. If you go deep enough into the Drow, you get caught up in everyone else and forget yourself. It's how she had me under her spell for so long.'

'It sounds horrible,' Nigel said, gripping Felix's hand.

'It's not,' Felix said. 'Not really. It's just overwhelming. The Drow aren't like Lillith, Nigel. They're so full of love. They're like children, really, afraid of the dark. That's why she could control them so easily.'

'So...you sort of felt Lillith's secret?'

'I guess, yeah. I let her in. I opened up to her. That's the special power of the Drow; once you let your soul become a window for others to look through, you look straight back through it into theirs. *I* knew Lillith's secret because *she* knew it. It was as simple as that.'

'What is it? The secret?'

'Magic lives,' she said softly. 'The Sacred Flame of Magic is alive, a living force that has been wielded and used for centuries by magicians. It's like a slave, Nigel. Trapped here. It wants to go home.'

'Home? To the Third Plane?'

'To Felixia Solis nebula, yes,' Felix nodded. 'Perhaps that's why the nebula is getting closer; it's trying to find the Flame.'

'But...how do we send it home?'

'I have no idea,' Felix said. 'And neither did Lillith. It's not as simple as just setting it free; it needs to be returned. But Lillith had no interest in setting the Flame free anyway. She just wanted to use it to protect the Drow, somehow.'

'Maybe the 'true Firelighter' that Linus wants to find, will know what to do? Maybe it really is all connected.'

'I think so,' Felix nodded.

'We need to tell Linus,' Nigel said, standing up.

Felix rose with him.

'We need to tell everyone,' she said. 'No more secrets.'

Nigel looked down at her and tenderly stroked his finger over her spirals. He felt them glow under his touch.

'I love you,' he whispered.

'And I love you,' Felix smiled, standing on her tiptoes to kiss him.

It took the rest of the day in the telling, with everyone asking questions and raising concerns. Aubrey had the most questions, of course, and it took two hours of discussion alone to satisfy her. But in spite of the time it took, a decision was soon reached.

They had to find the true Firelighter.

If it was their only shot at saving the Planes, then they had to try.

'Who goes, then?' Aubrey had asked.

Felix had looked at her brother sat at the table next to her.

'We both do,' she'd said.

Linus had smiled at her.

'No,' Aubrey said, shaking her head so that her hair puffed up to twice its normal size. 'You're the Firelighter and the Grand Vizier. We need you at the Citadel.'

'With respect, Aubrey,' Felix said, as carefully as she could, for she did not want to upset this woman who had guided her and cared for her. 'I'm not asking for permission. I'm going. The Flame is safe with Linus and me and together, we'll give it to the true Firelighter.'

So it was agreed.

Linus and Felix would go together. Slingsby would take them to the Ashfjord, and Nigel would accompany them.

'Thanks for that. For saying we'll do this together,' Linus had whispered to her afterwards.

'Linus,' Felix then said tentatively. 'I'm not sure if you know, but I first heard about Felixia Solis from Corbin...from your father.'

Linus had looked confused.

'I think that Fiddle told Corbin his secret,' Felix had explained. 'Fiddle was his tutor when Corbin was a boy and Fiddle trusted him, foolishly, believing that knowing the secret would make Corbin a better man.'

'Right,' Linus had nodded, tight-lipped.

'Don't you get it?' Felix had continued. 'In his own misguided way, Corbin, your father, he was trying to save everyone when he made that machine. He figured that magicians are made of magic so they can withstand the force of Felixia Solis...so it stands to reason that if he turned the commoners into magicians, they'd survive too.'

'But he hated commoners,' Linus had said. 'And it doesn't excuse what he did.'

'No,' Felix had agreed. 'But it helps us to understand him, a little. And maybe it can help us to forgive him.'

Linus had looked at her as though she was crazy, and Felix had laughed a little.

'To paraphrase a wise man, magic is more powerful when it comes from love, not anger. You are angry at him, I see that. But you loved him, too. That's your biggest secret, isn't it? That you miss him.'

Linus had looked down at the table. Felix had seen the wobble of his throat.

'Forgive your father, Linus,' Felix said. 'And forgive yourself for loving him. Love should never be a regret. In Corbin Godspell's dark life, your love was the only light he had. Be thankful for that.'

The day after Yule, the crew of the Skyskimmer said their goodbyes on the dock of the Ardere Academy.

'You can't leave,' Linus said in a small voice.

He barely dared to speak, fearing the emotion that somehow seemed caught in his throat.

'Och,' Captain Kildare said with a smile. 'You'll be fine, laddie.'

She wrapped an arm around his shoulder awkwardly and was taken aback when Linus threw his arms around her, holding her fiercely.

'Thank you,' Linus said into her neck. 'Thank you for everything.'

Captain Kildare pulled away, sniffing loudly, her eyes gleaming.

'You weren't much of a pirate, lad,' she said. 'But you will always have a home on the Skyskimmer, should you want one.'

'Y'aarr,' called out the crew in agreement.

Pinks grinned and nodded, holding out her hand in a thumbs up gesture.

'Keep taking your Fleetwater,' Captain Kildare said, pulling down Linus' waistcoat and neatening his collar. 'Be careful with it. Pace it out.'

'I will,' Linus nodded with a sniff, as Captain Kildare brushed his hair out of his eyes.

'And don't go doing anything I wouldn't do,' she said, wagging a gloved finger in his face.

'That doesn't leave much, then,' Linus grinned.

'Less of that lip, lad!' Captain Kildare barked, but then she smiled a wobbly smile and pulled Linus towards her, wrapping her arms around him and quickly kissing his crown.

'Take this,' she said gruffly, handing him her silver whistle. 'You call us if ever you need us, you hear?'

Linus nodded and attached the whistle to his belt, next to his Fleetwater.

The captain and her crew climbed aboard the Skyskimmer and began loosening the cleat knots.

'Where will you go?' Linus called out, as the ship began to drift from the dock.

'Wherever we want, lad,' Captain Bonny Kildare shouted back, with a joyful smile. 'Magic awaits!'

After the crew had departed, the Ardere was much quieter. Memorials were held for Paris Lovelock, Sigbert Goodnight and Principal Duncan Ellis. Felix gave instructions to Aubrey for the ruling of the Magistry, and it was with great satisfaction that she gave her a document, written by Linus, declaring that he gave full permission for Fiddle's home, Fenton House to be turned into the first library for both commoners and magicians.

'Make sure it happens,' Felix said to Aubrey, pressing the parchment into her hands.

'I won't let you down, Felix,' Aubrey said.

She had shadows under her eyes and Felix was sorry. Aubrey had never wanted to lead, she had said that once. But Felix was beginning to learn that the greatest leaders had responsibility thrust upon them, rather than seeking it out. For that reason alone, she trusted Aubrey and knew she would do her best in her stead.

Soon, it was time for Felix, Linus, Nigel and Slingsby to leave. They had packed bags with supplies, and Slingsby had told them to wear clothing suitable for icy conditions, for the Ashfjord was a mountainous realm of ice and snow.

Thaddeus had dutifully created a hatch for them, using a classroom door, that would take them to the Ashfjord boundaries. From there, they would be on their own.

They stood outside the door, dressed in long padded coats trimmed with fur and big, thick boots that were heavy to lift. There was no longer anything to wait for.

'Right then,' Felix said nodding her head. 'Time to go.'

She stepped forward towards the door, taking the handle in her hand, and the dire wolf stepped forward with her.

'No, D.W, you need to stay here,' she said, looking down to him.

'As if,' he snorted.

'I mean it,' Felix began, but the wolf fixed her with his golden-eyed glare.

'Open the hatch, Felix,' he snarled.

Felix sighed and tried to hide her smile, but it won out. She grinned down at him. D.W grinned back with his toothy mouth.

She reached down and held a tuft of his fur and then looked behind her. Nigel held out his hand and Felix brushed her gloved fingertips against his. Deep inside she felt her heart sing.

Felix opened the door and together, they stepped through the hatch.

Epilogue

The girl pulled her shawl tightly over her shoulders. The wind was bitingly chill, and the shawl provided little protection, but the girl had been raised in the snow; she was used to the cold. Besides, it eased the burning in her skin.

She looked down at the gravestone and knelt down on her thick skirts. She started to pull out the weeds which were peeping through the snow and ice. It was unusual for there to be weeds growing, what with it being midwinter, but the weather had been strange of late. Still freezing, yes, but not as cold as yesteryear or the annum before that.

The girl looked up to the sky. It was dancing. Lines of red and blue and purple and yellow swam across the sky. It reminded her of the time her mother had poured oil into water. She'd shown her all the pretty colours, like a rainbow hidden inside the liquid. Her mother had not known much magic, but she had been clever and learned, though she had never explained how she knew so much.

It was the sky that brought the weeds. With the dancing colours came the heat. Not enough to melt the snow completely but enough to make the seedlings grow and to bring the fireflies when it wasn't their season. The colours were brighter than yesteryear, too, like they were closer, dipping down into the sky like they were looking at her the same way she looked at them.

She examined the sky a lot. There was little else to do in the evenings when she had completed her chores. There was nobody else to talk to; nobody would talk to her anyway. Ember the magical dunce, Ember the freak, they called her. And maybe she was. She couldn't do magic like they could though she could see it, sure enough. Surely that made her a magician? And her skin burned daily. Each footstep she took was like standing on a funeral pyre. The only thing that eased the pain, was the magic water that her mother always made her drink. Vials and vials of it, she had, all stored away in the padlocked cabinet in their wooden hut. It was her mother who had told her how much to drink and when, telling her that the effects of Fleetwater were dangerously addictive. It came from some magic river on the First Plane, her mother had said.

Ember had never been to the First Plane. She couldn't. She had no special glasses that made her see the other world. Her mother had never seen it either though, and that comforted Ember somewhat. Even though her mother could do some small magical tricks, it always comforted Ember to know that she was a magical dunce too. She'd never felt lonely when her mother was around.

Now, she felt lonely all the time.

She had never known her father. Her mother didn't talk about him. Ember didn't care much at the time, but now she found herself wondering about him often. She thought it might be nice to know if she had family somewhere. But she'd had a happy life, a simple one, but happy; farming the land in the summer, selling the spoils at the weekly markets in the little town where everyone knew her name.

In her final deathly delirium, her mother had told her she'd been married once. Not to her father. She had never married Ember's father. But she had wed another man. She'd called out his name, when she was in pain that not even the Fleetwater could numb.

'Forgive me, Bertrand!' she'd cried out.

Ember wondered what she needed forgiveness for. She no longer bore the man's surname. She used her maiden name and Ember, too, went by that same maiden name. When Ember asked her mother why, the woman had gone quiet, flushed in fever.

Ember tugged at some weeds, clearing the space around her mother's name. She traced her bare fingers over the letters, feeling the rough stone on her skin.

Sometimes, Ember would go several days without speaking. There was simply no one to speak to. Fireflies would sometimes creep into the hut and she might say hello to them, and on her treks around the fjord, the firefoxes nuzzled against her skirts, instead of running away like they did with the townsfolk and she'd talk to them, occasionally, whilst she stroked their bushy tails. But she realised, now, tracing her cold fingers over her mother's name that she had not spoken in nearly ten days. That was a record.

'Hestia,' she whispered slowly, testing her voice to make sure it still worked.

She rolled her tongue over each syllable lovingly, as though there was magic in the word, as though her voice might bring her mother back to her, even if only for a moment.

'Hestia,' she repeated again, a little more loudly this time.

And when she was confident in her voice, she spoke her full name, in a longing whisper.

'Hestia Farynor.'

The words left nothing but resounding silence. The wind blew.

Ember Farynor stood up, brushed the snow off her skirts, looked up.

Above her, the sky burned.

Acknowledgements

So much has happened since A Spark of Fire: book one of The Firelighters was released that it feels only right to acknowledge the myriad of people who have made A Curse of Smoke and Flame possible.

Firstly, thank you to my family and friends who have offered me continuous support and encouragement all of my life and never made me feel that this crazy dream of mine was anything but possible. Thank you to Dean, my husband, partner, soundboard and proofreader; always will never be long enough. Thank you to Sebastian who unwittingly shares my time with Felix. This is all for you, baby boy.

Secondly, to Lisa Greener, my editor and publisher who saw something in me and took a chance and to whom I am immeasureably grateful. Thank you to Anthony Kelly for a second book cover that made me cry.

Finally, a heartfelt thank you goes to the NHS, the teachers and nursery workers, the police, the fire departments, the careworkers, the supermarket workers, the staff who kept our lights on, our water flowing, our bins empty, our public transport running and our food delivered. In a year that has felt like a dystopian fantasy, you have been the true magicians.

About The Author

Jennifer L. Rothwell always wanted to call herself an author.

She dreamt of saying it one day, back when she was scribbling stories in her endless piles of notebooks and back when she would sneakily read whatever novel she was immersed in by hiding it inside the dust jacket of To Kill A Mockingbird at school.

(Don't worry, she'd already read it. To Kill A Mockingbird remains one of her favourite novels.)

She is also a teacher, a coffee drinker, a cat enthusiast, a keen foodie and most importantly, a mother to Sebastian.

Jennifer writes Young Adult fantasy because she never really grew up and she still can't believe that she's an adult. But at least now she can call herself an author.

P.S: She's sorry for being so sneaky in your English classes Mr Kerr!

For more information about our books, or to submit a manuscript, please visit

www.green-cat.shop

GREEN CAT BOOKS

Printed in Great Britain
by Amazon

69952331R00208